WHERE DID THE WIND GO?

THE GHOUL GANG · BOOK ONE

WHERE DID THE WIND G?

J. M. FAILDE

BOOKLOGIX
Alpharetta, Georgia

ISBN: 978-1-6653-0622-5 - Paperback
ISBN: 978-1-6653-0623-2 - Hardcover
eISBN: 978-1-6653-0624-9 - eBook

These ISBNs are the property of BookLogix for the express purpose of sales and distribution of this title. The content of this book is the property of the copyright holder only. BookLogix does not hold any ownership of the content of this book and is not liable in any way for the materials contained within. The views and opinions expressed in this book are the property of the Author/Copyright holder, and do not necessarily reflect those of BookLogix.

Library of Congress Control Number: 2023902404

∞ This paper meets the requirements of ANSI/NISO Z39.48-1992 (Permanence of Paper)

Illustrations, cover, and layout design by Anto Marr (@anto_marrt).

0 2 1 5 2 3

To my own Ghoul Gang, you know who you are. Thank you for putting up with me while I fought my inner ghouls to make this possible—and for your undying support.

Masses of black bark passed my line of sight with each hurried step. Panting, the stitch in my side begged me to slow down. I felt a cool trickle of sweat dribble down my forehead, making my hair feel glued to my face.

I didn't know what I was running from, only that I needed to go. The thump-thumping of my heart was louder than it ever had been before—and I knew it wasn't from the running but the fear that whatever was behind me might catch up.

And it was getting closer.

The crunch of leaves and branches below my feet masked the galloping sound of the giant beast behind me. I wanted to scream—but not even a yelp would escape my frozen lips. A chill air passed, the trees above me trembling with the sudden breeze.

My eyes grew wide as I felt this thing on my heels, its breath hot against my neck. All at once, my body came to a sudden halt, as though I had been paralyzed, each muscle straining for the slightest ability to move, to twitch, but instead, they remained still as stone. The wind stopped mid-breeze, the leaves stayed precisely where they lay on the ground. There wasn't a sound anywhere. I couldn't hear my own breath—I wasn't even sure I was breathing anymore. The woods were filled with nothing more than a heavy, daunting silence.

And then came the voice.

A cold, shrill, unexpected noise probed through my ears and pierced my very being.

Found you, it hissed.

PART ONE

THE
NEW LIFE

CHAPTER ONE

SIMON

The lingering sound of a raspy voice quickly ebbed into a blaring alarm. I woke up with a start in an unfamiliar room, filled with boxes and my scattered belongings across the floor. It took a minute, but I soon remembered that this was my new room, in our new house, in a new town. And today was my first day at my new high school.

In their infinite wisdom, Mom and Dad decided it was best we moved a week into my junior year. You know, the year when you finally have your established friend group, when you're not a top-dog senior yet, but you're *so close*? It's just *so* awesome that I won't be able to experience any of that. Mom got a new job in a speck-of-a-town in North Carolina, called Ravenswood—which meant we all packed up everything we knew in sunny Miami, Florida, my home for sixteen years, to come here. When they said our new house would be like a "cabin in the woods," I literally thought *Cabin in the Woods* or *The Evil Dead*, ready for an artificial horror or Latin-speaking zombie to jump up out of nowhere. But this was different. Like, completely different. The house was huge and bright, spacious yet cozy, and completely surrounded by trees.

Looking at the map on my phone during the drive here yesterday, I groaned in protest, "You can't even find this place on maps! Is it in the middle of a national park or something?"

"Oh, Simon, it's going to be nice to be in so much fresh air and green. And seasons!" my mom exclaimed.

"No more traffic," my dad chimed in.

He's the type of dad you could never tell was joking or not. Dad almost always had a straight face—but that could just be the Korean American in him. He was born in Seoul until he moved to Miami for med school where, shortly after, he met my mom. She's also Korean but was born and raised in New York City. During her twenties, she decided to leave home—breaking her grandma's heart—and moved to Miami to study veterinary medicine, which leads us to today. She wanted to open her own practice, so when something became available, we decided to all follow along as she pursued her dream. I just wasn't expecting her dream to lead us to Nowheresville, North Carolina.

"Plus, we'll only be three hours away from Atlanta and four hours from Charlotte! Just like a drive to Orlando's theme parks!" Mom gleamed.

"Except we *won't* be driving for four hours to the most magical place on Earth. We'd be driving for four hours to *Charlotte*," I huffed.

I thought back to better times, the good ol' days, where seasons didn't exist, and the only greenery was in palm trees and alligators.

No more *café con leche* before class from the janitors.

No more traffic at all times of the day because of the never-ending construction.

No more Miami.

I begrudgingly got out of bed and looked at myself in the full-body mirror that hung behind my door. My black hair was formed into an unforgiving wave from sleep. My dark brown eyes reflected at me; the tiny freckle under my left eye peeped through. I flexed my muscles and was yet again disappointed at the results of my tall, lanky body. I inspected myself and discerned that I had not been probed by aliens during the night.

Oh well. One day it'll happen.

I hated to admit it, but my new room was awesome. Bigger than my last, it had dark carpeting, my computer desk was already set up to the left of the entrance, my dresser on the right-hand wall, and my bed pushed against the left corner with a window directly behind it. In the middle of the floor, in a box labeled "ghost hunting stuff," sat my prized possessions.

A little fun fact about me: I'm *obsessed* with the supernatural—everything from ghosts and demons to Romero's zombies. A self-proclaimed ghost hunter, if you will.

When my parents and I took trips to Key West, with Robert the Doll, the ghost tours, and all the other spooky things on the *Island of Bones*, it was like my own supernatural playground. I even saw a real-life ghost orb in the Shipwreck Museum! I wasn't sure if my parents believed in the metaphysical stuff as I did, or if they were just trying to appease me, but somehow, we'd done all the tours and returned to a few of them each time we went.

I looked down at the box on my floor in its neatly packed glory. It signified home and all the memories I didn't want to forget.

I threw on a pair of jeans, the first T-shirt I could find, and my favorite black beanie with a white ghost stitched on it. As soon as I ran downstairs, I knew Mom had my breakfast on the table. Waffles. Obviously, she was trying to compensate for this big move. What could I say? She knew the way into my heart.

"Where's Dad?" I asked as I shoved the first bite of syrupy goodness into my mouth.

"Oh, he had to go to the hospital to check-in. It looks like you're both getting an early start." Mom ruffled my hair, the tips of her almond-shaped eyes pointing downward, as if to say, *I'm sorry.*

"When do you start?"

"I'll probably go to the new clinic today. Make sure everything is in order, but I don't start until next Monday," she said, placing her hand on her chin.

"I wonder what the animals will be like here."

"We gotta take a tally to find the most popular dog breed of North Carolina."

"I'll miss all the yippy Chihuahuas of Miami."

We both laughed at the thought of the little dogs that seemed to dominate our old stomping grounds. After eating, we gathered our stuff, and she drove me to Ravenswood High, home of the Ravens.

Yay.

I walked into the school, and, of course, all eyes were on me. Not in an "Oh, my gosh, who is that total hottie?" kind of way, like I'd hoped. It was more of a "Who the hell is that? Does he even go here? We know everyone who's ever stepped through these halls, and you don't fit" kind of way.

I grabbed the straps of my backpack and took a deep breath.

It didn't look like I was off to a good start. Not that it mattered, but I hadn't seen any other Asian students. In fact, I didn't really see too many different races or ethnicities either, other than white. It was a stark contrast to my high school in Miami, which was a melting pot of diversity. An innate part of me was a little concerned, but I decided to try to be positive. I was one-of-a-kind, it seemed.

Based on the schedule we got in the mail, my first class was history. Having it first thing in the morning was going to be rough. Luckily, I had it only three times a week, thanks to block scheduling.

History, history. Room 1407. Oh, one number off from Room 1408! *Where is Stephen King when you need him?*

I darted around the building looking for my class. I quickened my step, and as I came up to 1407, I noticed a small woman standing in front of the class. She had obnoxiously dyed-red hair tied up into a bun on the top of her head. She was also wearing red-framed cat-eye glasses that sat low on the bridge of her nose, the color matching her hair almost perfectly.

"Ah," she said in a cracked tone. "This must be our new student."

She ushered me over and placed her hand on my back as if to present me. She took a second too long to look at me, and I could see her brown eyes narrow, with a puzzled look on her face. I think she noticed my reaction and quickly glanced at the paper in her other hand.

"Class, I'd like to introduce you all to our new student, Simon Woo." She pronounced my last name as "whoa" before correcting herself and prolonged the "OO" in *Woo.*

She stared me down for a second longer. "Dear, do you speak English? Do you need a translator?" She began to speak very loudly and slowly, pronouncing all of her words as clearly as possible.

Aghast at her little performance, I decided it simply wouldn't do. She must have thought I was an exchange student coming fresh from Asia and not Miami.

I turn back to her with sad eyes. "*Si, por favor. No hablo inglés.*"

You pick up a few things growing up in Miami, and where this was extremely basic Spanish—to the point where even a non-Spanish speaking toddler would know what it meant back home—here it was just another foreign language.

Her mouth dropped open and her eyes grew wide, and the room became deathly quiet for what felt like an eternity. I hadn't even noticed my classmates until their silence struck me. They all deftly looked up at this teacher and me. Then, at last, I heard two distinct snickers. I glanced up at my classmates. One of the two people with a good sense of humor was a Black guy with hazelnut eyes. He was sitting down, but I could tell he was probably around my height and about my body type—a fellow lanky. What caught my attention about him was his shirt. It was a graphic tee of Jordan Peele's *Get Out*. I instantly felt like he and I would resonate. Not to mention that he was the only other person of color in this room, other than myself.

I turned to the other snicker-er and found a girl. She had crystal blue eyes surrounded by dark makeup. Her hair was unnaturally light blond, and she was paler than pale. She also was wearing all black.

Ah, I thought to myself, *the resident goth girl.* She looked at me with approving eyes. She liked my joke, and I felt my heart skip a beat.

I had found *my* people.

I smiled back at the stunned older woman. "I'm sorry. Force of habit. Yes, I speak English."

The teacher—Mrs. Wilson—looked flushed for a moment, embarrassed at her cringe-worthy performance. Without another word, she pointed me to my seat, which was perfectly in the center of the room. I made my way there as I felt some straying eyes. I saw that *my people* were about equal distances from me on either side. The goth girl glanced up at me and flashed me this sort of evil smirk like she still appreciated my joke. She looked away and continued to gnaw on the edge of her pen.

God, I wish that were—

Mrs. Wilson's voice broke through my thought, "So, please open your textbooks . . ." and her voice droned on.

Being the new kid sucked. I got lost once the bell rang and we had to go to our next class. As I rushed to the second floor of the building, I realized five minutes between classes was not enough to get anywhere on time. It didn't make it easier that my next class was chemistry, and I really didn't want to go. I'd always been into science, but chemistry had become my weak point.

I finally walked into the room as the bell rang. The room was arranged differently than history. The tables had two seats each and were raised higher. This meant partners.

I looked around the room. Most of the seats were already filled, of course. It was already the second week of classes.

I finally laid my eyes upon my soon-to-be best friend from history class, the guy who laughed at my joke. I pretty much beelined right in his direction for the empty seat next to him.

"Hey, does anyone sit here?" I held my breath for a second. I knew that this was the deciding moment— whether I would be a total loner during high school or have a friend.

He smiled up at me. "No, you can sit."

I sat down next to him, ready to introduce myself, but then, he did it for me.

"I'm Miles. You're the new kid, right?" Miles's voice had a slight accent to it. Not like a foreign accent, but an accent I couldn't place, yet had heard many times before.

"I'm Simon, and yeah, I'm from Miami. Hence the Español in history." I gesture with a Latin snap of the hand. He laughed again.

"Yeah, that was great! She was totally caught off guard. Serves her right for assuming."

"What was up with that?"

"You're in North Carolina now, buddy." The sentiment kind of scared me.

I remembered his shirt and decided to ask him about it. Was he just a cinephile? Or was Miles a fellow pop culture aficionado?

"So, Miles, right? Like Miles Morales?"

"Yeah! Man, *Ultimate* is crazy. Love Miles, but not that big of a fan of that universe. And, truthfully, I've always been more of a Miguel O'Hara fan." He laughed. I raised my eyebrow instinctively. He knew his Spidey stuff!

"Ah, yeah! Both are great. I'm an originalist, though. Peter Parker will forever be my Spider-Man," I said as I felt an instant bond forming between us. But just as he was about to continue, the teacher walked in.

He was a thinner middle-aged guy. He looked like an old-school rocker-turned-teacher. I could almost see the tattoos he had hidden under the long sleeves of his white button-up. He seemed like a fun guy.

"Hey, class, we have a new student. Simon Woo, are you here yet?" I raised my hand. "Ah, good. Welcome, welcome. You already met Miles, I presume? You two will be lab partners for the year. Everyone, say hello to Simon."

A grumble came out of everyone that formed some kind of greeting as Miles patted me on the back. This was not going to be as bad as I thought it would.

During class, Miles and I realized we had similar schedules—we had six out of eight classes together— which also told me how much smaller the school was here compared to my high school back home, at least in terms of students.

I asked about the girl in our history class as well. Miles told me her name was Riley and, apparently, she's pretty much a loner from what he can tell. All he knew was that she didn't talk to anyone—other than herself—and people thought she was weird.

I also found out that Miles moved to North Carolina over the summer, so this school year was also his first here. His dad was a cop in New York City where they lived (finally pinned his accent), but after his parents' divorce, the two moved here, and now his dad was the chief deputy of the town.

"So I haven't met anyone either. Thank God you came along. If not, I'd be the only person with an actual personality in this whole place," he said as we left chemistry and went to the cafeteria. I was so thankful we became friends before lunch. Now I had someone to sit with.

"Us outsiders gotta stick together, man," I said, giving him a light fist bump. He laughed, but something instantly broke that laughter. A huge guy, definitely finished with puberty, with light-brown hair and green eyes, shoved right between Miles and me. He looked back directly at Miles, giving him the nastiest look I'd ever seen.

"Watch it," he barked. It was like I didn't exist, and all of his disgust was directed at my new friend. The tension was high until Mr. Puberty turned the corner and left the hall.

"You know that guy?"

Miles shrugged. "Nah. I've seen him around a couple times. Dude always looks pissed. But forget him, I'm starving!" Miles led the way into the cafeteria before I had a chance to ask him anything more.

The lunchroom smelled like watered-down cleaning supplies and processed food. Nearly every table was full of obvious cliques and groups of friends chatting and eating. Miles and I grabbed our food—tacos—found a rare, empty table, and talked about movies, mainly *Get Out.* He wore the shirt for an ironic effect. We both felt like we could relate to the main character, as though we were living out the movie in Ravenswood. But most importantly, Miles was a fellow lover of horror movies.

"There's a new one coming out over the weekend. It's about ghosts. Do you wanna go see it?" he asked me.

"Yeah! It gives me something to do." I chuckled. "Plus, I've been itching for a new ghost movie. Everything lately has been about zombies and vampires. I just want some good, classic hauntings."

"Right? Or about dolls. New *Annabelle*, new *Chucky*. There's some doll fetish going on in Hollywood or something. Plus, I haven't gotten to explore much of 'downtown Ravenswood,'" he said sarcastically.

"Totally! So, before we become best friends, I need to know one thing." I shifted my face to be as serious as possible. Miles looked at me. It was make or break time. "Do you . . . believe in ghosts?"

Without a moment of hesitation, he said, "Hell yeah!" in the loudest tone I'd heard from him. "There ain't no way ghosts *don't* exist. Too many people have had experiences for them not to be real. Now, I don't know what kind of ghosts I believe in. I feel like ghosts may live their deaths over and over again and never cycle out." He pondered, his hand on his chin, looking up. I laughed to myself because he looked identical to the thinking emoji. "Or if they're more like vengeful spirits and have a purpose to complete before they can pass on. The second one sounds more fun, the first just sounds . . . sad."

"I agree. I'm kind of a ghost hunter," I said, nervously. Miles's eyes and smile grew with excitement. I continued, "Back in Miami, I would drag my friends to abandoned and haunted places. I have a whole bunch of tech at home. We used to put up videos online and everything." I pulled out my phone to show him one.

"Have you ever caught a ghost on camera?" Miles asked.

"Um, not yet. I feel like they have some kind of power where they're only visible to the naked eye. I've caught EVPs of them though! And ghost orbs!"

"What's an EVP?"

"Electronic Voice Phenomenon. It's how you catch spirit voices. Here, listen close." I put the video up to his ear. "Nothing visually happens in this scene. We didn't even hear the recording until later, but it's so clear." At that exact moment, Miles shivered, and his eyes widened. He heard it.

"Did it say, 'help me'?"

I nodded.

He dramatically shivered. "Spooky." He paused. "I think my apartment in the city was haunted. I kept telling my dad, but he never believed me. And if he did, he did a damn good job at hiding it."

"Oh, man. What made it haunted?" My curiosity was piqued.

"Just . . . a bad feeling. Kinda like feeling watched all the time. Eventually, I got comfortable with it. I used to think, it ain't doing nuthin' to me yet, so I figured I was safe, or it minded its own business. Every so often, though, lights turned off when moments earlier they'd been on and no one else was in the room. I bet it was just walking around the house, doing things as if it still lived there." He looked at me as if asking for approval.

I nodded.

"So, which state do you think ghosts live in?" Miles asked.

I had to think about it for a moment. The truth was I believed in all of it. "I think vengeful spirits are poltergeists—they're the same thing. Violent, angry, and typically pretty evil." I saw Miles nodding in agreement from the corner of my eye as I looked down at my tacos. "And I think ghosts *could* do the whole loop thing, but more often than not, I feel like they're here because they left something unfinished while they were alive. That could range from watching over family members to maybe something a little more precise."

"You're right," a girl's voice came out of nowhere, joining our conversation. My eyes instinctively followed where it came from, and there she was.

Riley, the goth girl from history, stood over us with a tray of food in her hands. She was fairly short, only a bit taller than us in our seated states. She awkwardly placed it down next to mine, aggressively pulled out the seat, and flopped down next to me.

Her voice was a little raspy and deeper than I had expected as she asked, "How do you know so much about ghosts?" Her face was close to mine; I could see how her eyes had specks of green in a sea of blue, and how her lips looked chapped under the dark lipstick she wore. She elbowed me, and I snapped out of her spell.

"I-I'm a ghost hunter," I fumbled my words out. She eyed me up and down for a second, analyzing me. *Think, Simon, think.* "And you?"

Her eyes rested on my beanie—particularly, the classic design of the ghost. Suddenly, I felt my cheeks run hot; I felt so embarrassed and wished I could just throw my hat in the garbage disposal that crushed all the lunch trays. But then, she looked back at me.

"Because I've been a ghost. I like your hat." She flicked the stitching. "I'm Riley Silverstein. What're your names?"

"Miles Allen," he blurted out and shifted in his seat.

"Your dad is the deputy, right?" She nodded in Miles's direction.

He quirked his eyebrow. "Yeah. How'd you know?"

"My mom's his boss. The sheriff." She closed one eye and made a gesture with her hands as if she were pointing a gun at Miles, then shot. "Bang."

"I'm Simon Woo," I nervously added. This broke Riley's role-playing. She glanced at me again.

"The new kid. I liked your joke in history. Mrs. Wilson is the worst. She seriously needs to get laid."

"Preach." Miles nodded.

I gaped at Miles and Riley, unsure of what to say. Yeah, no one had a filter in Miami, but I was taught to respect my elders, even if they were a tightwad.

Without picking up on my weird tension from what she had just said, Riley said, "Anyway. You were right. Ghosts exist. They stick around due to something they didn't accomplish in life." Not even a hint of sarcasm or doubt in her voice. She was serious.

It's kind of hot.

"How do you know?" I asked, but just after, the bell rang. It was time for the next class. Riley got up and started to walk away, leaving Miles and me still seated. She turned on her heels, milk almost spilling over, but she didn't seem to notice.

Riley just smirked, turned, and walked away through the crowd of bustling students, entirely out of sight. I glanced over at Miles, who looked as bewildered as me.

"What the hell was that?" he asked. "No wonder I've heard all those rumors about her. She's nuts!"

"I think . . . I think she's kinda hot."

"*You're* nuts! But I get it," he said with a sly smile. We both got up and threw our trays away.

The next period was computers, which I didn't share with Miles, but he showed me where the class was and told me he'd meet me in front once it was over.

The next and final class of the day was math. Luckily, Miles and I shared that as well. As luck would have it, Riley was in both of those classes. She sat away from me, but every so often, I could feel her eyes on me. I wanted to talk to her more. But I didn't know how.

My first week of school went by pretty quick and, thanks to Miles, it wasn't nearly as bad as it could've been. We both had some run-ins with Mr. Puberty. It didn't help that I have a wonderful attitude and tested my limits on how much I could say during almost every interaction. Let's just say I've been shoved into *many* walls.

It was the last period of the day on Friday, math. I sat next to Miles, while Riley sat across from me. The teacher droned on and on about sines and cosines, but in truth, I barely heard a word of it because Miles and I had been texting the entire class.

Miles: Apparently, there are rumors of this huge animal-like creature in the center of town, he started, adding an emoji that had big staring eyes.

Me: Really? Like a bear?

Miles: IDK? They say it has giant antlers tho BUT it stands upright on two legs instead of four.

Me: Ah, the ever-popular bear-deer.

He scoffed next to me a moment later.

Miles: It's maimed some animals in the woods. It's probably just a giant elk, but still crazy. I don't think they even have elk in North Carolina, so the real mystery is how the heck it got here.

I turned in Riley's direction, only to see her lazily resting her head on her desk, her eyes half-closed. As the week progressed, I noticed she seemed more and more tired. Instead of kicking doors open, as she had at the beginning of the week, now she was shouldering into them, like all the energy she had drained away. She was wearing a worn leather jacket, which was fitting due to the cold bite in the air. It made me once again realize just how cool she was. At that same moment, Riley turned her head toward me. I quickly looked away, toward Miles, who was already eyeing me with a sly smile on his face.

That's it. He knows too much, now I have to kill him, I thought.

A second later, I felt my phone buzz again.

MILES: INSTEAD OF SEEING THAT GHOST MOVIE, WANNA GO GHOST HUNTING? I HEARD ABOUT THIS SPOOKY SHACK IN THE WOODS

I felt my eyes get wide and a moment of rapid heartbeat.

ME: DUDE YES! SAY LESS, I responded.

I turned back to Miles who was already giving me a thumbs-up. He mouthed, "Saturday?" to which I quickly nodded my agreement.

This Saturday, I'll make Ravenswood my own and go catch some ghosts.

CHAPTER TWO

I rolled around in bed until I smelled the sweet and spicy aroma of breakfast coming from downstairs and almost immediately ran to the kitchen and saw my dad in front of our new stove, making a traditional Korean breakfast. We usually did this for special occasions, and I *loved* it. Korean breakfast (and food in general) is all about the side dishes and is all served family-style. Dad had put all the dishes out, and I saw—and smelled—the leftover *galbi* from last night's dinner. My mom was already sitting at the table with a bowl of rice, *kimchi*, *pajeon,* and fresh eggs in front of her. She looked at her phone, her light brown, straight hair perfect.

"Morning," I announced.

"Hey, Si. How'd you sleep?" My mom looked up from her phone, glowing. She'd had a great first week here, setting up her practice and hiring new employees.

"Great—knowing today was Saturday helped."

"But your first week of school was good, wasn't it?" Dad chimed in. He had slight salt and pepper on the sides of his hair but looked great for his age. We were blessed to have those anti-aging Asian genes. He placed the *galbi* on the table and pushed the cold cucumber soup closer to me. He knew it was my favorite.

"It wasn't as bad as I thought it'd be. I made friends

so I guess that's something. But people are pretty weird," I said while digging into everything.

"You're going to go meet up with your new friend today, right? Was it . . . Miles?" Mom tapped a finger on her chin as Dad sat down next to her.

"Yep! We're going ghost hunting!"

"Are you taking your camera to make one of your little videos?" Mom asked. Why was it that moms always unintentionally degraded everything by simply using the word "little"?

"That's the plan."

"Well, just be careful, okay? You'll call us if you need us, right?"

"Of course. We'll be fine." *Famous last words, Simon.*

"And you have the location on your phone turned on just in case?" Dad raised his eyebrow.

"Yes," I groaned.

"What's our only rule when it comes to ghost hunting?" Dad asked.

"Don't become a ghost too," we all chanted.

After breakfast, my parents and I watched TV for the majority of the day. Well, I watched, and they sat with me. We saw my personal favorite ghost hunting shows with over-the-top hosts—which has been my gateway into searching for the unexplained. The shows got me even more pumped for our ghost-hunting sesh tonight. I texted Miles to make sure we were still on.

MILES: DEFINITELY!

He and I had already texted back and forth during the week and played video games together online. We killed it and our team dynamic was on point.

ME: WHAT TIME DO YOU WANNA MEET UP?

It was just nearing sundown, and I knew the things that go bump in the night would be most active . . . well, at night.

>**ME:** HOW ABOUT IN AN HOUR? DOES THAT WORK?

MILES: SOUNDS GOOD, SHOULD I BRING ANYTHING SPECIFIC?

>**ME:** A FLASHLIGHT MAYBE? WATER. AND SNACKS. DEFINITELY SNACKS. OTHER THAN THAT, I SHOULD HAVE EVERYTHING WE NEED.

MILES: SWEET! SO PUMPED, DUDE.

I smiled down at my phone. Going on a ghost hunt made me feel like I was truly in my element. Maybe this town wouldn't be so bad after all.

I stood up from the couch, stretched, and started putting all my gear together. Camera, flashlight, EMF meter, spirit box, audio recorder, two bottles of water, and bear spray—ya know, just in case my pal Bigfoot decides to make a special appearance. After the backpack was set, I threw on a dark pair of jeans, grabbed a jacket, and put on a worn baseball hat saying "Ghost Hunter" my mom got me two years ago for my birthday.

Just as I ran downstairs, ready to go, my phone buzzed with a text from Miles letting me know he was on the way. I quickly laced up my sneakers, called goodbye to my parents, and jetted through the door.

The place I was meeting Miles was super close to my house, walking distance evidently, and the weather was way too nice to pass up. The cool air of North Carolina at night added the extra pep to my step I needed. I glanced at my phone and saw the pin on my map Miles shared with me earlier today. I stood with my back to the woods, but it seemed like I was in the right place. There was a worn trail through the trees behind me that seemed to be used pretty often, though it didn't look official. I guess our haunted shack was also a hot spot for others in Ravenswood.

Not even five minutes later, a cop car pulled up with the emergency lights off and Miles jumped out. He didn't drive yet. He said growing up in NYC, driving wasn't a skill you ever needed.

Through the open passenger door, Miles's dad, the deputy, flashed me a smile. "You must be Simon. It is a pleasure to meet you." Mr. Allen had the same accent as Miles but even heavier. I could *feel* New York City emanating from him. He put his hand out and I shook it.

"It's nice to meet you too, sir." And it was. I felt like now that I'd met his dad, Miles and I were actually best friends. It'd only been a week, and maybe I was moving too fast, but what can I say, I loved this guy.

"All right, I'll be back to pick you up later, Miles. Simon, do you need a ride home?"

I almost said yes, but Miles cut me off.

"He lives right around the corner. I'll walk home with him. Thanks for the ride! We gotta go before it gets any later. Love you, bye!" Miles shouted and started toward the foot-marked trail.

"All right, all right, be safe guys!" His dad chuckled as he drove off. I waved and turned to catch up to Miles.

"In a rush to leave your dad?"

"Only so he wouldn't embarrass me. Trust me, another two minutes with you and he'd be showing you baby pictures."

We climbed uphill, through dirt and trees, along the path others had left for us. "It shouldn't be much farther up," Miles said, as he pointed his flashlight around into the darkness.

"How did you hear about this place?"

"Ravenswood is a small town. It seems like there's

not that much to do for people our age—other than going to the movies or traveling to the mall a town over. So, lots of people come here. It's spooky, isolated—"

"So high schoolers come here to smoke and drink, huh?"

Miles laughed. "You got it. Plus, the creepier the place, the more guys think they're likely to get laid, I guess."

"Note to self, if we hear a moan, don't automatically assume it's a ghost. Got it," I scoff. "So, what's the lore behind this place then? Other than half of Ravenswood High losing their virginities here." We were still trekking up the hill, each step crunching the leaves and twigs below us, but I decided to pull out my camera. Might as well get the whole story filmed. I turned it on and pointed it at Miles, the flashlights acting as our only light source for now.

He began, "Well, it's said that a woman was murdered here—"

I cut him off, "Typical."

"Shh, let me continue." Miles cleared his throat loudly. "It was a long time ago, back when they were still hunting natives and old gods dominated the land. There was a woman who lived in the shack with her brother. The two were very close due to their parents dying when they were only seven and five, and after being ostracized from the rest of the town for believing in herbs and superstition rather than the Holy Gospel, they realized they only had each other. The two were like wild things, hunting and foraging for themselves, relying only on nature and each other for support. They had a very strict rule that helped them survive for twenty years together in that shack. *Never* be out after the sun sets—"

"Let me guess, one of them stays out after dark and finds a monster!" This was going to be good. I could already feel the goose bumps.

"Close," Miles continued. "One day, on a late and cold Autumn evening, the sister stood at the front door, waiting for her brother to return with food for supper. She watched the swaying trees, her eyes directed at the farthest point they could see. But as the sun lowered, no one came. She stood there until the last rays shone on their small shack, but her brother didn't come home.

"The sister waited three nights. Each night risking more and more time in the dark, waiting for her brother to come home. She would call to him in hushed whispers, 'Brother! Brother, where are you?' But she never heard a response.

"On the fourth night, she continued her new routine. 'Brother, where are you? Can you hear me?'" Miles whispered in a high voice. "For a while, it was silent. The wind wouldn't blow, the trees wouldn't sway. Not even crickets would respond, in fear of what hid in the dark. The sister, tired of being fearful, took one singular step off her family's property and that's when she heard him. 'Sister! I've been lost! Help me, I've hurt myself and cannot walk.'

"Though she couldn't see him, the sister felt rejoiced to have her brother home and alive. They would overcome any wound he had, the sister knew her way around herbal medicine, after all. She ran toward her brother's voice, calling for him to speak. 'Sister! This way!' he shouted. But no matter where she looked, she could not see him."

Miles stepped on a thicker twig, and the crack caused me to gasp as I felt my heart stop and chills raced all throughout my body. Instantly, I laughed it off.

"Scared already? Aren't you supposed to be the ghost hunter here?" Miles teased.

I punched him lightly on the arm. "Shut up, I'm just getting into it. Tell me the rest."

Miles cleared his throat and went on. "The sister

continued to follow her brother's voice, but the more she followed, the farther from the light inside the shack she went. It is said that on this fourth night, the moon couldn't be seen in the sky, and it was as dark as pitch outside."

As Miles spoke, the small cabin came into sight. It looked . . . different from what I imagined in the story. Definitely not as old as early America. It was covered in ivy, but a small bench that looked like it would break if someone sat on it sat outside, below a broken porch light. I was about to scoff when I heard what sounded like a crunch of leaves come from the thickest part of the forest we just left.

Miles must've not heard what I did, because he continued the story. "Finally, the sister reached a spot where she was absolutely positive her brother had to be right in front of her. No matter how hard she squinted, she saw nothing. She reached out her hand, trying to feel for her brother since she couldn't rely on her eyes. In front of her, she felt the leathery feel of skin. 'Brother! There you are. Why did you make it so difficult to find you?' she asked, attempting to grab his arm to help him home. But her hand felt something slick and warm. The sister pulled back, but it was already too late. 'Sister, there you are. Why did you make it so difficult to find you?' the thing repeated in her brother's voice, but as it spoke, it morphed into something else. Something like a monster."

I kept trying to listen to what was around us, placing my camera on night vision and pointing it toward the trees behind us. *It's probably just an animal*, the rational part of my brain said. *You're in the woods, at night. It could've been a deer or a raccoon. Even a bug could make that kind of sound out here.* But something in my gut knew it wasn't just a bug. *What's out here?*

Miles pushed open the decrepit shack's door putting some weight behind each shove. After finally coming loose, it creaked open to reveal a dusty interior. Footsteps lined the floor, beer bottles rested in a corner, and shabby blankets I wouldn't touch with a ten-foot pole lay vagrantly across the floor. We made our way inside, and I panned the camera around the main room.

"The sister managed to pull away and ran as fast as she could back to the shack. All the while, she heard the rushed gallop behind her of whatever killed her brother. *As long as I get home, I'm safe*, she thought. But that wasn't the case. She ran inside and slammed the door. For a moment, the galloping steps stopped, the crickets continued to chirp, the fire still cracked. But only for a moment.

"Years later, people still think they hear the sister's scream throughout the woods. They still hear her calling for her brother. And scariest of all, they still hear the voice on a rasp of wind, 'There you are. Why did you make it so difficult to find you?'" Miles mimicked the raspy voice of the monster. He looked into the camera. "There have been reports of knocking on windows while people are in here, apparitions of a brother and sister staring at intruders, and the smell of a fire still burning in the hearth."

"Do we know the names of the brother and sister?" I asked, attempting to steal my voice.

Miles shook his head. "They were lost to time."

I let out a deep breath. "All right." Inhaling and preparing to yell, I blurted, "Hey, ghosts! Come on out! Show yourselves!"

"What are you doing?" Miles asked, raising an eyebrow.

"Ya gotta antagonize them a bit, if not they won't budge. Come on, try it."

"No way, dude. I respect the dead."

"Come at me!" I yelled to nothing. "You better watch out, or that monster will come get your ass again!"

25

We both stayed silent a second, but these ghosts were playing hard to get. I set my backpack down on the floor and pulled out one of my favorite devices.

"What does that do?" Miles asked. "I've seen those on ghost hunting shows."

"It's an EMF meter," I said, passing it to him. "It reads electromagnetic fields. Basically, it can sense when ghosts are around since they release energy. The higher the read, the closer—or sometimes stronger—they are."

"It says it's on a two right now." Miles looked at me, fear creeping into his eyes. "Does that mean something's here?"

"Not necessarily. It could be picking up anything, even our phones. I usually feel like it hits three or four when something's close."

"Have you ever gotten a—" but his words died on his lips. The EMF meter blared and shone an angry red light. It was at a five.

CHAPTER THREE

"**W**hoa, whoa, whoa!" Miles yelled, nearly dropping the (very expensive) EMF from his hands. "What's going on?"

Panic set in, but only for a moment. Then, a grin as wide as a crescent moon spread across my face. "It looks like we may have a ghost on our hands! Ooo, maybe even a demon!" I could hear how giddy my voice became. "Spirits! Now's your chance, show yourselves! Possess me—"

"Dude!"

"—Push me! Do whatever ya gotta do, just come out!"

Just as I said this, flailing the camera around worse than in *The Blair Witch Project*, I heard another creak at the front door. I swung around, ready to catch my first ghost on video, the camera following my line of sight. But . . . standing before me wasn't a ghost at all.

It was a girl.

"Riley?" I asked, lowering the camera.

"Miles? Simon?" she looked back and forth between the two of us.

"What are you doing here?" she and I both said in unison.

"We're ghost hunting," Miles said casually, lifting the EMF meter. "What about y—"

"You guys need to leave. Right now." Riley's eyes were harsh, and I saw her throat bob from a gulp.

"Is . . . everything okay?" I took a step toward her, the floorboards grating below my feet. She immediately took a step back, farther away from us. "Riley?"

"Leave! Now!" she urged. "It's not safe here."

"What do you mean? People from school come here all the time," Miles questioned.

"It's not safe *right now*." She pointed to the door, but neither of us took a step in that direction. She pressed her fingers to her temples. "Okay, I just need to be alone right now, all right? And this is the only place to do that. Get out of here, *please*."

"Riley, right before you walked in, this thing went off the charts," I said, pointing to the meter. "You're right. It's probably not safe in here. But it's not safe for *you* either." I attempted to take another step forward, but Riley gasped, grabbing her chest.

"What's going on?" Miles said. "Are . . . are you hurt?"

Riley yelled and threw herself to the floor, completely hiding her face. I ran and bent down to her.

"Don't touch me!" she screamed, causing me to fall back, my palms scraping against the floor. "Please leave, please leave, please leave," she begged. But Miles and I didn't move.

"Riley," I whispered. "Talk to us, what's happening."

She slowly lifted her face, her eyes meeting mine—but something wasn't right. Her eyes looked as if they had a film over them. Her pale skin grayed, turning almost blue and . . . translucent? "I'm sorry, this happens sometimes."

"What happens sometimes?" Miles asked. I couldn't see his face, but I just knew it was riddled with fear.

"This." Riley lifted herself from the ground and stood before us. I could see right through her, almost like she wasn't even here.

"Uhh, Simon. You're seeing this right? We're awake?"

"Uh-huh," I agreed, mouth agape.

"Cool. Coolcoolcoolcool. Okay, not dreaming. Great. I just—uh—have the invisible woman in front of me. Cool." Miles sounded like he was suppressing a scream. I couldn't blame him, I had one lodging in my throat too.

"So, you turn invisible?" I asked, trying to wrap my head around what was happening in front of me. Clearly, Riley *wasn't* okay. And whatever was happening wasn't new to her.

"Not invisible . . . although that can happen too."

"What does that mean? What, are you a ghost?" I chuckled, trying to lighten the mood.

"No, not exactly. I mean, right now I am. But not always."

"Riley . . . I was kidding." A cold breeze followed my words and a strike of pain through my chest.

"I wasn't."

"Wait, are you saying you're dead or something?" Miles's eyes widened in horror. "Are we in *Sixth Sense*? Was she a ghost this whole time?!"

There obviously had to be a logical explanation for all of this.

"No, no. I'm not dead," Riley held her hands in front of her, her voice was soft. It made me feel like I was a kindergartener being soothed by his teacher. "But someone nearby is." She looked over at Miles and me and saw that we didn't understand. With a heavy sigh, she continued, "I call myself a Viber. Like a medium, I can sense the supernatural. You're right about ghosts, Simon. They're real. But so are a lot of other things. Vampires, cryptids, sirens—pretty much all of it. When they're close enough, I not only feel them, I *become* them too." She paused.

Miles and I didn't speak. We couldn't. What could either of us possibly say?

29

"I try to help them. The ghosts and stuff, I mean. When I feel them, I try to find them," Riley continued.

I felt a rush of blood to my head and my ears drowned out Miles's constant freak-out. "Everything is . . . real?" I whispered to myself. "Everything is *real!*" I was in disbelief, even though it was standing right in front of my eyes, in the form of the hot girl from school.

My heart leaped from my chest, and I didn't know if it was from excitement or fear. Everything I had ever believed in, all of my time spent hunting and searching, it wasn't just a waste. Ghosts were *real.* Monsters really *did* lurk in shadows and under beds. I felt another smile creep across my face, the adrenaline from the new discovery pumped through my veins. I felt antsy and ready to see *more.* Ready to see it *all.*

"I tried to get you guys out of here before I vibed. I didn't want you guys to know. But you can still turn around, pretend this *was* just a dream, pretend you never saw me here. Ugh, I'm so sorry."

I felt bad. I wanted to hug her, but I knew that I couldn't because, logically, I'd phase right through her. I was at a loss for words.

Miles coughed, bringing me back to reality. "Well, my mind is officially blown, and I still think Simon drugged me or something. But I don't think I can turn around and pretend *this*—whatever this is—didn't happen. You said you help people you . . . vibe to? Well, if you're a ghost right now, does that mean there's another, eh, ghost near us?"

Riley nodded.

"I know we don't know each other well or anything. But this is pretty big. I think it automatically qualifies us as friends. And as a friend"—he took a deep breath—"I'm willing to help. I don't think I would've survived in this town or school much longer without meeting Si. And who knows, maybe we're meant to be the three amigos. The ghost girl and the ghost believers. We could be like the Ghostbusters, but hot."

Riley smiled.

Finally standing, I patted Miles on the back and looked at Riley. She stared at me for a moment, and I knew she was waiting for me to say something. But instead, I thrust my hand in the middle of all three of us, outstretched, like a damn '90s sports movie. Without a moment's hesitation, Miles placed his on top. We both turned to Riley. Her eyes fell on our hands, and for a moment she didn't move.

"Aw, what the hell." She sighed, placing her delicate, ghostly hand at the top of the pile.

I looked up into ghostly eyes. "Now, how can we help?"

CHAPTER FOUR

We had a mission: to find the ghost and figure out what to do with it. That was all Riley told us. I admit, it was a bit vague considering everything Miles and I just had to swallow.

Ghosts were real, obviously, but so were all the fantasy creatures I grew up with in fairy tales. *Wait, were fairies real too?* I'd have to make a mental note to ask her. It was a lot of information to process in such a short amount of time.

Riley explained more about her gift as we trudged through the forest. She also seemed to have a mental compass for these beings and, according to her, the ghost we were in pursuit of was north.

She compared herself to a "medium," like the ones on TV who communicated with spirits. But this seemed like there was more behind it than just calling herself a ghost whisperer. She not only felt the being and communicated, but she *became* the being as well—as a replica, a *viber* she called it. Kind of like a copycat, only she held the value of her true self. Like right now, she was a ghost, but also still Riley. She wasn't lost and she wasn't dead. She wasn't haunting anyone.

"I've been like this for as long as I can remember. I don't really know what started it. I don't remember the first time it happened, the moments of me as a kid muddle together," Riley said as we all walked uphill toward the ghost.

We had been walking for a few minutes. The moon was high but shaded by clouds. Miles and I had to use our flashlights, while Riley provided us with a faint blue glow around her. Each step she took looked more like a hover. Her impact made no noise, no leaves crunching underneath her. Her breath was also non-existent, while Miles and I were basically gasping for any breath we could.

It was all surreal. One thing I did know for sure was that the forums, and my friends back home, wouldn't have believed me if I had told them.

"How does it feel?" I asked with sharp heaves. "How does it feel to be . . ."

"Dead?" she finished. "I can't explain it even if I wanted to. It happened a lot when I was a kid. I would always freak out. Once or twice, I actually became invisible, like *The Invisible Man*. My mom couldn't see me and I remember trying everything in my power to get her to notice me. It was terrifying. Once it ended, I thought about other ghosts—the real ghosts—who go through that when they die. I decided I wanted to help them."

"Like Jennifer Love Hewitt," I remarked. They both shot me a look with raised eyebrows.

"So are you like this"—Miles motioned to all of her—"until the ghost 'moves on'?"

"Not exactly. It's more like when they're close. A certain radius sets it off. When they're out of that radius, I go back to normal ol' Riley. The closer we get, the more I feel them, the more I know them. We're pretty close to him now."

"Him?"

"The spirit. It's a man. He's older, I think. He's not evil, just sad. I don't feel a traumatic death. Just one *he* wasn't quite ready for yet." Riley's voice was back to its usual self. Relaxed. *If I touched her, would I phase right through her?*

"Hey Riley," Miles's voice boomed, breaking my thoughts. "I was wondering, have you changed into the other stuff that you say exists? Like, maybe . . . werewolves?"

She turned back to look at him, but still seemed to be floating upward, toward our destination, and so we continued to trek behind her.

"Once," she rolled her eyes. "They kind of lose themselves with the first couple transformations and wreak total havoc."

"Do *you* also . . . lose yourself?" Miles's voice sounded shaky like he was afraid of the answer himself. She looked at him, contemplating.

"For a few minutes, in the beginning, I do. The transformation is excruciating. Blinding pain. I feel like those first few minutes are more adrenaline-fueled than the curse itself." She paused. "I think the same is said for the werewolves, but they have less control since they're actually under the curse and I'm just a cheap knockoff of the same product."

"Are there werewolves in Ravenswood?" I asked, and her gaze shifted toward me. She stopped floating upward and we stopped our climb.

"I haven't seen a werewolf in a long time, but I wouldn't be surprised if they showed up. I hate to say this, guys, especially since you both just moved here. But Ravenswood is kind of like . . . a nesting ground for the supernatural. Weird is born here and also flees *to* here. Don't ask me why, but they like it here. I feel like I was given this power, and if they're all here, maybe it's my job, my duty, to help them."

"Like a supernatural sheriff," Miles said in wonder.

She laughed. "Yeah, like the supernatural sheriff. Like mother, like daughter, I guess. We're getting close, by the way."

My heart was pumping. I was about to see a real-life ghost. My dream was finally being realized. I was shaking from excitement. Or was I afraid? Would he look like a hollow shell of what he used to be, perhaps? Would I be able to see him at all or would he be invisible like the first few times Riley changed? The more I thought about it, the more excited I got.

I think the other two noticed my mood, because Riley turned to me quickly with her index finger on her lips, telling me to shush. I looked over at Miles, and he disapprovingly shook his head at me but smiled.

Through the tree line, we saw a house at the top of the hill. One dim light was seen through a window on the second floor. Riley turned back to us.

"He's in there. I'm going up. You guys stay here."

"And miss all the ghost action?" I complained.

"Look, I need to see if he's dangerous or not. I don't feel ill intent coming from him, but sometimes they react differently once they see me. I'll try to bring him down here. First, I need to talk to him, alone."

Riley floated up to the house and phased through the wall. Miles and I sat and waited.

Miles's head was bobbing back and forth from sleep with soft snores coming from him as a bit of drool slid onto his fist that was propping his head up. I sat, shaking my right leg in anticipation. Riley had been gone for almost an hour. What if something went wrong? What were Miles and I supposed to do then? And how would we help her if it came down to that? I checked my phone again, only one minute had passed. A text from my mom asked how I was doing and when I was coming home.

Good. And soon, just hanging out a bit longer, I replied.

Truth was, I didn't know when I'd be home. And I was anything but good right now. Another minute passed. Was Riley okay? I just couldn't take it anymore. I stood up, accidentally waking Miles.

"Everything good?" he said, wiping the drool from his mouth and standing up. He adjusted his pants and pulled his jacket in closer. The air was getting colder with the passing time, and I saw Miles shudder as he rubbed his eyes.

"I'm worried about Riley. It's been a while. I'm going up there."

Before Miles could protest, I began to climb the last bit of the hill. I took about four steps and, just before I could go any farther, I saw the same blue glow emerging from the side of the house. Only this time, there were two glows. As they approached, I immediately knew one was Riley (I sighed with relief), and the other was an elderly man. Probably in his eighties. He slowly walked, without his feet touching the ground, same as Riley. He held onto her, arms linked. She helped him walk down the mountain toward us. He was short and plump. Even with his faded transparency, I could tell he had little hair, and what he did have was now all white. His skin was pale, and he wore square-shaped glasses that sat on his round nose.

Finally reaching us, the man gleamed.

"Frank, these are my friends, Miles and Simon," Riley introduced us.

"Hello, boys! Sorry to keep you out here so long. You must be freezing!" His tone was so comforting. Miles and I said hello and waited for Riley to explain.

"Frank was taking care of his granddaughter when he . . . passed," Riley said carefully.

Frank's head fell and he shook it. "My damn heart. It hadn't been doing well the last few years. Too much bacon." He chuckled. Something about him touched me. I felt bad for this man and his granddaughter, but I also found him endearing.

"So, he felt like he needed to keep looking after her. It's been a few weeks, however. I'm never this close to this part of the woods so I didn't feel him before. But we think it's time. Rachael is going to be just fine, Frank. We can watch over her for you now."

The man nodded. "Yes, I think she will be. She don't need me no more. I'll watch down on her from the other place." Frank smiled and turned to Riley, grabbing her hands together. "Thank you, dear. You've made this old, dead man feel okay about this all." He shook her hands and smiled again. A tear came down his cheek. Riley wiped it from his face before he turned to us. "Thank you, all of you." Frank smiled and looked up.

Riley chuckled. "This is my favorite part."

Just then, his blue glow turned into small dancing lights all around us, slowly sashaying up toward the sky. For a moment, we were transported to a different world. One filled with peace and wonder. We watched until they faded from existence, leaving our world and entering something beyond our understanding.

The gleam had vanished, and, to my surprise, Riley was back to herself again. Without thinking, I ran and threw my arms around her. She looked at me, wide-eyed.

"Thank goodness you're you again!"

"I was always me. I'm just not 'dead' me." She laughed.

Miles coughed and broke my hug.

"That's what I meant. We can touch you again." I caught Miles giving me that smirk again. It didn't dawn on me until that moment, I just hugged Riley. I just told her we can *touch her*. I quickly pulled my arms to my sides and shoved my hands in my pockets. She looked at Miles, then at me. Picking up on how utterly uncomfortable I was, she punched me in the arm. It kind of hurt.

"Means I can do that again." She threw her hands on her hips.

"Let's get out of here. I can take you guys home." Without another word, she started down the hill, through the woods. There were a million questions I was eager to ask her. How did she do what she did? Could I do that too?

We made the trek to Riley's car, an old olive-colored SUV that had definitely seen better days. As we approached, Riley stopped and turned to Miles and me. She stared down at the ground. "Look . . . I know everything that happened tonight was weird. You guys need to know that this kind of thing happens to me all the time. Other people at school don't know, so I would appreciate it if you didn't tell anyone."

We both nodded quickly. First off, no one would believe us. Second, hell—I couldn't speak for Miles—but I was still wrapping my head around a floating Riley.

"Cool, thanks. Also, I just want to say that I totally understand if you guys don't . . . you know . . . wanna hang out anymore. You two are probably shitting bricks right now and these situations usually get weirder and more dangerous. I'd understand if you guys want to bail."

Miles and I looked at each other. He lifted his head, wanting me to take this one.

I walked up to Riley and put my hand on her shoulder.

"I thought we already said that we're with you. No matter how weird. It suits us and we wanna be here." I smiled at her.

"Although the danger part kinda does spook me. We're with you, Riley," Miles chimed.

"I think we should make this into a formal thing. Your talent would be awesome on my channel." I grinned. She rose her eyebrows and laughed.

"But . . . wouldn't it be bad if it gets out?"

"Please." Miles walked up to us and threw his hand onto her other shoulder. "No one is going to believe his whack-ass videos. The internet is too cynical to believe in the supernatural. Have you *been* online recently?" He laughed and put his other hand on my shoulder. With this, Riley and I put our hands on the remaining shoulders to complete the circle. "Plus, we still need to come up with a dope name. We're real ghost hunters now."

"Real *supernatural* hunters," Riley corrected.

"Right, you need to tell us everything you know," I said with the utmost urgency.

Miles let out a huge yawn. "Maybe tell us tomorrow because clearly, we've had enough fun for today."

Miles was dropped off first. He waved with a sleepy hand and turned to go inside. I was next. The ride to my house was mostly sitting in silence. We pulled up and I hopped out.

"Good night, Riles. Thanks for the lift."

She smiled at the nickname. I think she liked it.

"Miles . . . Riles . . . You can be Smiles," she smirked again. "G'night, Smiles."

The rest of the weekend flew by. Sunday was mostly spent sleeping and eating. Not to mention lowkey reliving the ghost hunt in my mind. I wanted to jot everything down in my notebook, but it was still in one of my boxes. We were all still tired from the first week of living in Ravenswood (albeit, some more than others), we still hadn't fully unpacked.

I wondered if Miles was also fangirling about our new friend being a medium. Or the fact that my dumbass rushed to hug her. I mean, I barely knew her, yet I was so glad she was okay. Of course, the supernatural was everywhere, but to have a town as small as Ravenswood be an epicenter for this stuff seemed far-fetched. Then again, people believed aliens weren't real and they're clearly wrong, so maybe I was too.

Monday reared its ugly head. There was no difference in time when it came to waking up for school in Miami to here, but I had come to the conclusion that I just wasn't a morning person.

It was a colder day than I was used to but I was happy to be wearing my ghost beanie again. My ears were warm, and that made for a happy Simon. I also noticed I accidentally grabbed my dad's jacket in the morning—a giant, black, zip-up hoodie. I looked as if I could get lost in it. Lucky for me, oversized clothes were in style now, so I decided to make it my jacket.

Today I had English, PE, art, and Spanish, and Miles was in each class with me except for art. Turns out he's more of a band kind of guy. Riley shared English and art with me.

I bumped into Riley on the way to first period.

"Hey, Smiles." She walked in rhythm with me. She's back in her all-dark and heavy black eye makeup. "How was your weekend?"

"Oh, you know. I was pretty much in a supernatural vegetative state. I didn't do a thing and it was amazing." I chuckled. "How was yours?"

She giggled in response. "I also slept most of it. Becoming dead rather than undead takes a lot out of a girl."

"I know how that feels." I playfully elbowed her. Our laughter came to a stop when we heard a loud noise.

Across the hall, we watched Miles being pushed into the lockers, his collar gripped tightly by none other than Mr. Puberty—Austin Rhodes. He glared at Miles, giving him the nastiest look I'd ever seen. Miles's bag was on the floor, open, and his books sprawled across the floor. *Where the hell is a teacher when you need one?*

Through the crowd of onlookers, I saw a guy from our history class, Jake, look between Miles and Austin, and take a step forward. He was an athlete of some kind, I never paid enough attention to figure out which sport he played.

"Hey!" he said, nearing them. He was shorter than Austin, but bulkier, and had darker features. Dark hair and even darker eyes, with tanned skin from the countless hours he must spend outside.

Thanks to the interruption, Austin loosened his grip on Miles's collar, jerking his head in the direction of the other guy. I saw an opportunity and stomped up to them, with Riley on my heels, and as we neared, Mr. Puberty let Miles go and turned to leave, stepping on the fallen books.

"What was that about?" Riley asked. Her arms crossed over each other. She seemed pissed.

"Dude's a jerk. You okay, man?" Jake asked, turning to him.

Miles nodded. "Thanks, dude."

Jake flashed an awkward smile at us all and raised his hand in a wave before disappearing back into the crowd.

"Why does Mr. Puberty have it out for you?" I reiterated.

"Guess he hates me." Miles shrugged.

"Why? What'd ya do?" I said in a motherly tone to ease the tension. Miles chuckled and sighed.

"Nothing, nothing. But . . ." he stopped for a moment and shrugged again. "I'm Black and gay—so that probably hurts his ego."

For the briefest moment, I thought back to all the movies I had seen. When the best friend comes out, the friend being told usually says some speech like, "Wow, I'm so proud of you and accept you for you,"

41

or "That's so cool," but to be honest, I found that pretty cringy. And I had only recently met the guy and became the best of friends. So I responded the only way I knew how: I looked at my new friend and placed my hand on his shoulder. "He probably has a crush on you."

"He is *so* not my type." Miles chuckled, his shoulders finally relaxing. He glanced back in the direction Mr. Puberty went and said, "That guy just keeps buggin' me. I don't get it. He has been since the first week of school. I haven't even spoken to him." He looked down at his hands. They were shaking. He *was* afraid.

"Austin's not usually a bully," Riley began. "He keeps to himself, but . . . he *always* looks angry. Like something's up with him. I actually—"

Just then, the bell rang. We were all late. Riley grabbed the two of us by our wrists and trotted off to English. We all sat relatively near each other, which was nice.

We had just started reading *The Crucible* and, of course, Miles and I ragged on Riley, saying she would definitely be burned at the stake if we lived in that era. Witches *had* to be real, so . . . was Riley an actual witch? Was that the reason she had these powers? Were there more people who went through the same thing? Maybe then Riley wouldn't feel so alone. Luckily, however, she had Miles and me—sans powers, but we're still pretty great.

At some point, class ended and it was time for PE Unfortunately, Miles and I shared this class with Austin. We all exchanged angry looks and we avoided the tall brute as much as we could. He was probably the size of the two of us combined, an Adonis of a high schooler. It didn't matter. If he approached Miles, even a tad, I had promised myself I would defend my friend as much as I could. We would go down together.

I kept thinking about what Riley said. Why was he

suddenly so mean to Miles? Was he just homophobic? Racist? Or was it something else? And was Miles thinking the same thing?

After PE, we all met back up for lunch. Riley, Miles, and I sat in our now-usual place away from everyone else. She had whispered to us suddenly as we left English. "I feel . . . something," she hissed under her breath.

Now, as we sat in the crowded and loud cafeteria, she was ready to dish. "So, earlier today, I felt something. I'm not quite sure what it was but it was strong and didn't feel like a spirit." She was a bit dazed.

"What should we do about it?" Miles's voice quivered a bit, poking his fork in his mashed potatoes. He seemed to be more afraid of creatures than spirits. Riley looked up at him, meeting his eyes, then to me, with the crevice of a questioning grin on her face. We all had the same idea.

"We go searching," I said, triumphantly. The two smiled at me with determination in their eyes, Miles's fear disappearing.

We were doing this.

We had all agreed to tell our parents that we were meeting up at each other's houses to study that night. Riley made up a huge test that we *needed* to pass, and thus the studying might take longer than curfew would allow. Since we just moved, my parents felt like I still needed adjusting, so they had been lenient on rules. They allowed me to go, without even questioning or calling the other parents to confirm. Which was a good thing, because Riley and Miles had told their parents they would be at my house. I told my parents I would be at Miles's studying chemistry until my brain rotted, but really the three of us would be neck-deep in the middle of Ravenswood's forest.

Vibing.

That was what Riley called it when she became the supernatural. She was a viber. She explained it as though she connected to the creatures and then vibed to their same wavelength, and that was what made her *become* them. I wrote all of this down in a small notebook I had decided to carry around with me everywhere. I used it to keep track of all supernatural notes and facts. Riley explained that the ghost the other night was definitely one of the easiest encounters she'd had to deal with. Some ghouls, such as the vampires she faced last fall, were exceptionally difficult tasks to overcome.

I waited for Riley to pick me up to go to the forest just after sunset. I wore a heavy brown jacket, hiking boots, a thick pair of blue jeans, and my signature beanie. I also carried a backpack, containing all my ghost-hunting equipment. I had my EMF ready, my video camera with night vision, and an extra battery just in case. I was eager and ready for anything. Riley agreed to let me film on the condition that if I posted it anywhere, I would say it was just good editing. Which didn't bother me. I would know the truth and that's all that mattered.

Riley's car pulled up to the front of my house, the window was rolled down and I could already see Miles sitting shotgun and waving at me. I yelled goodbye to my parents, who had been in the other room, and ran out the front door. Riley and Miles greeted me, Riley started her engine, and then we were off.

"Let's go catch this ghoul." She practically stomped on the gas. Riley had used this term a couple of times. She used it in lieu of "creatures" and "ghosts" because it was easier to categorize them all together. Another one for the Riley dictionary (which I nicknamed my own *Necronomicon*).

From the back seat, I saw Riley's hand grip the

steering wheel tighter and tighter. She started to breathe heavily, and continuously tried to crack her neck. Her knuckles were white from her tight grip. Riley suddenly stopped the car, pulling it over to the side of the road.

"Hey, Riley, you good?" Miles asked before I could.

She awkwardly, almost like she had a hard time controlling herself, nodded. "Yeah. I'm vibing hard right now. We're close. And—" She let out a yell that almost sounded more like a growl in between. She took a deep breath. "I know what we're searching for. You guys aren't going to like it."

"What is it?" I asked, my voice shaking the tiniest bit. Riley flexed her hands on the steering wheel, and as she did, I began to see small brown hairs growing on her arms and hands.

She stayed quiet for a moment, and then she looked at the both of us, her eyes turning a strange shade of amber. And her teeth had grown longer, sharper. Her eyes went back to the road—no, not the road. She looked up toward the sky. Looming over us was a bright, large, full moon.

"A werewolf."

CHAPTER FIVE

Miles and I jumped out while she stayed in, panting. I looked around us and we were once again standing right in front of Ravenswood's forest. The wind whistled through the trees as I gawked. In a strange way, I felt drawn to the forest also. Almost as if it was calling me, begging me to go in and uncover its mysteries. I didn't quite understand it but I felt as though I couldn't take my eyes away from it. Something was looking back at me. Something deep, deep in the trees. Something I couldn't see but felt instead. I knew that whatever it was, we were looking straight into each other's eyes. Without thinking, I took a step forward.

Miles broke the trance by grabbing my shoulder. I looked at him, fear written all over his face. Before he could speak, I glanced back into the forest, but the sensation was gone. It was just normal trees and a normal forest again. I shook my head lightly, brushing off what had just happened as a fluke and getting back to the matter at hand.

The night sky was dark with some clouds in sight, the moon like the beam of a flashlight. Miles stood close to me, looking utterly petrified. It felt like we had just stepped into an '80s horror movie, full of campy-looking fog and cawing crows. I eagerly anticipated the foley sounds of aluminum sheets to clap thunder and the random strobe effect for lightning.

"Hey, man, how are you doing?" I patted his back and he jumped a little at the sudden touch.

"Ye-yeah. Werewolves just freak me out. More than anything else . . ." he trailed off. He shifted on his feet back and forth like he couldn't stay still.

"We just need to stand back. After she transforms, she'll still be Riley," I reassured him, unsure if I was telling the truth.

We heard a deep growl coming from the car and watched the door on the driver's side burst open. Riley stumbled out and landed on the ground, hard. She hunched over the dirt on all fours, wheezing and growling in each breath. Her body was shaking and twitching. She seemed to be flexing her fingers and hands, continuously.

"Riley?" I whispered. I took a careful step forward. She threw her hand up, signaling me to stop, before clawing at the ground, clutching the dirt in between her fingers. The growling only grew more ferocious. She sounded like she was in so much pain. Her bones began to make loud crackling sounds and her body kept shifting. She hurriedly removed her jacket just as her shoulder blades popped upward, diving deep into her back. At the same moment, it looked like her arms elongated, her bones contorted in all directions. Her fingers got longer as her nails grew from her cuticles and became sharp, thick claws. Thick, coarse hair began to grow everywhere. She looked like she grew hind legs. She screamed as her nose and mouth turned into a snout, and her teeth sharpened into vicious fangs.

Riley was gone and all that was left before us was a werewolf. An actual werewolf. Riley was fully transformed. She looked up toward the sky, reaching up on her hind legs, and howled. It was iconic. Straight out of *American Werewolf in London*. Riley was the wolf.

She dropped back down to all fours and turned her gaze to us. Miles and I were frozen, we didn't move an inch. I didn't even breathe. She growled and crawled toward us. I took a slow step back and saw Miles do the same. Her eyes raked between the two of us and then settled on mine. I wanted to run, as far as I could. My feet were begging me. My heart raced, pumping feverishly against my chest, to the point of pain. I took another step back.

"Riley?" Her name came out of my mouth, but I didn't recognize my own voice. Riley growled again, taking another step closer. But then the snarl fell away, turning into something softer. She sat back, making herself look like a giant dog. She stopped growling and began to pant. Miles nudged me, asking me if it was safe. How was I supposed to know? I'd never had to deal with werewolves before, much less a girl-turned-werewolf. I looked back to the now-tame Riley. There was no menace in her manor. Nothing out of the ordinary. I stepped forward, reaching my hand out. Surely it would be better if she snapped my hand off rather than gnawing my face off, right?

Riley nudged my hand with her head. I felt her fur and she brushed her ear under my hand. It was surprisingly soft, like an actual animal. Her eyes were a vibrant, unnatural yellow but the shape was still Riley. Her fur was a dark blond, the color of Riley's roots.

Of course it was still her. I turned back to Miles who seemed more relaxed.

"She's Riley again."

He sighed, his fear slowly washing away. Riley gave an approving noise.

She started to walk toward the edge of the trees. I gathered my gear together, turned on my voice recorder to catch any EVPs we might collect, and finally turned my camera on, placing it on night vision. We followed behind her, leaving a gap between us just in case.

"Catch." I tossed Miles a flashlight.

He walked ahead of me and caught up to Riley, but something held me back. I looked past my friends, into the lush yet daunting forest. The thing that called to me earlier and the feeling of being watched was rushing back. The darkness that bled into the trees seemed . . . daunting. I tried to make out details but was overcome with uneasiness.

Riley howled and broke my concentration. I wanted to shake the feeling off, but I still felt on edge. I decided it was just paranoia and anxiety about following a werewolf around the forest. I had seen too many horror movies that made me feel like something was standing behind me. This was no different.

At least, that's what I was trying to tell myself.

We walked for a while, Riley's truck behind us, no longer visible to our eyes. Riley sniffed at the ground a few times, searching.

Her size was strange. She had a face like a wolf, but her back was hunched like a bipedal werewolf. So, when she was on all fours, she was the size of an above-average wolf. When she stood on her hind legs, tall and strong, she was nearly a foot taller than me. I thought back to her transformation. It must have hurt so much; I couldn't imagine someone under the curse going through the transformation every night.

Riley suddenly stopped; her head and ears perked up and she began to growl straight ahead of us. A huge and ragged ghoul stepped out from the darkness beyond. Miles went stiff and didn't move. Was he even breathing?

I shifted my gaze back to the giant beast. It took another step forward, the moonlight finally revealing its face. It had glowing green eyes and thick fur in a light shade of brown. He was snarling, baring his saliva-covered fangs. Honestly, it was kind of gross. He growled aggressively in our direction and dropped one of his large, clawed hands to the ground.

After seeing him, and looking back at Riley, it was clear this werewolf was male. He was twice the size of her, broad and muscular. Veins rippled through his forearms, and his hind legs were thick and powerful. Where Riley towered over me standing up, this male werewolf stood even taller than her. I understood why Miles was so terrified. My heart skipped a beat. I grabbed his arm and the two of us backed up, taking slow, precautionary steps.

The werewolf's eyes darted up.

Shit.

Before anything could happen, Riley leaped forward, claws drawn, jumping in front of the beast. While she was smaller, her face was utterly fierce. She snapped at the other wolf, who took a step backward. They seemed to be communicating.

The male wolf dropped onto all fours and began to recede. Riley pushed on, making sure it wouldn't try to attack. The male wolf bowed its head a tiny bit and Riley stood tall. It was clear she had asserted dominance. She looked back at us, and I knew it was time to continue our plan.

I let go of Miles, who had still been shaking, and placed my backpack on the ground. I put my camera in his hand, forcing him to hold it, pointing at the wolf. With my hands free, I pulled out a big, iron chain. It was one of the many things Riley told me to bring just in case. We didn't know what we'd be up against, but this apparently was a pretty big standard while searching for ghouls.

The chains felt heavy in my hands. I had seen enough movies to know if I were going to chain this guy to a tree, it had to be a big one, one he couldn't easily uproot. I looked to Riley, who already seemed to know exactly what I was thinking. She turned to a nearby tree. The trunk was thicker than any of the rest around us—it was our best option.

Riley ushered our new friend toward the thick bark. I realized at this moment how much trust and faith I had in a girl I'd only known for a few days. I couldn't tell if I was stupid for trusting her, giving into my dream of being a paranormal investigator. The strange bond I felt between the three of us—that made me feel like I was exactly where I was meant to be, that my whole life was dedicated to meeting these two incredible people.

Regardless, I was standing in the middle of a vast forest, in the middle of the night, with two were-wolves, and one chicken. One of which I was slowly approaching. I decided, for the sake of this moment, I needed to believe in the second option.

This was fate.

Right?

As I rounded up to the male werewolf, his piercing green eyes met mine. He snarled for a brief second but then turned his eyes back on Riley, relaxing. He was much scarier up close. His fur was matted as if he had been out in the rain for a long time. He had bits of blood under his mouth that dripped onto his chest. Fear rushed through me so quickly that I felt like I was going to be sick. I swallowed hard and lifted the chains. I looked over to Miles, who was wide-eyed and statuesque.

Well, Simon, looks like it's just you and the chains.

I wrapped them around the tree and the wolf, who took a step back, allowing me to make the chains tighter. It seemed like he knew what was happening. Maybe he was conscious like Riley? Once the chains were firmly around him, he slouched against the tree and turned to all of us one more time.

Riley made a noise in his general direction, communicating a final message. The male wolf tilted his head to the ground and lifted his eyes, making perfect eye contact with Miles. After a long second, the wolf closed his eyes. We stood there for a few moments observing him, but nothing changed. Miles was still standing far behind us, staring at the resting werewolf. I slowly walked up, not wanting to startle him, and rested my hand on Miles's shoulder.

"You good?"

"Too much for me, I think. I don't know why werewolves are so terrifying. The way they lose control and can't help it. In movies, you always see how much damage they do to those close to them, even if they don't want to. The human behind the beast."

He continued to stare at the wolf chained to the tree. His voice was softer, weaker than I had ever heard it. I saw a different emotion in Miles's eyes, something other than fear. "His eyes look familiar," he spoke again. His confidence was restored, and he was the same old Miles again.

With the werewolf fully chained up, Riley began walking past us and back toward the car, ushering us to follow. Miles and I walked back in silence. I know I wasn't the one transforming into a werewolf, but I was exhausted. It was late and the moon was high. We planned to stay in Riley's truck until morning to untie the victim of the curse.

By then, we would know who it was.

Finally reaching the car, Riley began shifting back into a human. She made a few agonizing sounds and squirmed on the ground. In seconds, a bare but very human Riley huddled on the ground. At the sight of her, I felt my face flush, and quickly turned around.

"It's okay, Simon." Riley chuckled.

Miles, unphased, jogged to the truck and pulled out a large, black sweatshirt from the trunk. He helped Riley put it on and walked toward the driver's door. I snapped out of my boyish daze and followed them.

I laid down across the back seat, Miles sat in the passenger, and Riley in the driver's seat with both their seats reclined.

"All right, good night, everyone. I'm dead. No pun intended." Miles slunk back in his seat; his eyes were fighting to stay open.

"How does it feel to help your first ghoul?" She looked at me.

"Was that really helping him? Like is that what you normally do?" I yawned. Sleep was calling my name too, but I wanted desperately to keep talking to Riley.

"Of course. Not all of the ghouls I encounter need to be 'sent on' like ghosts do. And not all ghouls I come across need saving; some need exterminating. You guys luckily haven't encountered any of the bad ghouls yet, but they're out there."

"I want to hear all about them," I interjected.

"One day, Smiles. You did a great thing by helping this werewolf. He probably doesn't really know what's going on. When they first change, it's like they lose a part of themselves and it takes some serious training to be able to control the wolf, and even more to unite man and wolf. What's even worse is that they remember everything that happens the next morning."

"That's pretty unlike the movies. Normally, they have no idea what kind of sins they committed but find themselves in a pool of blood or something campy like that," I whispered.

"Well, not in real life. They remember everything: every animal they killed, people they hurt or scared. It's some scary stuff. Now that we've chained him to the tree, he can't do any of that. And once tomorrow morning comes, I'll be able to explain the situation and see if he needs my help."

"How are you going to help him?"

"I'm not really sure yet." Riley cracked her neck as she spoke.

"And if we can't help him?" I mumbled, fearing the potential grim answer. "Is he going to need . . . *exterminating*?"

53

Riley laughed, causing Miles to snort in his sleep. "I haven't gotten to that point yet. No, if they don't want to accept the fact that they're a werewolf, I'll ask them to leave town. That's what I did that last time."

It sounded so simple, but clearly, it worked. I wondered how many other ghouls Riley had encountered.

"You did a great thing today, Si." Riley yawned. "Congrats on your first proper 'ghoul hunt,'" she air quoted.

I sat back and considered her words. I helped this guy, I *saved* him. Proud of myself, I looked at Riley one more time. Her eyes were already closed and she was breathing deeply.

As I rested on the door of the back seat behind Miles, my eyes wandered through the adjacent window, to the trees and forest we had just been in. It was late and the night air was thick and full, with a light haze of fog surrounding us. Comforted by the sleeping sounds of my two friends and exhausted from the day and adventure we just had, I relaxed my eyes and drifted off to sleep.

Tap. Tap. Tap.

Something was making a soft noise on the window.

It happened every other second. I calmly opened my eyes and scanned around. Everything appeared foggy, dark, and blurry as if I was wearing dirty glasses. It took a moment for my eyes to focus on the time on the car radio: 3:28 a.m. I rubbed my eyes and waited until I was able to make out the shapes of Riley and Miles, who were still sound asleep. My gaze drifted toward the window. The tapping seemed endless. *How do they not hear it?*

The outside world was even darker and gray, like

something straight out of a Vincent Price movie. The fog slowly poured from the forest tree line and surrounded our car. I inched forward, adjusting myself to see directly out of the window the tapping came from. Nothing.

I begrudgingly shifted to a more comfortable position and tried to go back to sleep. The tapping was replaced by a voice in my head. Commanding me.

Come.

My eyes jolted open and followed the voice's command to the tree line. No, not to the tree line, but *through* the trees, past the branches and trunks, and into the darkness beyond. The voice came back, calling me, beckoning me forward. My body reacted on its own and I solemnly shifted from my comfortable position and opened the back door.

In what felt like seconds, I was deep in the forest, going in a different direction than we had earlier. I couldn't make out where in the forest I was. My gaze was fixed, pointed in a specific direction somewhere out there. My mind raced and begged me to turn around, but my body didn't listen. The cold air stung the tips of my nose and ears, my fingers were going stiff. With each step, I could see my breath in front of me in a small cloud. The voice became louder and distinguishable.

Only, it didn't sound *human.*

It sounded like those smoking commercials, where the age-old smokers have holes in their throats and need special devices to speak, but it also sounded fluid. Like it was nothing more than a whisper—a very, *very* raspy whisper.

And it kept calling out to me.

Simon—come here. Help me. Please.

While the words were innocent, helpless, the voice seemed giddy, as if it were mocking someone. Mocking me. My body continued forward, and the voice only grew louder.

I came up to a small clearing in the forest when my body stopped. Looking around blankly, all I saw was the darkness surrounding the trees. It was utterly unnatural. Where light should be, there wasn't any. I was amassed by a large circle of trees and those trees were flooded by darkness.

Just like earlier in the night, the voice told me to look ahead. Immediately, the sensation of being watched captivated my entire body, sending tingles down my spine. I felt like eyes were on me from every direction, breathing down around me. I swore I saw shadows in the corners of my vision moving in all directions.

Then I was prompted to look forward, beyond the trees and into the darkness. I stared for what felt like an eternity. The voice had all but stopped suddenly. As if a reaction to my own thoughts, directly into my right ear someone whispered.

Simon . . .

I felt their hot breath on my cheek and smelled the awful aroma of rusting metal, of something rotting or decaying. It hit me then that what I smelled wasn't metal.

It was blood.

My eyes wouldn't move, no matter how hard I tried, they wouldn't turn in the direction the voice or smell came from. They only looked straight ahead, into the darkness.

Hello, Simon, I've been waiting for you, it whispered, each breath from the being wheezed louder and louder. I felt something gently run up my arm, making circular motions. It felt cold and stiff, but hard. Like a long nail attached to a frozen finger.

Welcome home.

The voice retreated and the smell shifted. The finger slipped from my arm and disappeared. I was alone, but I also wasn't. I felt as though I was meeting someone's eyes, having a staring contest to see who would last longer.

I was losing.

Something, or someone, was looking directly at me, directly into my eyes. But I couldn't see them. I couldn't see the pair of eyes that had been watching me so closely since the evening began.

Until I did.

In the depths of the darkness directly ahead of me, two eyes slowly opened to reveal glowing beams of red fixed on me. There were no pupils, no whites, just glowing red. The illuminating eyes contorted, the person they belonged to smiling, the teeth jagged, sharp, and misaligned. I knew in my gut the smile was wicked. Evil.

A cold chill ran along my skin and forced me to shiver.

Simon . . . the carmine eyes glistened.

Simon . . .

"Simon!"

I jolted up. It was early morning and I was still in the back seat of Riley's beat-up truck. Miles was stretching while Riley shook my leg. I looked at her and then at the radio. It read 7:19 a.m. My eyes shifted to my surroundings, my body's sleeping position, and the temperature on the car's dashboard. Everything had been as it was when I fell asleep. Nothing changed. So did that mean . . . it was a dream? All of it?

I searched the forest—it was bright and colorful. The only kind of fog was a light morning dew. My arm hairs were sticking up and I couldn't tell if it was from the memory of the cold finger that traced my arm or if it was from the brisk morning air.

Miles hopped out of the car, swigging back an entire bottle of water. Riley climbed out, carefully. She still wasn't wearing pants, only wearing the large sweat-shirt from the night before. She shivered and made her way to the trunk of the car, rifling through items until she found what she was looking for. The next I saw her, she wore skin-tight black leggings tucked into boots.

Someone knocked on the window behind me, and my gaze snapped to see what it was. Had the tapping returned; was it real? But my face was only met with Miles. He was offering me my own bottle of water. I opened the door and climbed out, taking the drink.

"We need to go. You guys got the stuff?" Riley rubbed her hands together, in a gesture to warm them up. Miles's mouth was full of a protein bar he'd been cramming down, but he nodded to Riley's questions. His hands were full with three more bottles of water, a gray sweatshirt and basketball shorts hung over his arm, and I counted five protein bars sticking out from his pockets.

"Great, I'll lead the way."

Riley started on the track back to where we had left the werewolf a few hours earlier. Miles followed suit.

Still dazed, I felt like I was forgetting something. Or rather, leaving something behind. I looked around, and back to the car. Nothing but a whisper from the dream, a fading memory. The voice I had remembered so easily now began to fog, to morph into something unrecognizable. The feeling I had shifted into what I *felt* I should feel versus what I had actually felt. The touch of the ice-cold finger turned more into a trace on my arm than a pressing cold. The breath on my neck simply became the breeze on this September morning.

Steering my attention back to my friends, I caught up to them, storing my thoughts away for another time. Miles was asking Riley questions.

"So, how are we going to help the guy?" he asked, climbing over a large tree stump that jutted awkward-ly from the dirt.

"Well, I'm going to help him learn to control the curse. If he gets it under control, he won't have crazy blood-lust anymore, he won't change unless prompted."

"Have you ever done this before?" Miles asked, a little wary.

"What, with another werewolf?" she questioned, almost in a scoff. "Not really. But I'll figure something out. I've encountered werewolves, but, like, once. They kind of just passed through," she explained. "I know I mentioned it before but, this place really seems to summon ghouls, even when they don't realize it."

I thought of the voice in my dream.

Summons them, even when they don't realize it? Was that what happened to me? But . . . I'm not a ghoul.

Before I could ask her what she meant, she stopped dead in her tracks.

"Look . . . I didn't want to tell you last night because I felt we all just needed to get some sleep. But . . ." Her eyes shifted to Miles, meeting them directly. "I think I figured out who it is, and you're *not* going to like it."

Riley walked forward a bit more and rounded a tree. We were in the same place we had been last night. Only, there wasn't a werewolf chained to the tree anymore.

A boy, who looked more like a man, stood half-naked, body chiseled. A guy I desperately didn't want to see. His brown hair, messy from the night before, was resting on his forehead, poking into his green eyes. He looked up at us, scanning us. His gaze landed on Miles, and he grinned sheepishly.

The werewolf tied to the tree was none other than Mr. Puberty.

CHAPTER SIX

"**A** ustin? Austin Rhodes!" Miles quirked his eyebrow. *"You're* the werewolf?"

He smiled at us as Riley untied him. I simply stared, dumbfounded, before noticing that Austin's eyes were locked on Miles. I didn't like the way he looked at him with what seemed like an insatiable hunger. Nor the way Miles's eyes lingered on the werewolf's stupid muscled body. I took a protective step forward.

"I had a feeling it was you under the fur," Riley said, releasing the final chain.

"What? How?" Austin asked.

"Dude. I've known you for years. You've always been . . . nice. A big dumb idiot, but nice."

"I think you mean a big dumb *racist* idiot, Ri," Miles said, folding his arms in front of his body.

"Um, about that . . ." Austin looked at the floor. This guy who had been a *literal* raging beast just hours ago was *fiddling his thumbs.* "I'm really, really sorry if I've been a bully . . . or if it seems like I'm targeting you. I promise, I'm not racist."

"Sure. Some of your friends are Black, aren't they?" Miles's voice dripped with disgust. I felt so proud of my boy.

All was silent for a minute. Guess Miles really told him.

"When you're around . . . it's hard to explain."

"Try," I demanded. Either he gave Miles a reason to care, or he only made more of a fool of himself. But saying nothing would not be enough.

Austin took a deep breath. "When you're around, my senses go a little wild. You . . . smell different from everyone else."

"Well, that's rude," Riley chimed in.

"No! Not like that, not a bad smell. Just *different*. You just make the wolf want to come out. I thought if I was mean, maybe you'd stay as far away as possible."

"But here we are." I gestured to the forest, the four of us standing together.

"But here we are," Austin repeated. "I really am sorry. To all of you"—he looked at each of us—"but mostly, I'm sorry to you, Miles."

"So, what, I make you hungry or something? Like the Big Bad Wolf?" Miles's voice was getting higher. I could tell he wasn't taking this well. The guy had a fear of werewolves even before being the sought-after main course.

Inappropriately, if you ask me, Austin smirked. "I'm not sure. I don't think it's that. I mean I'm not tempted to *eat* you or anything, but . . ."

"But?" Miles prodded.

Austin sighed and just shook his head, clearly unwilling to explain more. "I don't know."

After a moment of awkward silence, Riley stepped forward and spoke up. "Not to lessen the issue here, but I think I get it. When I vibed out last night, there was a certain . . . *need* to fulfill. Pulls on you like a magnet. If Miles really does smell—for a lack of better words—*better* than the rest of the Ravenswood population, it's sure to drive any wolf mad. I didn't feel a stronger pull to you any more than anyone else, but then again, I'm not really a werewolf."

"Yesterday, in the hall . . ." Austin's voice was barely

a whisper. It was so little for a dude so large. "I'm really glad you guys stopped me. The full moon always makes me a little extra beasty."

There was a heavy silence for a moment, as I looked between Miles and Austin and their stare down.

Finally, Miles sighed. "Fine. I'll accept your apology. But this doesn't mean we gotta be friends or anything like that." He crossed his arms, still surveying the weirdly ripped sixteen-year-old. "But we need to fix this whole . . . wolf thing you've got going on. Can't have you *Twilight*ing at our high school."

Austin, smiling now, sighed as well. "My 'wolf thing' is nothing like *Twilight*. Trust me."

"Yeah, buff, shirtless high schooler aside, it seems to err more on the side of *The Wolfman*—a classic—much more"—I put my hands up as if they were claws—"*I want to eat you*."

"Simon!" Riley scolded.

"What? It's true! He needs . . . wolf training or something. Control the beast within or whatever."

"That's—" Riley began but stopped. Her eyebrows scrunched together as she pursed her lips. "That's actually genius. I'd have to practice a little, but I think I could teach you how to shift on command, Austin."

His face lit up. "Really?"

"We'd have to practice a lot. Shifting on or around the full moon could be hard . . ." She tapped her finger against her chin. "I mean, if I could still be *me* right after turning into a werewolf, I don't see why you shouldn't be able to also be *you*."

Miles stepped forward, crunching the leaves still below our feet. "Si and I can cover for you guys whenever you need."

"And if you need a leash, I'll be happy to take you for a walk." I grinned. Austin rubbed the back of his neck. *Guess I made him embarrassed, oh no, whatever shall I do.*

Ignoring my comment, Riley said, "We'll keep prac-
ticing, see what happens during the next full moon.
But no more pushing Miles."

"Promise!" Austin said quickly. He started smiling
to himself. "Thanks, guys. Really. You have no idea
how much this help means to me."

"Just don't eat us, and we'll call it even," Miles
smirked. I caught Austin smirking right back, and
their eyes were locked for a moment, seeming as if
they were in a world of their own.

Earth to Miles? Anyone home?

"You guys done? We're going to be late to school at
this point if we keep dawdling." Riley sighed.

I threw the hoodie at Austin's face. "Cover up, will
ya? Not everyone wants to see all *that*." I motioned to
his eight-pack and biceps for days. *Note to self, go harder in PE and cut out the late-night snacks.*

After a few minutes of wrapping up, the four of us
made our way back down to Riley's car.

"Did you drive here?" Miles asked Austin as Riley
and I began to climb in her car.

"Nah, I ran."

"Ran?" Miles quirked an eyebrow. "How far do you
live?"

"About five or six miles from here."

"Of course you do," I groaned. "Just get in the car,
will ya, Hercules?"

On the drive back to school, Riley filled in Austin
about her rad vibing powers, and how Miles and I had
only found out her secret recently. He wasn't nearly as
surprised as Miles and I were when we found out, but
I guess he already knew some form of the supernatural was real, being a werewolf and all.

I, however, was near silent. I was exhausted from the
night before, sleeping in the car, and I couldn't shake
the foggy memory of having some kind of nightmare.
I remember the woods, but that could've just been

because we were *in* the woods. I remember a voice too, but the more I tried to grasp it, make it tangible, the more it escaped my memory.

As the four of us walked into school—no longer enemies, but not really friends either—other students stared at us in confusion. Raised eyebrows, looks between Austin and Miles, and quick whispers. Apparently, people noticed the bully incidents.

Between all the looks and stares, Jake—from history—walked over to us and raised a dark eyebrow in Austin's direction. "Hey. Simon and Miles, right? You guys good?" Jake asked, not taking his eyes off Austin. The two alpha males were squaring each other up, and Jake didn't let their height difference discourage him from a stare-off.

Miles stepped in between the two. "Yeah, man. We're good now. Thanks for asking."

Jake's eyes slipped to Miles before he took a deep breath and a step back. "All right. Cool. I don't know what changed, but you guys let me know if this clown ever needs to be put in his place." I could almost feel the fire radiating off both Jake and Austin. While I appreciated the jock's act of kindness and concern, I knew we needed to get out of this situation right now—unless we wanted the star athlete to become puppy chow. Riley seemed to be thinking the same thing, as she reached for Austin's arm and started to lightly pull him away.

"Will do. Thanks, Jake," I said hurriedly, as I pushed Miles and Austin away, with Riley guiding from the front.

As soon as we were out of earshot from anyone else, Riley said, "Well, it looks like Austin and Miles suddenly being buddy-buddy is a surprise to all. I would recommend coming up with a cover story as to why that is."

"Can't be telling people 'Oh, you know, it turns out he just wanted to *eat* me this whole time. No harm, no foul.'" I shrugged as I mimicked their ridiculous situation. Riley smiled, but I guess the joke didn't fly over very well for Austin or Miles. Still too soon.

"Just expect this to happen again," Riley warned as the first bell rang.

"I'll think of something," Miles said as he turned to walk to class, with me close behind.

Not even thirty minutes later, Riley created a group chat with me, her, Miles, and our newest addition— Austin. Now, I not only had to deal with him in my real life and my ghoul life, but also in my *virtual* life? Too much.

RILEY: LET'S MEET TONIGHT. WE GOTTA HELP AUSTIN CONTROL THE WOLF, AND I THINK THE ONLY WAY TO DO THAT IS TO SHIFT INTO IT.

MILES: SOUNDS GOOD. WHAT TIME?

RILEY: DOES FIVE WORK FOR EVERYONE?

AUSTIN: WORKS FOR ME.

ME: JUST LET ME KNOW WHERE AND I'LL BE THERE.

ME: ALSO, THAT GIVES ME ENOUGH TIME TO FIND SOME SILVER BULLETS.

ME: JUST IN CASE ;)

In our next class, PE, Austin came up to Miles and me and kept our pace as we ran a lap. It seemed like he was intent on joining us for everything now. When we were ushered to play our quarterly sport (basketball, in this case), I spotted the eyes of someone else staring the three of us down. Just as Austin made yet another score, a blond girl I recognized from our English class jogged over to us while her group of friends kept an eye on her back.

"Miles!" she smiled. "Is everything okay?" The girl's eyes shifted between him and Austin. It was the same look of apprehension Jake had given earlier.

"Hey, Beth. We're good. Austin and I talked it out. We're cool now." Miles flashed a smile, and Beth seemed to immediately release the tension she was withholding.

"That's great. I was worried he was over here bothering you again." She put her hands on her hips and eyed Austin up and down. "If he suddenly becomes a bully again, let me know, okay? I have no problem telling Coach Williams for ya."

Austin looked down, scuffing his shoes on the concrete; Beth was speaking like he wasn't even there. Well deserved, if you asked me.

"Nothing like what happened in the hall yesterday will ever happen again. Cross my heart and hope to die," Austin said as he made an X across his chest.

"And I'll make sure he keeps that oath," I smirked. "Right, big buddy?" I patted Austin's back, unexpectedly finding my own hand and wrist hurting from the stupidly durable back muscles. *Jeez, this guy needs to lay off the protein shakes.*

As the day dragged on, Austin stayed glued to our sides. At lunch, he sat with us, earning our table even more odd stares from classmates, and at the end of the day, he waited outside the classroom Riley, Miles, and I all shared.

I was slowly realizing that Austin wasn't the big bully I had him pegged for. He was more like a lost puppy who just found his new home.

"Hey! We're still on for tonight, right?" he said as he walked with the three of us toward the student parking lot. The four of us together must've made quite an interesting group. Two lanky BIPOC nerds, one short goth girl, and a jacked, well-meaning bully. Better than a modern-day *Breakfast Club*.

"Yeah, I'll pick the guys up and head to the woods a bit before sundown," Riley said, spinning her keys in her hand. "We want to get there before the moon rises if we're going to try to shift on command."

"Is that even possible?" Miles piped up.

"I don't see why not. I think it'd be harder for me than Austin." Riley tapped her chin. She seemed to always do that when she was thinking. "I'll look into it. Can't be that hard; I already morph into anything near me."

"But do you morph *back* into yourself on command too?" I asked, eyeing her up and down. We'd only gone ghoul hunting a few times, but I've yet to see Riley vibe back into a human on command.

She glared at me and I realized I should've held my tongue.

"It's not that I *can't*—I just haven't figured it out yet." She pursed her lips. "Do you have something better?"

I smirked. It was my time to shine. "Lucky for you, little lady, I just might." My friends all looked at me, eyebrows raised. "I've only lived my entire life for this exact moment. I've seen every werewolf movie out there! And they're not all good. But one of them has gotta be real-life-accurate!"

Almost in unison, they all sighed.

"Unfortunately, our lives aren't something out of a movie or TV show," Riley scoffed.

"Aren't they, though? You literally turn into a ghost, this guy's a werewolf, and Miles and I are basically a real-life Shaggy and Scooby."

"I better be the Scooby in that duo, dude," Miles huffed.

"Obviously." I grinned. "All I'm saying is, we just found out that everything we always thought was make-believe, the entirety of the supernatural is real. If we know about it, who's to say someone else out there doesn't? Maybe one of the countless things I've seen on TV is from someone who actually knows what they're talking about."

My three friends stared at me for a moment, silent. Either I just said the smartest thing of my life, or I really was dumb. I was hoping for the former.

Finally, Riley looked me in the eyes. "All right, ghoul boy. What do we gotta do?"

With a Cheshire cat smile, I said, "I'm so glad you asked."

CHAPTER SEVEN

"**O**kay, werewolf one-oh-one," I said, standing in the middle of a canopy of trees in the woods. It was nearing sundown, and as planned, Riley, Miles, Austin, and I all managed to meet up. I told my parents I had a group project for biology. Not really a lie, right? I just left the part about *werewolf* biology out.

Riley had her arms crossed, tapping her foot on the dirt below, while Austin seemed to be pumping himself up. He was shaking his arms and hands, bouncing on his toes. It reminded me of a boxer before he goes into the ring for a fight.

"The first thing we should try is meditation and focusing on our breath."

"Like . . . yoga?" Austin quirked an eyebrow.

"I was thinking more like anger management. But sure."

"I know some yoga moves," Miles said. "We can run through a few salutations before the moon rises?" We gathered around Miles, putting jackets and backpacks on the ground, to protect our hands from the rough forest floor, and did a number of weird stretches. "All right, now move into mountain pose. Yep—exactly like that. Remember, breathe deeply with each movement. Now we'll move into Downward Dog—"

"Heh, dog. Is that a special one for Austin?" I laughed, but all I got were exasperated sighs.

After a few minutes of different poses, Miles finished with five deep breaths just as the sun disappeared behind the horizon. I looked at Austin, and I don't know what I was expecting, but there wasn't anything different about him. At least not physically.

"Did it work?" I asked.

Austin stared at his hands, flexing his fingers, then wrists, and finally forearms. "I'm not sure. I mean, I guess I feel more relaxed but not really any different."

"It'll be hard to tell without the moon being out, I think," Riley muttered.

"Speaking of"—I pointed to the sky—"are Miles and I safe to stay out here with you guys if that yoga stuff didn't work? I mean . . . will Austin go all *hungry like the wolf* on us?"

Miles's eyes flashed with fear before he quickly glanced at me. "Do we need to get out of here?"

"I actually brought something that might help . . ." Riley's cheeks turned a shade of red I had never seen on her. She took a deep breath. "We can still use chains, like how we tied up Austin yesterday, but I thought about what Si said at school today." Riley picked her backpack off the ground and reached into it. "*Don't* laugh."

She pulled out a small bundle of purple flowers. They looked a little beat up but pretty ordinary. What would flowers have to—

"Wolfsbane!" I gasped. "Ah, Riley! I could kiss you!" Before I even realized what I said, my face turned hot, my ears felt like they were on fire, and my palms got weirdly sweaty. I heard a snicker from Miles and Austin at my side.

Idiot! I thought to myself.

"Yeah." Riley cleared her throat. "Wolfsbane."

Staring at the flowers and refusing to make eye contact, I said, "Good idea, we can spread them around you guys. See if it works." I quickly grabbed a bunch of the petals from Riley's hand and shoved Austin to a nearby tree, just out of hearing range from Miles and Riley if I whispered.

"Dude—" Austin smirked.

"Don't say a word or I'll shove these things down your throat," I huffed, but Austin kept smiling and patted my back.

"So, you just put this stuff around me?" I could tell he was trying to change the subject. I still didn't really trust—or like, for that matter—him very much, but I felt relieved to not have to prolong my embarrassment from the moment before.

"According to the movies, it could work. Big emphasis on 'could.'"

"Why's that?" Austin quirked his eyebrow.

"Well, every werewolf movie just uses it for something different. In some, it could kill a werewolf if ingested. In others, it relieves but doesn't cure lycanthropy"—I started to pluck the petals apart—"but in a few, which is what we're hoping for, werewolves can't cross a path made of wolfsbane. So if we circle it around you guys, ideally it'll keep you contained, almost like a barrier."

Austin looked at the flower and nodded. I could see him process the information. Since we didn't know what it would do, I wondered if it was already bothering his wolf senses just because of the close proximity.

"Do you . . . feel anything? Allergies? Sleepy?"

"Honestly? I don't feel anything. At least, no different than before. I think . . ." He paused and sighed. "I think I'll feel better if you guys chain us up along with the petals. Just to be safe. If the wolf did something to you guys, I—"

I placed a hand on his rudely large shoulder. "I get it, dude. And I appreciate the concern."

Before it got too dark, or the moon was fully out, I chained Austin to a thick tree trunk, and then Miles and I surrounded Riley and him in their own rings of the wolfsbane petals. Since we knew Riley could control her own wolf, we figured she'd be the real test on the wolfsbane. We took more than a few steps back, close enough to see them, but far enough that we could attempt to make a break for it if we needed to. Not that it would do much good against two freakin' werewolves.

"I hope this works." Miles rubbed his face, a look of fear mixed with exhaustion trailing behind.

"The chains kept Austin tied up last night. I think we're safe in that department."

"I guess now all we have to do is wait." He sat on the ground, pulling his backpack off and making himself comfortable.

"And now we wait," I muttered.

Only a few moments later, moonlight poked through the canopy of trees. Just as I noticed it, I heard two yells as the sound of cracking bones engulfed the air. Riley and Austin were shifting before our eyes.

"I don't think this is something I could get used to," Miles said, voice quivering, as his eyes grew larger, staring at the shifting forms of our friends. And he was right. As much as I've seen it in horror movies, the real thing didn't even compare. *They never got the sound right*, was the only thing I thought as the popping and ripping of bones, flesh, and fur broke and reformed filled the air. I felt bile rising in my throat and swallowed hard. The transformation was grotesque.

Fully werewolves now, both Riley and Austin surged forward. Austin tried to break his chains and Riley dug at the dirt near the wolfsbane. It seemed to be working.

Or so I thought.

Miles and I watched intently, afraid either of them

would break out, when Riley pawed at the petals, making an opening in the seal. Riley looked at the flowers, concentrating on them, as she hesitantly reached out a clawed hand.

"Riley? Are you back with us?" I asked, voice shaking more than I expected. Her pale blue eyes locked onto mine, as the werewolf nodded her response. Miles echoed my sigh of relief next to me. The shift took hold of her way less than the night before.

Riley continued to reach for the wolfsbane and swatted it away quickly. No smoke, no oozing werewolf skin, nothing. She walked over the circle of petals as if they were just leaves on the ground. The wolfsbane didn't work.

"Dang," Miles started. "Now we'll have to find something els—"

Suddenly, it felt like reality was pulled from beneath my feet. My ears rang and my head violently spun, giving me vertigo.

Something wasn't right. I didn't know what, but I felt like I wasn't even in my own skin. The hairs on my neck stood and a cold chill raced down my spine. I turned, looking into the dense forest at my back.

Something's watching me.

What's watching me?

"Simon? You good, dude?" Miles's voice returned in a full boom. All the noise of the forest, the birds, the crickets, everything except—

"Where did the wind go?" I mumbled, unsure if it was even my own voice.

Just then, I heard a loud shatter followed by *thunks* on the ground, like something heavy was falling on it. I turned to see Austin free from his chains, snarling at me. His hackles were raised and saliva dripped from his muzzle. It was easily the scariest sight I had ever seen.

I couldn't run—couldn't even move. His growl only

got louder as he walked over the wolfsbane petals and beelined right for me.

Riley tried to jump in front of me, but he dodged her easily. I squeezed my eyes closed, ready for impact.

But it never came. Austin ran past me, into the woods where I was just looking. He wasn't running away from us. He was running toward something. To the same something that was causing this eerie feeling.

My heart was pounding, I didn't even realize the half moons my nails created in my palms until I felt the hot sting of blood. We waited there, staring after where the werewolf just ran. There was only silence.

"What the hell is going on!" I heard Miles say.

And just as soon as that rush of feeling came, it left. The void in the pit of my stomach dispersed. My head didn't feel like it was deep underwater. And soon my breath felt even again. Whatever had caused that . . . oddity seemed to have disappeared.

I took a deep, refreshed breath. "I-I don't know."

Riley's ears pricked as she stood behind me. She moved to stand in front of Miles and me and growled into the tree line just as we saw the shuffling of bushes.

Austin trotted from the woods, the snarl on his face gone completely, and his tongue hung out from his mouth as he panted, more like a dog than a ferocious wolf. He seemed . . . himself. Well, as much as he could be in that form. Like Riley, he managed to tame himself and be conscious *as* himself. I think Riley and Miles saw this change from wolf to man as well, as they both eased up. Austin walked up to me and nuzzled against my hand. As soon as I petted him, the fur fell from his bones, revealing the young man underneath.

And, without delay, Riley shifted as well. Miles and I quickly tossed them blankets to cover themselves and the changes of clothes we had packed.

"Austin, you did it!" Miles exclaimed. "But how?"

After changing, Austin scratched behind his ear.

"I'm not totally sure. I felt comfortable and just knew I could shift back. I think I just had to show the wolf that I was the master here." Austin's gaze then fell to me. "I'm sorry it seemed like I was about to attack you. I just had this overwhelming need to protect you."

"Protect him? From what?" Riley said as she joined us.

"I . . . I don't know. I didn't actually see anything." His eyes met mine. "Did you?"

"No, but I felt like . . ." I paused, afraid to sound crazy. It was probably just the dream from the night before giving me the spooks.

"What did you feel?" Miles stepped toward me, concern riddling his face.

"I just felt like something was watching me. Something in there . . ." I pointed at the tree line and their eyes all followed. Turning to him, I said, "Thanks, Austin. I don't know what you did but I appreciate you running to face the unknown for me." I awkwardly stuck out my hand.

Austin's smile covered his whole face as we shook hands. Maybe Mr. Puberty wasn't so bad after all.

CHAPTER EIGHT

"**M**iles, do you wanna study together today for history? We have a test on Friday," Austin asked. Miles and I sat in the cafeteria while Riley was still in the lunch line. Austin took the seat next to Miles while I looked at him, wide-eyed. Something about the color on his face had shifted. He looked warm and . . . pleasant.

"Uhm, ye-yeah! Yes. I need to study. You can too. Let's do that," Miles stumbled out. I wasn't sure if he was into him, or still afraid of him. Whatever face I made, though unwilling, Miles noticed. "Simon, you can join us; you need to study too!"

"Or you can help Riley catch up. You are the best in history, and she's been sleeping in class again. I don't blame her; it was a long night," Austin smirked.

"Yeah, I think it'll be better for them if we teach them one on one. You can take Riley." Miles smiled. He thought he was helping me. I wanted to punch him too.

Riley dropped her tray next to mine and slouched in the seat. She groaned and started stabbing at the food with her fork. Her eyes shifted to everyone at the table and landed on me.

"What?" she asked, zero emotion in her voice. She had dark circles under her eyes that looked more like bruises against her fair skin. She and Austin had stayed up through the night, making sure they had the shift between wolf and human fully down, while Miles and I slept in her car.

"We were talking about the test we have on Friday for history. We're breaking off into study groups," I said through gritted teeth. "It's you and me, kid." I placed a hand on her shoulder. She glared at me as she took large camel-like chews on her food.

"Sure," she said, her mouth still full. "Your place or mine?"

Austin raised an eyebrow while Miles stifled a laugh.

"Whichever," I said, shrugging it off.

Play it cool, Simon.

"You can come to mine. My mom works the overnight shift, so it'll just be us. I'll order pizza." She took a sip of her apple juice.

Home. Alone? With Riley?

I looked across the table. Miles and Austin were already grinning at me. My ears flushed hot and my cheeks felt like they were on fire. I pulled my beanie even more over my head and shifted my face away from Riley.

I coughed. "Cool, what time?"

"Let's do seven thirty. I need a nap after school." She finished the last of her grilled cheese and stood up. "See you guys later."

The moment the door to the cafeteria closed, Miles burst into laughter.

"You? Alone with Riley? Oh man, I wish I could see that!" He laughed heartily, heavier than I had ever heard.

"Ha ha, you're hysterical." I rolled my eyes. "We're just going to study."

"Yeah, 'study,'" Austin chimed in, raising his eyebrows up and down. I threw him a dirty look; one he didn't pick up on or simply chose to ignore. "Do you have any moves?"

"What do you mean? Moves?" I asked with frustration.

"Yeah, you know. Like . . ." Miles's face contorted, thinking. "Like the yawn over her shoulder?"

"Like the five-second stare?" Austin countered.

"The triangle look."

"The pinky touch."

"Oh, that's a classic."

My eyes shifted back and forth between the two. It's crazy to think that only a few days ago, Austin was Miles's bully. Instead, here they were, being chummy and offering me dating advice.

Confusion must have been spread across my face, because the two broke out into heavy laughter. Flustered, I added, "Of course, I have a move. I'm slick. It works *every time*." Folding my arms across my chest, I winked at them.

Play it cool. It's only weird if you make it weird.

"Oh yeah? What is it? If it's so awesome, why don't you share it with the class?" Miles nudged Austin on the shoulder.

"It's uh . . . it's a family secret. A Korean thing, you guys wouldn't understand."

"Come on, you guys know I'm a werewolf, tied me to a tree, and basically saw me naked. There are no secrets here," Austin winked. "Plus, I've seen *Boys Over Flowers*, I've seen your Korean secrets."

I hated him. But he was growing on me. And I hated him even more for it. I thought for a moment, desperate for any idea that would come to mind. But it was failing me, betraying me. I sought through my memories of the popular Korean drama, but was only left with awkward kisses, much-deserved slaps, and one ill-timed pool scene. *Boys Over Flowers* would not help me win over Riley. I cursed at myself.

"Look," I said, finally confessing. "I've got nothing. Also, who the heck says 'moves' anymore? Don't you just . . . ya know. Go with it?"

Never in my life had I seen two people laugh as loud as they did at that moment. Miles wiped something from his eye. Was that a tear from *laughing*? I shook my head and sighed. Austin reached over and grabbed my shoulder gently.

"Don't worry, man. I see the way you and Riley look at each other. You don't need any moves; whatever you already do is good enough for her. You got this." He smiled.

Damn it, even his teeth were awesome.

I felt myself smile back. I winked at Miles, throwing him off. His face immediately shifted, remembering that he also had a "study session" with Austin tonight. Austin, who was nearly twice his size in height and muscle. Austin, who looked like an '80s horror-movie jock all the time, who always smelled like pine (whether it was pine cologne or the pine trees he was running through as a wolf the night before, we would never know). Austin, whose smile took up his entire face.

This time, *I* flashed the sly smile, leaving Miles, red in the face, and Austin to finish their lunch and plan their evening together.

With history books and notes in tow, I started up the path to Riley's house. From the outside, it looked like a normal, well-maintained home. It was painted olive green with a white trim, had two floors, and a deck that seemed to surround the whole house. The driveway was made of dark pebbles, and Riley's matching olive truck sat in one of the spots. Perfectly normal.

I knew that it wasn't, though. After all, it was *Riley's* house. This forest was *her* forest where she had done the bulk of her vibing. My heart throbbed in my chest as I knocked on the door. I was going to be in *Riley's home*, with *Riley*.

Alone.

A moment later, the door flew open. Riley stood there, smiling. Her hair was wet, and she had no makeup on. The normal black that surrounded her eyes was gone. This was a different Riley, one I hadn't seen before.

"Welcome to my cave, come on in. I was just about to order the pizza!"

I was immediately hit by the scent of autumn-themed candles. Spiced apple, fire pit, and pumpkin filled my nose and made me instantly relax. It's how I always imagined Riley's house would smell.

Just like Halloween.

"Toppings . . . and go!" Closing the door behind us, she turned and shot finger guns at me.

"Anything except bacon. Love pizza. Love bacon. Not a fan of the combo."

"Specific," she laughed, walking us to the kitchen. She leaned back into the granite counters and picked up her phone and put it to her ear.

As she ordered I walked into her living room. I placed my bag full of books down on the floor and sat on the dark-brown leather couch. It was cold at first, as if no one had sat here all day. The coffee table in front of me was low and matched the espresso-colored wooden floors beneath. It had the atmosphere of a log cabin while still retaining the homey feeling.

I also made a mental note to stop watching house shows with my mom.

Moments later she appeared next to me sitting on the couch. "Thanks for coming, by the way. These last few days have been rough." Her azure eyes were as full as the sky in summer. "Also, I can't afford to fail a class. Any of them, really. But this balancing life and vibes thing, it's hard to do alone, so I'm thankful for you and Miles. And now, I guess, Austin." She smirked as I cringed.

"No worries. It's awesome of you that you're letting us in on this whole ghost-hunting thing." I gleamed. "Could you imagine? Living your whole life believing in something that you don't know is real, but you believe with all your might—"

"That's called religion, Simon," she interrupted.

"Well, imagine a super religious person finding out their god was *real*. And having proof! Seeing it with their own eyes! That's how I feel," my voice trailed. I was embarrassed. I didn't want to fanboy too much, but I ended up vomiting words before I could stop myself. I cleared my throat, trying to rectify my blurting. "Well . . . I mean it's cool. What you do, I mean. And now I do it too." I was flustered.

She cocked her head. "It's nice to know that I'm not alone in this anymore. For years, I've just kept it to myself. And now, well. Now, I don't have to." She looked up, and finally, grinned back.

I shifted in my seat. We *were* on the subject. Now would be my chance to ask questions. Learn more about it, about her, about what's real, what's not.

But before I could, Riley said, "How about we study until the pizza gets here? After that we can talk, maybe watch a movie or play a game?"

I nodded and bit back my tongue. The questions could wait. I'll have another chance. I showed her my notes and gave a mini-lecture on the French Revolution.

"The Reign of Terror was badass."

"If by 'badass' you mean horrible, bloody, and brutally unnecessary, then yes. Badass."

Mischief sparkled in her eyes. "Imagine all the vibes we'd get in Paris. The Reign of Terror, the storming of the

Bastille, the Women's March on Versailles, and that's not even with the catacombs beneath the whole city."

The idea alone sent shivers through my spine.

"Yeah, we'd probably die. Very quickly, might I add," I chuckled. "What happens to you when two different ghouls are in the area? Do you become only one or a fusion or . . . ?"

Riley placed a finger on her chin and looked to the ceiling. "I don't know if that's ever happened. I feel like I'd either get to choose, or it'll be based on whichever is closest to me." She nodded, more to herself than me. "I *have* been around multiple spirits before, however. And that was a nightmare. I felt everything they were feeling. All the pain, anger, and confusion. But the worst feeling was all the nothingness. People— hollows of people—" she corrected herself, "who were just . . . nothing. And they didn't know. Didn't feel anything. Not cold, not alone. Just nothing." She shuddered and crossed her arms around herself. She gazed into the page of my notes. I saw the goose bumps that trailed her arms.

I placed my hand lightly on her arm, causing her to startle the slightest bit. I left my hand there, giving this one spot heat, easing her goose bumps. She nudged me with her shoulder. My heart raced as she did, and I felt my face grow warm. I couldn't really tell if Riley was interested in me back, but for some reason, it didn't matter to me. That thrill of just being in her presence and seeing her was enough.

But when her eyes lingered on me, or when she leaned into me, I couldn't help but imagine what it would be like if we dated. If she liked me. I felt a dumb smile creep along my face, and I pressed my lips together to try and keep it from showing.

"Come on"—I cleared my throat—"let's get back to the guillotine." I turned away once again to hide my tomato-like face.

After about an hour, the pizza finally arrived. We sat on the floor of the living room, pizza box sitting atop the coffee table. I told her about Miami and about my friends there. I made a mental note to call them soon. I missed the crazy paranormal journeys I dragged them on. In turn, she told me about her childhood friends, two of whom she had told about her gift. She said they had both moved away and were too young to stay in contact.

"I always wondered if they knew I was serious or if they thought I was just playing pretend. I mean if *I* were them, I would have thought that."

She said she believes if she moved, and went somewhere other than Ravenswood, she would likely see *more*. Ghosts were everywhere, but creatures—other ghouls—were sometimes based on location. The fairies and faeries in Ireland, for instance. The Latin American Chupacabra. The Black Dog from England. All were based on geological lore and myths. Riley, and I, believed they were real. She dreamed of finding out for herself if they were. I mean, we'd seen ghosts. We'd met werewolves. She'd seen vampires and goblins, unexplainable creatures that lurked in the darkness of the forest. She'd seen demons, incubi and succubi. Invisible people, keeping to themselves. She said when she was a kid, she and her mom went to the beach. She stood on the shore and swore she saw a mermaid's fin flick out of the water, almost as if it were waving *hi* to her.

Every time we rambled too long, we kept trying to get back to studying. After reading about Jean-Jacques Rousseau for a bit, we circled back to the conversation from earlier. This happened more than once. Somehow one conversation led to another, and every new tidbit of history was brought back to the supernatural. We had been talking about dragons, the fact that she believed Europeans stole the idea from Asia (and that they might still be found there) when she received a call.

"Oh, hold on. It's my mom. Hello? . . . Hey, I'm here with Simon." She paused. Her face fell. "Oh, shit—Sorry . . . I know . . . Okay. Yeah, I'll look . . ." She glanced at me. "Yeah, he knows . . . I'll ask . . . I'll text you . . . Bye, Mom." She took a heavy sigh as she dropped her phone from her ear, and said, "So, I haven't really told you guys this, but my mom knows about the vibes."

"Have you vibed in front of her?"

"Yeah, all the time. After that story I told you about, when I was invisible and she couldn't see me, I tried telling her, and well, I was a kid. Of course, she didn't believe me. It happened again a few days later, only this time it was in front of her. It turned out to be that the ghoul was a different kind of ghoul, not a ghost like I originally thought, but more like from *The Invisible Man*. Just a normal guy, except he could become invisible. I was so young that I couldn't control it. The guy was using his power for super messed-up things, which the police eventually became involved with. Stealing from stores and being a Peeping Tom was how it started. Eventually, he moved on to bigger things. I knew how to find him and my mom used that to her advantage." She paused, taking in my reaction.

I was absolutely engrossed in her story.

"Holy crap! Did she catch him?"

Riley nodded. "Yep! Don't get me wrong, my mom is an awesome cop. She was able to move up the ladder to eventually become sheriff."

"Do you still get to help her every once in a while?"

"That brings me to this, actually. She needs my help again. There was a murder. A weird one. She thinks it's supernatural more than anything else. Her colleagues assume it's an animal, but she doesn't buy it. She knows too much about this town to believe that.

She's on her way here now to pick me up," She stood up, reaching her hand toward mine. "I know it's a lot to ask. But . . . do you want to come?"

I scrunched my eyebrows a bit instinctively. Of course, I wanted to go. A chance to be a part of a murder investigation? Much less a ghoul-related one? Sign me up! I grabbed her hand and got up.

"Am I allowed?"

"My mom knows that you guys know about ghouls, and she even knows about Austin. But she said this thing is . . . intense. She's also in a hurry. If you don't want to come, she'll send one of her officers on duty to take you home, but it might be a while. It's kind of an all-hands-on-deck thing with this case. The news hasn't even reported it yet."

I had never seen a dead body before but at the same time, I would be able to hang out with Riley more. *And* I could maybe help her with a vibe session. Just us. And then she would ask me to help more. A part of me was also just morbidly curious. I had hunted for ghosts my whole life, and this might be the first chance I got to see the shell of a ghost, the *pre*-ghost. Maybe I would even see the ghost lingering around. Plus, I would like to learn more about Riley's world, what to look for, how to help. So that whatever this ghoul did to this person, it wouldn't happen again.

I looked up to Riley, meeting her blue eyes as I did. She cocked her head to the side, waiting for my response. I nodded to her.

She gave me a shy smile (which sent my heart fluttering through my chest) and glanced at our interlocked hands.

"Ya gotta let go first," she laughed.

"Right, lead the way." I coughed, releasing my grip.

"I think she's almost here. We can take our study stuff. I'm not sure how late this will go."

The two of us began to pack our things and waited

for Riley's mom. A few minutes later, we heard a car beep. Outside, leaning against a white-and-black cop car, was a woman who was like the older version of Riley. Her dark-blond hair was tied back into a ponytail. Her eyes were blue and kind, with light crow's feet at the edges. She had smile lines and pale skin with its fair share of sun damage. She stood relaxed; I saw now where Riley got her calm demeanor from.

"You must be Simon," she said with a bright smile. She walked over to me, gave me a warm handshake, and then pulled me into a light hug. "I've heard so much about you from Lee."

"Lee?"

"That's what she calls me," Riley said, her face flushed and embarrassed.

"I like it. It's nice to meet you!"

"I hate to rush, but we need to get to the hospital where they're performing the autopsy ASAP. Hop in," she said, opening the back door of the patrol car. Riley and I both got in. I had been in the back seat of a cop car before, at school career day, but the dividing metal cage still made my chest twist in discomfort.

"What are the details?" Riley asked once we were all settled and on the way.

Her mom glanced at me in the rearview mirror.

"You sure you're okay with this, right, Simon? It does get a little . . . wild."

I took a deep breath in and exhaled. There was no going back now. "I'm good."

"Her name was Addaline Alberts. She was found in the forest by an afternoon walking group. No clothes were found around the victim, and her entire body had been scraped down to only bones and ligaments, all still connected to each other. There are no signs of flesh or organs anywhere. The only thing untouched was her head. Her teeth are all accounted for, both her eyes and ears are still attached, no marks or wounds anywhere on her head or face."

"And the others think it was an animal?" Riley asked, completely unphased by everything.

"It looks like Addaline's tissue and muscle layers were wiped clean from the body, which they think could have been caused by animals eating away at it. I don't buy it. It looks too clean. There's not a single piece of flesh attached. It's almost as if they peeled everything off and then cleaned the bones. Wanna know the weirdest part? The bone marrow had been sucked out of everything."

I shuddered at the thought. Riley's mom saw and stiffened up in the driver's seat. "You okay, kiddo?"

"I'm all right. So, if it's a ghoul, what do you think it could be?"

Riley laid her head back against the seat. She stared up at the roof of the car for a while before she spoke. "It could be a number of things. Werewolf. Shifter. Very hungry vampire."

"Do they eat humans like in the movies?" I whispered.

"Shifters do. Vampires drink blood. If they are in a frenzy, it could become more cannibal-like. And werewolves might eat or attack anything that moves." Her face was deep in thought, her response to me almost like autopilot. "She was found in the woods, you said?"

"Pretty deep in, too. I figured it could just be an animal, but . . ."

"Could it be a person? Like a normal human?" I asked, awkwardly.

"It could, but they'd have to be insanely strong, with too much time on their hands to rip her apart like that."

"Other than her body, is there a crime scene?"

"Her tracks are everywhere. Broken branches. Stepped on plants. Footprints that led from her normal walk home to where we found her."

"This is strange. I'm not sure." Riley hummed.

"Have you felt anything lately? Anything new?" Sheriff Silverstein asked.

Riley shook her head. "Not since we discovered Austin."

Her mom sighed. "Well, we're almost there now."

We pulled up to the hospital my dad worked at, but he thankfully wasn't on duty tonight. Apparently, this hospital was the only one in town and, due to the general size of Ravenswood, also served as the medical examiner's office and morgue. We got out of the car, and Riley and I took our backpacks with us. We walked through a bunch of different corridors—some full, some totally deserted—until we reached the final hall that had been flooded with cops. It all felt very official, walking around with the town sheriff.

"Why are you guys all out here?" Sheriff Silverstein asked. Her tone had shifted a bit, becoming ever so slightly sterner.

"Deputy Allen told us to wait out here until you returned. Should we go back in now?"

"No, no. I'll handle this. Everyone, go take a fifteen. Get some coffee. It's going to be a long night."

Officers grumbled as they all made their way out of the hall. Some greeted Riley as they passed, I assumed they must have known her for years. In a way, all these people were probably like her family.

Riley's mom gently stopped a female officer by the arm before she could pass her.

"Where's Walsh?"

"He went to talk to the parents in the lobby. Trying to find out anything he can."

"All right, thanks, Kady."

Once everyone was out, Officer Silverstein looked at us.

"All right, it's go time. I'll distract Jason. Riley, you know the drill . . . I think Simon should maybe wait out here."

"Mom," Riley groaned. "He's part of the team now! He's already seen ghosts and werewolves!"

"Riley Silverstein. This is a dead body we're talking about. It's different."

"How?" Riley crossed her arms, sticking her bottom lip out.

"I-I don't know. It just is. Simon, wait out here." And with that, Sheriff Silverstein left us in search of this "Jason" she mentioned.

"It's okay—" I started to say when Riley nodded and suddenly grabbed my wrist.

"Come on, she's just saying that 'cause she's being a mom."

Riley waited until her mom walked out of the large, white doors in front of us with a tall, lanky man who looked like he may have spent just a little too much time indoors—his brown hair was massively disheveled on his head and his glasses were rather small for his face. The man had one of those faces that simultaneously looked super young but very old, like he could've been anywhere between thirty and sixty.

As soon as her mom and who I supposed was Jason turned the corner, Riley darted into a small room with a window and a door leading into a larger room. Through that window, I could make out a wall of silver drawers, one bright light overhead, and a metal table with a body covered by a white sheet.

I suddenly felt a sense of entrapment. And I felt it contort my face. Riley noticed.

"You don't have to stay, Si. You can wait outside if you want, like my mom said."

I wanted to be brave. Strong. "No. I'll stay."

She shrugged, then passed me a face mask and a small capsule of scented gel.

"What do I do with this?"

"You pop it open like this and put the gel directly under your nose. You can even put a little into it if you'd like. It's supposed to help with the smell." Riley cracked it open and demonstrated. After that, we were ready.

The room felt like an icebox. I couldn't tell if my shaking was from the cold or my nerves.

"They keep it cold on purpose," Riley informed me. "It keeps the bodies fresh and helps slow down the decomposing process."

"Gotcha," I said through chattering teeth.

"You ready?"

I nodded and Riley pulled back the sheet.

The girl—Addaline—was exactly how Sheriff Silverstein described her. But real. And *right* in front of me. Her corpse looked artfully grotesque like a painting. Her head looked utterly normal, if not kind of haunting, her auburn hair sitting perfectly along her jawline. But beyond her neck, Addaline was the embodiment of those school skeleton models they used for science. I immediately began to feel sick to my stomach. I wanted to vomit but I tried to hold it in.

Don't do this in front of her, Simon. Get it together.

Riley picked up the clipboard at the base of the metal table. "No claw marks on the bones. No blood samples, nail clippings, not even saliva, nothing to indicate what attacked her. It's like her body just evaporated into thin air, while her head and face remained perfectly intact."

"Any ghouls you know about that can do this, Riley? Or maybe it was, like, her body got abducted by aliens but they miscalculated their transport beam and so it left her head," I said, thinking it a very likely possibility. Would aliens be considered ghouls?

Riley didn't answer for a moment, raising an eyebrow at me and pouting her lip again. She shook the confusion off her face and scanned the body from head to toe as if she were taking it all in. Then she took a step closer and I followed her eyes to the seam where Addaline's head split from the rest of her body. I noticed it was basically a clean-cut.

"I . . . I don't think it was an animal. There's a strong aura. There was an insane, gluttonous hunger. Which, yes, an animal could have, but there was something else too." She paused, her expression seeming like she was searching for the right word. "There was greed. It didn't *need* to do this to her, to eat her. It *wanted* to. This was clearly out of pleasure."

"Murderous intent?" I asked.

"Something like that."

"How are you seeing the aura and intentions of what killed her?"

Riley stood at her full height and cracked her fingers. "Just can. But if it was truly hungry, why only this? Why wouldn't her face be marred and her bones all shattered or gnawed on?"

For some reason, I thought of the dream I had in the woods a few nights ago. The thing that stood behind me, and those red eyes.

"You doing good?"

"Huh?" I asked, dazed. "Oh, yeah. I'm fine." *Great going, Simon, she noticed.*

"I'm done. Let's get outta here before my mom and Jason come back." She grabbed my hand and for a second, I really thought I was going to puke. I couldn't tell if it was from the dead body a few inches away or from the warmth of Riley's hand in mine.

Out in the waiting area, the nausea subsided and I could finally breathe steadily. Riley and I sat in the waiting room, attempting to study but we ended up failing miserably. We talked about everything, from Addaline, ghouls, life, her mom, and my parents, until my eyes started to feel heavy.

Riley sat next to me. We watched shows on my phone as I leaned my head back against the wall. It was getting late, almost midnight. We sat there until her head slumped onto my shoulder.

I looked at her for a moment, unable to move out of fear of waking her. I held my breath, afraid that the slightest movement would interrupt this moment and that she would leave my side. I could feel my heart pounding against my chest, the weight of Riley against me, and I hoped she couldn't feel it too. Her warmth radiated into me as her deep breaths lulled her to sleep.

For a moment, I wondered what it would be like to hold her against me, my arms around her curves. Imagining her soft, warm skin against my own sent a thrill down my spine. But if I couldn't have that, I would settle for her body against mine right now.

Her presence was a comfort, and as tiredness crept in, my head swayed back and forth pulling me into the blankness of sleep. I rested it on top of her head, smelling the residual scent of roses on her hair. I closed my eyes and sleep took me.

I woke to the light shaking from Sheriff Silverstein.

"Hey, buddy. It's late, or rather early—but I'm gonna take you home now, okay?" Her voice was soft, a tiny whisper that barely echoed throughout the hallway. She lightly shook Riley as well, pulling her upright.

I checked my phone as we walked to the car. It was already 1:30 a.m. Riley was still half asleep with her eyes closed, as her mom half-guided, half-carried her to the car. It was dark out, but I could tell it was closing in on morning by the smell of the dew.

I breathed it in, vividly remembering the smell from the dream in the forest a few nights before. This was much nicer.

Sheriff Silverstein helped Riley into the back seat. Riley crawled in and laid down across the back. "You can sit with me, Simon. And please, for the love of god, call me Alice," Sheriff Silverstein whispered. "Sorry to get you home so late. It's been a hectic shift." She rubbed her neck. She seemed tired and had dark circles under her eyes.

I wondered if she did that—working late—all the time.

"It's okay, Offi—Alice. Thanks for driving me home."

"Of course! Thanks for coming and putting up with all this craziness.

"Did you . . . um . . ." I started without being able to stop myself.

Alice glanced at me, questioning. "Figure anything else out?" Alice sighed again. "Unfortunately, no. The poor girl." She was holding something back. It was the same face Riley made when she did but didn't want to say something. But it was almost two in the morning, and Alice just needed to vent to *anyone.* Fortunately for me, I was the only one awake. "We think she was murdered. The autopsy ended up showing . . . a bit." She glanced at me again. I could tell she was trying to read if she should continue or not. Her face had the question, *How much do you want to know?*

I looked back at her.

Everything.

"Like what? You said you think she was eaten, right?" I paused and remembered the taste of blood and heart in my mouth, remembered the noise-defying *thump* that managed to make the wind sound like it disappeared.

"We think—God, it's awful. We think she was eaten alive. There were no wounds on her body to indicate another cause of death. Nothing found in the little blood we could muster up to indicate drugging."

"But she didn't have a body."

"And only her brain was left. It showed . . . signs. I don't know the science behind it. Jason said he believes she died *after* bites were taken."

I shuddered. Being eaten alive was horrifying. I thought back to the hundreds of zombie movies I've seen and the bath-salts guy who ate the homeless man's face in Miami back in 2012. I remember imagining how it would feel to be eaten alive and the horrid pain and confusion you must feel as it happened. The idea now made me sick.

Alice saw my face, saw me processing.

"I'm sorry, I shouldn't be telling you all this. You don't need to be thinking about this kind of stuff. Ravenswood is a small town, Simon. We don't see this kind of thing here often. Everyone knows each other— hell, that girl's dad works at the printing shop right next to the station. Her mom works at the diner I get my coffee every morning. Murder doesn't just happen in this town, no matter how much weird shit goes on. Every death here is personal." She paused and sighed deeply.

I could tell she was trying to ease the tension in the car, shaking off the heavy emotions from the death of a local.

"You have a test coming up, don't you? That's why you came over today? To help Riley study?"

I nodded.

She quickly glanced back at the sleeping girl in the back seat. "Thanks, by the way, Simon. Riley's a good kid, it's nice to see her actually have . . ."

"Friends?" I laughed.

"Well, yeah. People who could look out for her."

"Trust me, she looks out for me way more than I do for her."

At this, Alice smiled. The same smile I'd seen Riley do a hundred times.

"You look like her, you know?"

Alice's smile widened. "Less goth, I hope. I have an image to uphold as the sheriff," she said sarcastically.

Moments later, we arrived in front of my house. Alice pulled the car to a slow stop.

"Go on in. I'll stay here until you get inside."

"Thanks for driving me again, Alice. And thanks for having me over today. I think Riley and I are gonna do great on the test."

I climbed out of the car, waved a final goodbye, and entered my house. Thinking of whatever ate Addaline, I quickly locked the door behind me.

Within seconds, my phone chimed. A text from my mom. She was awake, or at least somewhat awake, as she had always been when I came home late. Riley texted her a while ago, while we were in the waiting room, that I had fallen asleep on her couch and that her mom would take me home when I woke up.

MOM: GOOD NIGHT. LOVE YOU.

I texted her back and crawled up to my room, slumped onto my bed. I had a few more hours of sleep, but every time I closed my eyes, all I saw was Addaline's blank face staring back at me.

CHAPTER NINE

Something was off. I felt it in my bones.

I was dreaming but it all felt so real, so vivid. The biting cold ached in my fingers and crept along my ears—sensations I didn't wish on my worst enemy. Something was watching me again. Lingering eyes stalked me, but this time, I knew. I knew where I was going. The path was clearer and my body acted on its own accord, but I couldn't tell if it was determination or control. The hairs on the back of my neck rose up and a violent shiver rattled my spine. My heart was beating fast—too fast to be possible. I didn't feel pain, I only felt it *thump*. That was when I realized it wasn't only my heartbeat I was hearing.

Two sets of hearts. Two people. Where was the other one coming from?

This time, no red eyes shone from the darkness beyond, but I still knew they were there. I felt them. Everything was eerily silent. I was heading for a clearing. My footsteps made no noise against the forest floor. No crunching leaves, no cracking of wood. Just silence. The only noise was my rising heartbeat. *Thu-thump, thu-thump.* I let out a shuddering breath, a cloud of vapor appearing before me, and still, it went on.

Thu-thump, thu-thump.

Up ahead the fog thickened and the air was much

heavier than before. It twirled and danced, moving like a flame without restriction. It was hiding something; I just knew it. Protecting *it*. My feet were betraying me, leading me somewhere only *it* knew where to go. Vile screams echoed around the fog, sounding like a girl in trouble.

I quickened my pace and ran directly into the twirling tendrils of smoke, expecting to find a girl. A body. Anything. But nothing was there. I exhaled and took a deep breath in.

I instantly regretted it.

The air pervaded the scent of rotting flesh. Bile burned my throat, blurring my senses, and made me nauseous. It engraved itself on my mind as it began to claw through my lungs. I swayed back and forth before hitting the ground hard on my knees. The raw earth below scraped my skin as small beads of blood began to coil on my skin. The smell was still terrorizing my mind. Wet leaves clung to me as I pressed my palms against my forehead, so tight that I was hit by a burst of phosphenes, feeling as though my brain would slip out of place if I didn't hold tightly enough.

The pounding wouldn't stop.

My next step was to cry out, but no matter what sound I tried to make, nothing came out, as though my voice was getting stuck in the back of my throat.

Make it stop. Please, make it stop, I begged.

I can make it go away, Simon.

That same, raspy, fluid, taunting voice from the first dream. I looked up, knowing what I'd see. Two glowing orbs were staring down at me. In a flash, my headache was gone, replaced by something else entirely.

Taste.

My mouth filled with a metallic, coppery taste. Blood. It swam through my mouth and down my throat. I slowly, fearfully, lifted my hand. My face was covered in blood, as if I had been eating viciously.

Dragging my tongue against my arm, I tried to spit, to make myself sick, anything to get this taste from my mouth.

Do you like it? the voice asked. I wanted to curse. I wanted to mangle whatever was doing this to me. The eyes cocked its head. It must have been inches away from me, right beyond the veil of the fog. Their eyes were massive, and the glow was bright. It blinded me.

You'll learn to like it. You'll learn to need *it.*

The orbs stepped forward. I could almost see the outline—tall and thin. Too thin. Its ribs protruded outward while its waist was hollow. Its arms were long and its nails razor sharp. While I saw the head of a man, I knew this thing—this creature—was far from human. It was a ghoul.

The creature stood upright on its legs. They looked almost like deer legs—thin, delicate, but fast. I couldn't make out any facial features from the creature, only the round eyes that glowed red, like a cat at night. My eyes shifted up, above his eyes, above his head—they went wide.

Attached to the creature's head were huge elk antlers that reached high above the fog. The creature was already tall, but these made it seem giant. They had to add at least an extra foot. They spread out into sharp pointed ends and staggered all around.

You'll soon be like me, Simon, it cackled, a terrifying, haunting noise. Like nails on a chalkboard. My ears rang in pain. I was crying, sobbing, and I hadn't even known it. I was afraid; there was blood all over me. I was in pain, and cold. I was wet from the forest floor. I wanted to wake up. I wanted this nightmare to end. I didn't want to see what came next. I felt sick to my stomach.

The aroma of flesh came hauntingly back. The taste of blood was stronger than ever. I couldn't keep it down. I heaved and gagged.

All the while, the ghoul laughed at me.

Yes, good boy, Simon.

I heaved again, one final time, and felt something large come out of me. I jumped back at the sight of it. Before me, in a puddle of my vile, laid a human heart. I faced the ghoul.

Tasty, right? it rasped jovially.

I was frozen, gawking at it. Whose was it? Why was it *in me*?

All around me the cold bit my skin, the smell protruded my nose, the taste violated my mouth, and the laugh haunted my ears. I begged myself to wake up. I clawed at my arm, slapped my face—but nothing worked. I was stuck.

I'll see you soon, Simon, the voice whispered.

Everything went eerily silent again. No wind, no birds or animals, not even my heartbeat. I was left alone sitting on the cold forest floor, staring at the catatonic human heart for what felt like hours, days.

But nothing happened.

Until it did.

The once-still heart suddenly pumped.

Thu-thump.

CHAPTER TEN

found myself drifting off to sleep throughout the next day. Miles had to nudge my elbow to keep me from collapsing onto the desk. We hadn't spoken about last night and our "study sessions," but I promised myself I would ask him the first moment we were alone.

During lunch, I rested against my propped-up fist on the table. The noises of the chattering students drowned away and sounded like a collective embodiment of just noise. Even Riley's voice—who was right next to me—sounded far. I sat through lunch, motionless and silent. The others must have noticed the dark circles around my eyes because they didn't question why I was falling asleep.

Before I knew it, the bell rang, and I was off to my next class: computer lab. As soon as I got up, I felt a burning sensation on my knees. *Is this from the dream?* I felt as if I was in an in-between state where I couldn't differentiate between dream and reality.

While everyone tapped away at their keyboards, a noise that generally played like a lullaby to my ears, my eyes grew incredibly heavy. My head bobbed up and down. In my mind, a battle between sleep and consciousness played out like a valiant, swashbuckling sword fight. Of course, sleep was winning.

It wasn't until that moment that I realized just how

afraid I was to fall asleep. Would I see that ghoul again? Would I hear the scream? Taste the blood? Smell the rot? Vomit another heart? I didn't want to find out, but it was becoming more and more inevitable. Every time I blinked, I thought I saw the tall, decrepit figure. The antlers attached to its featureless head. The glowing circles protruding from the darkness. The absurdly long and thin arms leading to the curling fingers, fingers that always seemed to be reaching for me. Except this time, it stood at the front of the class, next to the teacher. It cocked its head, looking only at me. No one else saw it. Not even Riley. I blinked again; it was gone.

If Riley didn't sense the ghoul, I concluded that it *was* just all in my head. After all, I'd only seen it in dreams. Maybe learning that ghouls were real affected me more than I realized. Maybe it did something to me subconsciously, making me see and feel things that weren't there. Maybe, just maybe, it had the same effect on Miles.

I couldn't even understand why I was this tired. I'd done countless all-nighters and been more than fine the following day. I'd gone on three hours of sleep on school nights and never once fell asleep in class. And, truthfully, I had slept the majority of the night. Granted, of course I would be tired from the whole night, but not *this* tired. And Riley was fine.

Fighting sleep wasn't doing anything and my rationality as to why I was tired wasn't helping. Sleep was creeping ever deeper into my mind, fogging my vision.

Finally, I gave in and let it win.

With a heavy drop, my head fell to my shoulder and my eyes closed, making everything go black. All I could hear was the *tap-tapping* of my classmates' keyboards.

"Simon . . ."

My name. My name was the faintest whisper. So low and inferior, so utterly minute I couldn't hear the tone or sound of the voice. It passed through like an autumn wind—quiescent and bleak. Only I was asleep and in an enclosed classroom.

I heard it again, my eyes opening in automatic response.

My monitor was black. In fact, all the monitors were black. The keyboards looked as though they hadn't been touched in years, a heavy layer of dust residing along the letters and numbers. All the chairs were neatly tucked away under the desks. It felt like a relic of an old classroom: touch starved.

Something was off. The lights weren't on, but I could see clearly. The room had a dewy aroma.

I stood up and instantly felt a chill around my ankles. Below me was a thick layer of fog covering the dirty tile floor. A sound suddenly came to me—the sound of keyboard tapping. Only this time, instead of the cacophony of endless boards, just one was croaking.

Looking around the room, I was sure I was going to see someone. The room seemed endless. I walked row by row, hoping to find the culprit. Something kept whispering my name. This time it didn't sound like the nightmare's voice as I was expecting.

It was a girl's voice, soft and gentle—which scared me even more. For a moment, I thought it was Riley calling out to me, but the harsh, cool tone was missing. Each time my name was said, it sounded melodic. I must have passed fifty rows; the computers were still endless. The fog seeped up my jeans and I felt as though my shoes had become puddles.

But the tapping was getting louder.

The voice too.

Finally, I saw it. I saw a dim blue glow coming from a monitor. The hushed sound of a computer fan droned with the tapping. And someone's face stared at the screen. The blue of the monitor reflected onto her face, casting her already pale skin into a whitish glow. Her eyes were wide and frantically moving back and forth, reading the screen. She never looked at me. Not even a glance. I took another step forward.

Her face looked familiar. A lush of red hair was pushed to her front, covering her neck and shoulders almost completely. Where had I seen her before?

I rounded the corner of the last row and turned to face the girl.

Her body was a skeleton. Her typing fingers were nothing but bone. Her ribs sat perfectly, resting against the desk. Her spinal cord arched in perfect posture.

"Simon?" Her gaze shifted from the monitor to me in a flash. The cloudy green eyes of Addaline Alberts investigated mine. Her voice rose. "Simon, why? Why?"

"Wh-Why what?" I stammered out. Her fingers continued to type.

"Simon, why did you do this to me? Why?" Her typing seemed robotic. I dared myself to step forward. "Why, Simon?"

Her gaze was unwavering. Her eyes focused with deadly precision. Her voice still grew louder and the gentleness was lost and replaced with panic. I took one more step. As her voice grew almost into a scream, I broke our gaze and glanced at the screen. She had been repeatedly typing.

SIMON ATE ME ALIVE. WHY? WHY? WHY? WHY? WHY?

I looked back at her. Her face had contorted from calm to furious.

"WHY, SIMON? WHY DID YOU DO THIS TO ME?"

Her voice pierced my ears with pain so sharp, I thought my eardrums would explode. She wailed again. This time, her "why" dragged out the pitch of a horror movie scream queen. My ears rang so loud.

I clamped onto them as fast as I could before feeling something warm trickling down.

I was bleeding.

I turned to look at Addaline one last time. She was still screaming and full of anger. Only this time, she stood up. I thought about running but as soon as I turned around, something quickly made me hesitate.

Before me, the computer lab fused with the nightmare forest. Branches grew on the desks like ivy, vines consumed the computers like an invasive species. Below me, the fog transformed into dirt and mulch. No, not dirt—a trail of flesh and organs. A liver was a few feet ahead of me. A spleen lay about a yard away, and the smell of rot ran up my nose and made a home for itself.

I immediately felt sick. My hearing had vanished, my ears still ringing from Addaline's bellows. All I could smell was foul; death and decay were my new surroundings.

I turned around again, deciding the screaming corpse would be better than this, but it was gone. No longer was the computer lab a familiar place. All that was left was a mound of trees, tightly knitted together, making it almost impossible to pass through. I swallowed hard, knowing what I had to do. I had to see the dream through.

Following the trail of organs, I passed the liver and spleen, a stomach, and a few torn pieces of flesh. The taste of blood slowly grew in my mouth. I clutched my stomach, hoping to not get sick. I continued down and finally, at the end of the path, I saw the heart.

I knew the ghoul would be nearby. He always was.

Another step forward and I was ready to hear the heartbeat again when something viciously shook me. I tried to regain my footing, but I was shaken again.

All at once, I was opening my eyes. Clean air was filling my lungs, only the faint hum of air conditioning ran through my ears, and light nearly blinded me.

I was in the computer lab. The real one.

I looked up; Riley was shaking me. "Simon. The bell already rang."

I blinked at her. There were just a handful of other students, all ignoring our presence. Riley looked worried, with a tiny bit of annoyance creeping through now that I was awake. I followed her out of the room before she stalked off in the other direction.

I dragged my feet, almost colliding with Miles as we happened upon each other in front of the next class.

"Si, uh, are you okay?"

"Yeah. Just really, *really* tired." I wiped my face with the palm of my hand.

"Did something happen at Riley's?" Miles raised his eyebrow.

"What? No." I lightly shoved him, and he laughed. "Just didn't get good sleep." I paused. I wanted to ask him if anything strange had been happening to him. We were now in a classroom full of people and the teacher stood to begin the lesson.

The class ticked by, trying to welcome the end of the day. The teacher was still droning on when I decided to lean over and whisper to Miles.

"Hey, do you wanna hang out after school? Just us, no love interests. I'm in definite need of coffee."

"Hell yeah, I'm in." He nodded.

I wanted to tell Miles. He would understand. Even if he wasn't having weird dreams too, he'd get it. He'd have something to say.

Plus, even with everything going on in my head, I really wanted to know what was going on with him and Austin. I wanted the *chisme*.

According to Miles, Matty's Diner was known as *the* town diner. On the way, we talked about school and I told him about my night with Riley, carefully leaving out every detail about Addaline and the ghoul from my dreams.

"So, did ya make a move?" he asked, raising an eyebrow.

"She slept on my shoulder, so I'd definitely call that a win."

"My man!" His New Yorker accent peaked through. He playfully elbowed me as I smirked back.

The walk to the diner from school was quicker than I expected. This town really was tiny. Tiny, but full of trees. My hometown had lush palm trees, but this place was full of natural color.

"We didn't have seasons in Miami. We had summer and a slightly cooler summer," I explained. "Seeing the leaves actually change colors is impressive. It feels like Halloween already!"

"In New York we had seasons. But damn, did winters get cold. What's annoying is that you can't really appreciate them. Summer is too hot. Winter is too cold. Fall and spring are lost to concrete and construction." He paused, reminiscing. "Except for Central Park. Every season is nice in Central Park. Even with all the duck poop everywhere."

"Do you miss it? New York, I mean. Not the, er, duck poop." I laughed.

"I miss how fast-paced everything was. Everyone minded their own business too. It was, in a way, very comforting and *very* isolating," he said. "So, I miss it. But I'm also happy about the change of scenery. I think my dad's happier too. He never really cared about being a cop in the big city, but when he came here, he initially seemed to regret it a lot. He's back to his old self now. He has more responsibility as a deputy, and I think it's good for him. I miss my mom and brother, but I think it was for the best."

"Whoa, wait. You have a brother?"

Miles smiled. "He's older. My parents had him young. He was already in high school when I was born and then lived at his university for a few years. He got his degree, and a job in his field, but realized marketing just wasn't what he wanted to do."

"That's rough," I said. College was daunting. How they could expect eighteen-year-olds to already know what they wanted to do for the rest of their life was beyond me.

"I would've said the same, except Anton is definitely the go-getter of the family. He does *not* back down. Which made my dad and him butt heads on a few occasions. He ended up figuring out that he wanted to work in the fashion industry."

"Well, if New York isn't the place for that, then I don't know what is. Other than Paris, I guess?"

"Exactly. He went back to school, studied at FIT in the city, and ended up getting a job in the industry after. He couldn't give that up to come . . . *here.*" Miles gestured to the rising trees and winding road around us, to the small shops on either side and the pick-up trucks that suddenly reeked of tattered jeans and flannel.

"How old is Anton?"

"Twenty-six. He lives with my mom, but the two pretty much have opposite schedules. Plus, they've always gotten along real good."

"Are you and your mom *not* cool?" I raised an eyebrow. I hadn't heard Miles speak much about her, but the moment I asked, his face flushed.

"No, no. We are. I think I just felt a little mad when I moved here. She didn't come with me and she didn't really fight for me to stay. In fact, she's the one who encouraged me to move with Dad. She's come to visit three times already, and I only moved in June. So, I'd say we're good. She knew I needed something different."

He paused. We both took a moment to embrace the silence. Deep conversations with your best friend always carried a heavy but warm air. Like another door has been opened, whether you wanted it that way or not.

Miles turned to me as we walked. "What about you? Do you miss Miami?"

"Hmm, yes and no. I feel like this whole supernatural town has been everything I ever wanted. And like I already said, I'm super happy with seasons. Sometimes, I miss Miami. It was just so different. *No one* minded their own business and it was awful, but it was also home."

It was a windy October afternoon and sunset was teasing its way through the sky. We walked the rest of the way to Matty's in silence. Not an awkward silence, but something comfortable, something filling rather than empty.

We made our way into the restaurant and found a perfectly empty booth at the edge of the diner. The atmosphere was melancholic, to say the least. Alice had told Riley and me that Addaline's mother worked here.

We sat in the vinyl-covered seats and a stout, middle-aged woman with a little too much blue eyeshadow came up to us. She threw two sticky menus in front of us and held up her steaming hot pot of a thick, brown liquid.

"Coffee?" Her voice was raspy as could be and I could smell cigarettes with each syllable she spoke. Miles and I both nodded. She flipped the ceramic coffee mugs that had already been set at the table and poured us each a cup.

"Cream, sugar," she said pointing to two different containers at the edge of our table before walking away.

For a moment, the two of us looked at the menu. Miles put it down and made his coffee. He put a splash of creamer and grabbed three packets of sugar. After mixing it a bit and tasting it, his face contorted into disgust. He quickly grabbed three more packets of sugar, took another sip, and finally seemed content. He put the mug back down on the table and looked at me.

"Tell me, what did you want to talk about?" Everything from his posture to facial expression screamed that he was ready to listen, ready to know what had been bugging me lately. I opened my mouth to speak, closed it, and opened it again.

Our waitress came back to the table with a notepad and a bored expression on her face, breaking my hesitations.

"You the deputy's boy?" The waitress nodded at Miles.

"Yes?"

"I heard your pop's been working on finding who done that unspeakable thing to poor Addaline. Dessert's on the house. What will you boys have today?" she stated more than asked.

Miles perked up. "Oh, I'll have the two eggs, sunny-side up, with bacon and sausage. White toast, please. And can I get an orange juice on the side?"

The waitress jotted down Miles's order and hummed a quick "mhm" at his request. She looked up at me. "And you?"

"I'll have the Matty Burger. With provolone, no mustard please."

"Anything else to drink?"

"Uhh . . . Water is fine."

And without another sound, she grabbed the two menus and disappeared.

"Breakfast for dinner?" I asked Miles once we were alone again.

"It's my favorite!" He smiled. "So, you were saying?"

"Before I start," I say, trying to push back the conversation about Addaline and the ghoul as much as possible. "How was it with Austin yesterday?"

Immediately, Miles's eyes darted to the floor. He blushed wildly and stammered on his words, trying desperately to conceal a smile. I give him *the smirk.*

"It was . . . fun! Cool, I mean. Taught him a lot. About history. Obviously, and—"

"You are totally in love on him."

"What! No. He was a total dick not so long ago, remember?"

"Hmm." I sat back and crossed my arms. Miles looked at me, with fake annoyance written all over his face.

After a few minutes of complete silence, Miles finally broke the silence. "Okay, okay. I maaay have the tiniest crush on him. No big deal. He did apologize for the bullying after all. An-and . . . he only did it because he's, ya know"—he leaned in close and whispered—"a werewolf. That *has* to do some kinda damage to you." After the dreams I'd had, I didn't need convincing of that.

I nodded. "So, like, has he made a move?"

Miles's shoulders dropped. "I don't know. It's hard to tell. I can't just be like 'Hey, uh, do you like guys?' now can I?"

"Why not?" I frowned. It hadn't really occurred to me that not everyone was comfortable in their masculinity, and here in North Carolina, some might take that a lot more offensive than people from Miami might.

Miles sighed loudly and just shook his head, planting his face in his hands. "I think," he enunciated, "he flirts with me. Last night especially. He was definitely trying to get us alone, right?"

I nodded again. "Yeah, I think so. He seemed like he was trying to get the two of you alone more than get me and Riley alone. So, I don't know. What happened last night?" I questioned, raising my eyebrow.

"We just talked, a little too much. About his life and feelings and, well, not normal 'bro' stuff."

"Hey! I talk to you about my feelings."

He laughed. "Okay, yes, but with him, it felt different. He sat *right* next to me. We were touching the whole time!"

"Oooh, the old touch trick. Very clever, that one."

Miles stared at me for a moment as if he wasn't sure if I knew what I was talking about. So, instead of waiting for his ridicule, I threw one back at him. "Do you want me to ask him?"

"What! No! Definitely not. Then he'll think I begged you to ask! That's, like, best friend code."

"Okay, okay," I laughed. "I won't say anything, but you gotta keep me in the loop, okay? I wanna know every detail, every text!" I pointed at Miles, aggressively.

He smiled and nodded. "Okay, deal. Same for you and Riley." He stuck out his hand, and we shook, making our deal into a pact.

Miles shifted and took his phone from his pocket. "He actually texted me something after school. Look." He turned his phone screen to me.

AUSTIN: HEY, I WAS THINKING . . .

AUSTIN: I KNOW I'M NOT "REALLY" IN THE GROUP YET.

AUSTIN: SO MAYBE WE CAN HANG OUT THIS WEEKEND?

AUSTIN: I MEAN, WITH EVERYONE IF YOU PREFER.

AUSTIN: YA KNOW. WHILE WE'RE NOT DOING VIBE SESSIONS AND STUFF.

AUSTIN: JUST NORMAL TEENAGER STUFF, LIKE GOING TO THE MOVIES OR SOMETHING?

AUSTIN: OKAY, JUST WANTED TO GET YOUR OPINION. I'LL STOP TEXTING U NOW, HAHA :)

After a moment of reading through the messages a second time, I looked up at Miles. "Jeez, he texts a lot."

Miles nodded and grinned.

"Austin's asking you for your opinion. That's something. He's spent the most time with Riley in the group, but he asked *you* if *you* wanted to hang out. He added the 'everyone' bit to not seem suspicious."

"Plus, the smiley face. That's flirty, right?"

"I hope so."

"Here you go, boys." The waitress brought out our food and we both chowed down. I finished my burger in a flash and slowly began picking at my fries and dipping them in ketchup.

With a full mouth, Miles knocked on the table and gestured toward me.

"Your turn."

I sat up straighter. I felt my heart race a little and my hands grew sweaty.

I took a deep breath. "I've been having these dreams lately and I can't explain them."

I didn't feel ready to talk about them out loud and every horror fan knows that once you do, it brings them into existence, sans *Nightmare on Elm Street*. But I needed to do this. I needed to know if he was having these weird dreams too, if he thought the ghoul was real. I just needed someone to know. Someone to talk to.

I told him everything. The first dream that night in the car the night we found Austin. Everything about Addaline. The horrible sounds and smells. The taste of blood in my mouth. Most importantly, I told him about the glowing red eyes. Miles tensed when I spoke of this. He folded his arms and shuddered. I finished telling him about the ghoul with the dream I had during school today. Silence reigned between us for what felt like an eternity.

"That's some spooky shit."

I nodded in agreement and ran my hand through my hair, pushing it back.

"So . . ." I tensed before asking the question I needed to know. "Have you seen him too? Is this my brain freaking out, learning that ghosts and werewolves and everything are real?" I was hopeful. More than anything I wanted to feel like it wasn't just me.

Miles's eyes fell. His face changed from horror to sorrow and concern. He opened his mouth to speak a few times, but no words made it out. Eventually, he just shook his head.

"Oh . . . so I am crazy."

"I didn't say that, nor do I think that. Based on what you've said, it sounds real. Plus, who are we to say it isn't? As you said, we just learned all these things exist. Maybe this is something too. Something we don't know about yet!"

"But, if it was a real ghoul, Riley would have vibed with it. She would have sensed it way before my first dream."

"Have you talked to her about it? Maybe she has."

"I didn't want her to feel bad about introducing me to this world, in case it is just manifested anxiety."

Miles looked at me for a moment, thoughts clouding his face. He nodded. He understood my fear of telling Riley. "So, what do we do?" Miles asked. We both remained silent. He peered down at his empty plate as I stopped to just think for a moment.

"I'm not ready to tell Riley just yet. Maybe that has to be the next step. If I have one more dream tonight, I'll try to get to the root of what's going on." I scratched my head. "I gotta say, I'm really hoping I'm just crazy."

Miles scoffed. "Honestly, so am I."

My stomach started to twist into knots. I felt something trying desperately to come out of my stomach.

"Dude, are you—" Miles started, but I didn't stay to hear him. I jumped out of the booth and ran as quickly as I could to the restroom, and vomited up everything I had just ingested.

Moments later, I heard someone come in. I hugged the toilet tightly and felt a hand on my shoulder. Miles.

I heard him walk toward the sink as he pulled out paper towels and brought them to me. He stayed with me, waiting for me to expel everything. After I was done, I slouched back on the floor and rested my head against the stall wall. Miles handed me the paper towels. I wiped my mouth, feeling utterly grossed out. He crouched next to me and placed a hand on my forehead. I felt my hair stick to me in a cold sweat.

"Since when have you felt sick? You looked fine a minute ago."

"I felt fine a minute ago. I don't know what happened." I wiped my mouth again.

"This is all getting to you, Si. Let's get you home, man." Miles's look of concern was written all over his face. He helped me get up, flushed the toilet, and we left after saying thanks to our waitress.

Thankfully, the diner wasn't far from my house.

He paused at the doorway and shifted on his feet.

"Maybe—maybe don't go looking for the ghoul in your dream tonight. Focus on feeling better."

"Yeah, I'll do that," I lied. As soon as Miles left, I knew what I had to do. I didn't plan on listening to Miles. I couldn't avoid the ghoul anymore, I had to find it. Tonight. I knew he was the reason I threw up. It was making me sick.

A little voice in the back of my head—his voice—whispered to me. *Meat is your only substance now. Human meat. Like little Addaline.*

Miles had made sure my parents knew I wasn't feeling well before we even made it home. They both had concerned looks on their faces as I walked in.

With both my parents being doctors in their respective fields, the amount of cleaning my parents do all the time was sure to slowly wipe all germs from the planet someday. Dad was huge on vitamins, and at the slightest cough or sneeze, Mom would tell me to take some form of medicine or tea. So, walking in with the color faded from my face, hair stuck to my forehead with sweat, and the slight but disgusting aroma of vomit, they were incredibly and utterly nervous.

I was ushered upstairs at once, stripped of my clothes, and thrown into the shower. Moments later, I was dried, pajama-ed, and finally tucked into my bed so snuggly, I felt like a caterpillar going through a metamorphosis.

Maybe I *was* going through a metamorphosis, like *The Fly*.

My parents seemed to be taking turns coming in and out of my room, bringing me things, and asking questions.

"What did you eat?" asked Dad as he gave me a little white pill and water.

"Are you okay?" Mom placed a damp towel on my forehead.

"Did you get enough sleep last night?" Dad took my temperature.

If only they knew I barely slept anymore.

"Is something going around at school?" Mom questioned as she handed me a hot cup of lavender tea. I could smell the honey steaming up into my nostrils.

This went on for a while until, finally, my parents seemed to take the hint of I-just-want-some-peace-and-quiet. My mom left the door slightly open, and I didn't see either of them again for a while.

I stayed in bed, sipping my tea until the sun went down. It was Friday, which meant I had the weekend to recover. I sighed in relief. Whatever was going to happen when I eventually fell asleep would be bad, and I needed all the rest I could get. My stomach calmed down right after finishing the tea. The urge to vomit calmed.

Must be some kind of Korean magic.

Miles and Riley—and even Austin—had texted me throughout the evening to check up on me. I responded to all of them.

ME: I JUST NEED SOME SLEEP. I'LL BE FINE.

They kept trying to carry the conversation, but I didn't respond. I knew it probably wasn't the best decision, but I figured I would just let them believe it was food poisoning. They would worry less than understanding the alternative. Plus, I needed to get myself mentally prepared for this dream. I went through a phase in my freshman year when I got really into trying to lucid dream. I had done it successfully a handful of times and I felt like it'd be a helpful skill to have. Maybe I'd be able to control my own body this time. I was facing a demon Freddy Krueger who made me eat people. I needed every resource I could find.

Based on the dreams, I tried to think of every detail, from what I was wearing to what things physically felt like. In my dreams, I wore whatever I was wearing in real life. Maybe if the clothes followed me in, other physical things could too. I got out of bed, dug around through my ghost-hunting gear, and grabbed my video camera and recorder. *Maybe I could take this into a dream with me, if not visual, then audio. Like* A Nightmare on Elm Street.

If this worked, I'd have proof the ghoul was real. This way, I could show Riley and she'd know I wasn't crazy.

This way, *I* would know I wasn't crazy.

I got in bed and turned off the lights. It was now or never. I threw the blanket over myself and clutched my camera and recorder as close to me as possible.

Please let this work.

CHAPTER ELEVEN

Everything felt heavy. The world closed in around me and slowly faded from existence altogether. All that was left was me, standing on a patch of grass with a vast emptiness of darkness and tendrils of fog wisping about. Around me was nothing. Or better yet, a lack of something. I knew I was standing in the forest, the same way you just seem to *know* things in dreams. Names of people with different faces, settings you're in, who you are.

I was standing on a small patch of grass that I knew expanded into the forest I'd been in so many times now in my dreams. I looked down at myself. I was in the same sweats and T-shirt I was in when I went to sleep. In my hands were my camera and recorder.

Holy shit, it worked. I smiled to myself; my experiment was successful.

I turned the recorder on and placed it into my pocket with the mic facing upward, then turned on my video camera. The screen revealed the forest, past the patch of grass I stood on. The quality was lower than it usually was but revealed more than my own eyes could see. I looked back and forth for a minute and decided to follow my gut.

Using the camera's screen to guide me, it seemed like the patch I could see followed and shifted with my every move. The forest was my stage, and I was the spotlight. With each step, a loud crunch sounded beneath me—the leaves were dead.

But the weirdest aspect of this dream was my senses.

Without my camera, I could only see a small perimeter of my surroundings. I couldn't smell a thing; there were no sounds, not even that of forest-dwelling creatures, only the echoing crunch of the leaves beneath me. I felt as though I should be cold, but I wasn't.

I weaved between trees, with nothing but the oddly pleasant and comforting sound of the leaves. I knew I should be terrified, but the truth was, I felt nothing. I didn't sense the darkness or terror I usually felt while in these dreams. I didn't let that deter me. I needed to catch a glimpse of the ghoul.

I needed proof that I wasn't going crazy.

The forest was familiar now and the more I walked, the more I wanted to see, the more I wanted to know about the ghoul. I was well-versed in my ghosts and "things that go bump in the night," but I had never encountered a beast with human anatomy and antlers.

I thought of the biblical "horned beast" but knew those were ram horns. Plus, it would smell like brimstone and have a pitchfork, right?

Then I thought of a satyr, but it would have goat legs. Just nothing seemed to fit exactly. Nothing I could think of. Not to mention that Riley didn't vibe with the ghoul.

Could it be human? I felt like this theory made the slightest sense. No human could make me feel how this ghoul did. To make me feel paranoid in my own body, to make me think perhaps I was the monster that ate the girl from the morgue.

I simply couldn't fathom it.

Something was on my camera screen just beyond my circle of sight—but it wasn't the ghoul. Sitting on an old tree stump was Addaline. She was staring directly into the camera lens.

"He's not here. Not right now," she whispered.

Her voice was soft and echoed throughout the darkness, creating a shudder in the tendrils of fog.

"'He' who?" I asked bravely. I could feel myself trembling but wouldn't let it dip into my voice.

"The one who killed me. The one you're looking for."

I inched forward enough to see her with my own eyes. I let the camera drop but held it at my side. I made sure the lens was still on Addaline, even if it was a bad angle.

"He was the one who killed you?" I asked.

No response, just a nod of the head.

"I had a dream earlier. You said I killed you." I thought back to the screaming girl who swore I was the one to kill her.

"Simon, it's his fault you're like this. Don't let his greed overpower you." She stood up and walked toward me. She placed her hand on my chest. "You're one of the good ones. Don't let it corrupt you."

"What do you mean?"

"Don't let *him* corrupt you. He's never satisfied."

Just as I was about to answer, she swiftly spun away. The white dress she wore hovered just above the ground. She was floating. I noticed only now that there was a slight shimmer radiating through Addaline, a transparency that gave way to the trees behind her.

"I'm angry, Simon. Really angry. What happened to me shouldn't have happened." I could hear the rage growing. I thought back to the shriek. She reminded me of a banshee.

"Addaline, is your spirit bound here?"

She turned to me, her red and tear-stricken eyes contorting into fury. This wasn't right. Not only did the ghoul kill her, but now she was trapped here.

Just then, we heard something dreadful deep within the woods.

"He's back!" Addaline cried. Our heads jerked toward the trees.

At first, it sounded like a very guttural growl and then it resonated as if something was charging directly toward us. With each second, it got closer. *Stomp, stomp, stomp.*

Holding out my hand, I called out to her. "I brought these things in," I yelled, holding up the camera. "Maybe I can pull you out!"

She looked at my hand and then back at me, hesitating. The stomping was getting closer.

"I know it's scary, but this is the only thing I can think of. Let me help you!"

She took my hand.

The last thing I saw before squeezing my eyes shut was the movement of trees and something charging through them. The last thing I heard was a loud and agonizing shriek. Addaline's scream.

In a jolt of panic, I forced myself awake. I blinked a few times and saw that I was in my room and the sun was coming up. I looked at my hand, but there was no one at the other end. My gut told me that it worked. I felt her fall back into this world with me.

I remembered my ghost-hunting equipment. I pulled out the recorder from my pocket and ran through the EVP.

"He's not here. Not right now." I heard Addaline say after a moment of nothing but white noise and crunching leaves. It wasn't crisp and perfect—there was a static overlay—but it *was* her voice. Everything was there. And then, I heard the growl, stomping, and the scream.

I checked the video camera. Everything was there: the forest, the trees, Addaline, the leaves. Everything. I was relieved to have proof, but then the end of the video came. In the final seconds, something made the trees shudder violently. There he was. The ghoul stood, eyes glowing red, antlers towering as tall as two of me.

I caught him. I had proof. Solid, actual proof.

I spun around and reached for my phone. It was eight in the morning, and my friends were asleep, but it didn't matter. I opened the group chat and messaged.

> **ME:** HEY GUYS. WE NEED TO MEET UP TODAY.
> I NEED TO TALK TO YOU.

It was time to come clean.

CHAPTER TWELVE

I t took a while to successfully convince my parents to let me out of the house after last night's vomit-fest. A lot of "you could be contagious" from my dad trying to get me to stay home, but even more "you just need rest, sweetie," from Mom, who seemed a little more than nervous at the idea of her one and only son being even slightly ill.

I lied and stated that it was food poisoning from the diner and promised to never get that burger again. I mean, to be honest, I didn't even really know if this *was* a lie. I technically was poisoned by the food—but in more of a terrifying supernatural way than a normal North Carolina way. (Truth be told, I was starting to not see the difference anymore.)

The gang and I decided to meet up at Riley's today. I remembered to bring the camera and recorder from last night. I had to show them my findings.

My mom begged to drive me and I agreed, even though the trek was wildly awkward. My mom usually spoke a mile a minute but today she seemed as if she was in a small room with a sleeping baby, afraid that the smallest of noises would wake it.

"Mom, are you okay?"

"I should be the one asking you that." Her face said it all: worry, fear, love.

"I think it was just the food, honest. I won't eat any-thing unless it's at home, just in case."

Though truthfully, I wouldn't eat anything, even if it *was* at home. Earlier today, Dad made a light breakfast. Most of it was bland food just to keep my stomach full. Toast, crackers, and water—the usual. None of it stayed down. I cleaned it all up as quickly as I could, and nei-ther parent noticed. They assumed I finished it all.

Now, as I sat here in a confined space with my mom, I started to feel her doubt tread in.

"Just call me if anything happens, okay?"

"I will."

"Promise?" She glanced at me again and I started to see her grip tighten on the steering wheel.

"I promise."

I didn't want the awkwardness to continue, so I de-cided to do what every parent wants of their child: to care.

"How's the vet going?"

That put a huge smile on her face.

"It's going really well. I've been getting a lot of cli-ents already!"

"That's good! How are the wild animals? And the cows?"

"I prefer the deer to the livestock; chickens can be kind of mean." She scowled, and I couldn't help but chuckle. "Cows and goats are cute though! But the best cases are healing injured deer and bats and setting them free again. It's so refreshing to feel like I help na-ture just that much more. I'm hoping for a mountain lion one of these days."

It was so comforting to hear her talk about what she loved. Her job never felt like a job. It was home to her, and watching her eyes shine relaxed me.

"Any cute dogs?"

"Oh, so many. There's this one named Bear. He's a Rottweiler. He's so funny, he chases his tail around constantly! I think he truly believes he's a small dog because he's always trying to squeeze into the smallest cabinets or he walks in between people's legs—it's the cutest."

"They really are adorable, big goofballs, Mom."

"The biggest in size and love. The owner has a young daughter, and you should see this dog with that girl. I think Bear thinks *he's* her dad."

Ever since I was a kid, my mom and I have bonded over our love for animals. She taught me that every animal was precious. She would let me go with her to work to see what she did and to play with the animals who needed some extra bit of love. I was taught not to be afraid of them from early. A bite is just a bite, and they always have a reason. A scratch is typically an accident. Animals are never inherently bad.

This made me think of the night we first saw Austin in all his werewolf glory; how scared he was, and why he was so mean to us at school. He was alone and totally out of his element. He simply acted how any dog would react to strangers coming upon him when he was scared and alone.

I need to be nicer to him; he's just a big—a really big— dog, I thought. *I wonder if he likes belly rubs.*

"So why was Bear at the vet in the first place?" The more we spoke about work, the less we would talk about me.

"Well, that family owns another dog. Much older than Bear. He has his ways that he's used to, and the owner feels bad trying to change them."

"Like what?"

"The dog is what I like to call an 'outside dog.' He kind of wanders around the neighborhood whenever he wants. He's extremely good with people, so he won't ever attack, but he's not so good with other dogs," she explained. "Apparently, even he and Bear don't really get along.

"So, one day this dog was roaming the streets, as he always did, and he came across what the owner described as a 'beast of a dog.' This dog—Ramsey, by the way—always came home safe and sound, so we assumed he was a good fighter or just didn't get into many conflicts. But this time, Ramsey and this beast-dog got into a fight.

"I'm not quite sure how or what really happened, but dogs have such a keen sense for these kinds of things. Bear sensed Ramsey was in danger. He jumped over their fence—which was something he often did, usually just to greet his owners—to save Ramsey. He helped the older dog fight off the other. Unfortunately, it was a bit too late for Ramsey. He had a nasty gash at his side, larger than I had ever seen another dog make. Too big for bite marks, but also too big for a normal dog's paw. It was strange."

She paused for a second. I wondered if what Ramsey encountered was actually a dog, or something more Ravenswood-y. *Was it a ghoul?*

"Anyway, Bear rushed back to the house and got the owner, barking at him and ushering him to follow. Bear led the owner to Ramsey. Bear wasn't too beat up but had a pretty big cut on his snout. So the owner came in and explained everything. Like I said, it was too late to save Ramsey. The daughter was hysterical, I'm pretty sure he had been around even before she was born. He was such a good boy." My mom smiled, and I did too. Dogs really did have a way into people's hearts.

"Did anyone ever find the big dog that attacked Ramsey?"

She hesitated but slowly shook her head. "No, and truthfully, I don't think they ever will."

I turned to her, but before I could ask what she meant, we pulled up to Riley's.

"All right, Si. You know what to do. Call me if you

need anything. Call me when you're coming home and if you need a ride."

I nodded, blindly agreeing with everything she said.

"Text me if you guys go anywhere. If you feel sick again, I'll come get you."

"Okay, Mom. Thanks, bye." I kissed her cheek and got out of the car, but before I could close the door, she stopped me.

"Oh, and Si? Ravenswood is a little . . . strange. Try to stay in the house after dark, okay? Be careful of the *dokkaebi*." She winked, blew a kiss, and reached for my door to close it, before I could even process her words.

I turned slowly, calculating what she had just said.

Dokkaebi? Korean goblins . . . in Ravenswood? Does she know about ghouls?

Austin's car was already in the driveway. I knocked three times, and before I could knock a fourth, Riley threw the door open. She wrapped her arms around my shoulders and pulled me into a tight embrace.

"Miles told us you got sick," Pulling away, she punched my arm. "That's for making us all worry!"

"Yeah! And what was up with that same shitty response you gave us all?" came Miles's voice from within the house.

"'I just need some sleep, I'll be fine' was scarier than hearing you were sick in the first place!" came Austin's voice, with a mocking tone.

Uncontrollably, I smiled. Riley saw my face and smiled back, ushering me into her home. As I walked in, I saw Austin and Miles sitting on one of the couches in the living room with a bag of chips and soda sitting on the coffee table in front of them. They both looked up at me and grinned.

"You want anything?" Riley asked from the kitchen.

"He's going to say no, but he should definitely drink water," Miles stated, and as I turned to argue, I saw Riley nodding her head in agreement, pouring a rather large glass of water, and forcing it into my hand.

I stood there for a moment, awkwardly, not sure what to say, where to begin, or what to do. But that quickly broke when Riley lifted my arm and raised the glass of water to my mouth, forcing me to drink. After a moment of chugging—and also getting water all over my shirt—she pointed her hand to the couch we sat on the other night, silently telling me to go sit. All eyes were on me, and I felt incredibly uncomfortable. I took another large gulp of water, stinging my throat in the process.

"Sooo, how have you guys been?" I asked, trying horribly to break the awkward silence.

"I haven't told them anything," Miles started. "Just that you have something to tell us, and it's a lot."

"Spill," Riley said, rather harshly. It was obvious she was not playing around by the scrunched look on her face.

I lightly scratched my head and put the glass down on the table. I reached for my bag and pulled out both the video camera and recorder and placed them on the table in front of me, next to my water.

"I'm just going to come right out and say it: I think a ghoul is haunting me." I braced for the worst.

All three of them looked at me with different expressions.

Riley spoke first. "I'm waiting to hear more before I make any decision on what to think. I'll just say if it's a ghoul, I would have felt it."

"That's what I thought too, and honestly, that's why I haven't said anything. This . . . *thing* I've been encountering is more ghoul-like than anything I've encountered. But you didn't vibe with it—him. I was scared he wasn't real. I was scared that maybe I was just *so* excited for the supernatural to be real, that maybe I created all of this in my head. I thought I was losing my mind." I paused, not wanting to voice the next part out loud. "But I was more scared this *wasn't* just a conjured-up dream. And now I'm starting to see that this ghoul . . . he's real."

Staring at the gang, I tried my hardest not to cry. Letting out a deep breath and closing my eyes, I felt Riley place her hand on my shoulder.

"This all started a while back," and then I told them every gory detail. All the dreams. All the feelings. The woods, the girl, and the red-eyed beast. "I had a sick feeling that I was—am—being possessed by this thing. Getting sick yesterday was just an add-on to the craziness. It was my first real meal since the initial dream with Addaline and my body immediately rejected it—it wasn't human, it wasn't blood. I don't think I was allowed to eat anything else. That leads us to last night's dream."

I pointed at the recording device on the table. Everyone's eyes shifted toward the video camera.

"I realized that in all the dreams, I've been wearing whatever I was wearing at the time I fell asleep. I thought maybe physical items could go in with me too, so I tried it out. The dream consisted of Addaline mostly, but at the very, very end, he was there."

Miles gasped.

"Before I show you this, I need to say something else. At the end of the dream, I attempted to pull Addaline out of her prison; she seemed to be stuck in there with the ghoul. I think it worked, but when I woke up, she was gone."

"We'll find her." Riley straightened. "She's either moved on or is a lost spirit somewhere. I'm sure I'll vibe to her."

"The thing is, I have a feeling I know *what* Addaline is. Have you guys ever heard of banshees?"

Miles and Austin shook their heads, but Riley's face

completely and utterly became devoid of color. "Why would you think that?" Riley asked.

"She looked like a ghost, but angrier. Her clothes were all white, her eyes were bloodshot from crying, and she wailed," I recollected. I turned to Miles and Austin. "Banshees are part of Irish folklore. They're vengeful spirits of women who were wrongfully killed. Their whole thing is that they have a piercing shriek. When you hear it, you're pretty much doomed. I think Addaline became that."

"Well, I hope you're wrong," Riley spoke as she avoided eye contact. "They're typically omens of death. If you hear them wailing it means that someone you know and love is destined to die soon. They're crying *for* you since they know how horrible the loss will be. In actual practice, they're full of rage. Their goal is to kill the one who wronged them, but they'll kill anyone in their path. The shriek is their weapon. We don't know in what state she came back in. She might not remember her time at all in the ghoul's world. She might even be after you, Simon."

The room fell silent. I felt a mix of fear and pity. Fear because a banshee coming after me was a truly terrifying idea. But pity because, in a strange way, I'd come to know Addaline. She was killed, untimely and gruesomely. She was trapped by a horrible beast. And then she was finally set free only to become this horridly vengeful spirit. How much more must she go through?

After a moment of silence, everyone clearly thinking about the whole situation, I reached for the video camera and began fast-forwarding to the end. Everyone positioned themselves to see the screen better and I paused at the exact moment the ghoul appeared before flipping it over. "That's him."

No one spoke for what felt like forever, instead, they all just stared.

Miles glared up at me. "What the hell is that?"

CHAPTER THIRTEEN

After a ton of back and forth, we concluded that we had no clue what the ghoul was. Austin voted for a deformed werewolf due to the claws, Miles swore it was a psychopath cannibal in a costume, and Riley thought it could be a fleshgait (which we learned was some kind of ghoul that mimics human voices perfectly and wears their skin after killing them.) But none of us were totally sold on any of these ideas since all we had was a pixelated silhouette.

It was something more. Something strong enough to create its own "in-between" dream reality that I had visited so many times, that Addaline had been stuck in. Something that looked slightly human but was further away from that than anything I could even think of. We were racking our brains, trying to figure everything out. I knew I should be feeling panicky as I was sure the rest of them were feeling, but I couldn't help but feel slightly relieved.

They believed me. I had my friends to help me now, and I had a strong feeling that nothing could stop us.

"I'll go to the library, see if I can learn anything," Miles said, pulling out a small notebook. I grabbed it and flipped through, reading notes and descriptions of the ghoul:

"TALL, THIN, GLOWING RED EYES, ANTLERS, HUMANOID,
LONG CLAWS, ATE GIRL, SIMON SEES DEAD GIRL,
WANTS SIMON TO EAT HUMAN . . ."

"The library? Why not just look it up on the internet?" Austin said, matter-of-factly. I nodded my head. I mean, what decade were we in?

"But if I search for 'human-eating creature with antlers,' I'll just get weird creepypastas or scary stories."

"Hey, the internet has helped me through so many vibe sessions," Riley defended as she stared at the ghoul on the camera screen. I heard Miles sigh as he pulled out his phone and began searching.

A bit of time passed as we all sat on our phones, looking through different forums, pictures, and any kind of media we could find. We threw out other ideas, and various creatures, but nothing stuck.

"We need to make a ghoul encyclopedia," I finally said before a long grunt of frustration and exhaustion.

Everyone weakly agreed. *Thud.* We all looked up to see Riley's phone fall from her hands. Her eyes were hazy, off. The same look as when she began to vibe with something.

Was Addaline finally making her presence known to us? Or was it the ghoul?

We sat in silence until she spoke.

"There's a ghost nearby. She isn't hostile. She wants us to find her." Riley blankly stared at the front door. She nodded her head in the direction of the exit. "Come on."

We made our way out of the house, across the street, up the small grassy hill, and into the woods just in front of Riley's house. Almost immediately after entering the forest, Riley vibed to the ghost nearby and became a living apparition. She studied her see-through hands and floating legs before turning to the rest of us.

"Well, the Ghoul Gang is back on the job." I pumped my arm in the air.

"Ghoul Gang?" Riley's voice had an overlapping echo, just like a ghost was simply an echo of the living.

"What do you think? We can't be the Mystery Gang. So, *Ghoul Gang.*"

"We do hunt ghouls," Miles added. "I like it."

"How'd you come up with that?" Austin asked.

I shrugged. "So, do you guys like it?"

"I can already see it on T-shirts," Austin grinned.

"I've always wanted to be part of a gang," Miles joked.

Riley looked down at her ghostly figure.

"I guess I'm in by default, right?" She smiled.

That was that. We were the Ghoul Gang.

"Well, this way, Ghoul Gang." Riley guided us toward the ghost, continuing our trek through the forest. We hiked through a dense cove of trees and mud, going uphill and then downhill, and uphill once again. The mountainous landscape of North Carolina was tiring to my South Floridian legs which were bred for flat land and humidity.

The trees were formed in a particular way to make the wind blow through hard and sharp. An array of branches, leaves, and twigs cascaded around the floor. Behind me, Miles nearly tripped on one, but just before he fell, Austin caught his arm and helped him upright. The two stayed close to each other for the rest of the hike.

Riley was up ahead, having no issues with the tough terrain as she floated above it. The rest of us struggled up, carefully choosing each step. Finally, I saw Riley stop up ahead at the foot of a large, round clearing. It was strange, out of place. The dirt in the clearing was so dark, it almost looked black. The trees seemed to have an invisible barrier where they could no longer pass. There were no dead, stray leaves that flew in. The clearing had no greenery, only the same almost-black dirt throughout.

"This is . . ." I started.

"Weird, I know," Riley finished my thought. "I've been in these woods my whole life and I've never seen this."

Austin seemed uneasy and Miles simply gaped at the empty void surrounded by life.

"Should we go in?" Miles asked, asking himself more than the group.

"I guess so?" Riley shrugged. She hovered into the clearing and we all followed.

We slowly walked—and floated—toward the center of the field. Nothing happened.

"Do you still feel the ghost?" I asked as we walked closer and closer to the center.

"Yeah, she's definitely here." Riley looked nervous.

We all got to the center of the clearing and stood still. We glanced at each other, expecting something to happen. For a moment, the forest was still.

"Hello, dearies," came an older woman's voice from behind us. It was harsh yet warm. Rich with life and beauty, but cracked and old and hidden away. We all turned around to face her. Her voice matched her appearance.

Before us levitated a small, older woman. Her hair was wild and fell around her face like a willow tree around its bark. I could see the silver sheen through the transparent blue hue of her spirit. Her eyes were large and something told me they were once a vibrant green. Her clothes were old-fashioned. Colonial perhaps? She wore no shoes, her feet tarnished with dark dirt that matched the patch we were standing on.

She smiled at us, warmly, with a hint of mischief. Around her neck was a small jar tied on a long string. In the jar was a bit of the same dirt and a few lavender buds resting on top of it.

She caught my eye and smiled even wider.

"It is for warding the evil away," she said with a wink.

I smiled back at her.

She then looked at Riley and began to shake her head. "We can't have you like that, dearie. I want to see you as you are." And with a snap of her fingers, Riley landed on the ground, fully opaque and human—and alive.

Riley's eyes widened as she patted herself down. Confused, she shot her head up toward the old woman. "How did you—" But before Riley could finish, the woman held her hand up and simply shook her head.

"For another time. I have much to tell you, with not a lot of time." Her face fell. It became somber. Her eyes then lifted to me. "You're cursed, dear. Marked. Even I can see that."

Everyone then looked at me. "What—What do you mean?"

"The beast has found you. He has chosen you. There isn't going to be much you can do now."

"You know about the ghoul we're searching for?" Riley interjected, a note of panic in her voice.

"Aye, I do. He has been lurking in Ravenswood since before it was Ravenswood. He is an evil, *evil* spirit. He possesses those he chooses. And bad things always happen." Everyone was silent for a moment.

"You know what I am, right?" Riley asked the spirit who simply nodded. "Why can't I vibe with him? Why can't I feel him?"

The woman stopped for a moment and looked up toward the sky. Night was slowly approaching.

"I believe that has to do with the type of spirit he is. He was once two, but now he is one." She paused and watched us. Everyone's expression must have been the same as mine because she continued to explain herself.

"The Spirit and the Human."

"The two," Miles said. He seemed as though he were finally solving a puzzle he had been stuck on. The old woman nodded.

"The Spirit possessed the Human, ate away at his humanity until nothing but the Spirit was left."

"Riley, you don't feel him because technically, he is still within the human," Miles concluded.

"Aye. That is correct. Listen to this one, he's smart," she said, gleefully reaching a wrinkly hand at Miles. She tried to pinch his cheeks but her hand phased right through. He blushed and nodded his head in thanks before the old woman continued.

"The Spirit has done this many times. Each time finding a new host, a new body to inhabit. He possesses them slowly, making sure they are worth it. And he is doing it again." She looked at me only. "Tell me, boy. Has he made you taste human meat yet?"

Everything went quiet. The wind stopped. The trees no longer swayed. I felt sweat begin to drip from my forehead.

"Only in a dream, he made me. But—"

Before I could defend myself, she dropped her head and nodded to herself. "I see. So, it has already begun." She watched me again.

I felt my heart begin to pound. My vision went dark. I wanted to run away and hide, but my body wouldn't move.

"How do you know all this?" My voice quivered, nearly breaking.

"What do we do?" Riley begged.

"Do you know what the creature is?" Austin asked.

"Can we help Simon?" Miles's voice was stern, all timidness had gone.

The woman placed her hand up once more. We all fell silent.

"One at a time," the woman mumbled. "I am old. Very old." She gestured at her clothing. "I am not just a mere spirit, as you may all have noticed. I am the spirit of a witch. When I once was alive, I was the witch of this forest, of this town. This was my home.

"That evil spirit has been around for nearly as long as I have been dead. He fouled my resting space with corpses and bones, making it his eating ground. He has taken many residents from Ravenswood, my people. I have watched him through the ages. He knows of my presence and I of his. But due to our lively differences, we can do nothing to each other but watch. And he makes sure he puts on a show.

"He once took my own kin—my brother—as his host when we were younger. And I have never forgiven him." Her voice began to trail away. She seemed lost in the memory of lifetimes ago. It sounded . . . familiar, and then I realized. The story Miles had told me on our very first ghost hunt. I glanced at Miles for confirmation. His eyes were wide as they connected with mine.

She then cleared her throat. "What you do, I cannot say. I suggest you get one of these." She lifted the tiny jar around her neck. "It won't stop him from coming, but it might help you keep your mind a bit longer till you can find out what to do. I do know what he is, but I cannot say. To utter the name is a curse in itself. Bad luck—bad, bad luck." The woman spit on the ground. "I'm sorry I cannot help you more. But you will find out soon enough," she said as she glanced toward Miles.

I looked at the rest of the Ghoul Gang. Everyone had a mixed expression of sorrow and terror on their faces. I wondered how I seemed to them.

"Who are you, and why are you telling us this?" Riley mumbled. The question was barely a whisper, quieter than I had ever heard her.

The older woman smiled at us and lightly shook her head. "For now, you can all simply call me Granny. I am invested in your win against this beast and will offer my aid when the time comes." Her voice was warm again.

Almost immediately, I felt better than I had before, with a new surge of confidence. She looked at me again, her eyes wrinkling as she did. She made a strange but sharp hand gesture and a small glass bottle on a string similar to hers appeared in her hand. It already had the dirt but was missing the lavender.

"Here, take this. The lavender plants surround my clearing." She nodded her head toward a small path behind us. I walked up and grabbed the bottle.

Typically, with a ghost, my hand would phase right through hers. But as my hand touched hers, I felt *something*. A chill raced through my palm and up my arm. She wasn't a regular ghost, that was for sure. I smiled at her again, in thanks, and placed the cord around my neck, letting the small glass jar hit the exact center of my torso.

"He doesn't like the smell of lavender," she whispered to me with a snicker.

I chuckled and thanked her yet again. It felt weird to receive such kindness from a ghost. Why was she still here? Was it a witch thing or was it something more?

I took my place back in the line of the Ghoul Gang. Everyone was quiet. The sun was almost completely down, which meant we had to head back soon.

As if reading our minds, Granny spoke one more time.

"Before you all go, there's one more thing. An omen. A warning. Something truly dreadful will occur on All Hallows' Eve. That is when he will make his move."

"On Halloween? Isn't that a little stereotypical?" Miles asked, trying not to sound offensive. But instead of Granny replying, it was Riley who answered his question.

"Believe it or not, ghouls are way more powerful on Halloween. It's the spirits' day. The reason we wear costumes is to mask ourselves as them. It's their only time to walk the Earth as the living do."

"She is correct. The dead get stronger, yes. But we also become more mortal. This 'ghoul' will attack you on that day, that I can see. But it will also be your chance to stop him. It'll be your chance to find the spirit as he is—human—and end him before the process of possession is complete." A shiver ran through my spine.

Halloween would be the deadline; it'll be the one and only chance we had at stopping this thing. Stopping it before it got me. And not only that, but Halloween was only a week and a half away.

"Simon," Granny's voice broke me out from my panic. "You'll be okay. Stay strong. And stay true to yourself," she said with a sad smile. "And for Earth's sake, get yourself some lavender."

The sun was gone. The sky was brilliant, but dark, and the stars were already bright. The air had a certain chill to it that only an October night brought.

The Ghoul Gang and I treaded down through the dense woods. With lavender around my neck, I felt a tad safer. But we all had a figurative cloud over our heads. We needed to figure out a plan and we needed to figure it out fast. We walked down through the forest and back across the street to Riley's. My mom had already asked when I was coming home and I felt it best to not keep them waiting too long.

For the rest of the walk, the Ghoul Gang spoke of normal things. We talked about school and classmates, Halloween costumes, and plans. I said I wanted to dress up as one of my favorite slashers—Ghostface from *Scream*.

"Ghostface is your favorite?" Miles asked. "Why him? Michael Myers is obviously the superior choice." He smirked.

"Michael is a top-tier choice. But Ghostface acknowledges the tropes in horror. He lives and kills based on them. Don't do drugs, don't have sex, and don't say you'll be right back." I held up one finger for each *don't*. "Follow the rules and you'll be safe."

"What about Randy? He was killed and didn't do any of those," Austin replied. I was impressed for a moment with his knowledge of the series.

"Randy survived until the sequel, which no character is allowed to do other than the Final Girl—and I guess Gale and Dewey. Also, he taunted the killer, he was basically asking for it," I explained.

The gang stayed quiet and I grew worried that maybe, *maybe*, I geeked out a bit *too* much. But then the gang all started to laugh.

"Maybe we should all be horror icons. I can be Michael. Austin can be Jason. Riley can be Carrie, or Reagan from *The Exorcist*, or Samara from—"

"I want to be Hannibal Lecter," she blurted.

"Or Hannibal Lecter," Miles smirked, nodding in approval of the idea.

"You guys can push me around in a little cart." She laughed.

"I'm cool with Jason too. I pretty much already have his ensemble, save for the mask. Big green jacket, check. Black boots, check," Austin said as he pointed to the black boots he was currently wearing.

"You can definitely find the mask anywhere," I said.

It had pretty much been decided. The Ghoul Gang was going slasher for Halloween. And as happy as I was to have plans, to have a potential reality for my favorite holiday other than the horror that was promised to be waiting for me, the dread of the night was still looming over me.

Austin offered Miles and me a ride home and we both accepted. The ride was quiet and normal. We joked about my crush on Riley. I poked Miles about his hidden crush on Austin without the werewolf noticing. For the moment, it felt like we were all just normal teens, normal friends, without a terrifying ghoul looming over us, over me.

When we pulled up to my house, there was an awkward air of things left unsaid.

I slowly opened the door, but before I could get out Miles spoke. "Have a good night, Si. Let us know if you have any dreams tonight."

"You can call me if you can't sleep . . . or if you don't want to." Austin turned back to face me. He smiled at me with a sort of sad smile.

"Thanks, man." I lightly bumped his fist with mine. "Good night, guys," I said and got out. I waved as the duo drove away down the road.

After taking a deep breath, I turned and faced my house. I clutched onto the lavender that rested against my chest, and for the first time in what felt like weeks, I wasn't *totally* terrified to sleep—I felt I needed it. But I only wished the ghoul could give me a night off. Just one. So that I could truly get a good night's rest.

CHAPTER FOURTEEN

woke up the next day in the afternoon and the first thing I did was check my phone to see if I had any messages from the Ghoul Gang. Most of them asked if I had another dream. Instead of sending a convoluted text, I invited them to a video call.

"Hey, guys," I said with a smile. Seeing my face in the bottom corner made me so happy. I looked rested, with no bags under my eyes, and for the first time in awhile, I didn't look like the Crypt Keeper.

"Si, you look—" Riley started.

"Great!" Austin finished.

"Did you dream of the ghoul?" Miles said getting right to the point.

"I did!" I thought back to my dream from the previous night. "It was short and a little hazy. The ghoul was angry and I think he was mad that Addaline wasn't there anymore. He kept hitting and clawing at trees. We were kind of far apart—he never came near me, so I felt as safe as I could be. Guys, I think Granny's charm worked!"

I saw Riley smile through the screen. "Anything else happen?"

"Nope. It wasn't a long dream. I feel better than I have in days! I'm just starving now."

"When was the last time you ate?" Miles asked.

"Real food? Not since the diner. I've had a couple of bites here and there. I got sick after breakfast yesterday morning. I really feel like I can't eat anything but . . ." Before I finished speaking, I realized how *badly* I didn't want to finish the sentence. And I think they noticed too, leading our call to an awkward silence.

"Do you want to come over today? That way your parents don't really question why you're not eating?" Austin offered.

We'd never been to his house before, but we knew his parents weren't frequently home. His dad traveled for business a lot and his mom went with him. According to him, Austin's parents knew nothing about his lycanthropy.

"Y'all can come. Maybe you can try eating a raw steak or something?"

I considered this idea. It's not human, but *maybe* it could work. I agreed to go, and so did the rest of the gang.

After we all said goodbye, I clicked off. I journeyed downstairs, both parents idling around the living room watching TV. They both shot up when they heard me. My mom asked how I was feeling after the weekend's illness while Dad checked my forehead for a fever.

"I feel fine. Better than fine, actually. Really good." I smiled.

Mom took an involuntary sigh of relief while Dad's body relaxed and settled back into the couch. We sat together, commenting on the shows we were watching, laughing together—it just felt so nice. It felt just like Miami, in the comfort of our old home. As if none of the craziness of the last month has happened. And I missed it. We just laughed at silly characters on a silly show that we all liked. It was perfect.

To think, in just a few weeks, I may never get to feel this way again. If the ghoul succeeds . . .

"Simon, you okay?" Dad asked, lightly tapping my

shoulder. I nodded at him, trying to push back the horrible thought.

I want to enjoy this moment, I told myself, *whether this is the last like it or the first of many.*

And so, I did.

The day passed fairly quickly and, eventually, I ended up finding myself standing at the front entrance to Austin's house. You might be picturing me standing at the front door to a perfectly average home, ready to ring the doorbell or knock on the door to find my friends inside. However, you would be wrong.

I was on the outside of a large and ornate black-iron gate. There was a perfectly paved and tiled driveway that passed underneath it, and to my right stood a callbox with one button. I tried to peek through the iron bars to spot the mysterious house on the other end, but the land looked like a fairytale forest within, large green trees everywhere. After a moment of taking it all in, I stepped up to the callbox and pressed the button. At first, a woman's voice came out.

"Hello, are you one of Austin's friends?" Her voice sounded sweet, I assumed it was Austin's mom.

"Hello! Yes, I am!" I could feel my voice crack like a pre-teen.

"Excellent! Just follow the path around the corner, we'll be here waiting. Oop—" she paused. I heard a sound buzzing from the gate as the doors slowly began to swing open. "It seems like Austin is going out to meet you. You should see him along the path! Don't mind the dogs, they're very friendly."

"I love dogs!" I said, realizing how awkward that response must've sounded. "Err . . . Thank you! I'll see you soon. Bye." I always felt awkward in front of other people's parents, and the fact that Austin's parents were the owners of this big-ass house made me feel even more nervous.

What if they give me two forks? One is for salads, right? But which one?

I started toward the house, passing large trees. Just like the woman on the speaker said, there were dogs coming at me, barking incessantly.

Dogs are great, but the sound of multiple, big barks coming at ya? Pretty terrifying. Before I could do anything totally stupid, like running away from them, I noticed Austin running in tandem and keeping them at bay. I laughed, realizing that he was just a big puppy like the rest of them. At least the pups knew who their alpha was.

"Hey, Simon!" he yelled as he began to slow down his pace, but the dogs surrounding him didn't. Two German shepherds, one that looked like a Labrador, a black French bulldog with a too-large spiked collar, and finally a very fluffy, golden Pomeranian. I looked at the pom-pom and then at Austin.

"Little Sophie is my mom's dog and the meanest of the bunch." He laughed. Sophie barked at me and then looked back to Austin and barked some more. The rest jumped on me and I gave them all some healthy and loving head pats. Dogs fill up your energy bar faster than health potions in video games.

"Are the others here yet?" I asked after getting tons of puppy kisses and wiping my face of doggy slobber.

"Yeah, Miles is. We're just waiting for Riley. Should be here any second now."

Just then, we all (dogs included) heard a horn honk lightly at the gate. Austin pulled out some form of clicker from his pocket and the gate slowly opened. He motioned me to the side of the driveway and Riley pulled up through and past us. After a short walk, we ended up standing in front of his insanely large house. His door was like a giant window, with a gold design that resembled crashing waves at the corners of the two doors. I gaped at the elegance of it all.

Austin Rhodes, the once-violent-wolf-boy-turned-lovable-puppy, lives here?

Austin opened the door for us as Riley jumped out of her truck.

"Whoa, holy sh—" Riley stopped when she noticed Austin looking down at the ground.

"Is it too much?" Austin scratched the back of his head.

"What, the house?" I asked, sounding utterly aloof.

"Completely." Riley made her way past us and into the giant spectacle of a home.

After a beat, I smiled over at him and lightly punched him in the arm. "Dude, it's fantastic. Why didn't you tell us you were rich? We should hang out here all the time!"

"Simon!" Riley yelled behind me. "You can't just say that. Austin, we love you for you, not your money. But also my birthday is in November." She smirked.

"Can't we love him for both?" I asked.

"Uh, no." Riley chuckled.

I looked over to Austin who nodded confidently.

"Well, are y'all coming in, or do you want to stay out here all day?" he said, giving a sharp and quick whistle directly after. On cue, all the dogs ran into the house and dispersed. My eyes trailed the little pom-pom, who struggled to jump up the carpeted, winding staircase just beyond the doors.

I gestured my hand outward, letting Riley go in before me, I followed after, and then Austin closed the door behind us.

After a short tour of the humongous house (seriously, this place had a theater room with its own popcorn machine), we ended up in what I assumed to be one of the family rooms. Miles sat on a brown-leather couch, eyes glued to the TV as he flipped through streaming videos.

"Miles, did you know this place was huuuuge?" I asked him, as if he weren't here with me, experiencing it for himself.

He shrugged. "It's pretty awesome, right? I kept trying to convince him to have you guys over sooner."

"Miles, not you too," Riley said, exacerbated.

Wait a second. Miles and—

"So . . . how often have you come here?" I raised an eyebrow. Miles blushed and stammered out a vomit of unintelligible words.

Riley burst into laughter and we all followed suit.

Man, did it feel good to be surrounded by friends.

Just then, I caught something in the corner of my eye, a shadow that darted past in the hallway leading to the next room.

"Austin, is someone else here?" I pointed to the hallway.

He scratched the back of his head. "Ah, yeah. That's my . . . well, honestly, I'm not quite sure what she is."

"Your mom?" I asked sheepishly. As soon as it left my mouth, I regretted saying it.

Learn impulse control, Simon!

But Austin took it in stride. He awkwardly chuckled. "I mean, she might as well be. I've known her my entire life. She's like our nanny-slash-housekeeper. Her name's Denise." He glanced at Miles. "Not that I still *need* a nanny but she keeps me and the dogs company while my parents are . . . out."

"What do they do again?" Riley plopped on the sofa next to Miles, grabbing a handful of chips on the table.

"My dad works in tech and his company works a lot overseas, so he's constantly traveling to China, Japan, Europe . . ."

"Damn, I gotta get into tech," I said. "No wonder my parents always want me to study coding languages."

"Preach." Miles nodded in agreement.

Austin called Denise, who was a plump, short, and super adorable middle-aged woman with thick brown hair and soft blue eyes, into the family room to ask if she can make us some snacks. Riley and I introduced ourselves, and she made some very warm-hearted mom jokes, then she left the room for us all to talk.

"I'll get the steak for you in a bit, Si. How have you been feeling today?" Austin asked.

We all sat on the couch and watched the mood change from fun and light-hearted, to sad and dreary in a heartbeat. It looked like they were all walking on eggshells around me.

"I've actually had a really good day," I boasted. Did they not believe me? "Honestly. I mean, in the dream, I truly *felt* safe. Typically, when I'm there I feel like I'm in a haunted house. Queasy and ready to run the moment something pops out. Last night, I didn't. I felt like I was at home, under the covers—which I was—watching a horror movie. The tension was still there, but with comfort knowing it was something I was *watching*, not something I was *experiencing*."

"Was it any different than your other dreams?" Riley asked, not looking at me and instead grabbing another handful of chips.

I thought back, trying to remember, trying to put myself back into it. "Remember the other night, that dream I had that I found myself under a spotlight? And I couldn't see anything past it? It was sort of like that, only I was in my *own* spotlight. The ghoul had his own. I could see him, but there was a dark, empty space between the two of us. A border neither of us could cross."

"Wow, that lavender really worked. Were you wearing it in the dream?" Miles leaned forward

"I remember looking to make sure it was there. Actually, now that you mention it . . ." I paused. "There was this strange trail of smoke or mist. I think it was the lavender. I didn't pay too much attention to it, but it wafted from my spotlight to his and he didn't like it. So much so that he was the one to 'disconnect' the dream. Granny was right," I said, clutching the pendant in my hands.

"The only thing is we'll need to get more," Austin spoke up. "Denise is really into natural herbs for teas and aromatherapy. She has to buy new ones every few days. Apparently, the smell fades. It might be able to last about a week or two. I'm assuming the more powerful the smell, the more it'll stay away. The weaker the smell—"

"The stronger his retaliation will be," Riley finished. Austin nodded.

It'd already been a day since we pulled it from the root.

"We'll find more. I'm sure they sell that, right? If not, we can harvest one from Granny's clearing. Maybe we can get you a whole plant for next to your bed," Miles suggested.

"We can. But I think Granny implied that he needs to be wearing it," Riley explained. "Right, Si?"

"Riley's right. It's only things I hold that come with me. Or on me. Like the camera equipment the other day, my clothes, and the necklace." I rested my elbows on my knees. Everyone around me stayed quiet pondering.

"What if—" Riley began, but before she could continue, she yelped and doubled over, gripping the sides of her head as if she was trying to prevent it from falling off. Immediately, we all stood and rushed over to her.

"Riley! Are you okay? What's going on?" I kneeled down next to her and rested my hand on her back. I heard the worry in my voice and my heart beat a mile a minute.

"Talk to us!" Austin pleaded.

That's when I noticed Riley wasn't clutching her head but she was covering her ears. Then it dawned on me, Addaline was here.

Riley grunted again, her face contorting, holding in a scream. If Riley couldn't control herself, we'd all be deaf within seconds. But after a moment, Riley finally spoke.

"I'm gonna vibe. Get me out of here."

In a rush of panic, Miles and I lifted Riley and escorted her outside.

"We're going—uh—to the movies!" Austin yelled before shutting the door.

"Where should we go?" Miles asked.

I looked around to see if there was any excessive foliage on the grounds we could hide behind, but before I could respond, Austin ushered us all through a set of trees farthest away from the front door. Riley's body started to jerk in a bunch of different directions.

"The screaming . . . in my head . . . it's so, so loud!" Riley yelled out in pain right before her head slumped forward. She was quiet, unmoving, her body weight completely shifting onto Miles and me. She was knocked out. I nudged my shoulder so that her head would rest on it. As she swayed, I noticed something wet on her hair. Something wet, and red.

My eyes lingered on her bloody ears. I felt Riley's pulse against my hand as I held her wrist around my shoulder. It was slow and steady.

Miles tried to say something in the background, but I couldn't hear it. It sounded as if I wore noise-canceling headphones. My breath staggered and my fast heartbeat didn't seem like it was going away anytime soon.

All I heard was the *th-thump th-thump th-thump* of Riley's pulse. I could smell Riley's blood and it was mouthwatering. My mouth quenched, and for the first time all day, I felt hungry. I felt myself *starving.*

149

My, how good that looks. And you're so hungry too. You haven't eaten anything in days. One little bite wouldn't hurt. Just one little taste. Just to hold you over until your first real *meal.*

I couldn't think; I tried to stop myself, tried to see reason, but all I could think of was how ravenous I was. Whose voice was that—my own?

I found myself ignoring the thought. My body was in fight-or-flight mode, acting of its own will. I leaned closer to Riley. Her hair brushed my lips, my breath hot against her neck and heavy in her ear.

Poor, unconscious Riley stirred, her head rolling to Miles's shoulder.

That's it, just a little bit more.

The closer I got, the more my ears rang.

She probably tastes delicious.

Before I could appease my appetite, something in the far, far distance screamed. No. Something shrieked. I jolted away in pain while Miles and Austin covered their ears. The wail snapped me from the daze, nearly forgetting every feeling other than the hunger.

In unison, all the dogs in the house behind us began to bark, loudly. Some growled, some cried. But they didn't stop. If that could affect us from this far, how would it be up close? Miles, Austin, and I exchanged worried looks.

"Was that . . . ?" Austin began loudly, his voice trembling and trailing off behind the noise in the house.

I looked over at Riley again, to see if the scream had affected her in any way. The blood began matting the hair around her ears.

One tiny taste couldn't hurt—

Control yourself, Simon! I told myself.

I looked back at the guys.

"We have a problem."

"What?" Austin held a hand to his ear.

"Riley's ears are bleeding. We need to get her to a

doctor!" I said, a little louder so my voice would carry over the dogs.

"*What?*" Austin asked again, stressing the word and taking a step forward. "Why are you mumbling?"

"Simon!" Miles turned to look at me. "His hearing is way better than ours. Maybe the scream is affecting him more than it would for us?" he shouted.

I hadn't thought of this, but dogs do hear better than us. If that scream was loud for us, it must have sounded like a high-pitched bomb going off to a werewolf.

"*What are you guys saying*?" He began to get aggravated. Miles pushed Riley's weight onto me, and I followed his lead. He unwrapped her arm from around him and walked toward Austin.

"Is one of your phone's going off? I hear a ringing!" Austin yelled again. He put his hand to his ear and started pressing on it, realizing what was stunting him.

"Austin!" Miles said very, very loudly directly in front of him. "Don't worry! It should pass in a few minutes!" He emphasized each word, making sure to mouth it carefully.

Riley began to get heavy and the smell began to waft into my nose. I started feeling my stomach rumble.

Just one bite.

I snapped myself back to reality. "Miles, help me get her onto my back."

Miles turned to me, and then looked at Austin, who still had his hands by his ears. He held up one finger and then came to me. We got Riley onto my back, slouched over me. "I'm going to call my dad. It would be easier than going somewhere. Can you reach the phone in my back pocket?" I asked. Miles grabbed the phone, dialed, and put it by my ear. After a second of ringing, he answered.

"Hey, Si. What's up?"

I heard neighborhood dogs barking in the background. "Dad, did you guys hear that scream?"

"Scream?" he questioned.

"There was a very loud scream, or noise, or something. It happened like two seconds ago."

"Wow, the dogs are going crazy on both our ends. Yeah, I heard it. I thought it was just the neighbor's TV. Some horror movie? Maybe it was a really powerful fire alarm somewhere." He paused for a minute. "But . . . you're not in the neighborhood still. How did you hear it?"

"I think everyone heard it. But that's not the point. It—er . . . had a really strange effect on Riley. She fainted and there's blood coming from her ears." I heard my voice crack. I knew I sounded worried. I felt worried. "Please, Dad, she needs help."

"Text me the address, I'll be right over," he said, urgency filling his voice.

Mom and I always said Dad had a split personality. Off-duty Dad was fun-loving and filled with horrible jokes. Doctor Dad was serious and stern, his voice always getting deeper when there was trouble. Like real-life (and not murderous) Dr. Jekyll and Mr. Hyde. Initially, we thought it was so patients and their families could take him more seriously, but over time we learned it was for him. It helped him get into the "act fast, be accurate" mentality he needed for work. Lives literally depended on him.

This man over the phone was the doctor, but the man coming to my aid was my dad.

"Simon, lay her down flat on her back. Press a clean towel to her ears." I nodded even though he couldn't see me. He knew. "Did she hit her head or anything?" His voice was calm, I heard shuffling in the background, most likely him getting his things together. He briefly explained the situation to my mom.

"No. But she uh . . . she had a really, really bad headache right before." I stuttered, finding it hard to explain the banshee scream going off in her head moments before. "But, Dad, I think it's serious. I think it's more of a head injury than an ear injury."

"I'm driving over now. I'll be there soon." And then he hung up.

"Is he coming?" Miles asked, his voice full of concern. I looked up and my friend appeared more worried than I had ever seen. It broke my heart a little. Austin looked stunned. He was sitting on the ground.

"Is he okay?" I said motioning toward Austin.

"I think he's really dizzy. Maybe motion sickness? He was swaying so I made him sit. We should take them inside."

Miles helped Austin up and slowly guided him back. As we entered, I called Denise.

"We have a bit of a situation," I said awkwardly as she came running to see half of us bloody, unconscious, and doubled over. As we sat Austin down and laid Riley on the floor, I explained the situation to Denise—the non-supernatural version. She had also heard the scream and just got the dogs to relax before we came in. I kept apologizing, feeling bad that the first time we came over, all of this happened. Sweet Denise continued to reassure us that none of it was our fault, just a fluke.

"Relax, it's probably a nearby power plant," she said.

"Right, power plant, yep." Miles gave a thumbs up.

Within minutes, my dad arrived. He swiftly opened his bag of tools and began to shift Riley's head left and right peering into her ears and pupils with a small light. Miles pulled me to the other end of the room.

"She knocked out before she changed."

"I know."

"Do you think . . . she did it on purpose?" he asked. My head tilted to the side; I hadn't thought of that possibility. "We all knew it was going to be really bad if she turned," he continued.

"Maybe she did too. She always has a hard time controlling the shift for the first few moments and this is powerful stuff. I don't know how she would've done it but it's possible."

"Addaline was screaming in her head," Miles said. "I mean it was so loud for us, I can't imagine how excruciating it must've been directly in her head. But you might also be right. I guess all we can do is ask her when she wakes up."

I began to turn away when Miles grabbed my arm. "And you? Are *you* okay?" His voice was stern. "Back there. Something happened to you, didn't it? I called out to you but the expression on your face was just so . . . dark when you saw her blood. No way you're a hemophiliac. So what was it?"

I turned back to look at him, carefully weighing my words before speaking. "I'm . . . I'm not really sure. I saw Riley, she was hurt, I got worried but then it was like I blacked out. All I could see was the blood, and immediately felt like I hadn't eaten in weeks. My stomach was begging me to . . . eat."

"Her blood? Is the ghoul a vampire?" Miles questioned.

"Maybe, but that wouldn't explain why *I'm* like this. I haven't been bitten, and I sure as hell haven't drunk any geezer's blood. No—this wasn't a thirst for blood. It was hunger for food. Hot and . . . " I found myself salivating at the thought, but when my eyes looked back up to Miles, his expression was enough to make my mouth run dry.

"So he *did* eat Addaline."

I thought back to the hunger and the voice. I thought for the briefest moment to keep it a secret, hide this pivotal detail. I knew better. I knew I couldn't solve this issue on my own. I knew no matter what I said, no matter what happened, my friends wouldn't abandon me.

I rubbed my eyes, sighing as I answered, "I heard

a voice while it happened. It was the ghoul. He was trying to make me—"

"Simon! Come over here, hand me the gauze," Dad hollered.

I began to make my way over as Miles grabbed my arm again. "Si, I don't know what you were about to say. But whatever it is, we're telling the gang tomorrow."

I had never seen him so serious before. I winced at his expression as he walked past me to lend a helping hand.

After a while, Riley woke up with a wild headache but was ultimately fine. Dad gave her some painkillers, just to be wary of any lightheadedness or bleeding for the next few weeks, and told her she could remove the medical wrap before bed.

Austin's hearing returned to him, with the slight sound of a ringing in his ear. He described it like how you feel after a concert: your hearing is a little muffled and there's a slight ringing, but relatively in perfect health. Doctor Dad told him it would probably be completely gone by the next day and just to get a lot of rest.

It was getting late, and Dad had an early shift in the morning. We drove Miles home, his dad came out and introduced himself, becoming fast friends with my dad. And then, it was just the two of us.

"Kind of a wild night, huh?" Dad said, sparking up a conversation.

"Oh, you have no idea."

"That sound was weird, right? You called it a scream earlier, you think it was a person?"

"Uhm . . . I don't know." I didn't necessarily

lie; Addaline wasn't *really* a person anymore. Not technically. "Have you noticed anything weird in Ravenswood?"

"Weird how?" Dad's eyebrow shot up.

"Um . . . just anything?"

"I guess the people are kind of unusual sometimes but it's probably just that they're so different from us Miamians."

"Anything unexplainable?" I pressed. He knew I was into ghost hunting back in Florida, I just assumed he knew I was asking about that.

"No, not really. Well, there was that thing in the news about the girl in the woods. Did you hear about that?"

"Addaline."

"Did you know her?"

I shook my head. "No, I didn't. People are just talking about it a lot."

"Ah, okay, okay. Horrible what happened to her. Like straight out of *Hannibal*. To me, it looked like something a serial killer would do."

Oh, Dad, how right you are.

"The way they only left her face intact, it's macabre. I feel so horrible for her family," he continued.

I felt a pang of guilt. What could I say? I looked out the window as the black outlines of trees passed us. My mind drifted. Was Riley okay? What happened inside of her head when she was hearing Addaline?

We came across a yellow sign with a deer on it. *Deer crossing.*

I kept running through the moment of hunger over and over again in my mind when something outside the window grounded me back into reality. It passed so quickly, I wasn't even sure if it was real.

Outside, in the darkness of the night, I saw what looked like a massive black elk, its horns so large, they blended in with the distant trees. Its eyes were reflecting the car's headlights, glowing.

CHAPTER FIFTEEN

For the rest of the week, I kept seeing short, subtle glimpses of the black deer. At school, I spotted it out the window, in the forest across the parking lot. On the bus, it showed up as a passing flash—one second there, the next, gone. Always the same, there in the corner of my eye. And now I know, it wasn't just the night making it appear black—no, its fur, antlers, everything was an intense pitch black. I never panicked when I saw it, instead chalking it up to a mix of hunger and overactive imagination. But the idea of the black deer never stuck long enough for me to acknowledge it as something eerie.

Halloween decorations filled Ravenswood High's halls, acting as a constant reminder that my time on this earth was possibly limited to one more week. The more I thought about it, the more the deer floated around my mind. Were the deer and the ghoul connected? Was he now able to walk around in broad daylight, outside of his dream world?

Friday morning, I caught up with Riley before homeroom. Standing next to her locker, she yawned so loud that the people that passed by gawked at her.

"Hey, Riley."

"Oh, morning, Si."

"Late night?" I asked, tightening the straps of my backpack.

"Addaline was up all night, constantly crying, all over town, but I haven't been able to find her. I can't keep going like this, I haven't properly slept since that night at Austin's."

We all had a pretty strange evening after the banshee's scream. Austin's got physically ill due to pressure built up within his ears. Riley was in and out of sleep and missed school Monday with a head cold. The only one of us who had relative normalcy since that night had been Miles. While nothing strange had happened *to* him, he himself had been odd. Distant to all of us. He always left during lunch to go do his own thing. He went straight home after school every day this week. Even Austin hadn't heard much from him in the last few days. I'd tried asking him what was up, but he always said he was busy with homework—which I knew was a lie. We have all the same classes, and what we don't have together, he has with Austin.

"How would you feel about running a solo op?" Riley asked, bringing me back from my thoughts. "Just us. Finding Addaline. Austin can't because of his whole hearing thing, he can't go through that again. Miles is MIA. And she might listen to you."

"Or kill me," I mumbled. Riley cocked her head at me. "That'd be fine, honestly," I said apathetically.

"Si," she said, totally over my mood. "You had another dream last night?"

I nodded. "The same weird shit as all the others. This time the black deer was peacefully eating a disembodied arm—an *arm*, Riley. I'm over it. I want to go back to thinking the supernatural was just for movies and pretend none of this ever happened. I'll never see *Ghostbusters* in the same light again."

Riley cringed back a bit. She looked sad, her shoulders drooping and her eyes falling. I hurt her.

"I didn't mean—" but before I could finish, Austin had walked up behind us, unknowingly cutting me off.

"Morning, y'all!" He studied me for a moment and frowned. "Simon, you've lost a shit ton of weight, man. You're a stick."

I turned and kept walking toward class. "Thanks. I hadn't noticed yet." I was being a dick, and I knew it. I felt so tired, so hungry, and I just didn't care.

Leaving Riley and Austin standing behind me, I heard their voices trail off.

"Is he okay? Was what I said mean?"

"I don't think so," she sighed.

I didn't have the energy to respond. My body was winding down too fast for me to process, and everything irritated me to the brink of utter exhaustion. Clearly, there was tension in the air between the Ghoul Gang, everyone was on edge.

During class, Miles nudged my arm with his elbow. "I need to talk to the Ghoul Gang at lunch."

I turned to Riley, who was diagonal to me. I tapped her arm, and she quickly turned to me. "Miles wants to talk to us at lunch."

"Okay." Her voice was softer than normal, and I wondered if it had anything to do with my comment this morning.

Soon enough, the class was over and we all gathered at our normal table after getting food. We sat the same way we always did: me and Riley on one side and Miles and Austin on the other.

"So, Miles, what'd you want to talk about?" Riley asked after sipping her milk.

"Well, not sure if you've noticed but I've been pretty distant the last few days . . ."

"We've noticed," Riley, Austin, and I all said at the same time. We chuckled for a moment and it felt good. It had only been a few days, but it all felt like we hadn't spoken in years.

"The truth is I got a pretty nasty stomach flu."

"How weird that we all got sick," Austin interjected.

"It isn't weird at all. That's what I wanted to talk to you guys about. I've been doing a lot of research on the supernatural. I read about banshees, and I might be on the right track to finding out what your ghoul is, Simon. After we heard the banshee scream, we felt sick. And there's a reason for that. As Riley said, it's considered a death omen if you hear a banshee's scream. The death of someone you love," Miles paused.

They all looked at me. I wanted to cower away and hide in my hoodie.

"But it could also be an omen in general. Usually something unpleasant," Miles continued.

"Hence why we all got some kind of damage," Riley completed.

"Austin and Riley's made sense. Austin being an oversized dog and Riley heard it directly in her head. But Simon and I being affected confused me. Simon's got some shit going on with the ghoul and thinking he's eating people." Miles glanced around to make sure no one was eavesdropping. "So he makes sense, somewhat. But then what about me? I didn't think I would be affected, but I was. I caught the stomach flu. Look around you . . ."

The cafeteria wasn't as full as it usually was, but those around us wore giant sweaters, holding tissues. Some people held their heads in their hands. A cacophony of coughing and sneezing came from everywhere.

I looked at Miles. "Everyone's sick."

"Or are out sick," Austin added.

"Exactly. We weren't the only ones that heard the scream. The whole town was affected by it. So, I don't think the 'bad omen' she's bringing has to do with Simon. I think it has to do with the town in general.

"Also, I'm thinking we call the ghoul a Skinwalker."

"Gross." Austin scrunched up his nose.

160

Riley put her hand on her chin.

"Have you ever heard of those?" I asked quietly.

She took a moment but finally shook her head. "No, I don't think so. I thought maybe a shapeshifter?" she asked, looking at Miles.

"Sorta. They're like shapeshifters but the lore behind them is different. They can turn into other animals, but in some myths, they can also steal the faces of people. They're from Native American culture, specifically the Navajo. They believe they are malevolent witches," Miles explained.

"What makes you think that's the ghoul?" Austin asked.

"Well, I drew this up." He pulled out a spiral notebook from his bag and opened it to a page with a rather large Venn diagram. On one side said "Simon's Ghoul" and underneath it, read:

- LARGE
- BLACK DEER
- LARGE ANTLERS
- CANNIBAL
- CAN SPEAK IN SI'S MIND
- MAKES SI HALLUCINATE
- DREAMS
- SMELLS LIKE DEATH
- RED EYES
- POSSESSION???

My eyes lingered on *possession*, setting my mind off. My leg shook up and down. I felt my temper beginning to spark. Seeing my gaze and expression, Miles pulled the notebook away from us.

"The Skinwalkers do this thing where, if you make eye contact, they can *possess* you and your body to do what they want. And I just thought . . ."

"Well, what? What did you think, Miles? Tell me," I

heard myself getting aggravated. Is this really what he thought of me? That I was being *possessed* by this thing? Nothing was supposed to happen until Halloween. I still had a week. "What do you think I am? Some kind of supernatural monster now? Are you just jealous because you're the only one in this group who isn't supernatural? Who *isn't* special?" I began to yell loud enough for anyone passing our table to hear and enough for Miles to quiver in his seat. He seemed so small to me now.

Good. I want him to feel this way.

I glanced and saw both Austin and Riley's faces flash red.

"Simon, relax. I'm sure that's not what he meant," Riley said. The moment she told me to relax, I rolled my eyes.

"Oh, so *I* should relax? *Me?* The one supposedly being 'possessed'? The one with the week left before all shit goes to hell? Yeah. I'll just chill out then, no biggie," I said sarcastically, shrugging and sitting back in my chair, crossing my arms.

"Si, that's not what either of them meant. You've been a little—"

I was getting angry. I sat up in my chair again and almost slammed my hands on the table. "*What* have I been, Austin?"

"Sensitive," he said with no remorse. He was mocking me. And I could tell he was getting angry too. It gave me pleasure. My blood was boiling.

"So you guys think a man-eating monster possesses me, and *I'm* the sensitive one? I'm the one who needs to relax? This is bullshit," I said, standing abruptly.

"Skinwalkers are also constantly on the hunt to turn people into one of them!" Miles interrupted. I remained standing, but I was ready to leave with one more insult.

"So?"

Austin, now standing, stared me dead in the face,

the hair on his arm began to grow, and his teeth extended and grew sharp, yet he made no move or sign he would do anything, his breath heavy, waiting for Miles to speak. "*So*, it means that it could be the reason you have the desire to consume flesh." Miles's voice was harsh and cruel.

Riley's gaze shot directly at me, alarmed. Her eyes were wide as they looked up at me. "The desire to eat flesh?" she said, horror riddling her voice. It made me feel extremely embarrassed, thinking about my hot breath on her neck. Thinking about the blood that ran from her head that day.

It also made me hungry.

I smirked. "Particularly yours, Riley."

Riley's face changed from fear *for* me to fear *of* me. I turned, glaring at Miles. I hated him for what he was about to say. I hated him for exposing me.

"That night, at Austin's. You were bleeding, Riley. And Simon, well—he got hungry. 'Starving,' as he said."

In a flash, before I could even stop myself, I nearly jumped across the table, grabbing and lifting Miles by his jacket collar. Austin grabbed my wrist and forcibly tried to pull it back, but I wouldn't budge. Riley jumped out of her seat. The chair she had been in fell behind her.

Everyone in the cafeteria had their eyes on us now. But I didn't care. My grip on Miles tightened.

How could he be doing this to me? He's supposed to be my friend, *and he's betraying me!*

Miles ignored me, acting as if I wasn't holding him up. "He wanted me to keep it a secret. But you guys should know. I think the ghoul is getting to him."

"Stop speaking as if I'm not right here. Look at me, Miles," I demanded.

But he didn't. "He was about to take a bite out of you, Riley."

Now he'd done it.

"LOOK AT ME!" I yelled, shaking him. His eyes shifted, but still no fear, no anger.

"I remember." Riley's voice was low and filled with panic. She ran one delicate hand through her hair. "I remember passing out after the scream and feeling something hot running from my ears. I remember Simon's breath on my neck." Her fingers absentmindedly drifted to her neck as her eyes fell on her food. She looked up at me, her face a mix of everything Miles's wasn't: fear, sorrow, and the tiniest hint of anger. I sensed that the anger wasn't toward me. "You were so close. I thought . . ."

Anger flared in me again. I shoved Miles away, yanking my hand back from Austin. He was quick to stabilize Miles before he could fall. Now, taking a step toward Riley, I looked down at her. She was so small. Defenseless. *Delicious.* Her eyes were wide, but she didn't retreat. I leaned down and asked in a hushed tone, "*What* did you think?" I closed the space between us. I could feel her chest against mine.

"I thought you were trying to kiss me," she said, almost in a whisper.

I glanced at Austin and Miles. Now they both looked angry. I smirked at them.

"Let me get this straight. You thought I was going to kiss *you*? And you decided to pull away? That's real nice."

"What the hell, Simon? I was unconscious! I didn't even think about it until right now. Excuse me that my knocked-out, bleeding brain just assumed—" She was beginning to get frustrated.

"You mean . . . you wouldn't pull away? If I tried again?" I leaned in closer, my lips hovering just over hers. And as I did, she backed up, nearly falling over the chair behind her, leaving me there. From the corner of my eye, I saw Miles and Austin step forward—as if they could do anything. "Tease."

"You're being a dick."

"Am I, Riley? Am I really? See, from my perspective, you guys are the assholes." I pointed at them all. The lunch bell rang. "I've had enough of this *belittling* conversation. I'm out. Have fun assuming the worst of me." I threw my backpack on and left the room. The last I saw of the three of them were their looks of total disgust.

Good, maybe now they'll get off my back. Who needs them, anyway.

I avoided eye contact (any contact at all, actually) with the Ghoul Gang for the rest of the day. For the first time, I skipped a class that we all shared. It was the final class of the day, and truthfully, I couldn't stand to see their faces anymore. So, in between classes, I just left. Going home seemed like the best option, but something urged me to take the scenic way home. This consisted of walking through the woods a bit. I knew this was probably dumb, especially with everything going on, but I needed a breath of fresh air. Plus, I hadn't explored Ravenswood on my own since moving here. I was always with the Ghoul Gang, wasting all my time.

But not today.

The way Ravenswood is set up is strange and half uninhabitable. Picture one large circle. In the center of the circle is another, slightly smaller circle, which is the woods of Ravenswood. School, the town, the precinct that Riley's mom and Miles's dad works in, and the movie theater are all on the south side of town. Miles is closest to the town being slightly west, but mostly south. Austin lives in the southeast corner, right off the woods. Riley lives east of the woods but has an entrance right across the street. And I live northeast, the farthest from school and the town.

I crossed the school's parking lot and entered the woods. It was going to be a long walk of just me and some much-needed fresh air to cool me down. The main road was visible through a few trees to my right, but it was still nice to feel like I was away from everything. Away from everyone. Alone with only the sound of leaves crunching filling the silence.

When I heard another set of crunching leaves, I thought nothing of it, until the sound moved toward me. I whirled around, and there it was, standing tall only a few feet away.

The black deer, in broad daylight, the sun shinning off his fur, making it the darkest shade of black I'd ever seen. Its antlers were large and complex, black like the rest of him. His hooves stomped on the leaves. Altogether, he towered over me by at least a foot. My gaze settled on his eyes, brooding, scary, and full of darkness.

I'd seen it so many times before. I should be used to it, right?

We both stood, frozen.

"What are you?" I mumbled, mostly to myself. The giant elk shook his head lightly. I raised an eyebrow, suddenly feeling really stupid. I straightened my back and decided it was time to confront him. "Why do I see you everywhere?"

Its silence was maddening.

"Are you goin—"

The more you look for me, the more I see you.

Shivers went down my spine. The deer's mouth didn't move, but it definitely came from his direction. I dared not shift my eyes from the beast.

It's only me and you here, Simon. You're without your friends this time. This is a first. Did you have a fight? the deer cocked his head to the side.

"How did you—" Before finishing my question, I

realized it was *him.* Miles was right. I *was* becoming possessed. "Are you the ghoul? Are you a Skinwalker?" I force my voice to remain strong.

I heard him laugh, but he didn't move an inch.

"Is this all in my mind?"

I am something far grander than a Walker. I am greed and hunger itself, ancient and proud. I am a god who eats the small and weak, a god who creates his own world. His voice was powerful and sturdy, much different than in my dreams.

"What do you want with me?" Taking a step back, my pulse raced and my mind went everywhere.

I want you. Just you.

"Like you did with Addaline?"

He laughed again.

No, child. I can have anyone; I would not go to these lengths just for a meal. No, I want to become *you.*

My body grew rigid, and a rush of cold air chilled my bones.

"How do you plan on doing that?" I knew the answer, I just prayed I was wrong.

My boy . . . it's already happening. The deer walked toward me. Fight or flight kicked in, and I began coming up with reasons this could be happening: it was a figment of my imagination, my anger from before materializing into this black deer. He wasn't real—he couldn't be!

I wanted to run away, but my legs wouldn't budge. For the first time in my life, I felt like I was about to die. In the dreams, there was always a surrealness to them all. A mist of fantasy. I hoped, wished, that I was dreaming. I tried to smack my arm, desperate to wake up.

No, this is the real world, Simon. I'm here. I'm real. I could feel the deer's hot breath against me, brushing my hair away.

I couldn't move. My body was frozen. All I could do

was shut my eyes. The last thing I saw was the deer inching closer. With them shut, I saw nothing. But in a way, it made all my other senses feel so much stronger. I could smell the scent of the forest, the slight stench of an animal, his breath, almost rancid on my face. I could hear him breathing, and the beat of his thudding hooves. But worst of all was the feeling of his fur against my skin. The weight of his antler rested directly above my head. I imagined his black eyes inches from my own, begging me to open mine.

I wouldn't.

His forehead was now against mine, his breath cold, and fur damp.

It was the last thing I remembered before my mind faded to black.

CHAPTER SIXTEEN

"**S**imon?" Riley sat on the edge of my bed. Her voice was soft as she looked up at me.

We were in my room, only it was freezing and everything was like an old '90s music video. Hazy, grainy, and far away. Cold. Except for Riley. The moon was full and bright, shining through the curtains on my window. I was by my door.

"Simon." Her voice was nothing more than a whisper meant only for me. Her eyes danced with the reflection of what little light my room held. She was mesmerizing.

It dawned on me: I loved when she said my name. Like water when you're thirsty, her voice filled me up with hope. She said it again, the heat rising up inside of me.

Did she read my mind?

I stepped closer and she reciprocated, shifting her body toward me. She was leaning back, using one arm to prop herself up while the other was draped across her, pushing against her cleavage. I gulped, praying that my body wouldn't react so quickly.

"Riley, I'm sorry about earlier . . . I didn't mean any of those things." Sitting next to her now, my body was running on adrenaline.

"You don't want to kiss me?"

Being this close was maddening. I wanted to close the gap. I ached to close the gap.

"N-No. I mean, yes! I do want to. I'm just sorry I was an asshole." There was no turning back. She looked from my eyes to my lips in a glance and for a moment, I thought about nothing but her lips tracing mine. Our breaths hot against each other. Her lips curved into a smile.

"Then do it."

In an instant, my lips were smashing against hers.

My hand reached up to caress her cheek and the other pulled at the nape of her neck, drawing her in closer. The kiss was harsh and strong. Within a breath, we pulled apart. My hand still cupping her face, she looked at me, her lips trembling. Her heavy breath tickled the cupid's bow of my upper lip. Her eyes were wide and helpless, pleading. She wanted more. Something surged inside of me again as her hands ran from my chest to my shoulders.

I leaned in once more, but this time, gentle and ready. Our lips met and danced around one another, teasing and bouncing off until I just couldn't handle it anymore. I grabbed her and pulled her on top of me, falling onto the bed. Her lips were soft and welcoming. Our bodies melted into one another. I felt every curve pressed against me, as the space between us became nonexistent.

Our kiss grew deeper as I felt her tongue wrap around mine, her breath heavy, acting as fuel. Every noise she uttered just made me want her more. I pulled Riley to the side and climbed on top of her, pushing myself against her and parting only for breath. My hands began to wander all over her body, sliding from her neck down to her waist. She pulled at my hair, kissing me with all the desperation she had while I complied. My lips crossed to her jawline, giving sweet kisses along the way.

Nibbling her ear, I whispered, "*I want you.*"

Riley let out a soft breath, driving me wild. I pulled back from her and began to lift my shirt off, feeling her cold hands against my stomach. Our eyes locked, her doe-like, stormy-blue eyes begged me to touch her. I reached for the hem of her faded black band shirt and began to lift. She obeyed, arching into it.

Panting, my lips crashed into hers once more, drifting to the curve of her neck. Making my way down, I wanted her touch so bad. I yearned for it. She gripped at the crunchy leaves on the floor and arched her back, ready for me to make the move. I smiled against her cold skin. I kissed and nibbled the crook of her neck again, but this time, I couldn't pull away. I tasted blood on my lips and heard Riley gasp louder than before. Her entire body was shivering with pleasure.

"Do it again," she whimpered.

Before I could stop myself, I bit her shoulder, my teeth digging into her skin, breaking flesh. Blood riddled my mouth and the next thing I knew, I was *pulling*. She screamed, but it didn't deter me. The meat on her neck came loose as I ripped it from her bones. I felt her blood drip from my mouth onto my chin. My stomach rumbled and begged for more.

Bite by bite, Riley screamed and thrashed, trying to push me away. Every time I realized what horrible thing I was doing—*eating my crush*—she would simply moan and pull me back into a deep kiss, like a siren lulling a pirate to his death.

The wind blew through the trees of the forest now—

Wait. The forest? I thought, hazily. *We were in my bedroom . . .*

I glanced around, but Riley kissed my collarbone, guiding me to her lips once more. I kept biting and eating, kept ripping her apart, licking my fingers of her blood and flesh.

This was a horror scene, why didn't I see it was a horror scene? And Riley? *What have I done; what am I doing? Why can't I stop? Riley. Riley. Riley, I'm so sorry.*

Just like that, the damage was done. I rolled off her, the smell of blood permeating my nose, the taste invading my mouth, the cold thickness of it plastered to my body. I looked down at Riley and my heart stuttered. Below me lay Riley's gorgeous head, connected to a bare skeleton.

What have I done?

The woods were cold and dark.

What have I done?

I killed Riley.

I jumped out of bed, sweat coating my entire body, as I scoured the room for blood and what was left of her, sunlight beamed through the window shade. It was late morning, I was in my PJs, and everything was exactly how it should've been, wasn't it?

I imagined that I could still feel her kiss on my lips, my teeth sinking into her, the taste of her blood, her flesh inside my mouth.

I have to call her. I have to know.

She beat me to it. I missed a number of calls from Riley, Miles, and Austin and even more messages. I sighed in relief. *It was just a dream.* I opened the group chat and one immediately stuck out to me.

RILEY: THE GHOUL KILLED AGAIN. SAME WAY AS ADDALINE. CALL ME.

My heart felt like it was about to leap from my throat. *It killed again. Or did I do this?*

Looking at all the other messages, their concern for

me pierced me like an arrow through the chest, seep-ing the guilt I had along with it. I knew I needed to apologize, I just hoped they understood that I wasn't myself yesterday—literally. The idea of losing my friends, of them figuring out this ghoul situation and then . . . abandoning me . . . it killed me. I shook my head. It was out of the question.

What was important right now was to get this ghoul and stop it from killing another innocent per-son. Calling Riley, each ring felt like an eternity until I heard the voice I had just heard in my dream. Different now—alive, well.

And concerned.

"Simon? Are you okay?" she rushed out.

"Ye-yeah. I'm good. I just woke up and saw your messages. Someone—"

"The same way. It's another girl . . . we knew her, Si. Beth Freenly. She was a junior, like us."

"The blond girl from PE class?" It was someone I knew. Someone I saw every day.

Addaline was shocking enough, but this was a bit too close. It made the danger more real. Who would it be next? Riley?

"That's the one. We're all here at the hospital. Miles and Austin got here an hour ago. I think you should come. I'm not vibing to anything because of whatever is blocking me from sensing this asshole, but maybe you'll be able to feel something."

The idea of sensing something Riley couldn't due to the fact that I was slowly becoming possessed by this nightmare was horrifying. But I wanted to see if I was the one who did this, not the ghoul. I remembered the taste in my mouth and I felt physically stronger than I had in days.

I felt *full*.

"I'll be there soon."

"Call me when you're here," she said, her voice

sounding as if she was pulling the phone away to hang up.

"Riley, wait!" I yelled. "Riley . . . I'm really sorry about yesterday. I was—"

"Just get here soon, okay?" Immediately after, the phone clicked off.

She had hung up.

I raced to get ready, throwing on whatever I could find. As I ran downstairs, both of my parents were sitting at the dining table, having what looked like lunch.

"Hey, Si, how are you this morning?" Dad said as he sipped his coffee.

"Umm, not too great," I said, walking up to them. "Riley just called me, she's at the hospital."

"Oh no, is she okay?" Mom asked.

Yeah, she's fine but this other girl in my class got eaten alive by a terrifying monster—which, by the way, is also possessing me, slowly driving me insane, and made me think I possibly got freaky with the girl of my dreams before eating her . . . and not in the way I would've liked.

"She's okay, I think I just gave her my stomach flu. But Miles and Austin went to visit her there. Can one of you take me?" The lie felt dirty in my mouth.

"I'll drive you. Give me five minutes to get ready?" Dad said.

"Do you want anything to eat before you go?" Mom asked.

"I'm good. I'll just eat later with the gang."

Within minutes, Dad was back in the kitchen with us, dressed in a heavy jacket and jeans that looked like they desperately needed a wash.

"Ready? It's cold out today. You're going to need your coat." He zipped up his jacket as high as it would go.

The moment we stepped outside, the air was icy against my cheeks and nose. It was biting and drastically colder than any other day since we moved here.

It's just because I'm from Miami, I told myself. *I'm not used to the cold.*

But somewhere deep inside, I knew this cold meant something different.

As soon as I was through the hospital doors, Dad drove off with a wave. The cool, blowing air within the hospital did nothing for my chilled fingers and toes. As I walked to the morgue on autopilot, I kept thinking, *What if I did this? What if I killed Beth?*

The thought alone hurt me. It wasn't possible, right? I woke up at home, but how did I *get* home? The last thing I remembered before the dream was the deer in the forest. The black, damp fur resting against my forehead. The sick voice that made its way into my head.

I tried to shake the thought off as I made my way into the cold, death-smelling room. The door squealed and three pairs of eyes shot at me, all full of different emotions. Which ones, I couldn't discern. I followed their eyes to the body on the metal table. Beth Freenly—or what was left of her—laid there. Her eyes were a hazy, empty brown, staring up into nothing. Her pale blonde hair was draped around her shoulder bones.

Bones. That's all she was now. Just bones, like Addaline, sucked dry once again of all the marrow within.

"Hey, Si." Austin was the first to break the silence.

"Hey, guys." I waved, feeling the social anxiety rising in my throat.

Damn, this is awkward.

"She looks just like Addaline, right?" Miles chimed. His eyes were sad and sick, his nose was scrunched

175

like my first time in the morgue. I realized this was probably the first time he or Austin had seen a dead body. Had *smelled* a dead body. They both stood as far away from Beth as this small room allowed.

"She does. Miles, were you friends with her? Besides just PE, I mean."

His shoulders rounded. "Beth was the first person to talk to me this year. She was really friendly. Helped me get my footing in Ravenswood. We didn't talk much but," His voice broke for the briefest moment. "She was nice. Caring."

The looming idea that I was the cause of this grew heavier and heavier by the moment. We all stood in silence for a while, heads bowed, honoring Beth. With a heavy sigh that awoke the room, Riley looked up at me.

"Do you sense anything?"

I had been focusing so hard on *not* feeling anything and now that all eyes were on me, I felt a pang in my chest and thought of Addaline.

Two. Two innocent people the ghoul now claimed. My legs, acting on their own, took a step back from Beth.

"It was definitely the ghoul's work." Looking at the Ghoul Gang wasn't an option. Panicked, my eyes glared at the floor.

Just then, I heard a voice only I could hear. *Was it me, Simon? Or was it you?*

Riley spoke, but I couldn't make out anything she was saying.

Was this me? I asked myself, pleading for an answer.

The more I looked at Beth's body, the more I remembered the taste of flesh against my lips. The more I envisioned myself eating away until only bones were left. The more full I felt. The more I could remember myself positioning Beth's bones in a perfect skeleton, only leaving her face untouched on the muddy ground of the forest.

This was me.

CHAPTER SEVENTEEN

Was I losing it? Was any of this real? I felt like it had to be fake. No way would I ever hurt anything or anyone, let alone someone I saw nearly every day in school. Chills ran down my spine and I felt myself start to sweat. I felt like I couldn't see anything—or anyone—around me, only Beth. I felt my hands trembling and hoped it wasn't visible to anyone around me.

Was I a murderer? Did I need to come clean to Riley's mom and Miles's dad? Was I going to be arrested? I tried to take in a deep breath, but it was so sharp and painful it hit my lungs like a rock and I immediately felt my vision darken.

I suddenly felt a hand on my shoulder and dashed around, scaring the owner of the hand. Riley's mom stood behind me looking slightly shocked. *When did she get here?*

"Simon, are you okay? Is this too much for you?" she asked, placing her hand on my forehead. "You've gone pale. Riley, please get him some juice or soda or something!"

"Uh oh, she's gone full mom mode. Let's go, Simon," Riley joked as she escorted me out of the room. I hadn't even noticed but Miles and Austin were already outside.

When Miles caught my eyes, I quickly darted them away. But not quick enough.

Riley ushered me to a seat in front of the morgue before grabbing Miles and walking off in search of a vending machine. Once they were out of sight, Austin turned to me.

God, I wish I could be alone right now.

"What, you wanna beat my face in too?" I snapped as he got closer.

"I'm gonna ignore that. What happened to you in there, dude?"

I started to answer, but before I could, Austin continued. "I know that expression. Back when I wasn't in control, before you guys found me. Back in the days when I wanted to do nothing but rip Miles's throat out because he smelled good." Facing away from me, Austin stared at the corner Miles and Riley had just disappeared behind. "I know what that face means."

"And? What does it mean?"

"You think you did this, don't you?"

Before I could think, before Austin could react, my fist was pounding through his face with a strength that was foreign to my flesh. Blood gushed from his nose onto my knuckles. I could feel his eyelashes, so close to where my fist landed. The next moment was another blur of events.

Riley dropped the drink she was carrying for me as she rushed over to the scene, with Miles a step ahead of her. The drink in her hand slowly fell to the ground. On impact, the cap burst open as the blue sports drink spilled across the floor. To my right, Riley's mom and Jason, the hospital pathologist, ran out of the morgue room to pull me off Austin, whose broken nose was dripping crimson drops all over the white tiles. *Drip, drip, drip.* My stomach growled.

Dog meat isn't our typical flavor.

"What happened?" Alice urged. I felt hands grab

around me and pull me up. The crowd gawked at my vacant expression.

Neither myself nor Austin said a word. Austin couldn't. He was fighting to stay conscious. The force of that punch was stronger than anything I alone could have mustered up. I knew in my heart my lanky arm would've shattered in multiple places if I'd ever tried to do that.

Miles and Jason slowly helped Austin up to find medical attention.

"Good thing we're already in a hospital," I scoffed.

"What the fuck is wrong with you!" Riley burst out. It wasn't a question anymore.

I hadn't noticed but my knuckles were bleeding, raw from the punch. Riley grabbed my wrist and led me out of the hospital. We went down two flights, turned into countless hallways, and finally left through the main doors.

"Talk to me, Simon. *Now*! What's been going on with you?" Her shoulders squared. A small, sick part of me thought about how hot her commanding tone was.

They are so *delicious when they're feisty, aren't they? Even more so when they* beg *for it.*

Riley's pleading moans from last night filled my mind. The thought broke me, cracked a part of my mind I hadn't felt in days. Tears finally slipped down my cheeks.

Look at that, Simon, giving into your human feeling.

"I don't know, Riley. I'm terrified. I had a dream last night. A dream that you and I were . . . and then I . . . but I didn't think it was . . . and now . . ."

Riley's face fell. "Please, just tell me, Simon. Tell me so I can help you," she pleaded as she grabbed both of my shoulders.

"I don't . . . I don't know how . . ." I said.

"Please," she added, looking into my eyes, her face filled with worry.

179

"I think . . . I think I did this, Riley."

She lightly gasped and closed the gap between us. She clearly didn't know how to respond. Who would? In the blink of an eye, she threw her arms around me and squeezed tightly. I could feel the wet drops fall onto my shoulders from her tears, and her warm breath tickled against the edges of my hair.

"I'm so sorry, Si. I shouldn't have gotten you into this. I should've never—"

Before she could continue, I embraced her, squeezing her to me. "No, don't do that. This isn't your fault, it's the ghoul's. Or maybe it's mine. But it's not yours, trust me. No matter what happens to me, no matter if I end up becoming the next murder documentary, never blame yourself."

I didn't know how badly I needed human contact. How badly I simply needed *this*.

A shattering noise broke my thoughts. I threw my arms over Riley and myself as the lights above our heads in the awning exploded. The cold air blew our hair into our faces as trees swayed and clashed against each other. It seemed to howl, but by the sinking feeling in our guts, we knew it wasn't an ordinary wind passing by. Riley clutched her hand against her temple and I felt the heavy despair of death. We heard the first wail and knew it was Addaline. Before Addaline's scream finished, a second scream belted.

Two banshees? Beth. They're coming here. They're coming for me.

Fight or flight took over. I wanted to escape but my mind—not the ghoul's—said, *Stay. Stay for Riley. Stay to make sure the scream isn't too much for her to bear.* But somewhere in between, a new voice gelled with my own. *You're at a hospital, Simon. She'll be safe. Now* run.

Thin mist curled through the luminosity of the street lamps. It looked uncomfortably out of place as it shifted into two perfect outlines of young women. As if we were mesmerized by the transition, Riley and I stood there, our arms still awkwardly wrapped around one another. Her hand slowly dropped from her temple as mine fell to my sides.

Before our eyes, two women in white appeared before us. One I recognized as Addaline, the girl from my dreams and the morgue weeks ago. Her skeleton was covered with pale, almost bluish skin and her eyes were a cloudy green. Her red locks had become pale and muted.

The floating spectral next to her was the girl I saw every day in class, Beth Freenly. Beth's appearance replicated Addaline's. Her skin, though pale, was still opaque and had a pearl's sheen to it. Her brown eyes were sharp, the color slightly faded. As their twisted, outraged expressions formed, and their eyes glared directly into mine, avoiding Riley altogether, I knew they thought I did this. I let go of Riley and without thinking, took a step back. Then another. And another.

Run.

My legs turned on their own, my body reacting with it. I was sprinting full force directly into the forest, leaving Riley, Addaline, and Beth behind me in the glare of the street lamp. Something, or someone, drew my feet to the brush of trees. My body was desperate to be in the forest, as if answering a summon.

I heard voices all around me: Riley's, Miles's, and Austin's ringing in my ears. *Help. Help us, Simon,* they said. I knew it wasn't them, but I went forward anyway. As I ran, I felt cold sweat dripping from my forehead. The husky voice in my head crept back in and kept saying *run run run*. Over and over again, the words matching the sharp inhale of each breath, the pounding of my heart. I felt the splint in my side after only a few moments of running through the trees, and I knew this was the fastest I had ever run before.

I didn't know where I was going, what direction I

was running in, or how long since I had dashed away from Riley. I thought I still heard the banshees' cries but knew it was all just in my head.

The farther into the woods I ran, the darker it became. It had been afternoon when I left for the forest, but now it looked as if it were the middle of the night. I glanced up and could only see the midnight blue of the sky, not a star in sight, the moon glowing brightly behind the dark clouds. Something was off. Had I really been running this long? It felt like I lost any semblance of time—like I had only just started while simultaneously feeling like I had been running for hours, days even.

Slipping into darkness, a spotlight guided me through the path of the trees. Without command, my feet turned in a number of directions. I didn't know which way was straight anymore. The farther I ran, the hotter I became. I was burning from the inside out, like my organs, bones, and blood itself were on fire.

Eventually, I began to shed layers of clothing, throwing them on the damp, cold ground of the forest. My coat, my hoodie, and even my jeans were all left, laid around in different places, several steps apart. All that I was left with now was my gray T-shirt, boxers, and black sneakers that were beginning to rip at the seams and soles.

My feet hurt, and I could almost feel the hot and slick ooze of blood coming from welts underneath. The more I ran, the more I felt like I was losing myself, mentally and physically. My sight was fading to black more and more, the voice only getting louder. I didn't want to run anymore but my legs just wouldn't give up. I felt like Forrest Gump, only if he was in a horror movie and being chased by a ravenous, beastly Hannibal Lecter trying to *eat* him.

That was when I heard it.

Him.

It sounded almost like hooves beating against the cold ground. His steps were quick, too quick, like that of a deer. I could hear his ragged and hard breath, as the ghoul ran toward me. I begged my body to run faster, run home, run out of the forest.

The smell hit me next. It smelled like that first night so many weeks ago, that first dream in the forest. It smelled old, decrepit. The beast was behind me, gaining on me more and more.

I dared not look back, in fear of seeing those bright crimson eyes only inches away from mine. I still hadn't fully seen the ghoul in the light, only his silhouette and those haunting eyes—but still, I was even more afraid to see it as a shadow in this forest.

Simon, stop running. You're wearing yourself out, I told myself. I didn't know how I hadn't passed out yet. My entire body ached. It begged me to stop instead. I *couldn't* listen. Listening would lead to something horrible—I knew it in my gut.

You don't have a choice. The words crept along my spine like a long fingernail.

Without any warning, my body suddenly stopped. My feet felt raw and burned with agony, my joints cried in pain. It felt like my feet were on fire, the flames licking up to my legs. It was so hot and painful. I could almost feel my legs cracking under the flame. As I glanced down, there they were, perfectly normal, only completely bare—even my shoes had disappeared— on this irregularly cold October night. Small bumps lined my legs and arms. Goose bumps. Somehow, my body was cold, even though it simultaneously felt like I was on fire.

All at once, every feeling I'd had in the last few weeks, every hungry sensation, bloodlust, craving, anger, and fear came flooding back. My body finally buckled under the pressure of this wave of emotions and desires. My knees were wet and cold against the damp leaves along the forest floor and I just felt so *tired*. The lack of sleep, the nightmares, and the insatiable hunger weighed on my body now more than ever before.

I reached for the only ward of defense, except it wasn't around my neck. *Why did I take off the only thing protecting me from the ghoul?* A memory resurfaced in my mind: I had taken my lavender necklace off before sleep last night. I saw the moment vividly—like being shown a video. As if this memory was locked away and now something new to me. Strange that I couldn't remember anything else from yesterday after my encounter with the deer, so why was I recalling this now?

The ghoul's hooves inched closer and closer, yet still, I couldn't turn around. Slowing his pace, I felt his presence directly behind me. The beating of the hooves on the ground was replaced with the sound of cracking bones. I could only imagine the black deer's bones shifting into something even more horrid. It made pained grunts behind me and yelled in agony. I felt my curiosity rise as my head instinctively began to turn.

Don't look. Don't look, I begged myself.

A thump behind me and the smell of the ghoul became a million times worse. I nearly gagged at the stench alone. My entire body felt cold now. I knew part of it had to do with being outside with barely anything on, but this was a deeper chill, something that ran through my bones. My chest felt heavy and pained. It was hard to stay up as I ravenously shivered.

I imagined Riley, Miles, and Austin. I thought of them, wondering where I was.

They don't care about you. Not really, anyway.

You're wrong, I wanted to say, but the words didn't come out. Instead, there was a deep and shrill cackle. The laugh rang in my ears and shook me down to the core. I was living in one of my nightmares but I knew, this time, I wasn't dreaming.

Suddenly, the sides of my head were racked by pain.

It felt like something was *growing* from my skull and trying to find a way out, pushing on the flesh of my scalp.

I cried in pain, louder than I ever had before. All the while, the ghoul cackled behind me. I yelled until my throat turned hoarse and raw. I clutched at the sides of my head as I felt something beginning to break the skin under my hair. Blood gushed in my hands and slipped down my forearms. Whether it was from the pain or the fear, or something in between, I knew I wouldn't be staying conscious for much longer.

I clawed at the ground in front of me and tried to pull myself away. I crawled as much as I could but I knew, it was too late to get away from the ghoul. Everything around me looked like my dreams—only a spotlight could be seen, and the spotlight rested solely on me.

This was it. The moment I'd been fearing all these weeks. The ghoul's possession of me was reaching its completion. I felt an ice-cold hand close around my face as the ghoul lifted me back up toward him. The cold of his stretched skin iced onto my back, sending a violent shiver down my spine.

"Why me?" I managed to say, fighting to keep my vision, fighting to beat the cold growing in my heavy chest.

Why? Because, Simon, you were able to hear my call.

And then, everything went black.

PART TWO

THE GHOUL GANG

CHAPTER EIGHTEEN
RILEY

Saturday Evening

Shit.

It was all my fault. Simon wasn't himself. He was wrong, damaged, and I knew it was because of me. If we hadn't met, maybe things would be different. If I hadn't told him about my vibes, maybe he'd continue to be living his blissfully ignorant life. And now? Who knew where he was and why he ran away.

Something was up, and I was determined to find out what.

After Simon—literally—ran into the woods, I was left outside the hospital doors with two terrifying banshees screaming their spectral lungs out at me. My vision was going dark and something about their screams blocked me from vibing with them. Their screams hurt me so badly, they knocked me out before I would be able to change. Talk about the worst headache of my life—period migraines couldn't even dare compete.

"Why did Simon run from you?" I tried to ask with a brave face. But then again, I seemed to always put on a brave face. Neither of the girls had answered me; instead, they wailed and wailed.

I decided at that moment, *I hate banshees.*

The two of them looked to the woods shortly after Simon disappeared behind the tree line, their eyes focused on the creeping shadows growing with dusk. After a short moment, they both disappeared and I was left alone, Simon's face twisting into utter fear and horror ingrained in my mind.

Somehow, since I've known him, Simon became my greatest joy and pain. I wished I could vibe with a time-traveling ghoul to go back to that moment when I first laughed at his "*Si, por favor*" joke in history class. Or to that first day I had lunch with him and Miles, when I told them ghosts were real—that all of this was real. I should've just kept all of this to myself, again. Like I always did. I should've just stayed alone. But no. I messed up, and I dragged not one, but *three* people into my mess of a life. I was so pitiful and I knew it.

As I walked home, as far away from the hospital as I could, I knew what I had to do. I had dragged them into enough danger, I could leave them out of this one.

I texted my mom that I was going home on my own. I had driven with her to the hospital today so my truck still sat in my driveway. I needed time to think anyway. I stuck to the road, on the far side from the forest where everything weird happened. Where things called to me, things I shouldn't even be able to hear, night and day, every day.

Dusk quickly became night and by the time home was in sight, the moon was high in the sky. As I walked through the doorway, I left all the lights off in my wake. What I was about to do worked better in candlelight anyway. I locked the door behind me, drew the shades of the windows, and beelined upstairs for my room. Of course, my room was a mess. The bed was left undone, dark sheets wrapped between each other. Clean and dirty clothes lay rampant on the floor in puzzles of artistic complexity that only I had the key for. Candle wax spilled over bookshelves and nightstands leaving trails of white, purple, red, and black scattered around my room.

The mess may have been typical of a teenager, but that was about as far as it went as my bedroom doubled as the workspace for a girl who can commune with the supernatural.

Wards were drawn under my bed, behind the door, and under the window. No way was I letting a wandering spirit come in as they pleased while I was sleeping until the afternoon on weekends. To the average person, my room would probably look like an occult fanatic's dream, but it was my everyday life. I dropped my bag on the hardwood floor, kicked off my boots, made my way to my closet on the other end of the room, and slid the mirrored door open.

What I was about to do was my last resort solution. No longer would I let Simon go through this alone. I was done being left in the dark, I was done standing idly by as my friend was tormented by a hungry sleep demon. But I couldn't vibe with the ghoul, I felt like I had zero ammunition against this guy, zero ideas on how to even begin my approach to save Simon. I reached into the layers of black clothes, my arm fully engulfed in the fabric, until I felt what I was looking for. It'd been a while since my last use, a use in which I swore to myself would be the last time. As I pulled the item out, I lightly brushed the dust away from the words printed on the brown box: SPIRIT BOARD.

I groaned to myself at the idea of using it but walked to the center of my room anyway after sliding my closet door closed once again. I kicked away some of the clothes on the floor and placed the box on the floor. I grabbed four white candles and a lighter, all of which had been lazily scattered around my room but easy to find, and finally, I sat down cross-legged in front of the board.

I thought back to my last spirit board session. Through the full body mirrors on my closet doors, I had seen . . . something, with charred skin, sitting nude behind me, back to back. The demon mimicked me and sat with his legs crossed, his clawed hands resting upon his knees as my hands, with their chipped-polished nails, rested on my knees. He had been sitting so straight, it looked painful, and I could feel his back firmly pressed against mine, his skin hot like fire. The only qualities I noticed were his two horns protruding from the front of his head and dry, burnt, carmine skin that looked as though it might crack at any moment.

That was the day I threw my planchette under my bed and locked the board in my closet. Every time I thought about it, a phantom heat crept along my spine, just as it did that day, his breath on my neck from the smooth and deep voice that laughed as he whispered my name. I haven't touched the board for nearly two years. Until today.

Now the scene was set. The spirit board sat in the middle of the floor, surrounded by four white candles for protection. I grabbed the planchette and was ready. It was simple in design, save for a crescent moon and flaring sun on either end of the bottom and the small stars that lined the top. The crystal in the middle was clear and bright, ready to magnify my messages.

I adjusted back to where I'd been sitting in the room two years ago and placed the piece on the board, both hands attached, and took a deep breath in.

And then I remembered the demon.

I jumped back, unready for my journey to the world beyond. Vibing with ghosts, werewolves, vampires, even cryptids, was so different—so easy—compared to doing a spirit board session. And I was skipping one of the vital rules of communing with the dead.

1. Don't insult the spirit.

2. Never ask when you're going to die.

3. Always say goodbye at the end of a session.

4. And NEVER play alone.

Welp. I held the planchette in my hands, away from the board, and bit my lip. Did I really want to do this? I know I actually saw dead people all the time but this was terrifying. This was welcoming, *begging*, entities— malevolent or not—into my space. Vibing to them was one thing but, like Ravenswood, something about my powers seemed to call to them too. Using the spirit board was like turning on a lighthouse for all wandering spirits.

Except I was the lighthouse.

I was reminded immediately of Simon and his sweet, innocent face. He had a knack for always making me feel like I wasn't weird or strange. I wasn't doing this for me. This was for him.

I took a deep breath in and placed the planchette on the board again, both hands on either side, resting on the sun and the moon. I closed my eyes and began.

"Hello? I'm calling out to Beth Freenly and Addaline Alberts. If you can hear me, I need to speak to you, I need your help." I always felt awkward when I used the board. It was awkward enough talking to people I saw every day, let alone spirits who seemingly wanted to kill my friend.

For a while, nothing happened.

"I need answers. About Simon and why you're targeting him. What he did—what you *thought* he did to you. What the monster that's haunting him is." I waited but still nothing. My hope was draining as my shoulders sagged.

With less confidence, I mumbled, "I just want to know if he's okay. Where did he go?"

The jarring movements caught me off guard. My heart leaped and I jumped so high my entire body shook.

R-I-L-E-Y

"Ye-Yes! That's me. Are you here with me now?" I asked aloud.

The planchette moved to *Yes*. I sighed with relief, my calling finally worked and I didn't even have to hear them scream.

"Great. I have a few questions for you. I felt like this may be the best way to communicate. Are you both here?"

It moved to *No*.

"Am I talking to Beth or Addaline right now?" And while I was fully expecting the planchette to begin spelling out one of the two names, it simply moved off of *No* and back again.

An eerie feeling filled the air. I could feel myself gulp and my hands began to shake, rocking the planchette.

"Who am I speaking to right now?" I questioned, my voice quivering.

The planchette stayed in place for a moment, before it viscously moved across the board, stopping briefly on a set of letters.

S-I-M-O-N

My hands jumped off the planchette (another thing that should never happen when using the spirit board) when it finished spelling his name. I gasped and clamped my mouth in shock. It couldn't be . . . could it? I had just seen Simon a few hours ago. He was alive, he was fine, maybe a little scared, but fine. The planchette started moving on its own and I quickly placed my hands back on each side.

H-E-L-L-O

"Simon, are you—" Before I could ask if he was dead, the planchette moved to *Yes*. A sob escaped me and I could feel hot, wet tears streaking down my cheeks. My eyes strained to stay open as they became more and more filled.

"But, how did you . . . ?"

G-H-O-U-L

I tightened my grip on the planchette, my fingers digging into the wood as much as they could. I didn't want to believe this—I couldn't.

"But I just saw you. You were—I would've . . . Can I fix this?" I asked, desperate for a *Yes*. But of course, I couldn't. I could only connect to ghosts, not reverse death.

Wait a minute.

I could connect with ghosts. If Simon was a ghost, wouldn't I just . . . be one too? Every ghost I had ever been around, I vibed with. Why not now?

"Simon, if you're a ghost, why not reveal yourself to me?" My voice oozed with speculation.

W-E-A-K

Okay. This was bullshit. Even the weakest of ghosts I felt. Frank, the first ghost Simon encountered with my powers, was a weak spirit, barely anything, but I brought him out. My powers did that. Even the weakest of energies was able to commune with me—that was kind of the whole point.

Now I knew this was a sick and evil joke. My tone shifted and became harsh and aggressive.

"Who is this? I know it's not Simon."

The planchette began to move in fast circles around the board, another big no-no in the spirit board rules. The planchette kept halting at *O* and at *Z*. But over and over it moved. I stopped the planchette with my grip, my fear rising but my anger with it.

"What are you?"

D-E-M-O-N

I almost laughed to myself. Of course.

"The same one from last time?" The planchette moved to *Yes*. "And now you're back. For what? Why me?"

P-O-S-S-E-S-S Y-O-U

I sarcastically laughed at the demon.

"Yeah, not going to happen. Goodbye." I got ready to move the planchette to the *Goodbye* position, but before I could, it moved away from my hands and shook the board, moving so quick and hard that the nubs underneath the board to keep it from scrapping the wood dug into the wood now, making deep cuts all the letters.

G-O-I-N-G T-O D-I-E B-E-C-A-U-S-E O-F

Before it could say anything more, I forcefully dragged the planchette to *Goodbye* and once again removed it from the board. I even took the extra precaution to flip the board over.

I took a deep breath and exhaled. *Man, I hate demons.* I hadn't even noticed that all but one candle had gone out during my session. I rubbed my neck, which suddenly felt stiff and heavy, and stretched out my back.

I hadn't reached Addaline or Beth. I hadn't even come close. I shook my leg, my anxiety getting the better of me. I didn't want to try again—it was a stupid idea. But maybe. Just maybe . . .

Before I even considered trying again, I felt a buzz in my back pocket and slipped out my phone. It was a message from Austin. Austin and I had become close. In fact, I would probably consider him my closest friend. During the time we worked together to learn how to control the wolf within, we learned a lot (maybe even too much) about one another. It had all been pretty heavy information to tell someone you've never really spoken to before. But turning into wolves, going through that kind of raw pain during the transformation with each other, becoming like a small pack of our own as time went on, it made it *more*.

Though we'd known each other since we were kids, I felt like I barely knew anything about him. He practically grew up alone. His parents were rich, yes. But they were distant, and he resented that. To make up for it, they bought him animals. Conveniently, dogs were his favorite.

Austin's dad was some super strict, big-money guy with a really toxic view on masculinity. And Austin hated it. His mom did everything his father would say, agreed with everything, never put up a fight, and never fought *for* Austin. Austin loved his mother, but he was convinced she only cared about the money she had married into.

Austin's father snapped when he came out. So bad, that Austin went back into the closet. He had told his parents he was wrong and dated a pretty girl a few weeks later. He hated himself for so long.

And then the werewolf came into town.

Initially, Austin had followed one of his dogs into the woods. I assumed it had run in after hearing the howl of an alpha animal. But the dog was nowhere to be found, and over the course of the evening, Austin lost his way. A werewolf had wandered into the Ravenswood forest and attacked him. I remember Austin being in the hospital toward the end of our freshman year, and I guess it had dragged out all the way through the summer. When he came back at the beginning of our sophomore year, he had been . . . different. He was always a bit quiet, but he played sports, and he had friends. When he returned to school, he alienated himself.

That is, until he met us.

For a full year, Austin had been doing nothing but chaining himself in the woods every full moon. Getting loose on rare occasions and taking his familial rage out on the local wildlife. He'd never attacked anyone, and for that he was thankful. After he came out, things had never been the same. So his parents then left on business trips and bought a place in New York City by Central Park. Then they bought another place in Los Angeles, and another in the Bahamas. They went everywhere—as long as it wasn't Ravenswood. They feigned love and care by sending him money and gifts weekly and postcards and pictures of sunny beaches and snowy winter days. The house in Ravenswood stayed empty save for Austin, his dogs, and Denise.

When the Ghoul Gang first went to Austin's house, I remembered Austin lying about his parents. While his dad did work in tech, his absence wasn't due to work. I had known it then but supposed he hadn't wanted to tell Simon or Miles yet. After all, he had been trying to impress Miles since they met. If only the two dorks would just tell each other and get it over with.

Jeez, how blind could you be?

Austin had really wanted to get closer to Simon, he had felt like they were the only links in the Ghoul Gang that hadn't connected. He said he felt like he was causing the circle to be incomplete. I knew that with everything going on with Si, Austin was extremely worried. We all were. But due to the wolf, Austin had a harder time than most differentiating between rage, sorrow, and everything in between. He had lashed out at Simon, for good reason. That ghoul—whatever he was—had done a serious number on Si's personality. Austin's werewolf tendencies and Simon's Dr. Brundle transformation didn't match up too well.

Austin had been punched, rather brutally, in the face today by Simon and I hadn't even checked in on him with everything that had gone on. What a great friend I was.

I glanced down at my phone now, only two words appeared on the screen.

AUSTIN: YOU OKAY?

ME: YEAH. YOU?

But I wasn't. I was worried about Simon, and hoped he was home, but feared the worst.

That damn demon.

My phone buzzed again.

AUSTIN: YEAH . . . SI GOT ME GOOD, BUT THEY PATCHED ME UP ALREADY. I JUST GOT HOME NOW, WHAT HAPPENED WITH YOU AND SIMON?

I clutched my phone as I read the text over again. I wanted to hide the truth from him but knew it wasn't smart. I couldn't save Simon on my own, and I think I knew that deep down.

ME: A LOT. CAN YOU ACTUALLY COME OVER? I THINK I MIGHT NEED SOME BACKUP.

I knew I was being vague, but my head was still racing from everything that had happened today.

Another dead body—someone we knew.

The banshees.

Simon running into the woods like a madman.

The demon.

It was all just way too much for me. And where I normally would handle it all on my own—I didn't need to anymore.

Less than twenty minutes after I had texted Austin, I went to open the door for him. His nose had a large white bandage across the bridge and looked slightly bent out of shape. Both of his eyes had darkening circles and I could tell they would be black by tomorrow.

"Hey," he said out of breath. "Came as fast as I could. What are we doing?" Austin walked into the house and slipped off his shoes and coat.

"Well, I don't think you're going to like it," I said as I led the way back up to my room.

"Why is it so dark in here? Should I turn on the light?" he asked, but I shook my head.

"Not for what we're doing." I could hear the deep gulp from behind me as we entered my room. The candles had been blown out and the spirit board still lay in the middle, surrounded by my mess. "Ta-daaa," I said halfheartedly.

Austin's face fell.

I sat down on one end of the board and ushered him to go to the other side, and as he sat down, legs crossed as instructed, I gave him the details.

"Basically, I want to call Beth and Addaline here. It's too difficult to communicate with them when they just appear."

"Why do you want to call them at all?"

"Well . . ." I found myself fidgeting and picking my fingers, my cuticles screaming.

"A lot happened after Simon punched you."

Austin raised an eyebrow.

"I followed him outside of the hospital, and for a moment, he seemed like himself. A bit confused, but himself. And he was just so afraid that he had done something to those girls," I said, remembering the expression on his face, the warmth from his embrace.

"And then what happened?" Austin's soft voice crept in.

"The banshees appeared in front of us, but before they had even become fully corporeal, Si freaked out. He ran and disappeared into the woods."

"In the direction of his house?"

"I don't know. I think so. It didn't seem like a calculated dash, he just kind of ran. I can't help but think that it has to do with the ghoul. Remember, Granny said the woods were dangerous. And now he's in there. I've tried calling him a few times, but he isn't answering."

"How about we try his parents? See if he's home?"

"I don't want to freak them out anymore than they have been already, with Si going home sick all the time," I said, finding my arms wrapped around myself.

Austin nodded. "What do you need me to do? I'll help in any way I can," he said reassuringly, his eyes wide and eager to please.

I smiled back at him. "Well, basically, I'm going to try to call the banshees here using this." I pointed to the spirit board. "It didn't really work out as planned last time, so having you here will help stabilize me . . . I think."

He nodded.

"Then, once they're here, it should be easier to communicate. I think if I call them with the board, they'll be able to speak without the influence of rage around them. I'll get to ask what happened to them, how Simon is involved, and why they're banshees rather than just regular ghosts or poltergeists even."

"That is a lot. But let's do it." Austin lightly touched one of his ears. "Hopefully they don't scream into my ears again," he said with a sad laugh.

"Hopefully," I agreed, and then I placed my hands on the planchette and motioned for Austin to do the same.

CHAPTER NINETEEN
RILEY

Saturday Evening

"I am calling out to the spirits of Addaline Alberts and Beth Freenly. If you are here, I would like to speak to you, to help you. But I also need your help," I said for the fourth time. Nothing called back, the planchette remained still. But our focus stayed strong.

"Try again," Austin whispered.

I took a deep breath and followed his advice. "I am calling out to the spirits of Addaline Alberts and Beth Freenly. If you are here, I would like to speak to you, to help you. But I also need your help." This time, Austin repeated the words as I did. We tried once more, and before we could finish, the planchette moved. I opened my eyes and looked down at its movements and up at Austin. His eyes were wide with excitement. He laughed to himself.

The planchette moved and said, *H-E-L-L-O*

"Hi. Is this Beth and Addaline?" The planchette moved to *Yes*.

This felt different than before. I couldn't feel the immense negative energy and dread. Austin and I both smiled widely at each other. We had done it!

N-E-E-D T-O T-A-L-K

"Us too!" Austin said.

"We need your help. We need to know . . . what happened to you both. And how Simon is involved. If that's okay . . ." I trailed off. Demanding things from banshees seemed like a bad idea. But just before I could fix it, make it sound more pleading than demanding, something happened with the planchette.

Out of the glass hole in the top, a faint, soft, white mist rose. At first, it moved slowly. As Austin and I followed it with our eyes, our gaze slowly shifted from the board to each other to the roof. It kept flowing out, more and more until a pool of white mist rotated above our heads. The mist curved around itself, flowing and shifting until it became two separate, silent entities.

I could feel my heart begin to pound. Harder and harder, as if I was having a heart attack. I knew instantly what it meant.

"Cover your ears," I uttered through gritted teeth as my chest clenched.

"Riley, are you okay?" I heard Austin say before all sound drowned away. His mouth was still moving but I couldn't see a thing.

I was vibing.

And in order to become a banshee, I needed to die first.

My heart lurched—it felt like it was going to burst through my chest. My entire body felt numb and I caught the aroma of crisp apple cider, the scent I always smelled before I died in a vibe session.

While I may have told Simon, Miles, and Austin about the vibes, I never really explained how they worked. It felt private to me, like it was my pain to bear. Whenever I became a ghost, or any kind of undead, I died. And it was painful every single time. But it was short, fleeting, like waking up from a nightmare—you only remember the very end and then you wake up.

That's how dying felt. That's how becoming a ghost felt.

Only this time, I wasn't just becoming a ghost.

I felt my heartbeat quicken before it slowed. *Too slow*, I thought, but then it just stopped altogether. I felt my body go slack in Austin's arms. I consciously knew that I was dead, which didn't really make sense, but then again, what about my powers made sense?

Austin shook me, screamed at me, all around panicked. But I couldn't do anything, not until the vibe was complete. Next to us, Beth and Addaline floated. They were crisp white, Addaline's red hair was stark against her pale skin and white dress, while Beth's blonde hair looked lighter than it ever had.

And then my body shed its tangible form. My body exploded, leading way for a new one. I screamed a blood-curdling shriek, higher than I ever could, and wailed profusely until I caught myself again.

Vibing felt like being on a tightrope. I was up on the rope for minutes, a perfect copy of the ghoul I was transforming into. The same feelings, the same rage, but . . . I wasn't them; I wasn't on a tightrope. I needed to remind myself that each and every time. I needed to let go and fall into the net that was below me, the net that was *me*.

After what felt like an eternity, I did just that. I let go and became myself again. I heard the end of my own scream and stopped. I looked up to see the figures around me. Austin was covering his ears and staring at me, eyes wide, hands tightly pressed against the sides of his head. Addaline and Beth were next to him, patiently waiting for me. I took a deep breath in and glanced at myself.

I was intangible, my hair flowed around me as if I was underwater, and I wore a long white dress, so bright it hurt my eyes.

"Whoa," I said instinctively. My voice echoed, and Austin slowly removed his hands from his ears.

"Riley? You good now?"

I nodded. "Uh . . . hi?" I said to the two girls. They both smiled at me and then at Austin.

"Hi," they both said.

"You needed our help?" Beth asked.

A million questions ran through my head. Who was the ghoul, how did you die, *why* did it choose you? But only one question actually mattered.

"Did Simon kill you?"

The words spilled out of me before I could stop them, and I think everyone felt that. Austin's jaw slightly dropped as the two banshees blankly stared at me.

"No," said Addaline, breaking the silence. Her voice was soft and sweet. "Simon is being used. I don't know how, but he was there after my death."

"What do you mean?" Austin asked, trying to sound extra gentle.

"I was eaten. Alive. By that horrifying ghoul that smelled like death. I felt every pull of my skin, every bone sucked dry. I watched as he drank the marrow from my femur, and heard as he ate my kidneys. I don't remember dying, only the pain, the fear, the sorrow that I wasn't as nice to my mom that morning, that I hadn't said 'I love you' to my dog before going to campus. And then I woke up."

"Woke up?" I said, thinking of my recurring death every time I became a ghoul.

"Yep. Woke up. It was dark, and I knew I was dead. I felt like I was being watched, and I knew it was the thing that ate me. Only . . . he was stronger."

"Stronger?"

"Before, when he killed me, he was weak. Like a dying animal. On the day I died, I was incredibly sick. I had the worst cold I think I've ever had. I decided to call it a night and skipped the rest of my classes. I was going home when he . . ." she said, her voice drifting like it was caught in a breeze, unable to finish the sentence. But Austin and I understood.

"Where did you wake up?" Austin asked after giving Addaline a moment to collect herself.

She looked up at him, her eyebrows pinched as though she was confused, unsure of how to describe something or searching for the right words to do so.

"Well, I'm not really sure. I almost want to say that it was like the creature's own world. Simon would wake up in it every so often, only . . . he wasn't dead like I was. He tried to help me. But I was so confused, I think I scared him a lot the first few times I saw him. He shared the same . . . energy as the creature that killed me," Addaline explained. "But then he helped me out of there. And now here I am."

"So how did you become a banshee? Instead of just moving on, or becoming a regular ghost even?" I asked. Her eyebrow twinged and, for a moment, I felt like I had asked the wrong question. But then her face softened as she responded.

"I'm of Irish descent. Banshees aren't something that's new to me; it's a part of my folklore. My parents were both really into that stuff. I remembered when I died, and when Simon saved me, that I wanted to warn people of this ghoul. I wanted to make sure no one would get hurt like I was. I was angry, and I wanted revenge. I wanted to be an omen, a warning. The next thing I knew, I was screaming louder than ever."

"Did the same happen to you, Beth?" Austin asked, looking at the other girl who had been silently listening. She shook her head.

"When I died . . . I saw Simon. But, he wasn't the one who killed me. In fact, I don't even know how I saw him, he was just . . . there. Floating above me as whatever that creature was ripped me apart."

"You saw him? Floating?" I asked, my voice trembling. Beth nodded. *Simon was there? But how? It wasn't even Halloween yet, how could the ghoul reach him?*

"And then, just before everything went all black, he

disappeared, and I saw Addaline. She screamed and the creature ran away. But it had been too late. He had just finished his meal. Addaline took my hand and the next thing I knew, I was wailing with her."

We all remained silent for a moment.

"I guess when one banshee collects another lost soul, that soul becomes a banshee as well," Austin said. "Do you know what this thing wants with Simon?" Austin's voice was filled with worry once more. His face dropped, the concern for Simon showing through his tough exterior.

Beth shook her head.

"Not really," said Addaline. "I heard the creature talk about him a lot though, while I was in his world. I think he wants Simon to be like him, to eat people, but I'm not sure why. Simon put up a fight—every time I saw him, he was either running or fighting."

I thought of him now. His brave face whenever things got real. His smile whenever he laughed. I wanted all of that back.

I faced the two girls.

"Will stopping this creature help you both move on?" I asked. A new determination swelled within me. They both looked at one another for a moment and then back at me.

"I believe," Addaline said, "if the creature is stopped, and no one else can be hurt or killed by it . . . that we will be free of this form." She weakly smiled at me.

I turned back to Austin. "Okay. Then that is exactly what we're going to do."

After the two banshees fizzled back to their misty forms, my body became tangible again. My heart started beating, my breath came in hot, my voice became hoarse from the scream, my hair fell straight against my head, and my skin became slightly less pale than when I was *literally* dead. I was back to normal, and now I had a mission. I needed to stop this ghoul, but first I knew I needed to figure out what *it* was.

"This is pretty gnarly," Austin said, breaking my thought process. "And I mean that in the worst way possible."

"I know. I feel like I don't even know where to begin with this. It's not a werewolf. It's not a ghost or demon. It doesn't have a tangible form but then it also does? I don't even know what to think of it anymore."

"Maybe it's a cannibalistic Bigfoot." Austin's voice was thick with sarcasm. "And it's not like we can ask Granny about it, she can't even say the creature's name because it's bad luck or something."

"Yeah, didn't she say the more you know about *it*, the more *it* knows about you or something?"

Austin nodded.

This was all just too freaky. And I dealt with demons on a regular basis. Something about this ghoul, about this *thing*, was utterly and truly horrifying, and it was more than just the fact that it had total control over Simon.

As the night went on, Austin and I sat researching different kinds of creatures—mythological, supernatural, cryptids, you name it. But nothing really came up. Nothing felt . . . *right*.

We hit a dead end—and I hoped, more than ever, that this was just a poorly worded phrase.

CHAPTER TWENTY
ALICE

Sunday

I t was already midnight; Riley was home trying to find any *ghostly* clues about where Simon ran off to and about Beth Freenly and this monster eating my town away one by one. But over the last several hours, I was stuck in the *human* world—the world of paperwork and needed explanations. It was difficult, being the sheriff of Ravenswood, always having to explain the unexplainable to the higher-ups.

"How did this person die?" they would say.

Well, sir, a ghostly woman in white made herself visible as she crossed the street in front of their speeding car, and to avoid hitting the spirit the driver swerved off to the side and embedded themselves into a tree. That would get me one ticket straight to the looney bin and a plastic star so I could keep playing sheriff. Having a daughter *become* the supernatural while also keeping the town's head on its shoulders was a hard balance. But we'd managed to make it work so far.

But it seemed like the older Lee got, the more ghouls she connected to, and the more ghouls appeared. This whole ghoul-in-the-woods business was getting out of hand, nothing like we'd ever seen. And I'd seen her take on an entire horde of leprechauns. The amount of unexplainable glitter made the woods look like a wild night at Mardi Gras.

I drove through the windy yet familiar roads of Ravenswood. I had been born here, in the very hospital I was just in. Was raised here, with a mother and father, and all of my family had been just a five- or ten-minute walk away. But my parents moved to Florida after Nana passed away, leaving only me and Riley to fend for ourselves.

I had my girl when I was too young and too dumb. I had big dreams of making it out of the city, to follow my boyfriend—Riley's dad—across the world, wherever the wind took us. But the moment I found out we'd have a third partner on our hands, my young, dumb boyfriend up and left the city. Claimed he needed to "spread his wings" or "sow his oats" before he became too old and got stuck in this "shit-town," as he so eloquently phrased it. Not even six months after he left, the jackass got himself arrested for selling crystal meth one town over.

So it was just me and Riley from then on out. And I still wouldn't have had it any other way.

My cell buzzed in my pocket. Without even looking at the name on the screen (which would be illegal— no texting and driving), I swiped along the bottom. "Sheriff Silverstein."

"Alice, it's Walsh. Did you leave the hospital already?"

"Hey, Walsh," I heard my voice get a pep in its step. I didn't know this old heart could still do flips. "Yeah, I'm on the way home already to see how Lee is doing. Any word from the Woos?"

Walsh sighed on the other side of the line. "I just got off the phone with Peter. Hana was, naturally, in hysterics—"

"If it were Riley, I would be the same . . . Worse. I would be worse."

"Ditto. Don't trust a parent with a gun when it comes to their kids, right?"

"I would go full Bruce Willis on their ass."

Walsh laughed on the other side of the phone, his voice husky from the late hours of the night and the seemingly endless case we'd been working on. "Well, I know that little *Ghoul Gang* of theirs are always together. This whole thing with Simon has me . . . scared," *A man admitting to his own fears, be still my heart.* "Imma watch Miles like a hawk, but if I . . . slip—"

"I'll watch him like he was my own, Walsh."

I heard the man on the other side sigh with what could only be relief. "Thanks, Alice." I could almost picture the smile in his voice. "Get some rest, will ya? And then tomorrow—we find Simon."

"All right sounds like a plan. Have a good night, Walsh."

"Good night, Alice."

As I hung up the phone, I felt my heart leap at the thought of Simon, alone in the woods; at Hana and Peter and their confusion as to where their son ran off to, and why. But then I reminded myself that all I needed to do was get home and talk to my daughter. I'm sure she would tell me that there was some kind of supernatural explanation for all of this. That the kid wasn't missing; that he ran toward something, not away. That there is *nothing* to be worried about. But the closer I got to home, the more that panic settled in. The more I feared that my daughter's new friend would end up as just another cadaver in the morgue like the one we pulled in last night.

As I pulled up to the house, I noticed a familiar car parked in my driveway. Austin's parents were pretty MIA so, nowadays, he often spent evenings and weekends here with us, I guess tonight would be no different.

As I walked toward the front door, clicking my car locked behind me, I needed to steel myself emotionally and decide what hat I would wear into this upcoming conversation. Was I going to be the sheriff of Ravenswood tonight or the secret *X-Files* agent? Was I going to be Riley's mother or her Rupert Giles? Whatever it was, my daughter needed me more tonight than she had in a long time. And with a relationship like ours, I would *always* be there when she needed me. I'm the mom, and as the mom, I'm supposed to be strong for my child when they are going through a crisis. But it was never easy to see my child in pain and to know that something may or may not have happened to her friend made things even more difficult.

That poor boy.

As I walked through the door, I smelled the faint aroma of sage and candles. Clearly, she was already up to something. "Riley? Austin?" I called. The moment I said their names, the two came rushing down the stairs.

"Anything?" Riley asked before I was even able to put my purse down.

"I was about to ask you the same thing."

"We haven't seen or heard from him since the hospital, Ms. Silverstein," Austin said, his expression was a bit ghastly.

"Boy, call me Alice. So, Lee, what's going on? Whole story this time, don't leave anything out."

"It's . . . long."

"We've got all night, don't we?"

She took a deep breath and flopped onto the couch, Austin sat beside her. "Well. There's a ghoul."

"When is there not?" I interrupted.

"Mom. It's a ghoul I *can't* vibe to. I haven't even seen him—" Before I could ask what she meant, she shook her head. "That night, when we first discovered Austin was a werewolf, something called out to Simon from the woods. Initially, he thought it was just a dream—"

"But then the dreams started happening more frequently," Austin interjected.

"None of us were really sure what to make of it all. We believed him, of course, but we didn't know what to do. His body started rejecting food. He couldn't eat."

"Couldn't sleep," Austin said.

"And then he started getting angry and extremely defensive."

"Really angry." Austin tapped his already-healing nose. "But Simon started seeing things. Everywhere. A black deer in the forest, a dead body in his dream, only for it to turn up the next morning."

"When he saw that body today, Mom, he thought *he* did it."

Silence filled the room for a moment. Guess I needed to put on my Dana Scully badge.

"So, the ghoul that murdered Addaline Alberts and Beth Freenly is Simon?" I rose an eyebrow and began to pace around the room.

"Of course not!" Riley shouted. "But we think . . ."

"We believe that whatever this ghoul is," Austin interjected, placing a hand on Riley's shoulder, "it's somehow possessing Si through his dreams and making him *believe* he's the killer. We believe that this *thing* is trying to make him feel isolated and distorted."

"And if that is what this thing was trying to do then—"

"Then it succeeded," I finished. It was the only way to explain *why* Simon ran into the woods alone. Riley and Austin nodded in my direction. "Well, if he's out there, surely we can go try to find him. Right? Austin, do you need to be back home tonight?"

"No, ma'am."

"All right. Well, then I'll go get my flashlights out of the car. Let's go search the woods."

Describing Ravenswood to any outsider might make the town seem like its own special twilight zone. It was surrounded by trees and separated by trees, like a little island hidden away. The forest around us was large and wide, the makings of the Blue Ridge Mountains. But the woods in the center of town were densely packed, perfect for weekend hikes and, apparently, things that go bump in the night. The woods were about five to seven miles long, depending on where you started from. But tonight, we would start from the beginning.

I drove the kids back toward the hospital, where we left the car, and made the small hike up in the tree line where Simon initially disappeared.

Along the way, the two filled me in on the rest of the story. The strange video Simon managed to capture of the thing in his dream, their lunchtime argument yesterday—and the fact that he left school early after that. But things still weren't adding up. And it seemed like it wasn't for them either. Lee had never *not* known what a creature around her was, and if this thing was manipulating Simon to this extent, it had to be smart.

"Could it be a demon?" I asked at some point. I noticed Riley shiver and avert my gaze. She was scared, and I didn't blame her. Ghosts were one thing, but demons— *true* evil—well, that was an entirely different story.

As we neared the tree line, I heard a new kind of shuffling behind us. I swiftly turned around and yelled for Riley and Austin to get behind me.

But my flashlight didn't find a ravaging monster, nor a savage beast, or homicidal murderer. It simply landed on a rather winded Miles Allen.

"Miles?" Riley raised her eyebrow. "What are you doing here?" The boy looked between the three of us, his eyes lingering on me. As a mother and a cop, I could tell he was guilty.

"I . . . snuck away. Austin texted me that you guys were coming back here to look for Simon. I want to help. I *need* to help."

"Your dad told me to keep an eye out for you. It's like he knew you'd try this." I almost laughed.

Miles shrugged sheepishly, an expression I'd seen

Walsh do time and time again. "What can I say, he knows me too well."

"Well. I should tell him you snuck out. He's going to be worried sick," I said, watching the poor boy's face fall right before my eyes. His best friend was missing, who was I to tell him he couldn't help? "But he also told me to watch you like you were my own. And Riley is out here, so I guess that means you can be too. Just, stay close to me all right?"

Miles eagerly nodded and grinned at Austin. The taller boy handed him an extra flashlight. *Flirt*. The werewolf knew *exactly* what he was up to when he texted Miles that we were coming.

Within minutes, Austin turned into a werewolf and began trying to gain a scent as we all walked through the woods, looking for any kind of hint we could find, any sign that Simon had been through here—but we found *nothing*. Less than nothing.

Fact: Riley witnessed Simon running into these woods, right here. Fact: we have that proof on the hospital security cams placed in the parking lot and on the awning. Fact: if a human ran through the damp woods, there would be some kind of track—footprints, broken branches, crunched leaves. We were finding *nothing*, as though this piece of land had always been ruled by nature and nature alone. It was like the boy just . . . disappeared.

The night grew colder and our breath slowly became visible as the chilly dew of the slowly rising morning clung to our cheeks and ears. Riley and Miles looked freezing and red-nosed but they still didn't give up, not even as the bags under their eyes grew darker and heavier, refusing to call it a night until the sun rose.

CHAPTER TWENTY-ONE
AUSTIN

Monday

When I stumbled into my house the next morning, the sun was bright in the sky with hot and sticky early morning air for October. I felt sweat trickle down my neck and back as the dogs started barking and running toward me at the door. Denise hadn't come in yet, so I still had a few hours to be on my own.

The only company I needed were the dogs anyway.

As I walked through the giant, empty house, stripping off my sweat-soaked clothes to hop in the shower, they followed my every step behind me. The pack of them had always listened to me, always followed me around, but now it was different. Now, it seemed like they looked up to me. They awaited my commands and walked in a line behind me everywhere I went. Realistically, they didn't even need leashes for walks anymore, but I continued to use them for appearances' sake.

Sophie's small Pomeranian legs ran to try to keep up with me and the others as I climbed the stairs toward my room and bathroom. Bosco, the black Frenchie, always looked back to make sure Sophie was still behind him.

I had to admit, my house was huge. Too big for just me. So every few years, when my parents felt bad about abandoning me, they would ask what I wanted for my birthday, or Christmas, or just when they were feeling extra far away.

"Austin! We're about to board our plane to China!" my mom had said. "We'll be there for a month! And then it's off to Japan for another!" She would stall for a moment, but only a moment. She was the kind of woman who could not (and would not) tolerate awkward interactions. At the slightest hint of an awkward moment, she would spew out nonsense conversation or, in some cases, fill in the gap by loving me in the only way she knew how.

"Would you like anything from there? I know there are a few dog breeds that you've been interested in before!" Her voice trailed on the phone, the airplane attendant on the intercom above her calling for final boarding checks of the staff and crew.

My parents and I never really got along. We didn't *not* get along, but we just never had anything to talk about, nothing to share, as none of us were truly interested in each other's lives.

"Sure, I hear Shiba Inus are pretty good pets and tough to train so I would love to try that."

"Excellent!" I could hear the fake smile in her voice. "Once we get to Japan, I'll look for a cute one! I have to go; Dad and I love you and hope you're doing well. You can call our hotel if you need anything. Bye, sweetie!"

That was a month and a half ago. I hadn't spoken to them since. My mom had messaged me once, sending me a picture of a small, golden-brown Shiba Inu puppy. I guessed I'd be adding one more dog to my pack soon.

I hadn't spoken to my dad in probably five years, save for holidays. He was the opposite of my mom. Where she couldn't handle the awkward silence, my father seemed to thrive off of it. He had no issues sitting in a room with me for hours at a time with nothing to say. He would let it settle in and linger until you felt like *you'd* done something wrong, even when you hadn't done a thing.

At the top of the wooden stairs was my room. The master bedroom of the house. My parents gave it to me when we first moved here. We'd always lived in Ravenswood, but the moment they upgraded houses when I was in middle school, it seemed they had already planned to never stay one night in this giant place. And they hadn't.

All the dogs followed me into the room, some plopping onto the ornate rug, some hopping on the king-sized mattress in the center of the room. I finished removing my clothes, put everything where it belonged, and hopped into the shower.

I turned the valve to make the water as cold as possible, the heat still radiating off of my skin from the night before.

The moment I stepped into the ice-cold water, I felt all of my muscles, sore from the previous night, soften. All the stress and tension in my back, and my neck, subsided and eased. It was incredibly refreshing. I stood under the pouring water and just let it soak my hair and skin for what felt like an hour before washing up. I could have fallen asleep in there if the cold didn't keep me awake.

Last night was one of the hardest nights of my life. Riley, her mom, and Miles were devastated, frantic to find Simon. But the deeper into the woods we got, the more I knew we weren't going to succeed. Normally, I could smell Simon, Miles, and Riley from halfway across town. I was with them so often that their scents acted almost like beacons, small pins in the map of the city. But last night, I could smell Miles, and I could smell Riley. But my Simon pin was nowhere to be found.

I didn't know how to tell them, so I just searched. And I would keep doing that until something came up. Until *Simon* came up.

Something wasn't sitting right with me, though—even if Simon were dead, I would still be able to smell him. Hell, I would smell the body. I smelled Addaline and Beth before I got the calls from Riley on both occasions. With Addaline, I assumed it was an odd-smelling animal carcass. But with Beth, I recognized the smell. I knew it was the ghoul.

But this time, I couldn't smell a body. I couldn't smell Si. It was just the same old Ravenswood scent.

Miles, Riley, Alice, and I trekked through the woods, from the hospital to school to Simon's house and back. I had come to the conclusion that I would go out searching again tonight, school be damned.

Right now, Simon was the most important thing. I couldn't bear Miles and Riley's faces after we came home empty-handed. I couldn't stand the idea of Simon out there and alone. And I was the one most likely to catch a scent, maybe even find him.

I stepped out of the shower, full of resolve. I looked in the mirror and noticed the dark circles under my eyes from dealing with everything last night; my banged-up nose from where Simon punched me was almost totally healed except for the cut on the bridge.

I dried off and threw on the nearest pair of sweats. As I flopped on the bed, the dogs scuttled to make space for me. Sophie's fur felt soft against my face as she curled on the same pillow as me. Bosco became a tiny ball between my knees. Cali, the golden retriever, lay at my hand, nudging herself under for some pets. Cosmo and Wanda, the two shepherds, rested at my feet.

I felt myself drifting off to sleep, as the only sound around me was the whirling of the fan and the hot breaths from the dogs.

I'll go out to search again, I told myself, *after I just take a little nap.*

I ended up sleeping for nearly eight hours. The day had all but flown by, the dogs left me to my deep, much-needed slumber, and I awoke nearly an hour before sunset.

Denise had come over probably moments after I closed my eyes and had prepared food for me after she spent the day organizing the house and doing regular Denise things. I ate a hearty meal—pork chops, spinach, and mashed potatoes—before coming up with some excuse as to why I wasn't going to be home that night. I told her I had a really big test for school the next day and that my plans were to squeeze in a final study session before the exam came.

"Shouldn't you have been studying instead of sleeping all day then?" She had her hands on her hips and seemed more like my mom than my mother ever had.

I didn't really know how to respond to her so I just sheepishly smiled and hoped it would be enough. And it was.

I wasn't her *actual* son after all. We played house, but we both knew what our actual situations were.

I drove toward the hospital again, in hopes of starting my search in the same place Simon had run off. I parked my car in a guest spot and crossed the street, hoping no one noticed me as I climbed up the short, grassy hill and disappeared behind the tree line. I waited, leaning against a tree, for the sun to go down. I wanted darkness before turning into the wolf. The last thing I needed was for a pair of wandering eyes from the locals to catch the abandoned rich kid turning into a monster.

I counted down the minutes, the sun slowly trickling down the horizon, the trees losing the whimsical feeling of getting lost in an enchanted forest and instead being replaced by the darkness of a haunted wood.

I shook my leg in anticipation. Should I tell Riley or Miles I was doing this? Surely, if they knew I was out looking, they would want to be out here too. But if they were here, they would slow me down, cloud up the scent of Simon with their own.

If Miles were here, I wouldn't be able to focus. His sweet smell drove me absolutely mad when I first met him. Every time I got the slightest hint of his scent, I would need to find the nearest bathroom to adjust myself. This eventually turned into me trying to avoid him at all costs, shoving into him to make him afraid of me and stay as far away from me as possible. Of course, I wanted the exact opposite of that.

Apparently, actual wolves can sense their prey miles before they find it, and werewolves are the same way. Only our prey wasn't what we wanted to eat, it was *who* we wanted to be *with*. And my body knew it wanted Miles. It took maybe one conversation to realize that my mind wanted him too.

Though Riley taught me how to control the wolf within, it was taking every ounce of my being to not jump Miles when we were in close quarters, all of my strength to not rip all his clothes off. The heat rose in me just thinking about it.

If he had been here, my mind (among other things) would have been consumed by the thought, the smell, and the presence of him.

I stared at the screen on my phone and decided I would tell them *after* my hunt. I slipped it back into my backpack. The bag was stacked with replaceable clothes and a couple of water bottles and granola bars for the morning. I had to control myself not to eat anything during the night, so I always felt hungry when I became . . . normal again.

It was just about time, the sun was waving goodbye on the horizon and the woods were just dark enough that I could maybe be confused for a large bear. I slipped off my sneakers and shoved them in the backpack, then did the same with my belt, pants, and shirt.

I propped the bag up against a tree, a bit out of sight from the main road, and got ready.

Turning was always the worst. Each time was just as painful and brutal as the first.

I cracked my neck back and forth and tried my best to loosen up, though I knew it wouldn't help.

Here goes nothing.

In an instant, with less than a passive thought running through my mind, I doubled over to the ground. I could feel my fingernails *growing*, turning into claws. Each finger felt like the most painful thing I had ever experienced, but I knew this was just the beginning.

My spine felt like it was twisting underneath my skin, in between the muscle, as it elongated and grew out extra disks and bones that were unique to werewolves to make us longer, nimble, and stronger. I felt the coarse fur burst and grow from the pores on my arms, legs, and then everywhere else, each hair feeling like the prick of a pin as it poked through every part of my body. My limbs grew longer, as my legs broke at awkward angles to make room for new bones to be placed.

I wanted so desperately to pass out from the pain, unable to handle it. I screamed but knew no matter how much I did, the pain wouldn't stop until the transformation was complete. And while it didn't take long—no longer than a moment to anyone standing by and watching the transformation—to wolves, this moment makes it feel as though we slipped into a pocket dimension. A time that only we could feel, where everything around us stopped. Everything but the transformation and the agonizing torture that came along with it.

But the worst part was still coming, and I knew it.

I screamed in agony as my jaw broke from the rest of my face and waited to reconnect after my nose and upper jaw scrunched into a muzzle. My teeth grew through my skull, becoming long and sharp fangs. Turning had to be worse than death, and each time it happened, I felt every single twinge all over again. This time was no exception.

"Fuck," I muttered as the morph finally completed.

I lay on the ground, heaving and trying to catch my breath again. I had fully shifted and was letting all the pain from a moment ago wash away. That was the only saving part—the moment *right* after it all stopped. At that moment, there was a blissful feeling like no other, of total and utter freedom.

I looked down at my clawed hands as they rested against the cold, damp floor underneath me. I breathed, allowing my body to relax, and focused on unclenching each piece of myself. I relaxed my fingers, hands, arms, and shoulders, and did this all over my body.

This act seemed to have almost become a ritual for me. Each time I changed, I felt the need to ground myself. It helped me stay as—well, *me*, and not the wolf I had transformed into it.

After a moment of just *breathing*, I stood up. My height changed drastically when I transformed, I became nearly an entire foot taller and took up just so much more space. I got down on all fours and started searching.

About three hours had passed and it was now fully night. The darkness above took over, but I could still see everything in my path. I hadn't come up with a *single* whiff of Simon, absolutely nothing, and I was beginning to feel disheartened. I didn't see a single deer that matched Simon's description, nor did I smell anything strange around me. Just the normal animals and smells of the forest.

I knew I was running out of time. Halloween was on Friday, which just meant we all had a deadline to find our boy before . . .

But I kept searching anyway. I ran through the woods that lay within the center of Ravenswood. I tried to get as close to the outskirts of the trees as possible before any passing civilian would be able to catch a glimpse of me. I stayed a bit farther from Riley's house, fearing that if I got too close, she would have been able to sense me, vibe to me. And that was the last thing I wanted right now. I searched and searched, the moon overhead being my only indication of the passing of time.

I felt incredibly focused, everything moving out of my way in perfect timing. As the hours passed, however, I felt myself becoming wearier. My body began to slow, and my eyes grew heavy. The strain of seeing so much, so far, in such dark lighting was taking a toll.

And on top of that, the sky was beginning to change from the dark royal blue with bright white flecks of stars, to the light hue of the morning sky. The sun was coming out, and soon my giant wolfish appearance would be a lot more noticeable to anyone passing through the woods on a morning jog.

I raced against the sun back to my bag that lay nestled against the tree by the hospital. Once there, I shifted back into myself. The process was a lot more painless and felt more like a pretty gross shedding of skin, save for my jaw, which still needed to unlock and relock in place after the rest of the wolf peeled away. As hair and claws fell from me, they faded into nothing more than dirt to be added to the forest floor.

Through the extensive research of werewolf movies Simon recommended to me, I found the most similar representation of the transformation to be *An American*

Werewolf in London. They totally captured just how disgusting and painful that shit was. However, no film I saw really, *really* captured what the transformation back to human was like. They always just showed the guy naked somewhere, waking up after the night, or shaking it off to become themselves again.

They never showed the fur that peels off with a simple rub, or the dust it becomes once no longer attached, the only remaining residue of the transformation. Because I had no one to tell me otherwise, I called it "morning ash" since it was like my wolf form was dying away each time I turned back. That was how my time as a wolf had been, figuring it out on my own. Until the Ghoul Gang.

In all honesty, I couldn't even remember who the person to turn me was. I couldn't picture a face, a smell, or a voice. Nothing. I didn't even remember where I was that night, or what led me to be in that situation. I just remembered waking up the next morning, with morning ash laying all around me, and nothing but confusion and fear by my side.

I picked my backpack up off the ground and slowly changed into the clothes I had brought, shoved two granola bars in my mouth, and chugged three bottles of water. After I was all set, I went back to my car across the street, still parked in the hospital parking lot.

I had found no trace of Simon, but I still had a few nights to keep looking.

I turned back to face the forest. "I'll come back tonight," I said out loud. "I promise, Si."

CHAPTER TWENTY-TWO

MILES

Wednesday

I t had been exactly five days since Simon went missing. Five days since that late night in the woods. Five days since I snuck away from my dad's, hiked to Riley's and went searching with her, Alice, and Austin. Four days since my dad grounded me for leaving in the middle of the night while a murderer was on the loose. Three days since my dad took it all back and tried to comfort me as I worried for Simon. Three days since he took his car, off duty, to help me look for him. Two days since everyone at school thought my best friend was dead. Two days since Austin's been in the woods, searching for Simon on his own. And one day since Riley stopped coming to school to find Granny and look for Simon on her own.

I felt useless. Like I was doing nothing to find my best friend. His parents called me almost daily, sometimes crying, to see if I had heard or seen anything that could be relevant. But I had nothing. *Useless.*

Was this how every character in a horror movie felt when facing an unbeatable villain?

I wasn't a werewolf that could fend for myself in the woods. I wasn't a medium who could connect to the supernatural. I was just . . . Miles.

And that had to be good enough for something.

I sat all day today at school just *thinking*.

What can I do? I asked myself.

Austin was the brawns, Simon the heart, and Riley the power. I knew in my gut I was the brains.

I had to be the one to find out what this ghoul was. I knew based on my countless hours on the internet I'd be able to do this.

Years ago, before I moved to Ravenswood, back when I was the king of my apartment complex in Brooklyn, I had found out there was a ghost living in the apartment with us. My dad thought it was my imagination and my mom pretended to believe me. But I knew it was real.

The ghost was that of an elderly man. I found out he lived there two owners before us and died in that apartment. Hell, I found his obituary online. His name was Bill Johnson. He was eighty-seven and died of a heart attack one fateful November evening, totally alone. He was a pretty normal guy, not terribly haunting or poltergeist-y in any way. But a ghost is still a ghost, and it was terrifying to know that I might have been watched at any point while I was home.

I saw his shadow every so often from the corner of my eye. Bill really liked to watch TV, it seemed, as he always appeared whenever it was on, and would occasionally turn it on himself.

So, I spent the majority of my teen years in a house with a ghost.

And then the divorce happened.

My parents hadn't been happy for a long time. But they weren't enemies either. My mom was just a free spirit who didn't like being in a cage, whereas my dad loved the ordinary. He thrived on structure and schedules. He'd lightened up with me, but my parents just could never see eye to eye with one another.

For about six months we awkwardly lived in the

same New York apartment together. My dad slept on the couch and often picked up night shifts at the station. When the news of a promotion came, he couldn't have been happier.

Until he realized that this meant who I would live with was up in the air. I couldn't decide between my parents. I love them both. But my mom suggested I explore something new. The school in Brooklyn wasn't the best and the neighborhood only seemed to be flooding with more bad. But she couldn't leave. She was a born-and-raised New Yorker, didn't know how to drive and didn't want to, went wherever the A Train took her, and lived off street hotdogs and too-greasy pizza. My mom would never part from the city, just like the city would never part from her.

But there was something about growing up in New York that the movies don't tell you. The winters are too cold and the summers too hot, it smells, the people are *always* rude, and you pretty much always gotta watch your step. So I decided a new adventure may be worth it.

After moving, my dad and I hated it at first. I remember I couldn't sleep for weeks because of how silent it was in comparison to the always-awake city. But as time went on, only I hated it. He had gotten suspiciously close to Sheriff Silverstone and that seemed to alleviate a lot of the pressure he felt to fit in. Now, Dad loves the quiet life of the suburbs and the comparably slow beat of things in Ravenswood compared to Brooklyn.

My first summer here was dull, to say the least. I didn't adjust until I met the Ghoul Gang. The day I met Simon changed everything about living here. We spent countless nights playing games online together deep into the night, only to see each other a few hours later at school.

It was my first time having a friend group like this. Sure, in Brooklyn I knew the other kids in my building.

We hung out together, played basketball down the street, and sat on the stoops all day until it was time for dinner. But they were friends by circumstance. Not by choice. Not like Simon, Riley, and Austin were.

"Miles, hey." A familiar voice came from behind me in the halls of Ravenswood High. I turned and saw the familiar gleaming smile of Austin. He wore his smiles like a mask—a mask that couldn't conceal the dark bags under his eyes that made them shine an even brighter green and the mess of his dusty-brown hair going in every direction. Every time I saw him lately, my heart felt as though it would lurch out of my chest, and my cheeks turned hot. This time was no exception.

I pressed my lips together as he caught up to me.

"You looked deep in thought. I thought about just letting you go, but . . ." He trailed off and I got even more embarrassed.

"No, it's cool. I'm surprised you're at school. You look exhausted," I said, before realizing how awful that sounded. "Err, I meant—"

"Dude." Austin placed his hand on my shoulder. "It's cool. I think we're all a little washed lately. Were you thinking about Simon or the ghoul just now? I didn't wanna bother in case you were having a brain blast." His mask dropped and became a more authentic look of general concern and fatigue.

I shook my head. "I honestly have nothing. And it sucks." I felt so frustrated with myself. Straight As in school all the time, but I couldn't even figure out what this thing *killing* my best friend was. Austin looked like he wanted to say something—he opened and closed his mouth about three times before he watched his feet as he stepped.

After a few moments of silence, he simply said, "I've got nothing either."

The bell rang to usher students to their next class. As the hallways cleared up, I waved to Austin and turned to walk away. But before I could take more than two steps, Austin gently grabbed my hand. It felt so warm, so tender. His fingers were delicate around my palm as if each finger desperately wanted to be noticed but at the same time were too shy to do so. I felt my face turn hot once again as I looked into those pleading green eyes.

"What if . . . I help you tonight?" Austin's words dripped out slowly as his cheeks turned pink and his ears became strikingly red against his brown hair. His eyes continued to shoot to the floor and back at me.

Why is he so cute?

I didn't know how to respond. Not because I didn't want to—*of course* I wanted to. But because I was afraid if I opened my mouth I would say something really dumb—or worse, tell him that I liked him.

But before I could say anything, it seemed like he had enough of the silence.

"I just feel like I really need a break from hunting, you know. So, I thought maybe I could . . ." He scratched the back of his head, which only made his messy hair messier.

"I would really love that," I blurted out. Now I also stared down at the floor. I saw him adjust his weight on both feet as he rocked back and forth.

"Great!" he said with excitement in his voice, and he cleared his throat. "Um . . . where do you want to go?"

I looked up and saw the eyes of a puppy dog. He seemed excited, but as if he was trying to conceal it all away. He pressed his lips together and it was hard to look away.

I couldn't help but smile at him. "How about the library? I know it's old school, but I just keep finding creepypastas online. Nothing that's been proven to be fact," I said. "They all just seem like stories."

"To be fair, maybe some of them are real. I mean, if I didn't *know* werewolves existed, I totally would have thought it was all bullshit too." He laughed. "But okay.

The library sounds perfect." He paused for a brief moment and looked directly into my eyes now. "It's a date." He smiled brightly and then quickly turned away and jogged down the hall to his class before I could say anything else.

I had a date. With Austin Rhodes. To the *freakin'* library, to figure out what monster possessed—and potentially killed—my best friend. Well, if that didn't make for a memorable first date, then I didn't know what did.

My leg shook the rest of the next class—and the next after that. The minutes ticked by so slowly, feeling like another hour passed within each one.

I didn't want to feel happy right now.

Simon was missing, possibly even dead. I knew the cops, other than Alice, thought he was dead in the woods somewhere. Another body to add to the killer's count.

But they didn't know what I knew. They didn't know that the things that go bump in the night, the things they only thought existed in movies and comic books, were all real.

I knew in my gut that Simon was alive. That wasn't what I was worried about. I was worried *for* him. Would he come back the same, would he still be himself? Halloween was in just two days—no, a day and a half now. And we still didn't even know what this thing was.

I remembered Granny's warnings. Replayed them over and over again in my head.

He was once two, but now he is one.

My math notes were cluttered all over with numbers and letters, with this phrase scratched all over.

THE QUADRATIC FORMULA IS TWO BECOMES ONE = X.

I hated messy notes, but my mind needed to see it on paper to understand, and this was the only thing in front of me.

Granny had explained that the ghoul was once a human, now a spirit. But it wasn't a ghost, because if it were, Riley would vibe to it.

On top of that, the ghoul had some kind of *Nightmare on Elm Street* thing going on. It possessed people by their dreams, not by physically being there.

The thing wanted to possess Si, because it was in a weakened state and would "make its move" on Halloween when it was strong enough to do so. So, if it already had Simon, what was he doing with him?

I felt like I was wracking my brain—the more I thought about it, the more strained I felt. I kept trying to let it go, focusing on the equations in front of me, but the words "He was once two, but now he is one" continued to drift through my mind.

Eventually, the day finally came to an end. The bell rang and everyone was getting up to leave their classes. As I gathered my things and left the room, I glanced down at my phone to see if Austin had texted me where, or when, to meet up. But he hadn't. I continued to look as I left the room when I felt a tap on my shoulder. Austin was propped up, leaning back against the wall, waiting and smiling.

He slouched off the wall in such an effortlessly cool way, as was everything Austin did.

"Do you need to stop by your house before the library to get anything? I thought we could go to a café beforehand too. I figured it's gonna be a late night, with lots of coffee."

I blushed again. The way he phrased everything, the air in his breath, he made this feel like a real, genuine date and not a monster-hunting mission.

"Yeah, if it's okay of course. I'd like to pick up my

laptop. Don't want to be cluttering the library's computers with murder history and vampire lore." I laughed.

Austin smiled brightly at me and chuckled. "If they only knew, right?"

The two of us left school and jumped into his navy-blue sedan, which was this year's model, and still had the smell of a new car. The first time I asked about it, he said his parents bought it for him for his birthday and then quickly changed the subject. Austin didn't talk much about them, even though he had said they were close.

As I got into the car, I fumbled with my too-big bag and books and struggled to latch the seatbelt on. One of my books slid off the other and fell to the floor and I struggled to pick it up.

"Here, let me," Austin said as he, once again, effortlessly reached down, picked it up, and swung it in the back. He looked at me for a second longer before tilting his head. He chuckled again, and I wasn't sure why. I looked down at myself and the pile on top of me, feeling embarrassed all over again. I tried to quickly grab the seat belt to put it on, and then organize myself, but Austin reached in front of me. His arm was well-defined. Muscular with veins protruding in all the right spots. Austin reached around me and pulled on the seatbelt, snapping it in place.

"There you go." He smiled. "Here." Austin grabbed my books off my lap and placed them on the floor behind my seat, then grabbed my bag and rested it in the backseat.

"Comfortable?" His chest was turned toward me, one arm resting against the steering wheel as the other was propped up against the armrest between us. My eyes couldn't help but wander to his corded arms, the way they almost glistened in the afternoon sun.

God, I am so gay, I thought to myself as I nodded in Austin's direction. He threw another warm smile at me before adjusting in his seat and starting the car.

We drove to my house while having a casual conversation about life and classes, forgetting the impending doom over our heads. It was a quick pit stop; I hopped out of the car and ran inside, threw my school books on the couch in our living room, ran to my room and grabbed my laptop and charger, tossed it into my bag, and ran back out.

Dad was at the station again. He had worked pretty much all day, every day since Simon disappeared. He was definitely as worried as I was. My only solace was that I knew Simon was a fighter, and I knew the ghoul wouldn't strike . . . *yet.*

I got back into Austin's car, the engine still running as I slid into the front seat again, and put the bag at my feet. This time, I buckled my own seat belt before Austin had the chance to. He was watching me when I looked back up at him. I sheepishly smiled. Austin smiled back.

"So, the café? There's one right next to the library," he said as he started driving toward our next destination.

The drive was quiet. Austin was playing some music but I felt my mind wander to the ghoul and all of the possibilities it could be. I thought back to the idea of the ghoul possibly being a skinwalker. Simon had said no but . . .

"What's on your mind?" Austin's voice crept in and brought me back to the car, the passing trees, the low music. I glanced at him as his eyes darted from me to the road and back to me again. His face expressed something softer than worry.

"Just really want to figure this all out."

"You don't have to do it alone, ya know?" he said, his voice cheeky as he threw me another of Austin Rhodes's signature bright smiles.

Each time I saw it, it was like a mirroring effect, I couldn't help but smile too.

"I know." I sighed. "I just feel a little . . ." I paused.

Austin didn't speak. He waited for me to finish, letting the awkward silence build until I was forced to continue. "I feel a little useless in the group." I looked away, avoiding eye contact at all costs.

"Well, you're not," he said without hesitation, causing me to turn back to him. "Miles, you're incredibly smart. You've been holding us all together *and* you've been the only one trying to figure this all out since day one. You're Simon's best friend," Austin gave me a reassuring smile.

I felt a twinge down my spine. Was this hope?

"We're going to figure this out. We're going to save Simon," he spoke as if there wasn't a doubt in his mind. "And I'm here. Bounce your ideas off me, no matter how silly they may sound. Don't get stuck in your own head." His green eyes were shining back at me. "We're going to find him," he said again, assuredly, nodding ever so slightly.

I let his words sink in as I deeply inhaled. *We* are *going to find him*, I told myself. I smiled at Austin. "You're right. We are."

After a few windy roads and soft music playing with fluffy lyrics, Austin and I arrived at the coffee shop. We both ordered our drinks, and as he waited to pick them up from the barista, I chose an open booth.

I placed my laptop on the table and started searching for skinwalkers again. Something in my gut told me that this was at least the right starting path, and maybe it was just Simon's words echoing through my head, his anger at the idea of himself being a skinwalker. But that made me even more curious.

As I read, the puzzle pieces were beginning to line up, but something still felt . . . off. As if I were forcing two pieces that didn't *quite* match to fit together. But I figured this was as good of a lead as any, and maybe it could take me to a different ghoul.

The clank of the mugs on the wood tabletop snapped

me back from the computer as I watched Austin carefully place the second mug down, then a muffin and croissant next to it. Austin glanced to the empty side of the booth and back to me. He hesitated a moment before he slid in next to me. I felt the warmth radiating off of him against my arm and leg. He turned to me, and our faces had never been so close before. He had the smallest acne scar on his cheek under his left eye but was perfect other than that.

A small imperfection on a relatively perfect boy.

Finally, my eyes raised to meet his, and the jade greens were staring right back into mine. I could feel his light breath on the tip of my nose and the cupid's bow of my upper lip. I saw as his eyes glanced from my own, to my lips for the briefest moment, and back up again. I wanted to study his light pink lips so bad, my eyes nearly drifted on their own fruition, but just before the temptation consumed me, I stopped. I held his gaze for a moment longer, my heart racing. *What's happening?*

But then he slouched back into the booth, clearing his throat and turning away. I saw the faintest glow of red on his cheek and the tips of his ears. He began rapidly shaking his leg and flexing his hand and fingers open and closed.

For a moment, I thought I caught a glimpse of fingernails becoming like claws.

"Thank you for the coffee, by the way. You really didn't have to get it," I said as I reached for my own and placed it in front of me.

Austin smiled while still not looking at me, "Nah, I wanted to." He glanced around the coffee house before uttering, "I'll be right back. Gonna run to the bathroom."

I nodded, happy for the chance to calm myself down.

I rapidly pulled out my phone and started texting Simon.

ME: I THINK AUSTIN AND I JUST ALMOST KISSED

Until I remembered I couldn't.

I sighed heavily, locked the phone, and tossed it across the table, away from sight. I needed to find him.

It was more than a few minutes before Austin came back, but when he did, he was totally himself again. Smiling brightly as he squeezed in next to me. He lazily picked up the muffin and took a few bites while looking over my shoulder at the screen.

"So, what have you found?" His voice had an edge I hadn't heard before. It sounded serious as if he were a business executive about to cut a deal. It was hot.

"Well . . . not much honestly." I began to scroll through the websites and tabs I left open. "I originally thought it was a skinwalker."

"Right. I remember Simon flipping out at that. And they're shapeshifters, right?"

"Yeah. But something feels off. It's the best lead I got, but I don't think it's the answer. My gut says it's wrong, ya know?"

"You must've inherited your dad's 'detective gut feelings,' huh?" He laughed.

I had never thought about it before, but in a lot of ways, I found I deduced my research and knowledge the same way my dad used to take on cases when he worked as a detective.

"Oh, wow. You're absolutely right." I cringed. "Just tell me if I end up acting *too* much like my dad, okay?"

"Deal." Austin smirked. "So, if it's not a skinwalker, what is it?"

Now, that was the main question, wasn't it.

"I found this page, it's all about something called 'Not Deer.' Pretty much, it's a thread of a whole bunch of different deer in weird places, doing weird things. The theory is that they're not actually deer at all. But something supernatural."

"Like the skinwalkers?"

"Some people think they are. Others think they're different—*other*."

Austin seemed to ponder this. He tapped his finger against his cheek as his thumb rested below his chin.

"So. What makes these deer Not Deer? Like, how do the people on the thread know that it isn't just a regular deer in a weird place?"

Good point. I stared at the home page of the site, scrolling through entries. And just like that—*brain blast*. My back straightened and I turned to Austin, using my hands to fully express myself.

"Have you ever heard of 'uncanny valley'?"

"Mmmm. I think so, but explain it again?"

"It's like . . . you ever see a movie, and they CG a human? You, as the audience, can tell that something is off. Wrong. But you're not really sure what it is until after?"

"Yeah, they did that to Leia in *Star Wars* didn't they?"

I nodded, thankful for his reference and understanding.

"Exactly like that. The uncanny valley is the degree in which something is *too* human-like, without *actually* being human, leaving observers just feeling uncomfortable about what they're experiencing because they know something isn't right."

"Okay, I'm following. It's *other*." Austin nodded as he took a sip of coffee.

"From my understanding, these Not Deer force an uncanny valley onto their witnesses. The people who see them just *know*." I paused, replaying the ideas in my head. "Of course, I don't know if this actually has anything to do with Simon's ghoul but—"

"It's one step closer," Austin finished as he took another bite of the muffin and then offered me some.

We finished our coffees and snacks and decided to continue the investigation at the library, hoping something could tell us more about the Not Deer and what Simon's ghoul might actually be. The library was pretty much across the street, so we walked and left his car where he parked it.

As we entered, my nostrils were immediately filled with the smell only libraries could produce. The smell of used book pages, old ink, and the millions of doors to other universes and worlds permeated the air toward me. I loved libraries.

"Okay, so what should I be on the lookout for?" Austin asked as he crossed his arms and leaned down just ever so slightly and became eye level with me.

"That is a good question. I think anything with the supernatural, folklore, or cryptids."

"What are cryptids?" he asked, his folded arms naturally pushing his defined biceps outward. "Isn't that a cryptocurrency thing?"

I snickered, "No. They're animals that just haven't been scientifically proven yet. A lot of them are like local folk legends."

"Like Bigfoot?" Austin asked, his head tilting in the most puppy dog of ways. I felt urged to pet his hair.

"Exactly like Bigfoot!" I smiled at him. "I'll go find a spot to set up and then I'll help you look."

"Okay." He flashed one more smile as he turned and disappeared behind one of the several shelves.

I found my usual spot in a corner in one of the vast rooms. This library was huge and had quickly become one of my favorite aspects of Ravenswood. One of them.

I opened my laptop and continued my research as I pulled out my spiral notebook that had all my ghoul and vibe notes. Lots of info about ghosts, even more about werewolves (with a sketch of Austin as a werewolf that I quickly skipped past before anyone around me could see). Finally, at the back rested my notes and theories on Simon's ghoul. It was time to get to work.

CHAPTER TWENTY-THREE
MILES

Wednesday Night–Thursday Morning

A s I walked through what felt like the endless aisles of books, my favorite scent permeating through the air, my hope began to dwindle. There weren't nearly as many books on the supernatural as I would've liked, and many of them were fiction and fantasy-based stories.

I had collected a few, however; one read *Cryptozoology of North America*, and another, more local, *The Carolina Cryptids*. It wasn't much to go on but it was a start. As I made my way back to the table where all my stuff sat, Austin was already there, a large stack of books in front of him and he was already flipping through the pages of one. His gaze was so focused, he didn't seem to hear me coming at all, nor did he move as I crossed behind him to sit on his left-hand side.

"Hey, listen to this. Apparently, one of the cryptids in North Carolina is called the Dogman," he said without looking up at me. Evidently, he had heard me. He pushed the book toward me so we could read on together. Under a chunk of text, there was a drawing that looked eerily familiar.

"When was this published?"

Austin quickly flipped to the front of the book, his eyes scanning the small text.

"Apparently, last year."

"How long have you been a," I lowered my tone and whispered in his ear, "werewolf?"

He cracked a smile as he turned his head toward mine. "A year and a half."

"Well then, it looks like you're famous!" I looked down at the image once again, the eyes of the Dogman were a violent and electrifying green, and the fur was a dark brownish tone. Everything about it resembled the boy sitting next to me. Or rather, the wolf that sat next to me.

"What does it say?" I asked, looking at him once again as his eyes read on, pursing his lips. His jawline had been so defined.

"It says I smell bad," he pouted. "Well, that's rude." He flipped over to the next page. "It also says I am a vicious monster that will eat your children on a full moon."

"Oh my god." I gasped. "That's sick."

"Tell me about it." Austin closed the book and pushed it away. "Did you find anything?"

"Less than you, I think," I said, pointing to the measly two books in front of me.

"Well, I guess we should continue digging." He pulled another in front of him and flipped open the front cover. I did the same.

Austin and I spent hours flipping through a number of books and pages, the sun had gone down and the sky outside was still a royal blue yearning to be navy. I sat back in my chair to stretch and heard a distinct loud *crack, crack, crack* coming from my popping back and fingers.

Austin glanced up at me, tearing his eyes away from the book. "Anything?" he asked while beginning to yawn.

I shook my head and yawned in return. It had been nearly three hours already. And we had absolutely nothing.

"Apparently, we have our own iteration of Bigfoot too," Austin said as he leaned his head against his propped-up arm as he read on. "Their name is Knobby."

"How cute." I pulled the next book close to me and flipped it open.

"How about this?" Austin pushed the book he was reading in front of me. The top of the page read in bold letters **GHOUL**.

"What're the odds?" I laughed.

"Well, apparently, a ghoul isn't the broad term for the supernatural like we had thought it was."

"Yeah, Riley calls them that, so we kind of all just stuck to it. I think she got it from late eighties and early nineties pop culture stuff. I think in 'modern' times it refers to some kind of undead monster?"

"Yeah, that makes sense. I always thought ghoul was just another word for ghost or monster, to be honest. Blame *Scooby-Doo and the Ghoul School*."

I nodded. That was where I had known it from too.

"But it says here that it's of Arabic folklore," he explained.

"What makes you think *that* ghoul is *our* ghoul?" I asked.

Austin smirked and lazily chuckled as he answered, "Well. It's an evil spirit."

"Check," I said lifting my index finger.

"It has a desire for human flesh."

"Check." I lifted my second finger.

"It's ancient. And in some mythology, it *could* change into animals."

I lifted two more fingers.

"However, the animals it changes into are dominantly hyenas, not deer." I lowered the fourth finger. "And it typically resides in cemeteries, which our ghoul is *not* known for."

I dropped my hand onto the table. "I guess we should jot it down just in case. It's similar but something about it still feels . . ."

"Off? I agree."

We both sighed heavily.

"Want me to get us some more coffee?" Austin asked, standing up. He towered over me now, and as he stretched even taller, I caught the quickest glimpse of the bottom of his torso as his shirt rose up. I felt my eyes go wide, feeling extraordinarily hot all of a sudden.

"Ye-yeah. That would be great. Can I get an iced coffee this time?"

"Sure! You do look a little hot." His cheeks almost immediately turned a brilliant shade of hot pink. "I mean warm! Wow, yeah. Okay. I'm going to get iced too. It is extremely hot in here, right?" He began fanning himself with his hand.

"Extremely!" I agreed, and with that, Austin grabbed his phone from the table and left to get us drinks.

After taking a few deep breaths and calming myself down—*god, why is he so hot*—I started glancing at the books in front of me again. I dragged the one I had picked earlier, *Cryptozoology of North America*, and began my search.

One of the first ghouls (our kind of ghouls now) to catch my eye was a cryptid of Kentucky, the Pope Lick Monster. The ghoul was said to live under a bridge, in the forests of the state.

Kentucky isn't that far, I thought to myself. While the whole bridge thing didn't really line up, the way it looked felt eerily similar to how Simon had described his ghoul. Sinister by nature. Though, the Pope Lick Monster looked more like a goat man than a deer man. I jotted it down in my spiral notebook. *Skinwalker, Ghoul*, and now *Pope Lick Monster*. I started making Venn diagrams for each, but there were still too many differences with each creature.

I sighed and continued reading.

A few moments passed by, the wind beating louder against the second-floor library windows. Halloween was around the corner and it was making sure all of the residents in Ravenswood were remembering it was a few days away.

"Hey!" Austin mock-whispered as he walked back toward the desk. "Hazelnut or french vanilla? I wasn't sure which you would like more so I got both." He placed the drinks in front of me. I reached for the hazelnut and took a sip. Austin watched, his head cocking to the side once again. Every time he did this, and it was a lot, I couldn't help but imagine a small golden retriever puppy looking for nothing but approval and love.

I grinned at him. "It's great! Just what I needed." He smiled widely, somehow managing to embody the expression of joy all over his face. His eyes crinkled, his nose lightly snorted—it was adorable and he didn't even know it.

Austin picked up his french vanilla iced coffee (he got us both the largest size available) and sipped it as he plopped into the seat next to me once again. I could feel the prickling cold from the outside coming off of him. It was definitely fall.

"Anything new?" Austin motioned to the books and notes in front of me.

I just simply shook my head. "Unfortunately, nothing fruitful."

"Bummer." He sighed.

We both continued to sip our coffees in silence as we got back to the books. On a number of occasions, I found myself staring at the same words over and over again—rather than actually continuing to read, my mind getting lost in thoughts of the ghoul, of Simon.

I put together all the things Simon has ever mentioned and began jotting them down on a fresh page in my notes.

RED EYES, EATS HUMAN FLESH AND ORGANS (AND SUCKS OUT BONE MARROW), DREAMS THAT LEAD TO POSSESSION, EVIL SPIRIT THAT WANTS A NEW BODY. HE WAS ONCE TWO, BUT NOW HE IS ONE. HE NEEDS A HOST. SIMON IS MARKED, CHOSEN.

I stared at the words over and over again and re-alized none of the things I had discovered earlier fit within this ghoul's description.

Austin lightly nudged at my arm, breaking away the deafening thought that I was still at square one. I looked at him as he held his phone up.

"I texted Riley that we were here searching when I went to go get coffee and she just responded."

"Oh, what'd she say?" I asked. Sometimes, I still doubted whether or not Austin was even into guys. I mean, he had never said it outright, maybe this was all just in my head. What if he was into Riley? What would that mean for Simon and me?

"She said, 'Cool. Out tryin' to vibe to anything I can. Either gonna find this son of a bitch or distract myself until I do. Let me know if you guys find anything. Tell Miles I said hi.'"

"Damn. She's been searching this whole time?"

"Yeah. She's really torn up about this. Don't tell Simon *when* he comes back," he emphasized, unblink-ing. "But Riley is pretty into him."

"Those two need to buck up and make a move al-ready." I laughed. "And my bet is that it'll be Riley."

Austin snickered, nodding his head. "No doubt about that. When this is all over, they better leap into each oth-er's arms. There's no use in wasting so much time."

I nodded in agreement, but I felt as though my heart was falling into the pit of my stomach. Something about his last words jabbed me to the core. If he felt that way, why was he wasting time? Austin had called this a date, and it hadn't occurred to me that may-be . . . maybe we are just friends. Maybe he wasn't into me in that way. Maybe he was straight. If Austin be-lieved that there was no use in wasting time, wouldn't he have already made a move?

I felt myself closing up. I shifted my body back to the table and noticed that it was already getting late and about time I called an end to this fantasy I was living and headed home. "I'm going to put these books back. Can you give me a ride home after?"

"Of course!" His expression changed from joking one minute to shocked the next. His eyes were wide as if he knew something he said bothered me.

I got up without another word and began carrying the books back to the shelves. I kept telling myself I was dumb for thinking this was anything more than a research mission, dumb for telling myself that a guy as hot as Austin Rhodes would like me. I thought back to all the moments in the evening I took for romance and reimagined them, seeing that in each situation Austin may have just felt awkward or uncomfortable. We were just friends, and I needed to remind myself of that.

I had two books left in my arms and was reaching to place one back on the top shelf when light and gentle fingers that yearned to be noticed grabbed it from my hands, lingered a moment, and placed it on the shelf.

I turned around to see Austin, mere centimeters away from me, looking down his nose and into my eyes. I thought the closest I had ever been to him was earlier in the café—this was even closer. Our bodies almost touched, his heat radiating off to me, filling me with warmth. Neither of us spoke, neither of us moved. We just looked at one another. I felt my eyes grow wide and my ears turn hot. He looked, once again, from my eyes to my lips, and back. I followed suit, his soft pink lips already parted ever so slightly, his eyes piercing as they scanned over my face.

The library behind us disappeared, and for that moment it was only us.

I expected Austin to inch forward, or back. But the longer we stared, the hotter his breath felt against the tip of my nose, the longer we stared, the more I smelled the sweet scent of hazelnut and french vanilla wafting between us.

I felt Austin's lips press against my own before I even registered he had moved. His hands drifted up to find perch on my face as he pushed himself into me. I felt the shelves and rows of books against my back, my legs. But none of that mattered.

Austin's lips were soft yet forceful as he slowly parted them and nibbled at my bottom lip to do the same. Within seconds, Austin lifted his hand from my cheek and slammed it against the aluminum shelf behind me, gripping it as he pushed against me even deeper.

I could feel all of him, each crevice and bulge of his muscles, as he held my chin up toward his. I dropped the book from my hand to the floor and lifted my arms around his neck, pulling him in as close as I could. He kissed me deeply, slipping his tongue between my lips without warning, but knowing he was more than welcome. The air between us grew hot as we gasped for breath each time we parted and reconnected. The scent of hazelnut and french vanilla kisses permeated through the air.

But the longer and deeper we kissed, the more aggressive it all became.

I felt the shelves digging into my skin, as I had been pushed harder into it. Austin was parting for air even less and slipped his hand to the back of my neck, eliminating any space that had been between us. My tongue caught on something sharp in his mouth, with an instant metallic taste, and the muscles that had been pressed against me felt like they were *growing*.

I pulled myself away from Austin, as best as I could, my lips still touching his but no longer kissing. Austin slammed his other hand into the aluminum shelf on the opposite side of me, caging me in with a loud *thump*. He pushed his body back and quickly averted my gaze, shifting his entire head toward his arm as he took rapid, deep breaths.

Austin's arms had grown thickets of hair and his eyes were glowing green. His canine teeth had become razor sharp, and as I felt the small cut against my tongue, I knew it had nicked one of them.

I glanced at Austin's hands that had been barring me in. His knuckles were white, looking as if they were about to burst. His claws had grown long and deadly as they punctured through the aluminum.

"I'm sorry," he said out of breath, still keeping his distance. "I'm so sorry."

I wanted to do something. To let him know it was okay. I gave him a few more moments to calm down before I gently kissed one of his knuckles gripping the shelf. And then another. And another. Until Austin's grip began to loosen. His claws slowly retracted. And slowly, very slowly, Austin became himself again.

He looked at me and took a final deep breath in. "I'm so sorry." Austin's eyes dropped. His forehead was covered with sweat. I knew how difficult it had been for him to control the wolf.

I took a step toward him, finally separating myself from the library shelf, and placed my hands on both of his cheeks. Austin's gaze shot toward me, his eyes nearly watering as I lifted myself up onto my tiptoes and kissed his head.

"It's okay," I said finally. "I actually kind of liked it." I felt bashful, silly saying it, but it was the truth. I laughed to ease the tension as Austin's eyes grew wide, realizing he was being accepted.

"Next time, we can maybe try taking it a little slower."

"Next time?" His voice sounded like he couldn't believe the concept of a next time, not after what he had done. But I hoped, more than anything, that there would be a next time.

Austin's face changed a number of times before he finally smiled warmly and looked at me, placing his hand against my cheek once again. "Next time, we can take it slower."

As I reached down to pick up the book I dropped on the floor, the title of another book caught my attention, *Algonquian Legends and Folklore*. Under the words on the spine was a hand-drawn logo of a stick-figure man with antlers. It reminded me of cave drawings I'd seen in textbooks.

"I'll put these away and take you home?" Austin said, pulling me from fleeting thoughts as he gently took the book from my hand.

I nodded. He left down the hallway, his face and ears still a bright pink from moments before. Once he had turned the corner, I gently touched my lips, smiling at everything—*everything*—that had just happened.

I went back to the table and gathered my things. In moments Austin returned to my side, still flustered, and sipped my hazelnut iced coffee to completion as we left the building.

We got back into Austin's car across the street, the café lights all turned off, the door locked, and not a soul in sight, only the bright reflection of the large library windows illuminating us.

Austin unlocked the car and we both slunk into our seats, our expressions wildly different than when we had arrived. I felt myself grinning from ear to ear and knew it wouldn't go away, no matter how much my cheeks were beginning to hurt.

As we drove through the dark streets of Ravenswood, we spoke about anything and everything. Music, books, TV shows, each of us slowly picking apart the puzzle that was us.

"So, why were you so weird when we first met?" Confidence trickled through my voice. I no longer felt scared to ask questions that could've been seen as awkward, not after the person I was asking stuck his tongue down my throat just moments before. I smiled at the memory.

"I-I told you guys, remember? I couldn't control it and . . . I was hungry?"

"Why did that sound more like a question than an answer, hmm? What about *me* smelled sweeter than everyone else?" I turned in the seat.

Austin cleared his throat once again and started adjusting in his seat.

"W-Well . . ." he stuttered. Austin's eyes shifted to mine for the briefest moment. "I wasn't hungry. You *do* smell sweeter and stronger than anyone else. But it's not . . . a physical scent."

"Huh?" Now I was the one cocking my head to the side. For a moment, I felt slightly offended.

"Lemme explain. So, I don't really know how or why but apparently specific people stand out to specific wolves—more than others. I smelled something on you that first day of school when we walked past each other in the hall. And each time I ran into you, the scent only grew stronger. Every single time I saw you," he dropped his head back against the headrest and looked out the windshield down his nose, "I would feel my heart ready to leap out of my chest. Each time, I felt my blood pumping through my veins. I just wanted to—" Austin glanced at me. "Well, now you know what happens when I get . . . excited."

I flushed.

"Basically, the wolf knows who I will want to be with before my mind even has a chance to register it."

"And it tells you by smell?" I raised an eyebrow.

"Yes. I know, it's weird. But I smelled you, and each time I smelled you the wolf in me wanted to come out.

I thought if I was mean, maybe you would steer clear. A lot of it was me just trying to get away from you as fast as possible before the wolf came out. But it was also so hard to stay away. Which was why I aggressively bumped into you all those times."

"So . . . what do I smell like?" I asked slowly, my curiosity peaked.

Austin broke into a laugh and looked at me, his face contorting with the second-largest smile I had seen all night. Without hesitation, he said, "Hazelnut and cinnamon."

Hazelnut. Wow, what are the odds? I thought as I smiled to myself.

"Do you, um, know how the scent is determined? I can't imagine I smelled the same *every day*."

"No, you did. Even now. It's still hazelnut with a dash of cinnamon. You're like a scented candle, all the other smells around me drown away—all but yours."

I felt a fluttering in my chest, and my hands get a bit sweaty.

"I think it's my favorite smell."

I had been so distracted by our conversation that I hadn't noticed when we pulled in front of my house. Austin slowly drove the car to a stop and put it in park.

Neither of us moved for a few moments, I felt like my feet had been glued to the floor. I didn't want to leave, didn't want this night to end. The moment I got out of this car, I would no longer know what the status was between Austin and me. I would have to worry about the ghoul again—I would have to worry if Simon was even alive.

As if he was reading my mind, he placed his hand on mine and lightly squeezed. When I looked up to meet his eyes, his were already waiting.

"I know we have Halloween looming over us, but I did *really* have a good time tonight. And I hope—once we get Si back—I hope I can take you on a real date."

He lifted my hand to his lips and lightly kissed just below my knuckles.

"I would love that."

"And hey. You're going to find the ghoul, okay? I just know it. Call it werewolf intuition." He slyly smiled.

I smiled back. "I hope so. Good night, Austin."

"Good night, Miles."

I turned to open the door to the car, slipping my hand out of his. But once the door was open, an impulse washed over me. I quickly turned around and cupped Austin's cheek in my hand, ushering him forward.

I gently and softly kissed his still-too-warm lips.

He wrapped his large hand around my waist, pulling me as much as the car would allow. After lingering for a moment, I pulled apart, a soft bounce between our mouths. Austin's eyes were still closed and as I pulled my hand from his face, they drifted open. We gave each other one more smile before I left the car and went into my house.

I was in bed, under the covers, scrolling through the internet, trying to find something, anything to possibly link me to the ghoul. It was already 2:45 a.m., and I just couldn't sleep. Not with all the excitement from today lingering over me, not with my best friend still out there, lost somewhere in the woods.

When I had gotten home earlier tonight, my dad was eagerly awaiting me. He had known I was with Austin, and he also knew how I felt about the guy.

"Sooo, did anything happen?" My dad was the first person I came out to. And he was the reason I had been so unabashedly fearless when it came to telling people of my sexuality. He had been supportive every step of the way, knew every crush I'd had and supported all of them—except for Craig. But *fuck* Craig.

"We, um—okay, he kissed me!"

"Heyyyy! My man." He gave me the highest of fives.

After we spoke for a bit more, my dad went to bed. His long work shifts had been catching up to him and he desperately needed some sleep. And by 11:30, he was out.

I showered and got ready for bed.

One more day until Halloween, one October Thursday left to try to discover what it was. I tossed and turned for hours, before finally deciding, to put my sleeplessness to good use.

I started recalling the notes I had taken before the kiss. I started typing things into search engines, social media sites, blogs—everything. And now, it was 2:45. I scrolled to the end of the blog post I was on, ready to call it for the night, when crudely drawn images caught my eye. It was then that I remembered the cave drawing on the book in the library. *Algonquian Legends and Folklore*. In the next few minutes, I found myself down a deep rabbit hole of indigenous creatures from Algonquian legends, and one, in particular, held my attention.

The image on the search site was a drawing of a towering yet incredibly gaunt man, standing among the trees at night. The image was dark, the features were poorly conveyed, however, the artist made it seem like its skin was decaying. There was no face, just shadow. But what really dragged my attention were the massive deer-like antlers protruding through both sides of the inhuman man's head.

The post with the picture read: *I saw something like this while hiking a few weeks ago on my trip to Nova Scotia in the woods. I saw it for the briefest second, the blink of an eye. It disappeared but it left a pretty awful feeling in my* gut. I left immediately and haven't really felt right since. I decided to draw it. It looked human but something about it just seemed . . . wrong. It also had these crazy eyes. They were like two red spotlights. I couldn't bring myself to draw them. I don't want this thing looking at me through my drawing. Anyone know what this is?

The note about the eyes pulled me in even more . . . was this it? I scrolled to the comments as fast as I could. A lot of them were bullshit.

Looks like something made by Lovecraft.

Fake.

You would be dead if you saw that.

Some of the comments were better. A few people in the thread mentioned that perhaps it was a Skinwalker. Others said it was some kind of Canadian Bigfoot.

But then I saw a new word, one I had never seen before. *This looks like a wendigo.*

I knew in my gut, before even continuing, *this* was it.

Several of the posts spelled the word differently— windigo, wendigo, windiga, windgo, weejigo. But they were all talking about the same creature. The same ghoul.

The most upvoted post in the comments section read: *It's a good thing you didn't draw the eyes, OP. This looks like a wendigo. They prey on the weak and socially disconnected—often making their prey feel alone. In short, they are cannibalistic monsters of North America that are savage for human flesh. They originate from Algonquian oral legends, and in some beliefs, the wendigo is believed to be a malevolent spirit that wants to possess others by filling their hearts with greed and an insatiable hunger for human flesh. When they possess a human, they usually haunt their dreams in order to drive them and make them weak. Get them to give in to their hunger quicker.*

In other cultures, the wendigo is an actual physical monster that was once human but became altered after feasting on human flesh.

They typically look tall and malnourished, so good job with the art. They also have incredibly sharp claws and teeth, long limbs to better attack their prey, and they are said to smell like death. They typically have red eyes and dried skin that is tightly pulled over their bones. Wendigos only want to eat, and if this thing didn't attack you, you should count yourself very lucky, OP.

EDIT: I mentioned it was a good thing you didn't draw the eyes because many believe that wendigos notice when they are being called for. The more you talk about them, research them, even think about them, the more aware of you they become as well. So don't draw the eyes, because it may just be able to see you through them.

The entire time I read, I felt like I was holding onto my breath. My chest went tight. My joints stiff. I felt like I couldn't move. This . . . THIS was it!

It was clear to me: the evil spirit possesses human, then human becomes the new physical wendigo. *He was once two, but now he is one.* This was it!

Everything in the post, everything, was so perfectly aligned with Simon's descriptions, Simon's condition.

There was a hyperlink attached to the first "wendigo" in the comment. I clicked on it, only to be led to an entire website dedicated to the ghoul. Pictures beyond pictures were leading me to new sources, new information. Everything tying back to Simon's ghoul. The only thing I couldn't find was how to stop it.

Somehow, it was now edging on four in the morning, but it didn't matter. I went to the Ghoul Gang group chat.

ME: I KNOW WHAT IT IS!

Impressively, Riley responded immediately.

RILEY: WHAT?

ME: IT'S CALLED A WENDIGO.

I then attached the links I found.

ME: IT FITS THE PHYSICAL DESCRIPTION SI GAVE US.
IT POSSESSES PEOPLE BY MAKING THEM GO CRAZY IN THEIR DREAMS.
IT ONLY WANTS TO EAT HUMAN FLESH AND IT IS ABSOLUTELY TERRIFYING.
THE REASON GRANNY COULDN'T TELL US THE NAME IS BECAUSE THE MORE
YOU SAY THE NAME AND THINK ABOUT THEM, THE MORE IT CAN "SEE" YOU.

RILEY: WHAT, LIKE FREDDY KRUEGER?

ME: EXACTLY.

RILEY: SO . . . WHY CAN'T I VIBE TO IT? IF IT'S A SPIRIT?

ME: BECAUSE IT ONLY EXISTS IN SIMON'S HEAD RIGHT NOW.
IT'S BASICALLY MASKING ITSELF THROUGH HIM.
I THINK IF WE SOMEHOW MANAGED TO PULL HIM
OUT THEN YOU WOULD BE ABLE TO VIBE.

RILEY: OKAY. HOW DO WE DO THAT?

ME: NO IDEA.

And I really didn't have any idea. I continuously tried to think of different solutions. Exorcism maybe? If those were even a real, helpful thing . . .

ME: I THINK MY BRAIN STOPPED WORKING FOR THE NIGHT.
CAN'T COME UP WITH ANYTHING.

RILEY: ALL RIGHT, NO WORRIES, MILES. GREAT WORK! I CAN'T BELIEVE YOU
ACTUALLY FOUND IT. I AM SO IMPRESSED.

ME: TO BE HONEST, I AM TOO. WHY ARE YOU UP SO LATE?

RILEY: OH, YOU KNOW.

But I didn't know. And she never told me. There were no more messages that night, and as if my body knew I had accomplished my goal, I felt my stress begin to drain, my muscles finally loosening up, relaxing into the plush of the mattress and pillow under me. I had found out what was keeping my friend hostage. Now I just needed to figure out how to stop it before it stopped Simon.

CHAPTER TWENTY-FOUR

RILEY

Thursday

I walked through the woods, my boots crunching the dry fallen leaves below me on the ground. Growing up in Ravenswood had made me accustomed to trekking through the woods more than I did the actual roads. Civilians of the towns found the trees to be a shortcut through town, the braver of the bunch using them to cut their travel time in half. Though most of them didn't see the things I did.

These woods were filled with supernatural creatures. I once felt like there must be a secret portal located in these woods that led to a fantastical world with fairy-tale creatures. But as I grew up in these woods, I realized there was no portal. These woods just *called* to the mysterious beings. They acted like a lighthouse to the wayward ghouls of the world. Ghosts, demons, werewolves, vampires, even leprechauns (those nasty creatures) had all been found in these trees at one point or another.

I took these woods daily to go to school. I followed the trees to the town. And now I followed them to Frank's house, which lay empty at the top of a steep hill, for sale.

Frank was the ghost that had started it all. He was

the ghost I vibed to, revealing my "secret identity" to Miles and Simon. *God,* I thought, *I'm like a freaking superhero.*

Because of that day, Simon had been exposed to the supernatural. Something he once claimed was his life-long dream but now felt more like the biggest regret of both of our lives.

But on that day, I made a promise to a ghost who was simply trying to pass on. I promised to check in on his granddaughter, Rachael, and Riley Silverstein never broke a promise.

It was a crisp Thursday morning. I hadn't slept the night before, and the bags under my stinging eyes were beginning to feel heavy.

I had been wide awake when Miles texted the Ghoul Gang the night before, trying to come up with my own answers for Simon's disappearance and feeling utterly stuck in the conundrum. But then Miles came through and provided the answers we had needed all along. And it fit perfectly.

The ghoul was a wendigo and I couldn't vibe to him because, well, he wasn't really *here* yet. He was inside of Simon, and we needed to figure out a way to pull him out before it was too late, before Simon officially became the ghoul's new host.

I climbed up the steep, mulchy hill behind Frank's house. Rachael's was meant to be just next to it.

As I rounded the top, I saw a small brick house directly next to Frank's log cabin. No wonder Rachael had spent so many evenings at her grandfather's while her parents were at work. They were so close to one another, they could almost be considered the same house, on the same property.

I pulled out my phone to read the time. *Seven a.m. sharp*, I told myself. And just as I did, a small blond bob walked out of the white door that parted the brick wall. Her glittery pink backpack glistened in the sun.

"Bye, love you!" she called inside the house as she closed the door.

Rachael had turned eight years old a few months before her grandfather passed away. Now, she walked to school, which was only two blocks away, on her own because her parents needed to be at work by eight a.m. and not a second later, and apparently walking their kid to school took too much time out of their morning routine to manage. But Rachael only followed her new schedule for about a week before I started showing up whenever I could.

"Hey, kiddo," I said, jogging to catch up to her.

"Hi, Riley. I brought you a banana." This was our morning ritual every day. I walked her to school, she gave me a piece of her breakfast. She never questioned why I started showing up, but she seemed grateful for the company. We would chat about school, her friends. Occasionally, she would bring up Frank. She would tell me stories about him, about the games they used to play, about the snacks he would let her have *before* dinner. And it made me feel even closer to them both, like I really was keeping my promise to Frank.

"How are your friends?" she asked me, her big brown eyes looking up as she peeled an orange.

"They're . . ." I didn't really have an answer. *Possessed. Sleep deprived. Dead?* "They're okay," I lied. "How are your friends? How's that Jenny Merrill been—should I give her another talking to?" Jenny Merrill was the third-grade bully who thought she owned Ravenswood Elementary.

"No, last time was good. She stopped bothering us." Triumph trickled in her voice as she smirked at me. *Oh no*, I thought, *am I a bad influence?*

"But Riley! Oh my gosh! Michael told me he liked me! Ew, right?"

"Yeah, wow, so ew. Who is Michael again?"

"Riley." She stopped mid-stride and placed her hands

on her hips, cocked her head to the side, and gave me the sassiest of looks. "He's only been my bestest friend since first grade! I told you about him! Remember?"

"Oh, of course!" I playfully smacked my forehead. "How could I forget! Wow, so Michael likes you?"

"Mhmm."

"Do you like him back?"

"Ew, gross! Boys are icky."

"Rachael, they are *so* icky. Always remember: boys are icky."

She laughed as we kept walking, her school now in sight.

"You don't have your bookbag again. Are you not going to school?" Kids are always too damn observant. Just when you think you get away scot-free, they come in with all the hard-hitting questions.

"I am, I am. I have to go meet up with someone first though so I'm going in late."

Rachael nodded her head. Apparently, my bullshit lie was enough to soothe her woes.

A short and skinny little boy with a bush of dark brown hair stood waiting outside of the school's main doors. I recognized him instantly, though I had admittedly forgotten his name, and nudged my elbow into Rachael's arm. She looked up and her eyes went wide.

"Do you think he's waiting for me?"

"Probably. What are you going to tell him?"

She thought for a long, hard minute. Michael kicked the dirt at his feet as he saw us walking toward him.

"I'm not allowed to have a boyfriend," she said, matter-of-factly. "But he *is* kind of cute."

I smiled at her—crushes were weird, and boys were icky.

Rachael started to run toward the other boy, which meant our morning walk had come to an end. She paused before she got too far and turned back to me. "Bye, Riley. See you tomorrow! Don't forget your

Halloween costume!" She waved and turned to catch up to her possible future husband.

I waved, my stomach dropping with each movement. Tomorrow was Halloween. Our time was almost up.

I found myself walking through the woods once again, my feet dragging against the dry, crunchy leaves this time. With each step I took, I realized I had no idea where I was going, my feet were taking me all on their own. I wasn't walking in the direction of my house, Ravenswood High, or the town, but deeper and deeper into the woods. The terrain looked more and more familiar with each passing tree. I was nearing a clearing that I had seen before, surrounded by small patches of sprouting lavender plants against the tree line.

"Hello, dearie." A warm and welcoming voice came from the clearing, but not a person in sight. I knew that voice.

"Hello. Did you bring me here?"

"Aye, I did." And suddenly, the gray-blue corporeal form of Granny appeared in the center of the clearing. "I wanted to chat. Just us girlies."

I crossed the branches and bushes of the tree line and walked to the center. While most of the woods were either uphill or downhill slopes, the clearing here seemed perfectly flat, making it comfortable to stand and rest on.

I walked up to Granny and smiled back at her already-warm smile.

"It's almost all Hallows' Eve," she said, her smile fading into a grim expression. "Did the bright boy who smelled of hazelnut discover the beast?"

Smelled like hazelnut? I thought. "Miles? The one you said would discover its name? He did actually. Last night. A wendi—"

Before I could finish the word, Granny threw her ghostly, cold hand over my mouth. One wrinkled and icy finger pressed against my lips as she shushed me.

"Do not speak his name in my forest. That will summon him and I do not want that *thing* anywhere near me." She gently pulled away.

"Okay, sorry," I said, touching my lips, trying to bring warmth back into them. "Well, the *Wendy* already grabbed Simon."

"What?"

"Yeah. The other night. Simon ran into the woods and never came home. You didn't mention that part in your warning."

"Hmm." She didn't look at me but stared at the ground. "Was he wearing the lavender?"

"I mean he hasn't taken it off since—" But then, I thought about it. Was he wearing it? I remember hugging him tightly, crying into his shoulder, worried that he was losing himself to the ghoul. I never felt the bottle pressed against me. I can't remember a spark of purple against his gray T-shirt.

"He needs to be wearing that. That is the only way you will stop the ghoul from consuming him, from *becoming* him."

I nodded at Granny. "I'll go to his house today. I'll get it."

"Good. Good. Take more too. I do not have more of the vials that I gave the boy, but the plant alone will ward the beast. That is why I have them lining my trees here." She pointed to the tree line encircling us. "To keep me safe."

"Was the vial special in any way?"

And suddenly, there was a twinkle in the old woman's eye. "It was. It was *magic*. A rather elaborate protection charm had been placed on the glass. But you already knew that didn't you?"

"Yes, I—wait. How did I know that?" I asked, my eyes darting up to her. She had the same mischievous smile as the day I first saw her with the Ghoul Gang. "And how did you make me . . . *unvibe* to you? Why aren't I vibing now?" I looked down at myself, the heat of life still pumping under my skin. I was my usual pale and not the blue hue of a ghost. I was *alive*.

"Because I willed it to be so. Have you never wondered *why* you had your power, dearie?"

"I-I . . ." But the truth is, I hadn't. "I just assumed . . ."

"I see." She slowly nodded her head. "You thought you were alone?"

I nodded.

For years I felt shame. Fear. I *was* alone in this. No one would really understand what dying and coming back to life was like. No one would really understand the pain of growing vampiric fangs one night and breaking my jaw to become a werewolf the next. No one would ever—could ever—understand the pain of sprouting horns or wings. Only me and my vibes would ever understand, alone.

"Well. You're not." She smiled. "You are special, yes indeed, but not alone, no. Though, I haven't seen a power like yours with my own eyes. I have only ever heard of others. A woman. Long ago, she lived in a faraway place. She took the immortality of the vampire she was in love with, the vampire who kept her as his own. But she could walk during the day. She could feed on any human delight. It was like she took the best part of being a monster and made it her own. You are the same. You walk between the lines. Between the veil. Between the worlds of this and the next."

I thought for a moment, taking in her story. "She was like me?" Granny nodded. "She vibed to the vampire?"

"Indeed. In her own special way. Just how you do so in your own special way. You, my dear, are what we call a Connector."

"A Connector?"

"Yes, but you may call it 'vibes' or whatever you like. But amongst us others, we call it Connectors."

"Others?"

"Yes, dearie." She paused. "I understand this is a lot to take in. But—"

"I want to know. Please." I reached out for her hand. For a moment, before I made contact, I thought that mine would phase right through her. But they landed. And I could feel her cold clash against my warmth. "I've spent my life having no idea what I was. I thought, maybe, it would be hereditary. Asked my mom. But she nor my grandmother had anything like what I have. No magic. No vibes. Just . . . normal. My whole life I fought, tried to force normalcy on myself. But it never took. Eventually, I accepted that I was weird, that I was strange. Finally, I found *my* people. The people who would accept me for who I was— Austin, Miles, and Simon. And I was happy. But I still *want* to know." I placed my other hand on top of hers, cupping her hand with both of mine. "Please."

She smiled sweetly. "All right. Get ready." Granny took a big deep breath in—not that she needed it—and exhaled. "You, my dear, are a witch," she said very matter-of-factly. "And you are correct. Being a witch is dominantly hereditary. In my time, nearly every generation had a witch in the family. My mother was not one, but her mother was, as am I, as were my children. But in your day and age," she scanned me up and down, "magic is weaker. It takes someone with a lot of power to muster up any kind of physical evidence. So while your mother and grandmother *may* have magic within them, it is clouded by the present. Same with the boy who smells of hazelnut. He has—today, you call it *instinct* or a *gut feeling*, but it is more of a third eye. Precognition magic, though weak. It is there."

"So, for me, it's strong enough to be seen? But . . . why me?"

"Magic doesn't choose anyone, dear. It simply *is* and it knows who will make the best use of it, whether good or bad. It knew to lend itself to you." She moved our hands toward my chest and lightly tapped at my heart.

"So I'm a Connector? Is that a *kind* of witch?"

"Oh yes. There are many kinds of witches. You are a Connector; I am a Charmist. I cast charms of all sorts, study different kinds and forms, and execute them to their desired effect. I cannot, however, 'vibe' to any creatures or beasts. I cannot commune with the dead. And I cannot foresee the future in any capacity like the sweet hazelnut lad," she explained. "I was able to stop you from using your magic because I have my clearing warded from other witches with my charms. I am able to thwart your magic in my space with a snap of my fingers." She snapped teasingly.

"How many kinds of witches are there, exactly?"

"Oh, many. And not all witches, dear, are like you and me. Not all have good intent, no. Like with everything, there is a balance. There is a good and there is a bad. And we witches can be *really* good, just as much as we can be *really* bad. Be wary of your own kind. Do not blindly trust just because someone may be the same as you."

I nodded. Of course, there was a bad in everything.

"Now, I will tell you the real reason I have summoned you here. *If* all goes according to plan, and you save your friend from that monster's possession, there is a chance that you will become one yourself."

"I . . . I had a feeling."

"If that happens. You might lose yourself. The spirit of that beast is strong and powerful. It knows nothing but greed. And to become it means to become Greed itself. You will have to fight and you will struggle. You may even hurt your friends in the process."

I gulped.

"But if you use the charm I gave the boy, if you force the monster to consume that charm, you will claim your victory. It will destroy him from the inside out. Lavender is a plant of love, and love will be the death of that creature. It will rot his greed from the inside and turn him into nothing but ash to be swept away in the cold of the night. Remember. It is almost All Hallows' Eve. He will be stronger, but so will you. Control yourself and you will win."

I found my hands gripping hers a bit too tightly and let go. My palms were clammy from the anxiety of it all. There was so much room for failure in this situation, and failure meant the death of Simon.

"And dearie?" Granny's voice brought my attention back to the clearing in the forest. "If you do succeed, which I really hope you do. A sort of . . . *beacon* will light. All of the creatures and witches *everywhere* will know where you are. They will come. This kind of evil isn't taken lightly; the supernatural world will feel its dark presence erase. Do not be surprised if others come to see who has flashed the light from the darkness."

My mind felt heavy. I appreciated all of the information. But it was becoming too much. Do I already have to worry about what happens next before we even save Simon? And then there was the matter of actually *saving* Simon. And becoming a wendigo. I felt my fingers twitch, my stomach upturned. I wanted to throw up.

"Grab some lavender on your way home, dearie. Use some of it to make tea for yourself. I would offer, but my ghostly figure can no longer do such menial tasks." She smiled at me, reached for my hand, and patted it reassuringly. "I know it is all too much, but you can handle it. I don't need to be a Seer to understand that."

"Granny, why are you helping us so much?"

She paused and looked to the sky, smiling at herself. "Because I know what it is like," she finally said. "Remember, this monster consumed my brother. He wore his face for Earth only knows how long. I want to see him pay. I have stayed in this land for a long time, Riley. I cannot leave. If I do, that will be the end of my time here. I knew I was meant to use my charms at least once more. And now, I finally have a reason." She smiled, warmly. Her smile made me feel like she actually *was* my grandmother.

"Why do you have us call you Granny? Is it to hide your real name?"

"Oh, stars no. My real name is Theodosia, quite the mouthful if you ask me. Shows my age, too." She giggled.

"Oh, okay. Granny it is." I chuckled, lightly. I grabbed her hand once more. "Thank you, Granny. Really."

"Of course, dearie. And know that when the time comes, when you think you might fail, I will be there. Remember the lavender and make that tea." Theodosia's eyes twinkled and her spirit faded from view.

PART
THREE

HALLOWEEN

CHAPTER TWENTY-FIVE
SIMON

E verything felt hazy. I felt my eyelids bat open, the lashes tickling my cheeks. But when I opened my eyes, I didn't see *anything*. All that surrounded me was darkness, a pitch so black that I felt like it was more so the absence of life than actual reality. I slowly tilted my head downward to look at my hands, but nothing was there. I couldn't see the hair that framed my face like usual, I couldn't see the tip of my nose, or the rounds of my cheeks. I saw *nothing*.

I knew it wasn't that my eyes were covered. There wasn't any foreign weight against me. It was just me. Looking out into the dark.

I started to panic, feeling my heart thumping in my chest. *Thump, thump, thump*. It was the only sound, other than the gulp that vibrated through my throat and ears alike. Normally, when I was home alone or in an empty room, there was a sort of white noise. A low hum, a soft ring, but now—again—there was *nothing*.

"Where am I?" I said aloud.

"Where am I?" my echo shot back through the darkness again and again until it softened and fizzled to nothing.

I tried to remember what had happened, why I was here. My body moved freely. I could take a step, but should I? What were the odds that this one step might drop me off a ledge? What were the odds that one step could lead me to a state that was worse than the one I was in now?

Once again, I gulped.

The woods.

That was what I remembered. I remembered the woods. Running through them. Leaving Riley in the streetlight's beam in front of the hospital.

As the memory came to me, a spotlight—radiant and blinding—flashed above me, blinding me for the briefest moment. And suddenly, I could see myself. The hair in my eyes, the rounds of my cheeks, the tip of my nose, red from the cold. I looked at my hands, and there they were, regular. Normal. I looked at my feet. I was barefoot, the soles bloodied from running, they were sore and each point of pressure stung, like a million pins and needles shooting through the blisters causing new wounds to burst open—but they were mine. I was stripped down to my gray shirt and boxers, and just as I noticed, I remembered the intense heat that ran through my body as I ran into the woods.

I remembered feeling like I was burning.

I shook my head and looked around me, maybe— just maybe—the spotlight would illuminate where I was.

I looked at the ground and saw the wet muck of leaves clinging together, the mulch packed tightly. I took a deep breath in and immediately recognized the smell. It was the woods, but not the woods that circled Ravenswood. These were the woods from my dreams. These were *his* woods. This was *his* spotlight. So why, now, did it shine on me?

I took a step forward.

Nothing happened.

So I took another, and then another. The spotlight followed me.

"Hello?"

Nothing.

"Where are you?!" My voice rose in anger.

But still, nothing came. I took another step forward, and then another. I walked through the trees, the black barks thick and smelling overly ripe. I touched my hand to one, resting for just a moment. But as my palm made contact, it *seeped* through the wood. *Gush*. It felt sticky yet thick, like pressing against a bad peach. It got all over my hand as I quickly pulled away. The tall tree sagged a bit as it got used to its new welt on the side.

I kept walking.

The forest was silent. No birds, animals, bugs, nothing. Just me and the crunching of the leaves beneath.

Everything felt hazy, unsettled, as though it were waiting for . . . something. It felt like the forest was asleep, and at any minute it would open its eyes and roar to life.

"Hello?" I called again, but this time in less than a whisper. I knew I was alone. I knew these woods were endless, and if I kept walking, searching for a way out, I would be walking in the same circles, forever.

After another minute, I saw a large rock by my side in a kind of clearing. I placed my hand against it, to make sure it was solid and not fruit flesh like the trees, and when my hand came in contact with the cold, hard surface, I took a deep breath in and out. *Finally*.

I sat on the floor and rested against the rock. Like the woods around me, I found myself waiting.

I felt my head jerk up, I hadn't even realized I fell asleep. My breath caught as my eyes focused on my surroundings. Dark trees towered over me, the cold of the rock still stiff against my spine. I was still in the woods, in the ghoul's world. But I no longer felt alone.

Standing up was harder than I thought it would be. I leaned against the rock and tried to take most of the weight off my feet. My calves and thighs were sore and my entire body felt as though it was only running on fumes. But my body and mind dragged me somewhere deeper into the trees.

In the dreams I'd had recently, my mind always knew when to be afraid, even before I did. My heart would race, my palms would get sweaty, and my breath would hitch. But right now, I felt totally calm. As if there was *nothing* in this world to be afraid of. I limped deeper into the darkness, my feet guiding me on their own. I didn't know where I was going, but I knew it was the destination I was *meant* to go in.

I slowly progressed as I limped past trees and trees. Each step felt like I was going in the right direction, with the spotlight still above me, following me, watching me. But the closer I came to my destination, the dimmer it became. The darkness behind the trees began to lighten, shifting from the darkest of black to charcoal, and then to a shadow and finally slate. Were my eyes just adjusting, or was there light ahead, some kind of break from this nightmare?

Beyond a circumference of trees, I saw the small glimmer of a tiny, dancing flame above a white, waxy candle. The spotlight was all but gone, and with each step, it was as though I was breaking the chain that bound me to the blinding light.

And suddenly, I felt invisible. The tingle that had been running down my neck since I found myself here was gone. It was only now that I realized I was being watched the entire time I was here, the ghoul's vermillion eyes that had been stained behind my own were no longer there, no longer watching.

As I took another step, I saw another candle. And then another. The darkness of the sky had become more like a mist of fog as I entered the clearing. It was bright against my eyes, but still gray.

Almost immediately I recognized the circle I stood in, the trees pushed far back to allow a large and flat area where bright brown dirt had been packed into the ground.

This was Granny's clearing. And the ghoul couldn't come—or see—here.

I got to the center of the glade and looked around me. It was barren but felt utterly safe.

"Hello, dearie."

I turned and saw Granny, floating in the air at eye level with me. She smiled warmly and I got to see the color on her face.

She wasn't transparent here, no blue glow against her. I saw the color of her pale green eyes, the wild gray of her curled hair, and the rosy cheeks under her pale skin. She kept her smile as she moved a bit closer.

"I figured you would be here. They all have come here, at one point or another," she said, the twinkle in her eyes diminishing as her words carried.

"Who?" I asked stupidly. It had felt like forever since I had human contact; I felt as though I had forgotten how to properly speak.

"The others he has chosen over the years. They all get stuck here." And she gestured to the woods around us.

"Are they still here?"

She stayed quiet for a moment and looked at me hard before finally exhaling and nodding her head.

"Yes. Those poor dearies. They wander into my glade every so often, much as you did now. But most of the time, they are lost in the darkness of the woods, I'm afraid. He watches them, you see. Makes sure they can be found whenever he needs them."

"He's still feeding off them." It meant to come off more as a question, but something in me simply knew.

Granny nodded sadly. "Aye, he is."

We stood for a moment in heavy silence.

"They are what led you here, to me," she said, raising an eyebrow. "They saw you asleep in those woods. They know you still have a chance, one they never got. They want to help you."

"They do? But how? I'm stuck here."

As she began to speak, black shadows from the woods crept through the tree line. The figures turned from hollow nothings to actual people—some old, some young, and each looking as though they were from different times.

"You are stuck. For now. But your friends will uncover how to help you. I have already met with Riley and offered the most advice I can give. They have discovered what the beast is. They are coming to try and save you, Simon. Do not lose hope."

The other spirits stood next to Granny now. She was protecting them. And she saw me watching.

"The beast may have created this place, but it is no more than a reflection of your world. He has made a replica of the woods you know. But there is only so much, and instead of drifting into a hollow version of the rest of the world, it simply repeats itself, endlessly. By making a replica of the woods in Ravenswood, he accidentally made a reflection of my glade. A safe zone. It is where these souls can come to hide, even if for just a bit."

"Why don't they just stay here?"

"The lavender. He hates it, it hurts him. And because they are a part of him now, it bothers them as well. They can only stand it for so long."

I studied some of their faces, most seemed uncomfortable while some even looked pained.

"Help," came a small voice to my far left. It was a child—couldn't be older than ten. He has an uncanny similarity to Granny. The shape of his eyes, the crinkle of his nose. *Was this her brother?*

"We," came another voice to my right.

"To."

"Want."

The different faces around Granny kept repeating the words, individually, over and over again. It was out of order, but I knew what they were saying. *We want to help.* I looked at the faces and painfully smiled. There had to be at least four dozen faces staring back at me. He had killed all of these people over the years.

"Addaline and Beth would be here as well. But you were able to help Addaline escape. And she found Beth before she was stuck here like the rest."

"But Addaline became a banshee? And made Beth one too."

"They died a horrible, gruesome death. Their spirits were consumed by rage. Addaline's rage spread to Beth when she saved her."

"I killed them."

"No, boy. You did not. *He* did. Remember that," she said, sternly. "These spirits would not stand in front of you as they are today if you killed them. They know it was not you. The banshees will aid you in your battle, as will I, as will they." She waved at the rows of people around her, their sad faces staring back at me. I found myself gulping before I nodded in their directions. Losing hope was worse than admitting defeat. Loss of hope—that was the real killer.

"Can I stay here? With you?" I asked Granny. I wasn't ready to brave the dark again. Not yet.

She smiled at me sweetly, sadly. "Of course, dearie." The figures around her already started to float back into the tree line, away from us, back into the darkness. Some stuck together, while others floated alone.

"How long have they been stuck here?" I questioned, more to myself, after the last one completely faded from view.

"Oh. That's a large question. Some have been here for years, others centuries."

"How long have *you* been here?" I looked at her, realizing that maybe my question was a bit too invasive.

"Oh, not much longer than you." She gave me a sly smile, a mischievous twinkle in her eye. The same look my mom had whenever she lied and claimed she was thirty-eight, *again*.

I chuckled and hearing the sound of my own laugh sent a burst of warmth throughout my entire being. *I'll be okay.*

"Do you know how long I've been here?"

Granny placed her hand on her chin and looked to the ground thinking. "To you, it probably has only felt like a few hours, less than a full day. To the outside, you've been missing for almost a week. It's All Hallows' Eve today."

A week? And just like that, my heart sank again. My poor parents must be worried sick. Where did they think I was? Did they think I was dead?

And what was worse, today was Halloween. Today was the day *everything* was supposed to go down. Today was the day the possession would be completed, which meant if the Ghoul Gang failed to pull me out of here, to save me from the ghoul, I would be stuck here *forever*.

I gulped.

"They'll come, Simon."

"But how do we beat this thing?" I rubbed my palms against my eyes until I saw a rainbow of dark colors bursting under my eyelids and dragged up my hands, pushing my hair out of my face with my fingers. I scratched my head a few times before I dropped both arms back to my sides. I turned to Granny whose expression was unreadable.

"You didn't wear the lavender."

I touched my hand to my chest, where the echo of the vial rested against my neck.

"I know. I messed up."

"I sent Riley to retrieve it. It will save you."

"But how? Magic?"

"The magic in the bottle will ward him. The plant will *kill* him."

"What, he's allergic?" I asked sarcastically.

"Sort of." She smirked, then her expression changed to one of complete seriousness. "It *will* kill him. But only if he *eats* it. Make sure he does that."

I pondered for a moment. So if Riley was bringing the lavender, then all we had to do was *somehow* feed the lavender to him. But all he ate was . . . people. And then there was the dilemma of me being totally stuck in here. How could I get him to eat it from here?

"Is there a way out of here?" I asked her, exasperated.

"Riley will do that part. You just figure out how to make him eat."

I nodded and then sat against the cold dirt on the floor. Time for more waiting.

CHAPTER TWENTY-SIX
RILEY

I woke up filled with dread. I considered going back to sleep, sleeping through the day and into the next. Sleeping through today would make today nonexistent. Nothing bad would happen, it would just be a regular, sleep-filled Friday, and I would wake up tomorrow and everything would be normal again. Right?

I sighed heavily and rocked my body up to sit on my bed.

Today was Halloween, today we would either save Simon or lose him forever to the Wendigo.

As I took the covers off of me and climbed out of bed, I spotted the small vial of lavender sitting on my nightstand. I had gone to Simon's yesterday, claiming to be there to see how his parents were doing. I tried to assure them we would find him, the words feeling vile on my tongue. They smiled at me, sadly, and they hadn't seemed to be doing too well. In only a week, Simon's mom had lost weight. The bags under her eyes were heavy and dark, and she had broken out around her chin. His dad looked tired and worn and seemingly gained a cluster of gray hairs. Both of their eyes had been bloodshot and tear-stricken. It had clearly been a hard week.

As I made my way up to Simon's room, I felt ashamed.

I felt as though I was invading something private. I had never been in his room, and though I was sure he would be more than welcoming, without him here it felt as though I wasn't allowed. I knew I would someday be in this room, but in my head I had always pictured Simon there, grinning like a Cheshire cat, from ear to ear. I had gently touched my fingers to the I Believe alien posters and against all the camera equipment by his desk. I picked up his journal that had *Ghoul Gang* scrawled on the cover in thick black marker.

It all made me feel as though he was still here. That he would burst into the room with all his warmth, carrying glasses of water or a tray of food, at any second.

I stared at the door, but no one came.

I looked around again, searching for the hint of purple until my eyes caught on something hung on his bedpost by where his head would be. The vial lay still, resting and waiting.

Somehow, this *thing* was going to save Simon. I grabbed it from my nightstand and threw it around my own neck, for safekeeping, while I got ready for the day.

That first day the Ghoul Gang met Granny, we had all talked about what we wanted to be for Halloween. And though I knew Simon would be a little disappointed that I wasn't dressed as Hannibal Lecter when I went to save him, I just hadn't had the time to get the costume. I was exhausted, my entire body ached, I hadn't slept for more than three hours a night, and I could feel the sting each time my eyes closed.

But today was the day.

I put on black jeans, black boots, and a black sweatshirt. While at Si's house, I saw a worn black hat that sat lazily on the floor. It said, "I'd rather be ghost hunting." I had picked it up and taken it with me with the lavender. It smelled like him, and I thought maybe his scent would come in handy for Austin.

But really, I just wanted it to feel like Simon was still with us. Like he was a part of this fight with the Ghoul Gang. With me.

I put the hat on.

I threw on some dark makeup, around my eyes and lips. My warrior makeup, as I liked to think of it, gets me through each vibe. It masked the bags under my eyes and covered how chapped my lips were.

I looked at myself in the mirror. The all-black attire made me seem even paler and made me look like a ghoul myself. I tugged the hat down a bit more and opened the door to my room.

As I descended the stairs, there came a loud knock from the front door. I reached the bottom and fluidly opened the door. Austin stood on the other side. He wore a big green jacket, brown boots, and black jeans. His nose was, thankfully, perfectly healed. He had a hockey mask in his hand. He studied me for a moment and then smiled widely at the hat as he walked past me into the house.

"Morning. Nice hat."

"Nice costume."

Austin looked down at himself sheepishly. "I mean, it *is* Halloween. Where's your costume?" After a moment of raising my eyebrow at him, he continued, "Simon is gonna be pissed when he sees that you're not celebrating."

"I'll apologize."

"With a kiss?"

I punched Austin in the arm. This wasn't the first time he mocked my . . . slightly-more-than-friends feelings for the new kid.

"Oh. Speaking of kisses. Um . . . I kind of kissed Miles the other night."

"What?! Really?" I smiled. These two dorks had been swooning after each other for months now.

Austin blushed and scratched his head. "Yeah. It . . . kind of just happened."

"How was it?"

"Great! Um, until I almost ripped his clothes apart and ate his face off."

I felt my face frown. "Wait. You had me in the first half. What was that about eating his face off?"

He scratched his head again, this time with sheer and utter embarrassment. I could almost see the tail between his legs in shame. "Well, I got a little . . . excited? And . . . the wolf *really* wanted to come out. But it's fine, we're fine, he's fine. We kissed again later. We're going to take it slow."

"Ease the dog into it."

He nodded.

"Well. Congrats on not eating your boyfriend's face off and finally growing the balls to make the first move." I snickered.

"Ah, shut up." He smirked.

After a moment of light laughter, another knock came at the door.

"Speak of the devil," I said as I spun to open it. On the other side stood a slender figure, a bit taller than me, wearing a dark blue jumpsuit, a Michael Myers mask, and a plastic kitchen knife raised in his hand.

"Happy Halloween!" Miles said, his voice sounding far underneath the rubber.

"Happy Halloween. You're really going to wear *that*? All day? Isn't that mask hot?"

Miles lifted the rubber to his forehead. He already seemed to be sweating. "Extremely. But it *is* Halloween. And look!" He walked in past me and placed his bag on the floor. He unzipped the big pocket of the bag and pulled out a ghoulish white mask.

"I brought this for Simon for after we save him. It's Ghostface from *Scream*."

"Nice!" Austin said. His expression shifted from

playful and teasing to supportive puppy dog eyes. He was so mushy.

"And Riley. I-I know you've been busy this week—"

"We all have," I cut in. Miles smiled at me.

"Well, I figured you didn't have time to get an outfit, so I brought you this." He reached into the bag one more time and pulled out a tan mask that would fit perfectly around the lower part of my face. It was Hannibal Lecter's mask from *The Silence of the Lambs.* "I know it's a bit ironic now. Dressing as a famous cannibal while hunting what seems to be the spirit of all cannibals. But . . ." He handed it to me, and I gratefully reached for it.

"Thanks, Miles. I'll wear it. It's like armor." I smiled.

"The armor for the Ghoul Gang is a bunch of horror movie masks. Seems . . . fitting." Austin chuckled.

"Simon would be proud." Miles smiled widely. "So. What is our plan of attack today?"

"Well. I hate to say it, but I think we go to school."

"Riley, you haven't been all week," Miles said, eyebrows raised.

"That's exactly why we go today. Ghouls aren't really active during the day. I mean, come on. We've all seen horror movies. Everything happens on Halloween *night*."

"True." Austin laughed.

"School ends at three. We can strategize there, and it'll make the waiting pass by faster."

They both nodded in agreement to the plan.

"So . . . what about *after*?" Miles asked, his lip pouting ever so slightly.

I took a deep breath. "That is the question. I saw Granny yesterday. Apparently, this"—I lifted the small lavender vial around my neck—"is the key. Granny put some of her magic in it. But she didn't tell me *why* this is important, just that the Wendi—" Miles's eyes widened and I remembered, *The more its name is said, the more it can* see *you.* "The *ghoul* hates the stuff. It pushes him away. This might be the way to save Simon, I just . . . don't know how."

We all stood in silence for a minute. All of our eyes looking at the small vial.

"I think this is going to be one of those things that we just . . . figure out as we go." Miles shrugged.

"Definitely a rough thing to 'figure out as you go' but . . . I agree. If we haven't figured anything out within the last few days, we aren't going to figure it out until something happens." Austin folded his arms over his chest.

"Okay. Then we'll wait to figure it out. We'll wing it." I sighed. "Granny also said that if we managed to split—"

"When," Miles corrected. I nodded.

"*When* we manage to split the ghoul from Si, that *I* might vibe and become a . . . Wendy also." I gulped. Both of their eyes widened.

"As long as you don't eat us, we're good," Austin said, trying to ease my worries, but making it *so* much worse. I exhaled.

"I'll . . . try. She said that the spirit is strong and I might lose myself initially. So if that happens . . ."

"It won't." Austin stood and placed his hand on my shoulder.

"We believe in you more than anything, Lee. You got this. *We* got this," Miles said as he placed his hand on my other shoulder. I smiled at both of them.

"We do." I pulled the Hannibal mask over my face and around my mouth. "Now, let's go to the real horror house. We're almost late for school."

The day passed surprisingly quickly, the hours ticking as the teachers had special lectures for Halloween, some even showing movies throughout the day. The ocean of students around me were all dressed up, but some had grown wary of the idea of going out tonight. After Beth, this small town was getting antsy with the idea of a killer hunting down teenagers and leaving nothing but their heads and bones. Parents were setting curfews, and we were probably one more death away from an absolute frenzy.

But I refused to let it come to that.

I sat in classes, thinking of *the plan*. Miles and Austin passed me notes each time I saw them, going over everything we needed to do tonight. Everything and anything we might need for the hunt and vibe session. Austin was bringing the chains we first bound him in for when I end up going full Wendy, and Miles was bringing all of Simon's ghost-hunting equipment, just in case.

But the more we talked about everything, the more I realized how little of an *actual* plan we had. I was going in blind, pretending that I had more than I did. I felt the need to keep a tough face, for the sake of Miles and Austin, and also for myself. The moment I cracked, we all cracked. But I was being eaten up from the inside out, my chest hadn't stopped pounding all day and my hands were constantly sweating. I found myself tapping my fingers and shaking my legs, every few moments. What was I supposed to do?

I knew I would somehow, *somehow*, pull Simon from the Wendigo. I would save him. But . . . how?

The bell rang, snapping me back to the present. It was the end of the school day; students all around me were jumping out of their seats, throwing on their bags, and running out the doors to celebrate Halloween with parties and trick or treating (for the younger bunch) and just enjoying the festivities of the holiday.

But I wasn't like these other kids. I couldn't just enjoy a day in costumes with my friends. For me, every day was like Halloween. October 31 into November 1 just happened to be the two worst days of the year, when all the spirits were at their peak.

I stood, watching those around me flood out of the main hallway until I felt a gentle press on my shoulder. I turned to see Austin to my left weakly smiling. With one look, this boy had read my face. There was no hiding from him. And it seemed like Miles was able to do the same with him, as I heard him come up on my right, both of them surrounding me.

"Happy Halloween to us," Miles smirked. "Let's go."

After a brisk review of our equipment and all the knowledge about the Wendigo we could find, we started making our way toward Granny's glade.

"So, it's ancient?" Austin asked as he drove, rounding corners of the curving mountain roads quickly, twisting up and around trees of the woods that rested in the middle of Ravenswood.

"Very," Miles nodded. "That's what Simon had told us once too. According to the Algonquin legends, they were evil spirits that would possess starving members of tribes during winter to drive them to madness. They would get so hungry that they would grow a taste for human flesh and become cannibals. Once they indulged themselves, their bodies would slowly change and they would become emaciated, always hungry for more and more. They become spirits of greed and glutton."

"So, is that how our Wendy started?" I asked. Though speaking the name makes them more aware, we figured giving it a little nickname was fine, belittling if anything. And if it wasn't, it had to know we were coming today for Si anyway. There was no time for hiding, not anymore.

"Not sure, but probably. We know he's old and has been tormenting Ravenswood maybe even before Granny's time. He probably only comes out every few years, which is why you didn't know of him, Riley. He feeds and feeds while waiting for some unfortunate soul to be his next host. Then he steals their body and continues to eat until the new body becomes like the old, and then he just looks for the new one," Miles explained.

Austin declared, "We can't let Simon just become another body."

"He won't be," I said. I clutched onto the lavender around my neck, Simon's hat feeling warm against my head, and the Halloween mask heavy at my neck. "He won't be."

Miles kept reviewing information about the Wendigo. Invading people's dreams in order to drive them crazy, making them angry and hostile to everyone due to feeling so exhausted, not letting them consume anything that isn't human, which added to the irritability and overall madness, and then once they felt completely isolated, alone, helpless, the spirit of the Wendigo urged them to run into the forest.

"It's said that once the victim is at that point, they'll run until their feet bleed, strip off all their clothes because they feel so hot on the inside when they're actually slowly freezing to death. There's a legend that the ghouls even have hearts entirely made up of ice. And the only way to stop them is to melt or shatter their ice hearts," Miles divulged.

"That's a bit dramatic, ain't it?" Austin mumbled loud enough for us all to hear as he veered the car off to the side of the road, just a short walk away from Granny's clearing.

Miles nodded and shrugged.

"Also, Granny specifically said that lavender had *something* to do with how we can stop him." I got out of the car, pulling a light backpack out behind me.

"Do you think we should, maybe, put it on Simon? And then they'll switch back?" Miles's voice was filled with hope. But . . .

"Possibly. But it sounds too good to be true. And there's still the issue of actually finding him." Austin folded his arms on top of each other after he locked his car. "I feel like we can't just *switch them back*. We need to *separate* them. Get Wendy totally out, so that Simon can just . . . be Simon again."

"And if we see Wendy in Simon's body, there's a chance I'll vibe to him and . . . become a ghoul myself."

"Don't worry, Lee," Austin patted the cap on my head, "we won't let you eat anyone."

We all chuckled a bit, full laughter feeling hard to find on a day like today. We hiked through the tree line, up and onward to Granny's clearing. The day was cool and breezy and there was a plethora of dry, crunchy leaves on the floor making the day feel like Halloween. I took deep, steady breaths, and with each exhale I could see a plume of fog in front of my mouth. I was glad I wore a big jacket.

We made it to the clearing and crossed over the moat of lavender, and almost instantly my body faded from physical to spectral. I looked down at my see-through hands, which shone blue in the dimming light of the day. Austin and Miles stared, the sight of ghosts and ghouls just hadn't seemed to become 100 percent normal yet, not even to the boy who was a ghoul himself. I gave them a smirk that said *I'm okay* as we continued on to the middle of the clearing.

"Granny?" I called out.

We waited a moment, and then another, and finally she appeared, with the same smirk on her face.

"Hello, dearies. Happy All Hallows' Eve."

"Happy Halloween," we all said in unison.

"Are you ready for tonight?"

For a moment, none of us responded, we all just looked at one another.

"As ready as we'll ever be," Austin said, the same smile painted on his face.

"That will just have to be good enough." She smiled warmly at each of us, and as her eyes landed on me, my feet became solid against the packed dirt floor once again, a wave of warmth filled my limbs under my skin before the cold of the air bit back. I was *alive* again.

"So," I said, taking a deep breath in and out, "how do I get to Simon?"

"I can only tell you; I cannot guide you through the process."

"What does that mean?" Miles asked somewhere behind me.

"You are the smart one, are you not? Surely, you can figure it out." Granny had the mischievous twinkle in her eyes once again.

"I have to vibe? To Simon?"

"You can do that?" Austin asked.

"I-I don't know. I've never tried to vibe to anything . . . or anyone for that matter. It always just . . . happens."

"Remember, dearie. You are a Connector. You can connect to those around you, ghoul or not. Simon is just beyond reach, I have seen him in the other world, in this very clearing. He is waiting."

"Okay. How do I do it?" Determination filled my voice. Whatever I had to do, I would if that meant I would be able to bring Simon back.

But Granny simply shook her head. "As I said, I can only tell you what to do, not how. I have heard of Connectors connecting to people from different places. But I do not know how it is done. I do not know the feeling or intention that goes within the magic." She sighed. "You will have to figure it out on your own. But I do believe having any of his belongings near you might help."

I touched the beak of the hat. *I knew this would come in handy.*

"Okay. Boys, pull out Si's ghost-hunting gear." I sat in the middle of the clearing, my legs crossed over one another, the hat pulled to cover my eyes, the necklace feeling heavy against the base of my spine.

I ushered the boys to lay the equipment around me. The spirit box sat in front, his camera to one side, the voice recorder to another; his EMF reader, his journal, everything, lay around me in a circle.

The boys and Granny stood back as I closed my eyes. I wasn't really sure what I was doing, but I knew I had to . . . *connect.*

I took a few deep breaths in, thinking of Simon. I said his name over and over again in my mind as if I were calling out to him, for him. I twitched my fingers before becoming completely still. I tried meditating, with only my breath and Simon on my mind. *In. Simon. Out. Simon.*

After a few moments of nothing, I began to drift into my vibes. I remembered the pain of shifting into a werewolf, the claws growing from my cuticles, my jaw breaking loose and reconnecting after it had extended, and the strange sensation of fur bursting through each and every one of my pores along my body.

I thought about dying, the last hitch of breath before I became a ghost, the lonely emptiness within my chest, the constant shudder and chill throughout my being, the inability to touch anything, and all the anxiety that came along with feeling . . . not real.

I imagined the pains and troubles of every creature I had vibed to thus far. The fangs growing in my mouth and the thirst for blood; the wings sprouting from my back, tearing my skin away; the flesh that became hard and scaly. All I ever thought about when I imagined the vibes were these feelings. But I just . . . felt like I needed to go deeper.

I tried to think about the feelings, the pull to the vibes. What happened *right* before the pain. *Right* before I became something . . . else.

In. Simon. Out. Simon.

I remembered the blur of my own being. I remembered the vibration I felt every time I was close to a ghoul, like my very own Spidey-Sense for the supernatural. Of course, the vibration wasn't exactly physical, but my core, my aura. My entire being would *vibrate* into something else. I *felt* them around me; they gave me their energy, their vibes, and I *became* them. I envisioned myself vibrating into monsters.

I envisioned myself next to Frank, the ghost. My . . . essence would vibrate, connecting and forming to him. But what was I even connecting to?

Stop, I told myself. *Slow it down.*

I mentally slowed the process. Each shift, each vibration, created a wave-like pattern. Frank had his own waves, and as I vibed, my waves shifted, changing to match his.

"Miles," I called out, breaking the deep silence that had filled my mind, filled the entire atmosphere of the clearing.

He startled. "Yeah?"

"What do waves have to do with vibrations?" I hadn't opened my eyes—I simply focused on the waves in my mind. I thought of Frank's again, they were open and swooping, with a steady and slow beat. I thought of Austin's, they were jagged and sharp, up and down and up and down, with little time for space in between.

"They have almost everything to do with each other. A vibration is what causes a wave. When an object is disturbed by the vibration of something else, there is a wave that is formed between the two objects to send the vibrations from one place to another."

"And every vibration has a different wavelength, right?"

"Yeah, usually. Wavelengths are the distances between the two crests of the waves. Sharper vibrations typically have shorter wavelengths."

I repeated Miles's words in my head. I knew they were wondering why, of all things, I asked about this. I had never explained how this felt. Hell, I never even thought about this until now. I'd never needed to. Vibing was just vibing.

But now, it was so much more. Now, it was *connecting*.

"Okay," I said in a low voice I knew would be loud enough for them to hear. The clearing was dead silent. No birds, no bugs—even the trees seemed to be holding their breath.

I took a deep breath in and closed my eyes.

In. Simon. Out. Simon.

I left my mind blank for a while, trying to imagine my own wavelength as easily as I was able to see Austin's and Frank's.

A line began to form. It slowly swooped up and down in a rhythmic pattern. Faster than Franks, but slower than Austin's. It had sharp edges that peaked like mountains, and as it moved, the same rhythmic beat repeating itself, it began to search.

I thought of Simon, his big personality, his warm smile, and kind demeanor.

And then I found it.

Simon's waves were soft and gentle, sweeping wide like massive smiley faces.

I felt my consciousness slip from my body, falling

deep into my mind, as I found myself walking, my own waves protruding from my chest, melding slowly into Simon's. I followed them. The large spotlight Simon had once dreamed was about over my head, and all around me was black nothingness. Only Simon's wave led me deep into the dark.

It had worked. I had vibed — connected — to Simon. I couldn't see where it was leading me, but I knew he would be at the other end.

CHAPTER TWENTY-SEVEN
AUSTIN

R iley sat motionless in the center of the clearing; her breathing had gone steady after a sharp inhale. "She's in," Granny claimed.

I released the tension in my shoulders. We were officially one step closer to finding Simon and ending this nightmare of a fiasco.

"So, I'm a little confused," Miles began. "I understand Simon is in the dream world Wendy created—an alternate, demented version of Ravenswood. But that's his soul, or whatever, right? So, where is his body?" He lightly scratched his head, the way he always did when he was thinking just a little harder than normal.

It's his equivalent to a Jimmy Neutron brain blast, I thought.

"Aye, his mind is in the other place. But his body is here. In these very woods."

"We gotta find it, don't we?" I urged. "He could be hurt out here, freezing to death, getting attacked by wild animals!" I began pacing. I felt so helpless, so useless. I couldn't smell him out, I couldn't find him, yet he had been here the entire time. "If he's here . . . why couldn't I catch his scent?"

Miles's eyes drifted up to mine. "Because . . ." he said slowly. "It's *not* him."

"It is the beast in sheep's clothing. Remember, the ghoul has possessed Simon. And that means he is out there, roaming in Simon's body. Feasting. Changing. He thinks he has won." Granny's eyes had changed somewhere between her words. Where once they were warm and sweet, they were now misty and sad. "He believes that as long as he gets through today, in the boy's body, Simon will become trapped in the dream world and simply become yet another victim to the beast's count."

"But we're not going to let that happen," I said.

"Exactly," Miles agreed. "We just need to figure out how to stop the monster once we pull him out of Si's body."

Granny hummed. "That is the trickiest of tasks."

"Can't we just, like, stab his heart or something?" I asked. I knew the words were dumb as they escaped my mouth.

"I mean, even though that's totally a vampire thing, it could work?" Miles raised an eyebrow.

I shrugged. "Stab anything in the heart and it's more than likely it'll die. Right?"

"And if the legends are true about the ghoul having an ice heart, then it'll shatter if we stab it," Miles looked to Granny expectedly.

But she only shook her head. "I like the ambition you both share. But your plan will not work. The beast's skin is old and decrepit, but though it may look brittle, as though it is about to fall off with the most delicate of touches, it is like rubber. If you stab him, it will not pierce—only bruise with the force of the impact. But he has had a lifetime of pain in all forms, a bruise will not stop him. It may not even slow him." She sighed. "He is weakest in his new host. You would be able to try that plan out as he is now, but . . ."

"But if we do that, then Simon will die as well," Miles finished.

I shook my head, but Granny simply, sadly, nodded. "Indeed."

I felt anger flare within me. The beast was playing dirty, he knew we wouldn't hurt Si, let alone kill him. He was using that. And he was assuming he would get away with it.

"I fear that the only way to stop this ghoul is to kill him from the inside out."

"Like, with poison?"

She nodded and Miles began to pace back and forth, looking at the ground as he rhythmically and slowly scratched his head. He paused and looked up to the trees and bushes that acted as a barrier to the rest of the woods.

"What if we fee—" He stopped dead in his words, and his eyes trailed up. Miles's face contorted from something almost like revelation, joy, to absolute horror. The lines between his eyebrows grew hard as his eyes went wide and unmoving. I followed his gaze and traced it with my own. My heart felt as though it skipped a beat.

There, in the shadow of the tree line, a pair of crimson eyes shone through, watching us, glancing from me to Miles to Granny and to Riley on the floor in front of us. None of us heard him come up, he had been silent. I felt a shiver down my spine.

How long has he been watching us? I thought.

My first instinct was to change. To become the werewolf. But then my eyes caught on Riley. If I changed now, would her body be forced to vibe to me since she was preoccupied? Would it pull her out of whatever trance she was in to save Simon?

I couldn't risk it.

I looked at Miles, gently pushing him as I whispered, "Stay behind me."

I dashed forward and swooped up Riley, her lank body lifting with ease. I never moved my eyes from the pair of crimson orbs that stared back at us. They looked like two shining rubies, two beaming brake lights. He never blinked.

With Riley in my arms, I slowly backed up and placed her on the floor next to Miles. "Watch her."

Granny had floated next to me, her eyes narrowed on the beast.

"I am unsure if he will be able to break the barrier in the new body," she whispered to me. "Be cautious."

"I can't change, right? It'll affect Riley, mess everything up?"

"Honestly, I do not know. Do so if you must, but try to hold out. We do not want to risk the girl coming back without Simon. Not now." Her gaze remained unmoving, her voice steady.

I looked forward, into the darkness, into the eyes.

And for a while, we all just stared.

Miles's breathing hitched. He was scared, of course. I forced my own to steady, but I could still feel the rapid thumps within my chest, my heart pounding faster and faster as the moments ticked by.

Though his movements were not fast or sudden in the slightest, I startled when the pair of eyes trailed from the Ghoul Gang to the barrier between us. He cocked his head and took short, slow steps forward. I could just barely make out the crunching of the fall leaves under his feet. It was as if he wasn't even there, and I knew if we weren't so dead silent right now, with our eyes glued to the glowing orbs, I might have not even heard him approach.

I stiffened, my muscles and limbs holding in all the tension they could. And though she was a ghost, I saw Granny do the same from the corner of my eye.

The eyes moved slowly toward the small brush of bushes. With each new step, the sun shining through the trees began to reveal new details of the face that was so familiar yet so different. Simon . . . or rather the

Wendigo in Simon's body walked out of the shade to reveal the face that had been missing for days.

It was Simon, perfectly as we always knew him, except for the glowing red eyes of the Wendigo, two small lumps on the sides of his head above his ears, and the cold, malice expression tainting his face.

I had seen Simon angry. I had seen him scared, worried, sad, and hungry. I had been at the other end of his rage due to this possession. But I had never seen such an expression on him as I did right now. And just by this expression alone, I knew this *wasn't* Simon.

The Wendigo in Simon's body smiled at us as he took a large step over the lavender bush and gently placed his foot on the packed ground of the clearing. He waited a moment, cocking his head again as he stared at his foot. It looked as though he was trying to make sure his foot was still attached to the rest of him.

I held my breath, hoping that somehow Granny's magic would repel the beast.

It didn't.

The eyes as slick as blood looked up at us once again. He smiled a sickly grin, an expression I knew Simon wasn't nor would ever be capable of. And after a moment, the Wendigo swung his other leg over, planting his foot gently next to the other.

Granny stiffened next to me even more. I stopped breathing.

I flexed my hand, the wolf claws begging to release. But I couldn't. Not yet.

For a while we all stood, staring at one another. I realized the small lumps on Simon's head were the beginnings of two antlers, like that of a baby deer. The two small nubs were slightly fuzzy, with light hair atop dark bone. The closer I looked, the more I noticed the dried blood that had run down Simon's head, past his ears and jawline, trickling along his neck.

The sides of his gray shirt were soaked in gore, but

it looked all dried as if it had been sitting on him for days. My eyes drifted down. His feet were bare and bloody at the soles; I could see broken blisters. His knees, toes, and fingers had gone red from how cold he was in boxers and a T-shirt alone, and his legs and arms had small cuts all over them, I assumed from the branches and thorns of the woods.

The Wendigo had Simon for the last week in his own clutches, and it was incredibly evident that he didn't truly care for his "new body."

But though he looked wounded, he seemed healthy. Healthier than Simon had appeared in weeks. The bags under his eyes had receded. His skin looked dewy and refreshed. Everything about him read "rejuvenated" and "whole," everything except the bloodcurdling eyes that stared back at us.

"Unfortunately, you are much too late." He smiled. The voice that slipped from Simon's tongue sounded twisted, dark, and hollow. Though the pitch may have been the same, the tone and mannerisms in which he spoke were different. There was a darkness there, something teasing and rueful. And the unnatural smile made it all even worse. It reminded me of the uncanny valley Miles had mentioned when discussing the Not Deer. Though this figure in front of us looked like Simon in every way, something about him just felt *off*. It *wasn't* him, and it was becoming clearer and clearer the more he pretended to be like him.

It sent a shiver down my spine, and I found myself desperately wanting to look away, but I couldn't. My eyes felt drawn to the mask the beast was wearing. The mask that was my friend.

The beast met my eyes and cocked his head. He smiled widely, in between his teeth were tons of bits and pieces of raw meat.

I gulped. If he had . . . *eaten*, that meant Simon—our Simon—had human flesh within his stomach already, which just meant the beast was already one step closer to full-on possession. I hoped—I prayed to any and all gods that would listen—that whatever the beast had eaten, it *wasn't* human.

"You are not welcome here, beast."

"Oh, come now, Theodosia, how long will we play this game today?" His smile could slice through metal. It was sick and looked as though it would ooze ink or blood at any moment. It was dark and simply not *right*.

"Do not act as though you know me. You are nothing but greed and hunger manifested at its worst, nothing but the skin suits you steal," Granny spat. Her words were slicked in venom and I was thankful she was on our side of the conflict. "*You are not welcome*." Her voice was hard and powerful. It echoed through me, through the clearing, as though they were targeted forcefully at the Wendigo in front of us.

A brisk wind came with her words and brushed against Simon vigorously, pushing his hair aside, revealing the small fur lumps jutting from the sides of his skull once again.

The Wendigo's spirit had already affected Simon's body, taking hold and changing it for his own. Soon, Simon's stomach would grow thin, his skin would shift from a pale, dewy complexion to something rubbery and devoid of nourishment.

The rush of wind was meant to be something grander. I could tell by the way Granny held herself. She had cast a spell in her words, but the spell seemed to have little to no effect on the Wendigo.

His head had been tilted back from the gust of air, but now he straightened once again.

"This new body of mine is stronger, Theodosia. Strong enough to withstand your little incantations and charms." He glanced at the lavender bush behind him. In a smooth motion, he plucked one of the lavender stocks, the small flowers a deep indigo, not quite purple and not quite blue. The Wendigo held the plant at arm's distance at first but slowly moved it closer to his nose. He took a deep inhale before cringing.

"It still smells quite awful." His eyebrows raised as he studied the plant. In a swift motion, his hand gripped the flower buds, strangling them. The tiny buds fell between his fingers and scattered on the floor in front of him. "But it no longer has an effect on me. It is simply unpleasant." The Wendigo smiled and threw the stock to the floor.

He took a step toward us, and then another. His eyes had shifted. Where once the red glow suggested corrupted mischief, they now held intent. Murderous intent.

"Give me the girl, forget the boy, and I will let the two of you live." Another step.

I knew he was talking to me. His gaze was unwavering with each slow movement toward us. Granny was a ghost, he could not do more to her. But he *could* kill me, Miles, and Riley. And he seemed like he had his eyes on the only other person here who maybe had a chance at stopping him.

"Never." I felt my fists clench, the fur of the wolf threatening to sprout at my arms. My claws dug into my palms, threatening to break the skin. My fangs elongated, piercing my lips. The wolf wanted to come out, but the moment it did, we would risk the failure of Riley's connection.

"Not yet, Austin. You must hold out a little longer," Granny spoke, voice and body unwavering. She stood her ground next to me as Simon's body neared.

The ghoul's eyes shot to the side, looking at Granny, and then once again at me. The smile as sharp as a knife returned to his face.

"You cannot defeat me as you are, boy. You cannot even slow me. You are nothing. I will enjoy ripping the flesh from his bones as you watch." He glanced at

Miles behind me. "I'm sure his skin is ripe and sweet, a perfect delicacy. You know. You have tasted it. Tell me, boy, what does the dark one taste like?"

I took a step forward, the rage blinding me for a moment before Granny's ghostly figure moved to block me. "No," she whispered. "Do not give in. Do not let him manipulate you."

The Wendigo took another step closer. "Hmm, is that hazelnut I smell? Mighty sweet. A sweet tooth, perhaps? I bet you simply cannot wait to sink your teeth into him, pull him apart inch by inch, savor each part of him, each drop of blood as it falls onto your lips. I wonder if the marrow in his bones would be as delectable."

My heart was racing, it felt as though it would explode from my chest at any moment. But as the beast spoke, my mind envisioned my kiss with Miles. His taste against my tongue, the smell of his skin invading my nose, making him smell . . . mouthwatering. I found that smell wafting toward me now and my mind drifted into a haze. My stomach rumbled, and my mouth grew wet as I licked my lips. My head slowly turned to see him sitting behind me. He was holding Riley, fear streaking across his face. First at the Wendigo, and then at me.

"You and I are not much different. There is a beast within you as well—a beast yearning to escape. To hunt. To feed. Give into the animal within you and see how much more fulfilled your life becomes."

The words made my mind hazier. I wasn't like him. I knew I wasn't nor would I ever be. But Miles was looking more and more *tempting* the more I stared at him. But it was different. I didn't feel hot or ecstatic like it normally did when I thought of him. Now I only felt *hungry.*

"Austin. Pull yourself out of this. He's manipulating you," Miles urged, inching back.

I knew he was. I knew this was some kind of spell or magic that came along with the spirit. This is what Simon must have been feeling all along.

"Just take one little bite. Just one. It won't hurt him . . . too much. And it will satisfy your curiosity," the Wendigo snickered. "Just one taste."

My eyes drifted to Miles's neck, the veins protruding as his heart pounded. I felt as though I could hear the blood running through his veins, trying to keep up with the anxiety. It looked like the perfect spot to sink my teeth into.

But as my eyes drifted up to Miles's face, as I saw the horror and betrayal in his eyes, the fear of *me*, something within had changed.

The hunger faded and my mind cleared. Miles sat in front of me horrified, I had become a monster to him in just moments. He was afraid of *me*.

I didn't know what to do. I knew I couldn't comfort him. I looked into his eyes and smiled weakly.

"No. We are not alike. I will not hurt him," I said as I turned.

But as my eyes focused on the change of direction, it was already too late. The Wendigo in Simon's body stood directly in front of me. His expression had shifted from sinister to bored.

I felt the hard impact on my cheek before I even saw him move, my body tumbled across the field as pain sprang into my face and blood welled from my lips and nose.

Sharp and sudden pain shocked my entire body as I struggled to find purchase in the dirt. All the wind had been knocked out of me the moment the Wendigo hit me and I struggled to find air. My ribs felt broken, and it hurt to breathe.

I raised myself to my hands and knees, shaking. If I wasn't a werewolf, the smack from the ghoul would have easily resulted in a broken neck. The wounds on my lip were already healing, my ribs mending, and my breath was slowly returning.

But as I healed, I looked up to where I had just stood a moment ago, and the spot was empty save for Granny watching in horror. My eyes followed her gaze across the field.

Miles lay limp where he was moments before, blood dripping from his head. My heart sank.

"No. Nonono," I mumbled, crawling toward Miles. This couldn't be real, it just couldn't. But before I could reach him, my eyes drifted.

The Wendigo held Riley by her hair and looked at me, one eyebrow raised in disappointment.

"Then you are weak. Like Simon. I hurt the hazelnut boy because you couldn't. And now I will hurt her because Simon couldn't."

He pulled Riley up toward himself, opening his mouth wide over her neck.

And all of a sudden, the wolf inside howled as I transformed.

CHAPTER TWENTY-EIGHT

SIMON

I sat on the floor, tapping my foot. It had been a few hours since I last saw Granny, which meant it had probably been a day or two in the real world already. I felt the anticipation growing in my chest with each passing moment. I couldn't stop fidgeting, looking around, over my shoulders to see if *maybe* Riley had appeared without my notice.

She would come for me like Granny said she would . . . right?

I shook my head. I had to have the confidence, the *belief*, in Riley and the Ghoul Gang, that they would come for me.

I stood, shaking off the dreadful anxiety. Pacing wasn't much better, but at least it would provide a better exertion of energy.

The ghosts from the beast hadn't been back, not even a simple sign of them had crossed through the trees. Granny was right, they really were bothered by the protective barrier.

Speaking of, I needed to figure out a way to get the lavender *inside* the beast. It would destroy him from the inside out.

"Maybe he'll have, like, a really bad allergic reaction to it," I wondered aloud to myself. I envisioned the beast foaming at the mouth and clutching at his throat. But could an allergic reaction kill a supernatural beast?

Maybe it would be like that scene in *Men in Black*, where Will Smith feeds the alien a bomb, and because it eats everything, it accepts and then explodes?

I looked at the lavender stalks swaying in a nonexistent gust of wind. Would those little things really cause a monster to explode? It seemed unlikely.

But the idea of a beast eating everything in its path *sounded* like this beast. Only exchange *everything* with *human flesh*.

I looked at my hands, ideas swelling in my mind. Bad ideas.

I could always sacrifice my own flesh, in order to get the lavender where it needed to be. And while the concept sounded heroic, like Luke or Anakin Skywalker, this wasn't *Star Wars*, where the loss of a limb had little effect on the character and his story, a fleeting moment at the end of the middle episode. No, this was real life and I would feel it every single day for the rest of my life.

I looked at my hands once again.

But if sacrificing this hand meant all of these ghosts would be free—*I* would be free—and no one else in Ravenswood would get hurt by this thing?

As I looked down at myself, wondering what it would all feel like after this was over, I felt the slightest tug on the front of my shirt. I looked down, but nothing was there. I felt it again, my shirt went unmoved.

I realized the tug wasn't on my shirt, it came from *within* my chest.

It was as though a string had been loosely tied around my heart, and the string was creating waves—as two kids did with a jump rope. It didn't hurt nor did it feel remotely unpleasant, though I knew that maybe it should. I clutched at my chest, worried that at any moment a chestburster from *Alien* was going to spring out of me.

But nothing came.

Instead, there was one more tug that pulled my gaze from my chest into the dark sky of the ghoul's forest. Above me, off into the trees just a short walk away, a spotlight shone down. But unlike the ghoul's spotlight which shone a bright yellow like the ones in cartoons, this spotlight had a light magenta glow and was headed straight toward the clearing. Toward me.

And I knew, like the tug at my heart, not to be afraid. Not to fear the ghoul, not to be afraid of the new beam coming my way.

Instead of fear, I felt warmth. It started from where I felt the pull, and spread slowly out, across my chest, down my arms to the tips of my fingers, spiraling past my torso and legs to the edges of my toes. It was a warmth that made me feel comfortable and fuzzy on the inside, the same as when I looked at a cute dog, or the rush of heat I would feel when Riley glanced at me.

And then I knew. That magenta glow was Riley. The spotlight was following her around, but instead of being harsh or cruel and blinding like the ghoul's light, it was soft, warm, and welcoming. It was filled with care and—dare I say it—*love*.

I clutched at my chest where I felt the tug. Realizing she was the one on the other side made the red string from my heart look like an ocean wave. And she was getting closer.

"Riley?" I called out, hoping to see her silhouette in the dark tree line soon. "Riley!" I yelled again. She had to be there. She just had to.

"Simon?" Her voice filled the clearing, sounding lighter than a feather falling, sweeter than music. Though I had only seen her hours ago—*No*, I reminded myself, *days*—it had felt so, so much longer.

"I'm over here!"

As I yelled to her, I began to see the thin shape of the girl I had been waiting for. My heart pounded, heavier than it ever had. I could feel the sweat on my palms through the stale and empty breeze of this stale and empty forest. But it wasn't a nervous sweat, filled with the anxiety of seeing a crush. It was the kind of excited sweat that comes along with seeing the girl who had your heart.

I never really analyzed my feelings for Riley. I knew I liked her, but that was that. I liked her look, her mystery. But over the time I'd known her, that need to seek out the solution to the puzzle of Riley became more of an overarching interest in her: her well-being, her worries, her fears, what made her happy, the way she laughed, the rhythm she spoke in. All that made this wonderful girl totally and completely unique.

And as I watched her shed that magenta glow of the spotlight as she climbed over the patches of the lavender bushes into the clearing, I knew that it wasn't the *mystery* I liked anymore. Nor was it the *resident goth girl* that my heart longed for.

It was Riley.

I took a few quick steps to grab her elbow as she climbed over the bush. After all four of our feet were planted on the dark grayish-brown floor of the clearing, we stood for a moment, just studying each other. She looked tired, but gorgeous nonetheless.

I eyed her as she did the same to me.

I had to remind myself that she was actually here, standing in front of me, over and over again. I read in her expression that she was doing the same.

Neither of us spoke, our eyes were wide, as I felt like they had been hungry, starving for the sight of her. A smile crept on my face as I gazed at her, and like an infection, a smile parted her lips moments after.

"Nice hat," I smirked.

She touched it gingerly. "Thanks, I took it from some guy I know."

"You should keep it. Bet it looks better on you than on that dummy."

In a flash, Riley threw her arms over my shoulders. She pulled me in and down snuggly. The warmth I had felt moments earlier as I looked at the magenta spotlight came again in brilliant folds and waves. I embraced her just as tightly, squeezing her as close as possible.

She smelled like rose-scented soap and shampoo.

I had the urge to hold her and never let go. My arms wanted to pull her into me, become one, feel her warmth spread through my body wherever we touched, and feel the rhythmic *thump* of her heart against my chest. But I knew we didn't have the luxury of such an embrace.

Every minute in here was longer out there, and today was the day to make or break this possession.

"I'm so glad you found me. Wait—" I pulled away from her, gripping her shoulders at arm's distance. "*How* did you find me?" The realization that Riley was standing in front of me, in this *place*, hadn't *truly* settled in. Not really. I saw her, and I knew she was here, but I also didn't quite understand how this all managed to actually transpire.

"It's kind of complicated. The short answer is I had to tap into the science-y side of what a vibe actually is. But it doesn't matter. It led me to you." She poked my chest as the words slipped from her lips. There was something in her eyes, a light I hadn't seen before.

I placed my hand over hers against my chest. "Well. No matter how, I'm so happy you did."

She smiled at me, and though she initially flinched at my touch, she now eased into it. Our hands interlocked against me.

"So. What's going on out there? Is it bad?"

"Oh, you know. Only an ancient cannibalistic monster taking over your body more and more with each passing second. No biggie." She smirked and playfully shrugged her shoulders.

"Yeah, ha-ha. No biggie." But I couldn't hold the same sarcastic tone as she did, even if I tried. And I knew she heard the fear in my voice.

"Miles figured out what the creature was. It's a wendigo. They—"

"Of *course*!" I cut her off, instantly connecting all of the pieces in my own head, feeling as stupid as can be. "I can't believe I didn't think of them."

"You know what they are?"

"Yeah. I saw them in a TV show once. I think the show was called *Paranormal*. It was like one of the first episodes of the show. I thought they were really cool, but also giant dicks. Go figure."

"Well, apparently, the spirit is taking over your body to make *you* a wendigo too." She rolled her eyes.

"That—that I *didn't* know. I guess you guys will have to fill me in later."

"Granny said you knew how to beat it?"

"Kind of. She gave me some hints. I think this lavender"—I pointed to the edges of the clearing—"will kind of give him an allergic reaction. If he eats it."

She took the necklace—my necklace—from around her neck and handed it to me. "How are you going to get him to eat this?"

I honestly still had no idea. It wasn't like I could hide it in some peanut butter and expect him to take his medicine. He wasn't a dog, he was a cannibal. And the only human flesh around for him to eat would likely be the Ghoul Gang. Whatever I had to do, however I was going to manage this, it was going to hurt.

"I don't really know yet. I'll wing it. But, Riley, we need to get back there. Time works differently here than it does out there."

"I know. I think . . . if you hold my hand, we can make it back to our own bodies. I think I know the way now." She gently touched her chest in the same spot she had touched mine earlier. With sudden and new resolve, she held out her hand for me to take. "The moment we get there, the battle *will* start. For all I know, it already began for Miles and Austin."

This was it. Do or die. The final countdown. The big finale to the end of the movie.

I felt my heart leap; my palms were clammy from the anxiety of what was on the other side of this world, what would transpire after taking Riley's hand. I hesitated, felt my body stepping back from Riley before I even had a moment to collect myself.

I looked down at the floor. The fear settled in like a weight against my chest, dragging each of my limbs down, down.

"Riley, I don't know if I can—"

But before I could finish, I saw her beat-up combat boots shuffle forward toward me. Her cold hands pressed against my cheeks as they lifted my face to hers. I felt the warmth of her breath against my cupid's bow before her lips touched mine. Riley kissed me, gently, softly. Our lips pressed to each other and I could feel the warmth radiating off of her, fueling me with a fire I had never felt before. I draped my arms around her waist and gently pulled her into me. She pressed harder, but just as quickly as it happened, it ended. We still clung to each other as she placed her forehead against mine. We smiled dumbly at each other without saying a word, as she shared her warmth with me.

Riley bit her lip as her cheeks flushed red. It was a cute look on her and I immediately felt the heat rise in my face, climbing up to the tips of my ears. She laughed and I just couldn't believe that Riley Silverstein kissed *me*.

"I've been thinking about that for a while," I confessed.

She giggled again, and it sounded like music to my ears, a laugh reserved for me to hear, and me alone.

She pulled me in again, wrapping her arm around my neck, and our lips collided again for a warm embrace.

I wanted to never part, to stay here, like this, with her forever. But I knew that if I wanted this to continue, I would need to take her hand and face my demons. Literally.

We parted again, and this time, she knew she had swayed me. She held out her hand, and I took it with ease.

"Anything for you," I smirked as our fingers interlocked for the first time.

"Anything?" she questioned, cocking her head while raising an eyebrow.

"Anything."

"Win."

I nodded, and she turned to lead the way back to the real Ravenswood, pulling me behind her.

With each step I took, a strange sensation began to push back against me. I felt like I had been trying to walk underwater, pushing the force out of my way.

Pushing the Wendigo out of my body.

CHAPTER TWENTY-NINE
THE WENDIGO

Suddenly, I was being pulled apart, a sensation I hadn't felt in nearly a millennium. And in a flash of heat, I was myself once again, detached from the humanity, the . . . *satiation* of Simon's body. The sickening hunger returned to my stomach yet again. I knew the pattern, knew how it would be more of an annoyance at first, a slight pang to the gut. But over time, it would grow. It would become painful, like death I assumed—only I would not die. I would only quiver, only *lust* for more.

I had been ripped from Simon's body, and the boy now lay hunched on the floor, vomiting from my feasts. I looked up, the girl with the light hair stared back at me. A look of vindication, not terror as I would have liked. The more afraid they were, the tastier their skin. If I killed her, surely Simon would come back to me, no?

The boy who smelled of hazelnut lay beat, bruised, the werewolf by his side, standing like the loyal watch-dog he was, defeated by my hand at the far edge of the clearing. *They* have the exact expression I would love to devour.

I felt my mouth begin to salivate. So many warm meals surrounding me. Maybe these three would be enough to satisfy the hunger for tonight. Maybe. But I wanted more.

My eyes glanced between the children—one, two, three, *four*. I would lick my lips if I had any remaining, but they had long since fallen off with this decaying body. I needed new ones. But this sorceress *stole* them from me.

I wanted to save her to be my first meal once I had Simon's body all to myself, but maybe now would be better.

I took a painful step forward, my frail leg buckling under the wasted weight of my body. And as I glanced down, noticing the prick of the accursed lavender against my parched skin, there before me, Simon stood perfectly, painfully *whole.* The boy, my host, had escaped my grasp. He was no longer mine. But *hers*.

And, oh, how I'd longed for a taste of his flesh. I had never eaten anyone of Eastern descent and wondered how the elasticity of his skin would pull, how his texture would feel on my tongue, how the flavors of his meat would differ from those I'd already consumed in the northeastern part of this god-forsaken land. How would his bones pop apart? Would they break like any other?

Long had I hungered for Simon but forced myself to control this curse. After all, Simon *found* me, and I was determined to make the young boy's body become my own. I lusted for lips that would smack as I ripped pieces off bone. How I longed for a complete nose to smell the ripe freshness of human flesh as I devoured, inch by inch, my victim's meat. How I longed for a stomach with the capability of feeling *full* once again.

I knew it wouldn't last. Simon's body would change, contort just like the last, but the idea of the short period of "in-between" was long enough to have me salivating at the mouth just by the mere thought of it.

But now, Simon was refusing me, casting me aside. Rejecting *me* of a host, of lips to smack, and a stomach to fill.

I decided, if I couldn't have Simon as a host, then I would have him as a meal.

CHAPTER THIRTY
SIMON

One moment I was holding Riley's hand, crossing through the Wendigo's woods, and the next, I felt the flash of heat as my body tore itself from the ghoul's pull. Flesh tore from flesh in one of the most excruciating seconds of my life. I wondered if this was how Austin felt each time he became a werewolf, and Riley each time she vibed.

But before I knew it, I was on the floor, my hands and knees rubbed raw from the impact. I was hurling. The slight taste of meat wafted through the bile as it made my throat feel sore and tender.

Pain tore through my entire body. I felt the heat of cuts all over my legs and arms, a striking pain on both sides of my skull, and the utter fatigue of my body spending a week in the woods, doing who knows what.

I wasn't Tarzan or George of the Jungle. My body was made for linen sheets and air conditioning.

I clutched the lavender in my hand, ready to strike at any moment. But I knew things wouldn't be that simple. The Wendigo was tangible now. Real. Which only meant . . .

I heard the scream before I could even finish the thought. I was on all fours between Riley and the

Wendigo as he took a step toward me, a look of pure desire glinting in his vermillion eyes.

On my other side, Riley had begun to clutch her head. Her clothing began to tear apart from her elongated limbs. Long, sharp fingernails grew from her own as her hair went an even paler shade of blond, making it appear almost white. Her teeth grew and grew into rows of razor-sharp fangs. Just like the Wendigo's.

Riley was vibing to the Wendigo.

She fell on all fours and began to vomit and vomit. It seemed like an endless downpour until I realized the spirit of her vibe was rejecting whatever was in her stomach. It needed her to be *hungry*. It was the curse of the ghoul.

Her skin was shifting, getting tighter and more wrinkly by the second, as though all of the elasticity, all of the nutrients, all of the moisture were being sucked out, leaving her completely dry like a sponge out of water.

She was yelping, crying, screaming, and all I could do was stand and watch. I hated myself at that moment, feeling useless, watching as she withered in pain. But I knew the Wendigo wouldn't take a moment's breath to let Riley shift. He would be on the attack.

I turned to the ghoul and finally saw him for all that he was. No forest fog to hide behind, no shadowy realm to blend in with. I was finally seeing *him*, and he was seeing *me.*

His body was long and tall—he was probably three or four heads taller than me. His skin was a black that looked as rough as coal and as slick as grease. All hair he had fallen out a long time ago. The Wendigo's lips, nose, and eyelids were also gone, as though he had ripped them away to reveal his sinister smile and starving glare.

His fingernails were just as I remembered, and the nails on his toes were equally long and sharp, digging into the packed earth of Granny's clearing. The ghoul's skin appeared as though it had been wrung dry like a towel.

The long, black antlers of bone jutting from the sides of his head into long ornate pieces made him look even bigger than he was.

The Wendigo smiled at me, and before I knew it, he was lunging.

I wasn't fast enough. Not even remotely. But I was just able to use all the strength I had to keep myself away from the beast's mouth. I struggled against the cold grip of the ghoul as I felt him grab around my waist, digging his nails deeper into my side.

I pushed hard against his jaw, forcing his ragged teeth away from me.

But he fought back, trying his best to take a bite out of me.

We tussled back and forth when I felt a sudden collision, a forceful push from behind the Wendigo. His claws retracted from my flesh and he let go.

The second I was no longer in his clutches, I fell to the ground and backed up, trying to get my bearings, preparing myself for another attack, grabbing the bottle around my neck and making a fist around it.

When I looked up, the Wendigo wasn't winding up for another lunge, he wasn't snarling those wicked teeth, ready for his next meal. In fact, he had his back to me entirely.

I glanced around the clearing quickly. I saw Miles to one side, Granny floating near him as a last line of defense in case the Wendigo decided to attack. Austin darted by, jumping into the fight and I noticed an inky puddle of bile from where Riley had just been. But as my eyes made their way back to the Wendigo, I realized that there were now two of them, face to face, snarling at one another.

The Wendigo and Riley.

Her hair seemed plastered to her head as it shone in that near-white color. Her skin had become paper white, and her teeth were large and sharp and seemed as though they had multiplied. Her claws hung low, prepped and ready to attack her enemies. Riley's eyes shone a haunting white and her waist looked too thin as her ribs protruded.

She seemed like a pale, healthier—if you could even call a wendigo healthy—version of the ghoul.

Riley flexed her claws and glanced at me before returning her gaze to the monster fighting off the werewolf in front of him.

In the blink of an eye, she jutted forward to Austin's side.

I backed up as far as I could in only a moment.

The beasts became an entangled mess of limbs, claws, and teeth.

It was like a violent dance as they came together and spread apart. Riley and Austin worked in tandem, as though every move had been choreographed.

Black gore gushed from the slash Riley made against the ghoul's chest. The Wendigo bit her shoulder, clamping his jaw shut. She yelped and kicked hard against his thigh when he buckled over, one knee dropping to the ground.

She thought she had him, but his antlers came into use as he swung his head to the side, trying to rip at her center.

Riley just barely dodged, getting the smallest nick from one of the tips of antler, as Austin punched the Wendigo in the gut. The beast only smiled wickedly. He stood tall and strong before backhanding Austin's muzzle, throwing him back toward Riley.

The Wendigo's face contorted instantly, going from a wide smile to a deep frown—in a way that made him seem like he was simply annoyed rather than worried or afraid. He may be older, better adjusted to living as this beast, but Riley and Austin were stronger.

Riley didn't suffer from the same hunger. And she knew it. She flashed a smirk of shiny white teeth, just before jumping into the air, toward the Wendigo.

She wrapped her long limbs around the beast's upper half and grabbed hold of his antlers, forcing his head to move in the direction she wanted.

He was held down and could do little less than puncture her skin with his claws. The blood oozed at Riley's side, and she yelped for a brief moment before yanking his antlers to the side, biting hard against the side of the ghoul's face.

I squirmed. Blood was nothing to me, but seeing her teeth sink into the ebony, decrepit face, and the black ooze smear across her face, made me think that his blood was like poison.

But it must have been fine, because Riley didn't react at all.

Instead, she bit only harder, deeper, into the ghoul's face. He yelled and tried to hit her off of him the best he could, but she just kept biting.

Austin jumped into attack, clawing at the ghoul and gnawing on his legs, but the Wendigo managed to swat him away. Austin may have had more muscle, but the beast had supernatural strength.

Eventually, Riley began to pull her head back, slowly pulling at his skin. I heard the sickening sound of tearing as she tore a chunk of his face and left ear from his head.

Riley jumped back and landed on all fours, spitting the Wendigo's flesh from her mouth. The Wendigo cried and withered, a sound so far from human, I didn't even know what to make of it. His eyes had gone wide with rage, with fear. He was furious and in pain, and he hit Austin so hard, the werewolf flew back toward me and was left in a daze.

The Wendigo dropped to all fours and lunged at Riley, but she was too fast. She had all of her senses, while he had been running on an angry rampage.

She dropped down low and waited. Waited until the ghoul was close enough. And just as he was about to claw at her face, she quickly spun and jutted out her leg to kick him. Her foot landed just at the base of his left antler, right above his torn ear. The sound of the impact spread throughout the clearing. With a loud *crack* like lightning touching the earth, and with a hollow *thud*, the antler crashed onto the packed ground.

There was a beat of silence. The ghoul stared at Riley, and she just stared back. And all I could do was watch. The black ooze began to rapidly squirt out of the crack in the antler against his head. The gore looked like something out of *Halloween* or *Friday the 13th*. Ridiculous and campy, but now it was real. The black sprayed all over Riley as the Wendigo clawed at his own head, trying desperately to cover the gush of carnage.

Riley stood, tall and strong, as she looked down at the quivering beast, who was maniacally attempting to reattach the fallen antler. But during his scrambling, she grabbed the other, jerked her body hard to the side, and snapped the second antler off. The same inky blood poured down, trailing along the Wendigo's face, his body, hands, and legs. I almost wanted to believe that the beast was crying.

As the ghoul helplessly looked at his fallen antlers, Riley punched and kicked the beast in his gut, his face, and everywhere it hurt him the most. She slashed across a final blow to the ghoul's chest, finally tearing his rubbering flesh and he went down with a *whump*.

We all remained still as he lay there, motionless, face down in the dirt.

But the Wendigo wasn't dead. It wasn't going to be that easy. If horror movies taught me anything, it's that the bad guy always gets back up. At least slipping a few lavender buds down an unconscious monster's throat would be a little easier than if he was still at full strength. I stood from the ground and gripped my side. In all of the chaos, I almost forgot about the puncture wounds.

"Is everyone all right?" I called, looking back to Miles, Austin, and Granny.

They all looked at me, their faces going pale.

"What? What is it?" I began to turn my head—

"Simon. Do not move," Granny yelled and threw her hand up to stop me.

I froze as I was, listening to Granny's warning when I heard the slow-approaching footsteps padding across the dirt. *How did the Wendigo get up already?* I thought, just before the wafting smell of decaying roses hit me. It wasn't the Wendigo. It was Riley. She was still vibing to the ghoul, and the hunger was setting in.

I heard a soft snarl as she placed her clawed hand on my shoulder. She violently spun me around to face her. Riley's eyes were wide, a look I had seen countless times in my dreams now. A look I knew well, as I had made it myself. The wendigo spirit was getting to her, greed and hunger taking over her mind.

She began to pull me in closer.

"The Wendigo is down! Spirits, now is your chance! Claim your revenge!" I heard Granny shout from behind me. She shouted to the sky, her voice booming throughout the clearing and spreading across the trees of the forest.

There was a strange silence after, like time had stopped. The birds were no longer chirping, the leaves weren't rustling in the wind. In fact, the wind was gone altogether. Everything was still. Frozen.

The silence before the storm.

Riley's clawed hand fell from my shoulder, making small scratches down my chest in their path, as she clutched her head.

She started screaming, pressing her palms against her ears as hard as she could. In her ghoulish state, it was utterly animalistic.

"Simon, come!" called Granny behind me, ushering me to run toward her and the boys. I took a step back from Riley, and then another, before dashing to Granny as fast as I could.

Just as I slid behind her, I saw them.

The faces I had seen when I was in the other world. *His* world. They had all been set free, no longer bound to him or his endless forest. They spilled into the clearing carefully, as though they were still wary, could still feel the sting of the lavender.

I saw Beth and Addaline, their faces contorted in pure anger, along with the young ghost who resembled Granny.

But before any of the ghosts could do anything, Riley's scream pierced through the clearing. My eyes fell on her as her body withered into different shapes. Her legs became transparent, while her hair turned white. Her eyes shifted between the striking of a wendigo and the pale blue of the dead.

She was vibing—to everything here. Wendigos, banshees, ghosts. And she was going into overdrive.

And then I remembered her words from the night we studied at her house, the night we first found out about Addaline. It all felt so long ago . . .

"I have been around multiple spirits before, however. And that was a nightmare. I felt everything they were feeling. All the pain, anger, and confusion. But the worst feeling was all the nothingness. People—hollows of people— who were just . . . nothing. And they didn't know. Didn't feel anything. Not cold, not alone. Just nothing."

I saw the nothingness in her eyes. She was shedding tears, but her face remained expressionless as she screamed a banshee's cry.

"This might be too much for her," Granny said, her eyes narrowed on the crowd of ghosts.

"She'll be okay though, right?" I looked at her and then at Riley who was scrunched over on the ground in pain.

"When she connects to a spirit, she dies for a brief moment, until she becomes a ghost herself. Her heart stops and starts again the moment it is over." She paused. "But right now . . . her heart is stopping every second, fluttering in and out, trying to connect to everyone, feeling everything they felt in death. At this rate . . ."

"Simon," Miles cut in. "You have to get these spirits to leave. They want their revenge . . . but they can't have that right now, not with Riley—"

"How am I supposed to stop them?" I felt helpless. "If I had my—"

"We brought your ghost-hunting stuff. It's in the backpack," he said as he threw it to me. "I don't know if there's anything in there that can help bu—"

I didn't listen to the rest. I immediately knew what I had to do, even if it didn't work, I had to give it a try.

I dug through the bag feverishly looking for the large tin canister. The moment I felt the cool metal against my skin, I yanked it out, dropped my bag to the ground, and dashed in front of Granny, through all the ghosts, through Addaline and Beth, past the fallen Wendigo, and finally to Riley.

Please don't fail me now.

I ripped off the lid and poured the small white crystals of my blessed salt in a circle around the both of us.

"I'm sorry!" I said as I kept pouring around us. "Please come again, thank you." After the circle was complete, I dropped to my knees and held onto Riley. In less than a second, her hands fell from her ears and her eyes drifted closed. She slumped against me— unconscious and human.

I held onto her and stayed in the circle with her. The spirits stayed, but their expressions had shifted. Somehow, the rage that had spread across their faces had become even more violent. I saw the bloodlust in their eyes. But also, the fear.

I quivered until I realized—they weren't looking at me and Riley, or my makeshift salt circle.

They were looking at the Wendigo, who stood tall behind us, smiling directly at me as he clasped his boney hands together.

CHAPTER THIRTY-ONE
SIMON

The Wendigo stood, his hands clasped together, a sickening smile spreading wide across his face.

The black ooze still dripped down his face, the antlers still lay on the ground.

But he was standing, as though he was perfectly fine. Because, it seemed, he was.

The Wendigo placed an arm against his torso and the other spread out like a wing as he slowly took a bow.

"Mesmerized by my performance, Simon? I dare say it may have been my best yet," he rasped, as he switched arms, taking another bow. "You're in shock? Was my acting really that superb? I've always dreamed of being on the stage." His head cocked sideways as he grinned, the blood spilling out of his broken antlers like a waterfall, a tipped jar of ink.

He took a step toward me, breaking me from my trance.

"Bu-but how are you . . ." I said, raising my finger toward his broken antlers.

"Simon, Simon, Silly Simon. Didn't you learn anything in school? Deer shed their antlers annually. They break all the time. They simply grow new ones, nothing to fret about. Wendigo antlers happen to be the same." He paused, his smile becoming more grotesque with each passing moment. "You would know that if you had just stayed where I put you." His voice was coiled with an edge of anger. "Plus, I can't die yet. I haven't had my main course."

The next few moments seemed to slow around me, as though each of my movements was an elaborate pose from *The Matrix*.

My eyes drifted toward the Ghoul Gang at the other end of the glade.

I glanced at Granny, her eyes wide with panic and fear. I knew she would jump in front of this bullet for me if she could, offer herself in order to stop the beast. But there wasn't any time—there was no physical way.

I kept turning, my eyes landing on Austin, his head still held up in Miles's lap. He lay there, battered and bruised, clutching at his ribs. His nose gushed blood down his face, his lip torn in the center, his eye blackened, the flesh around slowly shifting from pink to purple to blue. His eyes were pleading, begging me to run.

I met Miles's gaze with my own, expecting the same look of terror and fear spread across his eyes as everyone else's. But all I saw was resolve. He clenched his jaw and slightly furrowed his eyebrows. He was putting on a brave face, a face for me. We both knew what I had to do, and he wasn't asking me to run away. He was asking me to stand up and fight. He nodded, and I nodded back. We both understood.

I looked down at my hand, still clutching the small bottle of lavender. I had squeezed too hard—the glass, broken now, rested in my palm as pieces cut into my skin, while others were embedded in.

Small lavender buds rested in the tiny pool of dirt and blood.

I closed my fist again as I saw the Wendigo lunge at me from the corner of my eye.

I took one more moment to look at it, engrain myself with what it felt like to have both hands, before sliding Riley off me and thrusting my fist up to the Wendigo as a final offering. *Don't forget about me.*

I squeezed my eyes shut and waited to hear and feel the snap of bone, the tearing of flesh, and the pain of losing a limb.

I felt the puncturing of teeth sink in.

I didn't think it would actually work—the lavender, my plan to force him to eat it—until I saw the beast's eyes go wide in front of me. My entire fist was in his mouth and his teeth had been sinking into my forearm, painfully. Hot, red blood flowed from where his jagged, sharp fangs began to gnaw into me. But the moment his teeth pierced my skin, was also the same moment I unclenched my fist.

The lavender flowers spilled from my palm, falling deep into the Wendigo's large mouth, slipping past his tongue, and down his throat. In less than a second, the beast's eyes were large, not in the maniacal, menacing manner they had been when I first saw them in the dream that night we found Austin. Now they were wide with shock.

Shock that he had been outsmarted . . . by *me.* Shock that he had *lost.* Shock that his arrogance became the end of him.

The ghoul didn't want to unclamp his jaw, but his breathing had become even more ragged and forced than it already had been by his sickly demeanor. His teeth released the flesh of my arm with an audible *shink*, leaving several ruby welts all across the top and bottom of my forearm, as it fell to my side, limp with pain, pulsing where the blood trailed down to my hand and dripped from my fingers.

The Wendigo stumbled back before he coughed one single time. He raised his long nails to his throat.

"Simon." His voice was hoarse, cracked. "What have

you done?" He coughed again. And then again. It kept going, and he couldn't stop until he began to gag.

"You're so hungry, you want to eat everything in front of you. Well, hope you enjoy your last meal."

As if my words were a trigger, the Wendigo doubled over, his massive height reduced to all fours as he laid on his hands and knees on the cold, packed ground.

He began to vomit.

I expected gore beyond recognition to come from his mouth of all the flesh he had consumed over the centuries.

But instead, all that came from him was a black sludge. Something like ink and tar. Thick and grotesque. It smelled similar to rotten milk, the smell of mold or decay.

"Help me," he whispered as his body quivered.

He reached his hand up to me, his eyes pleading.

"You're dying from the inside. There isn't anything you can do. It's over."

"No, no. I am ancient, I am greed itself—you cannot kill a feeling, a thought of malice. You cannot kill hunger."

I crossed the salt barrier I had made and stepped up to the dying beast. I held onto my arm, as the bite now felt like it was burning. I crouched down, coming face to face with the Wendigo.

"That's the thing you fail to understand: *You* are tangible. *You* can be stopped. And it is your own hunger that led you to this."

I stood once again and looked at the spirits and banshees that surrounded me. "He's all yours."

"No—NO! Simon, PLEASE!"

But I turned around, walking back to Riley as the spirits moved forward, jumping at the beast that had claimed their lives. Even Granny jumped into the fray.

I sat on the ground next to Riley, pulling her against me as I buried my face in her hair.

I heard the beast yell and scream, begging for mercy, pleading to be saved. I heard the tear and pull of flesh as the ghosts worked on the ghoul, biting him, pulling his rubbery skin from bones as he had once done to each of them. I heard the gags and splash of the black sludge coming from his mouth, from his insides. I heard the loud hacks of organs rising up and out of his throat and onto the ground.

And then, there was only silence in the forest, not even the wind moved.

I looked at ghoul—or where he should have been—all that remained was a dark stain against the cold ground.

"The rain will wash that away, as it does of all things," Granny said, her eyes following mine. "Best to spread some of the buds across it, to ward this spot from evil."

I nodded in her direction and followed her instructions. Miles was with me now, lightly pulling at the small petals that made up the lavender flower. We yanked long stems as well, walked back to the dark spot, and scattered them across the floor. It made it look like a stained-glass window of purple and blue panels, which was so much more than he deserved.

"Come on," Miles said. "We gotta get them and you to the hospital." He gestured to Austin and Riley.

"I'll be fine. Just gimme a minute," Austin called, lifting his hand to the night sky and shaking his index finger.

"Oh, we can't really take a werewolf to the hospital, now can we," I said sarcastically.

"I'll heal. Eventually."

"Maybe the vet?" Miles grinned.

"Ha. Ha," Austin enunciated before dropping his hand back to his chest.

"Can we even take Riley to the hospital?" I asked Miles, but Granny was the one to answer.

"You can. She threw up all of the food that had been in her system so she might be low on nutrients. Also, make her some lavender tea, it will help with her *vibes*." Granny smirked.

"Granny, how can we ever repay you?" I took a step toward her.

"My boy, you already have. You have set all of these spirits, myself included, *free*. We are no longer bound to this earth and they no longer are bound to that beast. We can all go on in peace if we should choose." There was a twinkle in her eye.

Behind her, some of the spirits began to fade. One by one, they all disappeared.

The banshees, now regular spirits with all the rage taken from them, lingered. Addaline looked up at me.

"I'm sorry I blamed you. I think . . . you became muddled with the beast for a bit. I knew *you* didn't kill me, but in all my anger, I was blinded."

I tried to form my warmest smile. "It's okay. I think I was blinded for a bit too."

"Simon," Beth said, moving closer to Addaline, "I know we didn't know each other well. But thanks for saving us." She smiled.

Addaline held the other girl's hand as they both faded from view. All that remained was Granny now.

"You boys need to get going. That wound on your arm isn't going to heal itself."

"Granny, th—"

"Hush, boy. There will come another chance to say goodbye." She beamed at me, and then at Miles. "Be well. All of you."

And then she faded. Just like that.

The Ghoul Gang was alone in the woods.

CHAPTER THIRTY-TWO
SIMON

The moon had been shining brightly down upon us on this Halloween night as we trekked through the forest. Austin had an arm around Miles's shoulder for support while I did my best to carry Riley on my back with my one good arm. I didn't know what we would say once we arrived at the hospital, or how I would even begin to explain where I had been all week. But we called Alice to meet us outside the forest to drive us.

We saw the flashing blue and red lights as we neared the outskirts of the trees. She stood against her car, waiting, with her arms crossed.

"Alice!" Miles called, and immediately, her eyes shifted into a motherly gaze. She ran up the small mound of dirt that separated the road from the forest and aided us down.

"Riley! Are you kids all right? Why didn't you call me?! Is everyone alive?" She reached for Riley, pulling her into her motherly embrace.

"We're okay. Riley's okay. We won, Alice. It was all thanks to Riley," I assured.

"Well, I'm glad to know you all are safe at least." She gently patted my head, and where it was meant to be warm and tender, it seemed to strike some kind of nerve, as a hot flash of pain shot down my skull. I jerked away. "Oh, sorry! Come on, let's get you guys out of here and to a hospital. Simon, I'm so glad you're back. Your parents are worried sick."

We all limped to the car as we gave her the details of the night. She gave me a beat-up blanket from the trunk to wrap myself in, as I was still just in a T-shirt and shorts. I didn't even have shoes on, and my feet were aching with blisters.

"Simon, I took the liberty to call your parents. I told them you were found, but I didn't know if you wanted me to give a cover story or if you wanted to come clean." She looked at me through the rearview mirror. "Now, as you know, everyone in this town that knows of Riley's gifts sits in this car. But, that being said, you do whatever *you* think is best."

I nodded. "Okay. Thanks. I'll try to figure it out."

By the time we turned into the hospital entrance, which looked exactly as it had one week prior when this whole mess began, Austin was seemingly fully healed. His nose had reshaped, his lip formed together again, and he sat tall but relaxed.

"Hey, man." I nudged him gently, Riley's head resting against my other shoulder. "Sorry I punched you in the face."

"And broke my nose," he said, his eyes looking out the window.

I cringed. I felt so bad, I had been a monster. "Yeah, I'm really sor—"

Austin turned to me and smiled. "Don't be." His smile widened. "I healed really fast. That was a mean right hook though. You still got that in ya?"

I looked at my hand, all battered and bloodied. The bite was looking more and more furious as time passed, making it less and less passable for a simple dog bite. The rows and rows of puncture wounds made it look like a small shark bite.

"I'm . . . not sure."

As we pulled under the awning—now fixed—I saw a row of people, doctors, nurses, staff, and my parents. Everyone rushed to the car, pulling Riley and myself out and into the hospital. My parents ran with me to a room, my father already dressed in his scrubs. And like that, the party was split. Riley went one way, her mother and Austin following her, and I went the other, Miles trailing behind me and my parents.

Mom and Dad didn't speak. Nothing besides asking if I was okay, if I was dizzy, or thirsty, but nothing about where I had been, what had happened.

My father pushed the wheelchair I was placed in into an empty room and ushered me to sit on one of the blue hospital beds.

He stayed silent as he connected me to machines, placing an IV gently in my arm, and began to look at my forearm and my head. His expression darkened.

He grabbed some equipment and looked up at me.

"This may sting a bit." His voice was quiet. Soft. He sounded . . . different than usual. Utterly serious, like he was speaking to just another patient, not his son.

He dabbed at my arm and began to clean the bite. I recoiled at the violent stinging of the alcohol before I eased into it.

Miles and Mom stood at the edge of the room. Mom's eyes were wide with worry.

I wanted to tell them . . . I wanted to explain everything. To apologize for going missing, for making them worry. But before I could, she broke the silence.

"What, um . . . what did this?"

"Mom, I—"

"Was it a werewolf?"

My heart stopped.

"Ravenswood is a little . . . strange. Try to stay in the house after dark," I remembered.

My dad looked back at her. "Hana, what are you—"

"I know, Simon. I know what this town is . . . I've known since the second week we moved here. I saw them. And I know they're not the only things out here."

"Mrs. Woo—" Miles began.

But she wasn't letting go. She took a step toward me. "Come on, Si. I know you love that stuff. And now it's all real, and you've found it. And then you go missing for a week and come back looking like—"

"It wasn't a werewolf." But my voice was barely louder than a whisper.

"Simon?" Dad's eyebrows rose in disbelief. So, he didn't know. She hadn't told him.

"Then . . . what?"

"It was a wendigo," Miles said.

Both of my parents turned to look at him. His eyes went wide, and his cheeks turned pink. "I'm sorry—I'll go." He turned to leave but my mom gently caught his wrist.

"No, please stay, Miles."

"What are you all going on about?" My dad finally said, standing up from his chair.

"Dad, the supernatural is real. I know it sounds ridiculous. But you have to—*have* to believe me."

"Why are you feeding into this, Hana? He's been missing a week, comes back delirious, and you—"

I grabbed his hand. "Dad. Listen to me."

His eyes met mine and lingered for a moment.

"Peter," my mother spoke, "we swore not to be like our parents. We swore to be as understanding as we could. We swore we would *listen*."

I expected my father to speak up, to object. After all, this was crazy. And my dad was always a skeptic, only humoring my beliefs.

But he didn't say anything. He looked at me, and then at my hand in his, and remained silent.

I explained everything. The dreams, the ghoul, Riley's vibes, the bodies, the possession, the Wendigo's dream world. Everything. In the end, they both were wide-eyed. My dad treated my wounds and wrapped my head and arm in some bandages before moving on to Miles's scraped head.

Apparently, I had two small fuzzy bumps that may have been the beginnings of antlers growing from the sides of my head. My hair had covered them for the most part, but they were still tender, as they had broken the skin around my skull to pierce out.

I swallowed at the idea of living my life with these lumps, a forever mark of the Wendigo's possession, a mark to last longer than the scar he left on my arm. I hoped they would fade within the coming days.

In the end, my mom believed me, but Dad was harder to read. Which was odd, he was usually an open book. They now knew everything. And they made me swear that I would never run off like that again. I also probably wouldn't be leaving my house after nightfall for a while. Or ever.

Mom and Dad escorted Miles and me to Riley's room but waited outside, conversing with Alice and Allen. Apparently, Miles texted his dad that I was found, and Alice made up a wild excuse that I had gotten lost in the woods.

The adults spoke to one another kindly as Miles and I entered the room. Austin was relaxing in a hospital chair as Riley sat up, fully awake now, with an IV in her arm.

"What a Halloween this has been," I said sarcastically. The three of them looked at me for a moment before we all burst into laughter.

We all sat around Riley's hospital bed, talking about the night as if it were a movie. How unreal some of the moments were, how we couldn't believe we all made it out alive.

"He smelled like rotten cheese." Austin scrunched his nose.

"And was way scarier than I pictured in my head." Miles rubbed his chin. "No wonder you were so grumpy all the time, having to dream of *that* face every night? Yikes." He elbowed me and laughed.

"But what about those antlers?" Riley asked, pointing to the two new nubs.

I gently touched one, the bone felt fine but the skin around them had still been tender from where they jutted out. "I don't know. My dad wants to take some X-rays before we leave. See if it actually is bone. I hope they just go away."

"We did *just* defeat the guy. Maybe his weird possession will take a few days to leave your system?" Miles shrugged.

"Like a bad cold. Or drug withdrawals," Austin continued.

"Man, I hope so. I do *not* want to go my whole life with these weird little . . . things on my head."

"At least you like wearing hats, they'll cover them up," Riley suggested.

"And with your floppy, Asian-man hair," Miles lightly ruffled my hair, "they're, like, barely noticeable."

"Yeah, can barely see 'em." Austin waved it off like it was no big deal.

I could tell they were trying, and for that I was grateful. I guess I could live with two tiny bumps. None of it mattered anyway. We were all here, on Halloween night, together. Alive.

We won.

I woke up to the sun shining through the window in my bedroom. It was officially November. Halloween had come and gone, and with all the chaos, I hadn't even been able to watch my traditional horror movies to celebrate the holiday or wear the costume Miles brought me.

The Ghoul Gang was coming over tonight to hang out at my place for the first time.

I got out of bed, put on my best loungewear (a big hoodie and some sweats), and jogged downstairs. Dad was already making a big Korean breakfast as Mom began setting up all the side dishes on the table.

"Hey! Morning," I said as I entered the room. They both looked at me and brightened.

"Did you hear me last night?" Mom made an embarrassed expression.

"You mean when you came into my room every thirty minutes to check on me? Nah, not at all." I smiled.

"Well, can you blame me! I had to make sure you were still here." She lovingly threw her arms around me. "Plus, I only checked until three. Your dad took up the shift after me."

I gawked at him. "You too?"

In place of an answer, my usual-chatter-box dad grunted his response. "After breakfast, I'll rewrap the bandages. How do you feel?"

"Fine, for the most part. These things" —I pointed to the nubs on either side of my forehead— "were annoying to sleep with. Every time I turned onto my side, I got a jolt of pain."

Both of their expressions darkened for a moment, before my mom chimed in. "Well, lucky for you, I'm a vet. Your dad can handle the cuts and bruises, but maybe I should take a look at them? I mean, I've worked on so many deer since moving here."

"Really?"

"Of course. I'm sure I can figure it out." Mom ushered me to sit in the seat in front of her, and as soon as I did, she slowly removed the wrappings. They came away slightly bloody from the night before.

She poked around, moving my hair from side to side.

"Wow, you really can't see them with your hair."

"But be careful on windy days. The moment your hair moves, there they are," Dad said, washing his hands across the room.

"That's interesting," Mom said, as she rubbed on the new bone.

"Wh-what's interesting?"

"They have fuzz on them. Velvet, actually. When fawns first grow their antlers, they grow them with velvet. Over time as they grow, the velvet kind of sheds off—in a really gross way, don't look it up. But your little lumps make it seem like *you* are a fawn."

"Well. The Wendigo was in my body for a week. Maybe they would've grown more had his possession been successful?"

"Maybe. Just . . . we'll monitor them. I don't know anything about the supernatural, but I'm surprised you still have them, even after that monster . . . died."

To say we *killed* the Wendigo made *us* sound like the bad guys. None of us had said it since, and I didn't think we were about to start.

"What time are your friends getting here, Si? I thought we could order a few pizzas?" Dad said, kindly breaking the heavy silence that ensued.

"Um. I told them around seven."

"Okay! Great, we'll call at six thirty then. I'll pick up some chips and stuff."

"And alcohol. For us." Mom smiled.

"Of course. I *wish* I could find a Korean market around here. I would kill for some *soju*."

"Or *makgeolli*!" Mom sighed. Miami didn't have *that* much Asian cuisine, other than sushi, really. But the few places we had found were gems. "But really anything will do the job."

We all ate our breakfast as they asked me a bunch

of questions about everything I'd encountered here so far. I told them of Frank, the ghost, and how Austin was actually a tamed werewolf. Their eyes widened, but my mom expressed how the one werewolf she encountered had stolen the dog food from her clinic and ran off, not even touching her. *Could that have been Austin too?*

The day went on, Dad fixed my wounds again, the bite mark finally looking a little less angry and red. We watched TV and just enjoyed each other's company. Around six, I showered—which felt so, *so* nice—and threw on another pair of sweats.

At six forty-five there was the first knock on the door. Miles entered with splendid glee. He said hello to my parents as we made our way to my room. Riley and Austin stumbled in shortly after.

We watched horror movie after horror movie in the living room and ate pizza, chips, popcorn, and the greatest of Halloween candies before retreating to my room.

"How are your horns?" Riley teased.

"They're *antlers*. And they're fine. Apparently, they have velvet on them. I'm a young baby fawn." I sarcastically boasted.

"That's wild," Miles exclaimed.

"Yesterday was—" Riley began.

"Crazy," I finished.

Everyone stayed silent for a moment.

"Do you . . . Well, do you think he's really dead?" Miles asked, his voice trickling with uncertainty. "I mean, in horror movies—"

"I *do* think he's gone. That last plea . . . the expression he made. I don't know, it felt genuine." I absent-mindedly scratched the back of my head. "If anything, we can go back tomorrow and see if the black spot is still there?"

"*We* can go back," Austin said, gesturing to Miles, Riley, and himself. "I think you need to rest, bud."

"Plus. It's pretty unlikely that your parents are going to let you out of their sight for a while." Riley smirked.

"True." I sighed. "I owe them big time. I can't even imagine how worried they were."

"I can," Riley mumbled. Miles and Austin nodded their heads.

"Right. Sorry."

"Aye, man. It's not your fault." Miles patted my back.

We sat for a while, none of us really saying anything, when Austin's phone went off. He pulled it from his back pocket, his eyes glazing over the text.

"Oh, shit."

"What?" we all said in unison.

"My parents are home. They brought me a dog, look!" He flashed us all his phone. A picture of a golden Shiba Inu puppy stared back at us. The dog's tongue was hanging out as its head was cocked to the side, the iconic curled tail wrapping around as it sat.

"How cute!" Riley squealed.

"Do you know what you're going to name it?" Miles asked.

"Yeah . . . I wanna call him Ito. After my favorite Japanese manga artist."

"Oh, man. I love that guy!" I praised. "I *highly* approve of that name."

Austin smiled at me. "Have you read—"

But before he could finish, his phone went off again.

"Oh. It looks like I gotta go. Um, Miles . . ." He raised his head, looking at Miles, laying the smolder on thick. "Did you need a ride home?"

"Nah. I'm actually staying here tonight. But I'll walk you out."

I knew about his kiss with Austin in the library (and again in the car). Just like he knew about my kiss with Riley in the dream forest. We told each other the moment we were left alone in the hospital room. We had a lot to catch up on, but our love lives were a priority — of course. But, unlike them, Riley and I still hadn't even mentioned the kiss. And being alone felt . . . awkward.

"I'm the host, I'll walk you out too." I stood, but Miles immediately shot me a look.

"No, it's fine. I got it. Relaaax."

Austin waved at us and walked out of the door, with Miles behind him. As he turned to close the door, Miles shot me that same smug expression as he looked between me and Riley, and then he winked (or tried to) and left.

It was just me and Riley now.

We stayed quiet for a minute. I felt like it was too quiet. I had a lump in my throat and my chest.

My hands were sweaty.

"So," Riley said. Her voice breaking the silence like thunder. "How are you? After last night."

"I'm good, I guess. The antler thing is weird. But I can happily report: no more weird dreams. What about you?"

"I'm fine. That vibe was killer, but after I had the tea Granny left behind, I felt better."

I nodded.

She nodded.

Silence.

I saw her picking at her nails.

Should I bring up the kiss? Should I ask her on a date? What am I supposed to do here?

I ran through the catalog of romantic comedies in my head, trying to pick out the best option, my best comeback, to make this happen.

But she spoke before I had come up with anything.

"I think I should go. I'm pretty tired and . . . I just wanna get some rest." She stood, and I followed.

"Okay, yeah! I'll text you?"

She looked back at me and smiled as she nodded. "Definitely."

Riley took a step toward me and wrapped her arms around my neck, pulling me in for a hug. We embraced for a minute, and I noticed the smell of roses lingering on her hair again.

"I'm glad we got you back," Riley said.

"*You* got me back," I corrected.

"*I* got you back." I could feel her smile against my shoulder and neck.

And then she pulled away, kissing me on the cheek as she did.

"I guess thanks for coming back?"

"Oh, trust me, it was my pleasure."

She snorted and then grabbed her stuff.

"I'll walk you out."

We began walking out of the room, before Riley's eyes caught on my full-body mirror. She immediately jumped back and gasped, her eyes wide, as her entire face contorted in fear. I would've said it looked as if she'd seen a ghost, but she saw those all the time. What would scare Riley enough to cause this reaction?

"Whoa! You okay?" I placed my hand on her shoulder, looking at the mirror and back around the room. But I didn't see anything. "Is something here?"

"Huh?" She looked at me now, as though she had snapped back to reality. "No, no. I thought I saw . . . never mind. It was my own reflection. Ha . . . see? Tired."

She quickly walked out of the room, and after taking one more glance at the mirror and room, I followed.

We ran into Miles and Austin kissing right beyond my doorway, as they pulled apart.

"Get a room, you two," I scoffed. Miles and Austin instantly blushed, before we broke out in laughter.

We said our goodbyes to Riley and Austin as they both walked off to their cars, and Miles and I headed back upstairs.

"How'd it go?" Miles asked.

"We didn't talk about it. Maybe she forgot?"

"How could she forget something like that?" Miles crossed his arms.

"I don't mean like, 'Whoopsies, haha, I forgot.' I mean . . . like what if she *supernaturally* forgot?"

"Huh?"

"It's not like she was placed in that world like I was. She found it herself. She forced herself to vibe to me . . . maybe she doesn't remember?"

"I think you're coming up with excuses."

"Maybe."

"I think you should still talk to her about it."

"Okay, okay. I will."

"Promise?"

"Promise."

"Good. Now let's play some video games," he said as he pulled out his laptop from his bag and connected it to the wall.

"Okay. But I'm playing damage this time."

"You know I always go healer, baby!" Miles smacked his lips and started rubbing his hands together.

And for the rest of the night, all that could be heard from my room was the furious clicking of keys and mice, and the occasional loud, degenerate, screaming of two teenage boys.

There were no ghouls in sight.

EPILOGUE

The trees swayed back and forth, as leaves dropped to the damp ground in the crisp air, the branches up above were barren. Autumn had come and gone as winter was just beginning to peek through. The birds sang, the bugs chirped, and the squirrels raced for nuts and seeds. Everything was utterly peaceful.

Until the wind suddenly stopped.

The only movement came from the stain on the forest floor. The black tar oozed from the dirt and congealed together before disappearing entirely.

ACKNOWLEDGMENTS

I've always felt like the most daunting part of writing a book was 1) actually starting the book and 2) writing the acknowledgments. There is so much to be grateful for in this stage of the process, it's hard to write it all down without giving a little piece of my soul away in the process. But here goes nothing.

I have been working on *Where Did the Wind Go?* for a bit over three years, but the ideas of the Ghoul Gang going out for vibe sessions have been stewing in my creative well for over a decade. To have it finally complete is just beyond amazing.

I would first like to thank the obvious: my parents. Mom, Dad, Munky, Rick, Keila; you guys have put so much into making me who I am, and I give all my thanks to you for the endless support and love, and for always supporting my nerdy and spooky obsessions. You're the best team of cheerleaders a girl could ask for. An extra special and specific shoutout to my mom, Lizette Lopez. I love you to the moon and back. My love and appreciation for you is the one thing I can't express in words because there aren't any grand enough to express them.

To my wonderful family in New York: Ita, Papi Willie, Nana, Titi Ivy, Gaby, Dani, Mike, Alby, Tom, and our newest edition, Logan. Thank you for always being the best, most supportive family on the planet. Logan, I can't wait to teach you all about the Ghoul

Gang and create stories to inspire you to be the best little dude ever.

Next, to Mike Burke. You are the best boyfriend a girl could ask for and I love you with all my heart. I remember crying tears of joy with you the moment I finally finished my first draft and the countless hours you had to put up with me rambling about wendigos, demons, and a bunch of teenagers. I love you (and Maki) so much.

To my own gang of ghouls who have been with me on this arduous ride.

Brandi McGugan, you have been my ride-or-die since day one of this trip. Literally. I remember the night we thought up the Asian boy from Miami saying "*Si, por favor*" to his new teacher. Thanks for always being the best and constantly supporting me in everything I do. And thank you for being awake at three in the morning when I had a brain blast of an idea that I needed to talk out.

To Ludwin Vielman, not only have you been one of the best friends a ghoul could ask for, but you've also helped me flesh out Simon so much better than how he was originally written. His mannerisms are heavily based on you, and I thank you for being such a formidable role model.

Elsie Alarcon, thank you for being one of my first readers. Your support through this whole thing has been so appreciated I can't express enough how much I value your input and feedback on this story, and for constantly being a supporter of the Ghoul Gang.

I had a mighty team at my back while writing and editing this novel. Without them, this book wouldn't be what it is now.

Anto Marr, thank you for becoming one of my best friends in such a short time. I would go to the ends of the earth with you. You are the Phanto to my Ghoulie, forevermore, and I hope you know there is no getting rid of me. Thank you for making my book look exactly how I've imagined it in my head all these years. Your design work on the cover and layout is beyond amazing.

To my editor, Julia Lee, thank you for being so, so supportive through this and constantly reminding me that my words made sense on the page, even when I felt like they were a jumbled mess. I'd also like to thank Wren Blomeley, without your helpful guidance, a lot of this book would've fallen flat. Like Anto, you both have been a godsend in my life, and I am beyond grateful we met. As promised, I thank Caleb Jones for that one time he got me chicken nuggets when I *really* needed them. Thank you to Yesenia Roque for an amazing job at helping me turn my first draft into something so much more. And, of course, thank you to my BookLogix gang for helping make this into a reality.

Finally, as cheesy as it is, I'd like to thank myself. As a writer, it's important to acknowledge when you've *actually* completed your goal. It's real. I didn't give up, and I persevered. *I* made it happen. To all other writers, readers, and aspiring authors out there, you can do it too. Don't stop writing.

A final thanks to all my readers. I welcome you to the Ghoul Gang, and I already can't wait to go on another vibe sesh in Ravenswood with you.

ABOUT THE AUTHOR

J. M. Failde spent just over one hundred fortnights rigorously studying the complexities of the English language at Florida International University in her vivacious hometown, Miami. While she is not conjuring up stories, she can be found searching for *el chupacabra*, befriending the ghost in her house, or dying her hair a new shade of blue. Failde currently resides in her gothic manor on the outskirts of Atlanta, Georgia, with her partner, Mike, and her familiar—the round but feisty calico cat, Maki. Follow her on Instagram @jmfailde.

WWW.JMFAILDE.COM

CPSIA information can be obtained
at www.ICGtesting.com
Printed in the USA
BVHW032331050323
659706BV00006B/131